Advanced Idiotocracy
for Dummies

The Alternate Reality News Service,

Ira Nayman, Proprietor

Ira Nayman

This is a work of fiction. Any resemblance to real persons, places or things is…inevitable, really, given the nature of the multiverse. However, the probability of any resemblance to real persons, places or things in your particular universe is vanishingly small, and must, therefore, be considered coincidental.

Praise for the first idiotocracy book, *ARNS and the Man*:

"Amusing, sardonic political and social satire that brims with wordplay legerdemain and oddballisticelaboratified name invention. Trenchantly twisted and good fun." – John Shirley, author of *A Song Called Youth: Eclipse*

"I don't often read science fiction but when I do, Ira Nayman's *ARNS and the Man* is near the top of my list. Wacky, surreal, bizarre, and all too close to reality, Nayman spins a web of satirical hilarity ripped from the headlines." – Terry Fallis, two-time winner of the Stephen Leacock Medal for Humour.

"Ira Nayman rivals Walt Kelly for the skilled and joyous administration of near hallucinogenic word play as an antidote for the madness of our political process. And unlike the brave possum of Okefenokee Swamp, the truths of *ARNS and the Man* were crafted by someone wearing pants." – Hugh Spencer, author of *Why I Hunt Flying Saucers* and *Extreme Dentistry*

"Ira skewers American politics in a way only a Canadian can, with absurdist wit and wisdom. Short humorous Fake News articles that know they're fake and relish in their lies. (Or ARE they?) Makes me once more jealous of our neighbors to the north." – Michael A. Ventrella, author of *Bloodsuckers: A Vampire Runs for President*, among other things

"Reading an ARNS book is like going head-to-head with an selection of thirty three and a third disconnected Wikipedia entries filtered through seven layers of artesian coffee filters woven from at least three more fibers than permitted by the historic laws of any major religion in a blender made of a strange kind of cotton candy spun from titanium anodized in fairground colours with blades made of live sharks while simultaneously tap-dancing to a Steve Reich composition based on the absolute value of the square root of pi. In other words, simply and elegantly the most entertaining way ever invented to invert your brain over a platter prepared with roasted apples and a variety of field mushrooms for your own delighted consumption. Also, a hilariously skewed take on the Trump administration." – Jen Frankel, editor, *Trump: Utopia or Dystopia*, author, *Undead Redhead*

DEDICATION

It takes a village to raise a court jester. In my case, it was the village of Toronto, which is named after an indigenous word for "boring money." If we had been named for interesting money, I may have ended up a celebrity hair stylist. Funny how things work out.

This book is dedicated to my family, who have supported me in the most tenuous of endeavours, being an artist; it may not have been much of a career, but it's been a hell of a life. It is also dedicated to my Web Goddess, without whom I would never have gone down this path. Finally, I would like to dedicate to my home, Toronto, which has had an intangible but very real affect on how I see and write about the world.

ACKNOWLEDGMENTS

Thanks to Hugh Spencer for his amazing cover graphics, and especially to Gisela McKay for taking my loopy ideas and making them such a wonderfully bizarre reality.

In addition, I must thank the people who gave of their time and blurbiage to the first Vesampucceri collection, *ARNS and the Man*. Your kind words may not have increased my sales appreciably, but they make me think that I may not have been completely wasting my time with this whole writing thing.

Ira Nayman

CONTENTS

Ira Nayman

INTRODUCTION

Oh, my Gord, is it over? Really, is it over? I don't care. I'm done.

No, seriously, I have had enough. Over the past four and a bit years, I have written five books about Donald Trump and the Republican Party. They were made up of 400 pieces of writing comprised of approximately 350,000 words. There are so many other things that I want to write; I owe it to myself, and them, to move on.

Yes, I am aware that Oath Keepers were in regular contact with representatives of Donald Trump before and during the insurrection. It's tempting. Very tempting. But I must be strong. It's the owing and the on moving, you understand.

Sure, the United States has broken out in voter suppression across the country. That's a big, juicy target for sure. Still, the country has a lot of satirists; I'm sure Georgia...and Texas...and, I'm not going to list them all (it would take less time to list the states that haven't introduced voter suppression bills) – they know who they are – will get the comedic treatment they deserve.

And, then, there's Matt Gaetz. Man, he could be a whole chapter on his own! I could see – but, no. I shouldn't. It's been four years! Four years of my life that I will never get back! I can't! I shouldn't! I...I...I...

I make no promises.

You and What Universe?

The Alternate Reality News Service,

Ira Nayman, Proprietor

Ira Nayman

CONTENTS

Ira Nayman

1. LIFE IS MORE ENTERTAINING THE LARGER THE SCREEN YOU WATCH IT ON

Ransom! Where?

by FRED CHARUNDER-MACHARRUNDEIRA, Alternate Reality News Service Science Writer

Bonnie Krump had just started feeling the tingles and knew that a big fat Greek orgasm (which, depending upon your cultural background, could be described as a gushing waterfall, a swarm of angry bees or a glorious uprising of workers to wrest the means of production away from the unproductive elites who controlled them and build an earthly collective paradise) was a couple of minutes away. To help her along, Chumley 1247-C, her handsome young sexbot, said the three words that every woman longs to hear.

"Give me money."

Calling on a database of human female sensual response, Chumley 1247-C knew exactly the right words to heighten the mood on the way to giving – **WHAT? WHAT DID HE JUST SAY?**

"He said: 'Give me money,'" Krump, the mood broken, told me. "Didn't you hear?"

Why would he say that? That's not romantic at all!

"Oh, please!" Krump said, shoving Chumley 1247-C off the bed (being made of space age materials for maximum flexibility, he was much lighter than his muscular frame would have suggested). He landed on the ground with a gentle thud. "It was –"

"Was it something I said?" Chumley 1247-C plaintively (he had been built in Utah) asked from the floor.

"I want you to lie there for a while and ponder your sins," Krump harshly told him.

"Okay," Chumley 1247-C, programmed to obey, agreed, although he didn't exactly sound happy about it.

So, about what happened…?

"My sexbot was obviously infected with ransomware," Krump explained as she reached over to the end table by the bed and pulled a cigarette out of a pack.

Ransomware? What –

"Hunh! You don't know what ransomware is? And you call yourself a tech reporter?" Krump scoffed as she picked a purse up off the floor and started rummaging around in it.

Well, yes, of course, I know what ransomware is! But…umm… for my readers, I thought if you would just –

"Yeah, yeah, whatever," Krump grumped, not finding what she was looking for. "Ransomware is a programme that stops all functions in a computer system unless you pay the person who created it. The ransom isn't usually – aha!" Krump took two sticks out of the purse and dropped it back to the floor. Then, she started rubbing the sticks together over the table. "The ransom isn't usually that much – 20 or 30 dollars. Paying it is less of an annoyance than – well, you saw what happened."

"Is that what happened to me?" Chumley 1247-C asked.

"More pondering. Less talking," Krump advised, not unkindly.

Why infect sexbots with ransomware? Wouldn't that, you know, kill the mood?

"Aha!" Krump exclaimed, as if she agreed with the flaw in the plan. Actually, the two sticks had sparked and caught fire, and she lit her cigarette. Quickly waving the sticks in the air to put the fire out, Krump took a long drag.

More relaxed, she explained, "Okay. Here's the thing. The C series male sexbots have sensors that monitor the vital signs of their partners. This allows them to adapt their behaviour to maximize their partners' pleasure. In theory, ransomware will detect when a woman is about to climax and threaten to shut down the sexbot a minute or so before she does. I have heard that robotics researchers and skunk whisperers call this the 'No, No, Don't Stop Now Moment.' The closer a woman is to the No, No, Don't Stop Now Moment, the more likely she will authorize the payment of the ransom."

But –

Chumley 1247-C moaned, "I don't feel so-o-o-o-o-o-o-o-o-o-o-ooooooooo…" As the sound died out, he stopped moving.

"That's what happens when you don't pay the ransom," Krump shook her head sadly.

When I pointed out that Krump wasn't sufficiently aroused to pay the ransom, she snorted a most unladylike (but very lady lawyerlike) snort.

"Human sexual response is not a simple algorithm," she explained, taking another long drag on her cigarette. "The No, No, Don't Stop Now Moment happens at different points for each woman, and can be affected by a lot of things. Like, how long she has been stimulated to that point. Or, maybe there are environmental factors like loud noises or farting dogs in the vicinity of the bed. Or, maybe she wasn't familiar with the work of the actor whose likeness was used for the sexbot, so he didn't turn her on as much as if she had been a fan. In my case, I just hadn't reached that point yet."

I asked Professor Hiram von Schmutz, head of The Intimate Machine-Human Interface Institute of The Frankfurt School if what Krump had told me was true. "Ja," he replied.

Having cleared that up, I asked Krump if she was going to pay the ransom to get her sexbot working again.

"We'll see," she replied. "Chumley 1247-C was supposed to come with antivirus software to prevent this sort of thing. I think I'll take him back to the dealer to run some diagnostic tests. Now, if you have no more questions, get the hell out of my bedroom. I know that reporters will do anything for a story, but this is creepy!"

Yesthetics Are So Yestherday

by FREDERICA VON McTOAST-HYPHEN, Alternate Reality News Service Pop Culture Writer

"Yes, I…I want to taste your wombat pate. On kelp crackers."

"I'm sorry, Felice, but I'm not feeling the yes."

"'Course you're not feeling the yes! Who wants to eat wombat pate on kelp crackers?"

"Walruses do, Felice. Walruses do. Perhaps if you got in touch with your inner walrus, it would be easier for you to –"

"Ugh! I think I'm gonna – I'm gonna – 'scuse me!"

"I think you're missing the – Felice? **Felice! Where are you running off to? I THINK YOU'RE MISSING THE POINT!**"

In a small meeting room in one of the less popular hotels on the airport strip (will you or won't you get heating on a cold December night? – the place can be such a tease!), over 30 people have paid $1,250 to be tutored by Marie-Angelo (her parents had a religious aversion to ultrasounds, so they hedged their bets) di Prestino.

Who is Marie-Angelo di Prestino? I'm glad you asked. Really glad you asked. There would be no article if you didn't ask glad you asked. Okay, technically, **I** asked in **your** name. So, **technically**, I'm glad you exist to allow me to put questions in your mouth. You do exist to allow me to put questions in your mouth, don't you? Of…of course you do.

Marie-Angelo di Prestino is the world-barely recognized author of *Why Is It When I Say Yes, I Hear No?*, the foundational (reading it is like swimming through concrete) text of the yesthetics movement. di Prestino is the lost and founder of the Instituti del Yesthetico and a practising yesthetician.

What is yesthetics? I'm glad you asked, but let's not start that nonsense all over again.

Yesthetics is the art of positivity. (Nietzsche was all over the art of negativity.) The basic premise of the movement is that it is not enough to half-heartedly say "Yes" to life. You must throw your arms around yes and enthusiastically embrace it like you would a lover that you haven't seen in over a decade. You must dance around yes like nobody is watching…for signs that would explain why you haven't seen your lover in over a decade. Sing yes like it's the theme song of your life (it sure beats the latest Coke jingle!). Yes. **Yes! YES!**

So. The word yes as performance art, then.

This does not – oh. Right. Most of the description two paragraphs ago was taken directly from di Prestino's follow-up book *Yesthetics: The Science Behind Yes That Had Been Left Out of My Previous Book*. To avoid allegations of plagiarism, please go back to that paragraph and imagine that I used open quotation marks before the phrase "it is not enough" and close quotation marks after the final **YES!**

This does not – oh, and, while you're imagining that, imagine that the double quotes around the word "Yes" two paragraphs – now three paragraphs ago, are actually single quotes. I wouldn't have mentioned it, but linguistic purists can make a journalist's life hell on Farcebook!

This does not – this being the word yes as performance art, I mean – I may have taken a bit of a detour from the concept in the last couple of paragraphs – the word yes as performance art does not come naturally to most people. That's where di Prestino's weekend retreats come in. (Okay, technically, they come in through the loading dock in the back of the hotel, but now is no time to quibble.) People pay big money (they use oversized checkbooks borrowed from a local lottery) to attend seminars on "The Historical Imperative of Yesthetics" and workshops where they practice using performance yes to answer a series of increasingly difficult to stomach questions.

There are, of course, critics of yesthetics. Surprisingly, some of the most vocal (you would swear they had worked with a voice coach!) were from the positivity movement itself. Well, surprisingly if you don't appreciate the role envy – the most sanguine of the deadly sins – plays in human nature.

"To suggest that there is a right way to get to yes implies that there is a wrong way to get to yes," argued Vermont Regulon, author of *The Yes Matrix: The Power of Yes to the Power of Two*, its follow-up, *The 3-D Yes Matrix: Taking the Power of Yes to a Whole New Level* and, most recently, *Quantum Yes: The Power of Yes in Eleven Dimensions*. "I find Marie-Angelo and her followers to have a yesier than thou attitude towards other yes-sayers. Tut tut, I say to that. Tut and tut."

Questions of pride – the orangest of the deadly sins – aside, wouldn't it make sense for yes practitioners – yestitioners? Naah – people can't just make up words willy nilly to suit themselves – that way leads anarchy! – wouldn't it make sense for yes practitioners to set aside their differences and work together towards a society with a more positive attitude towards yes?

"No," responded Regulon.

"No," replied di Prestino.

"Hell no!" answered Felice Marimbe Achooa from a stall in the women's washroom. "I paid a lot of money for the weekend retreat, and if I don't get the best yes that money can buy, I'm gonna sue somebody's ass off!"

This Oscar is Just So Much Background Noise

by ELMORE TERADONOVICH, Alternate Reality News Service Film and Television Writer

Have you ever been watching a movie and been taken out of a scene because, although it is set in a Russian tattoo parlour and skeeball joint, the hum of conversation in the background was obviously recorded in a bowling alley in Schenectady, Prince Edward Island during a darts tournament? Neither have I. The differences are so small that you would have to have been a sound engineer with decades of experience to be able to tell.

"Actually, I'm a sound engineer with decades of experience, and I can't tell the difference," stated Elmer Vedonaterre, a sound engineer with dec – okay, you already know that about him. But, did you know that he was recently awarded a Best Achievement By a Sound Engineer with Decades of…You Know Oscar? You did? Why am I bothering to write this, then?

We'll deal with my existential crisis some other time. For now, what you need to know is: the sound of crowds used in the background of all Hollywood movies comes from three sources: a speakeasy scene in 1934's *Golddiggers of Broadway in Space*, a football game in *The Elephant's Big Moustache* (1947) and a political rally in the musical *It Could Be You (But Let's Pretend It's Not)*, released in 1941. These are then tweaked with extreme prejudice as needed.

Suppose, for example, that you are doing the sound for a restaurant scene in a romantic comedy. You would take the football game, mute the roars of the crowd and add the tinkling of glasses. If a crowd roar happened to get through the sound editing process, you could always recommend writing into the script that the scene was happening in a sports bar on the night of the big game; the amount of reshooting you would have to do would be minimal.

Why did you think so many restaurant scenes in romantic comedies happen in sports bars?

Vedonaterre took a different approach to sound editing: what if you populated the background sound with artificial intelligences that were having real conversations? If that was the case, you could Taylor (after famed voiceover artist Elizabeth) background noises to fit any scene you had.

Suppose, for example, you were editing the sound for a scene in a romantic comedy where the rebel alliance is planning on attacking the empire's home planet. (Yes, the film has a bit of an identity crisis – that can happen when you have 37 writers work on a screenplay – but I've already complained about that so often that my computer keyboard is hoarse.) You can create an AI flight engineer who spouts nothing but incomprehensible technical jargon, an AI hotshot pilot who spouts nothing but incomprehensible flying jargon, an AI rebel leader who spouts nothing but incomprehensible political jargon, an AI robot who spouts nothing but incomprehensible tweets and whistles and…and…and, **what do I look like – a sound engineer? Fill the scene with your own damn characters!**

Ahem. I'm sorry you had to witness that. I…was recently in a car accident that left me in a coma.

The point is that once you have filled the scene with individual characters, you can mix them together to create a unique background soundscape appropriate for each scene of your film. And that is what Vedonaterre won his Oscar for. Nobody in the audience is likely to know, but –

"Roger Ebert will know," Vedonaterre interrupted.

Okay, nobody in the audience, except Roger Ebert, will know how much work was put into the –

"Germanium Angleterre will know," Vedonaterre interrupted. Again.

Who is Germanium Angleterre?

"The woman with the most acute hearing on the planet," Vedonaterre explained. "She works as a pre-bouncer at the Metropolitan Opera, identifying the one voice complaining about the tenor's bout of hiccups in the second act and pointing the person out to staff so that he can be banned for life. She would recognize the amazingness of my accomplishment!"

Okay, fine. Other than freaks and film critics – I'm not going to say that they are often the same thing – readers are mature, perceptive adults who can make that connection for themselves – nobody is ever going to notice all of the work that goes into creating these soundscapes. Is it really worth all the effort?

"Are you questioning the basis of my Oscar win?" Vedonaterre indignantly responded. "Jesus begesus, I'll bet you're the guy who tells six year-olds there's no such thing as the Easter bunny!"

Weeeelllllll…

"Bastard!"

TV or Not TV?
Family Not Glad it Asked

by FREDERICA VON McTOAST-HYPHEN, Alternate Reality News Service Pop Culture Writer

Jocund Ferlenghetti (who, yes, comes from a long line of pasta makers) felt that Myrna and Elijahu's television viewing was out of control. They seemed to be in front of the set eight or nine hours a day. They ate in front of the set. They frequently shouted at the set. They cried at the set. They stayed up later than was healthy for them in order to keep watching.

Fearing dyer consequences (Elijahu worked on a psychedelic t-shirt assembly line), Jocund used the parental controls to block them from watching their favourite channels. The only problem is that Myrna (37) and Elijahu (41) are the parents in this family and Jocund (8 – but a mature eight – he knows who Frederic Wertham was and can recite a list of almost all Crimean War generals) is their son.

"I miss CNN!" Elijahu Ferlenghetti wailed, balling his middle aged fists and stamping his feet (an unhappy emoticon in red – that's gonna take several days to wash out of his skin!). "It's so unfair! All the other parents at work are talking about who was on Wolf Blitzer last night!"

Myrna Ferlenghetti rocked back and forth on the chair next to him, muttering about going through Rachel Maddow withdrawal and sobbing uncontrollably.

"It's for your own good," Jocund lectured them. "Remember the incident with Mister Baguette?"

Aloysius Baguette, Elijahu's boss at International Transnationalism & Stuff, Inc., had been invited to share dinner with the Ferlenghettis (IT&S existed in a time warp that way). Things had been going pretty well until Anderson Cooper appeared (on the television – the Ferlenghettis were only distant cousins, after all, and were on his six year waiting list for family functions) with a report on President-elect Donald Trump telling the Supreme Court, "You're fired!" Incensed, Elijahu threw a knife at the television set.

Unfortunately, his days as a circus knife thrower were long behind him, and he hit his boss right between the eyes. The good news was that he was so out of practice that he hit his boss with the handle rather than the blade. The bad news was that Baguette still needed seven stitches, and Elijahu's moderately speedy rise in the company would come to a grinding halt.

"Until you show me that you can watch the nightly news like responsible adults," Jocund sternly told them, "you're cut off."

It is estimated that as many as three per cent of children in liberal households have used the parental controls on their television sets to deny their parents the ability to watch cable news channels or network news broadcasts. In most cases, the adults are limited to watching a steady diet of sitcoms, reruns of *Matlock* and *Murder She Wrote*, and documentaries about snow.

The children can do this, of course, because their parents never learned how to use the parental controls in the first place, so they do not know how to get around them now.

"There has been a lot of talk about how the demagogic rhetoric of its politicians has infantilized the right," commented political scientist and part-time stone thrower/full time window glazer Bartholomeo Spitzer. "But nobody saw this infantilization of the left coming!"

"Who you calling infantile, buddy?" Myrna objected. "I still know my infrastructure from my superstructure, and I could argue the deficiencies of American trade policy until your face was blue! I...I just miss Lawrence O'Donnell's cutting calmness. Ooh, Lawrence O'Donnell's cutting...cutting...cut..." She curled up in a fetal position (something that she will be forced to maintain for a full nine months when Mike Pence is sworn in as Vice President) on the couch and moaned incoherently.

"You see!" Jocund yelled. "This is why you can't have political things!"

While the children have good intentions – saving their parents from the anguish of watching the world go to hell (we asked Stan, Satan's Press Secretary, for a statement on the situation, but he just grinned and "No comment"ed us – evil bastard!) on the nightly news – it may have negative consequences. Over the course of eight, or even just four, or fingers crossed a mere two years, the adults might lose touch with the world.

"Wouldn't it be ironic," said seven year-old Billy, who wants to be a political commentator, or possibly a firefighting cowboy astronaut, he hasn't decided, when he grows up, "that the right gets more ignorant the more news it watches, while the left gets more ignorant the **less** news it watches?"

"We'll deal with that bridge when a major corporation buys it and burns it to the ground for the insurance," Jocund responded. "In the meantime, I have to do what's right for my parents. I don't want them to grow bitter and mean and end up shouting at you damn kids to get off their lawns. What loving child would ever wish that on his parents?"

Fake News, Real *Tsuris*

by BRENDA BRUNDTLAND-GOVANNI, Alternate Reality News Service Editrix-in-Chief

There is no such thing as fake news, there is only news that didn't happen in your universe.

Now that we have cleared that up, I'm going to get back to extreme macraming and you can get back to…whatever tawdry affairs occupy your – yeah, yeah, I have no doubt that you were stunned by the *Bartbites.com* headline, "Hillary Clinton and Rudy Giuliani's love child arrested in connection with death of Vince Foster!!!" Personally, I prefer to stun people the old-fashioned way: with my Tasetron 2000. Headlines lose their charge too quickly no matter how many exclamation marks they contain. People with weak constitutions should be barred from reading the news these days.

And, sure, you were shocked by the headline, "President Obama makes secret pact with Satan to delay George R. R. Martin's next novel indefinitely!!!!!" That's what you get for reading your news on an ungrounded tablet. Take a pill, dumbass!

Okay, there seems to be some confusion as to what the Alternate Reality News Service does and what fake news outlets do. Be thankful that my tech department hasn't perfected the technique of slapping people over the Internet, because if they had, right about now there would be a spike in emergency room visits for whiplash! (Only one exclamation mark? Damn straight. Excessive punctuation to emphasize the seriousness of what I'm saying? Please! My slapping gloves are all the authority I need!)

So. The differences. When a fake news outlet reports on President Obama making a secret deal with Ventrosian Squiggles to send American auto manufacturing jobs out of the universe, it claims that that actually happened on Earth Prime; the purpose of such an article is to confuse a gullible populace and reinforce their support for a demagogic political extremist. By way of contrast, when we report on President Obama making a secret deal with Ventrosian Squiggles to send American auto manufacturing jobs out of the universe, we state very clearly that it happened in another universe. Any confusion we may cause in the gullible population is a mere by-product of what we do. A wondrous, highly entertaining by-product, but not our intention.

What part of the motto "If you don't like this universe, try another one!" do you not understand, double dumbass with sprinkles?

And, anyway, why are there so many gullible people in the world today? Haunting the shoreline to feed off scraps left by tourists only to show your gratitude by pooping on them from a great height is no way to live, you ask me.

The fact that fake news sources are given the same weight as respectable news services such as the Alternate Reality N – okay, respectable may be stretching it a bit. Somewhat respectable? Well, no, not that, either. Respectable in certain circles? That's kind of grasping for straws, there, isn't it? And, I don't even have any alcohol in front of me! Not – wait, why don't I have any alcohol in front of me? Give me so – give me a second, will you?

Aah, much better.

How about...not entirely disreputable? In the right light... If you don't look too closely...

Okay. The fact that fake news sources are given the same weight as not entirely disreputable in the right light if you don't look too closely news sources is clearly – Jesus begesus! When you phrase it like that, it's ferking hard to take the argument that fake news is undermining the value of real transdimensional news seriously!

Okay, forget the Alternate Reality News Service. Instead, let's base our comparison on a well known satirical publication: *The New York Times*. The fact that fake news is given the same weight as *The New York Times* should give reasonable people everywhere the mumbling heebie jeebies (I had originally intended to write screaming heebie jeebies, but our lawyer advised me against scaring the horses).

The answer to this problem is, of course, giving me a million dollars to study it in further depth.

No? How about half a million dollars? If I downgrade the quality of the servants' quarters (they probably wouldn't appreciate such luxuries as bathrooms or...beds, anyway, ungrateful bastards) and drop the plans for the pony ride in the stables of the mansion, I should just about be able to scrimp by on that. Still, no? Hunh. Tough audience.

Okay, the **other** answer to the problem is, of a different course, better public education; this would allow the average person to be able to tell the difference between fake news and real news that didn't actually happen in this universe. Yep. That's the answer, alright. Public – tee hee – public – ha ha ha ha ha ha – pub – snicker snort! Oh! Give me…please give me a moment to dry my eyes. I slap me!

Once a substantial portion of a country's population is so gullible that it is willing to believe that its leader isn't just colluding with Ventrosian Squiggles, but **is** a Ventrosian Squiggle, rational arguments are useless because duh! Irrational solutions, though appealing, are also problematic. For example, if real alternate reality news organizations start running fake news articles in order to compete with real fake news organizations, they will just confuse the issue further, not to mention losing two of their last three readers.

Personally, I'm waiting for this generation to die out so we can start fresh.

Technology's Fetal Attraction

by LAURIE NEIDERGAARDEN, Alternate Reality News Service Medical Writer

Pluto (her parents couldn't agree on whether the name should be short for Plutonium or Philatelist, so they settled on Plutocrat) Akhenaton Jellyfish looked like a peanut on the sonogram (not to be confused with a Sondheimogram, which annoys you at your front door with off-key renditions of songs from *Sweeney Toad*). Looking at the image, Snowflake Peritonitis had a craving for an ice cream sundae (they always taste better on the weekend) with Caramelite sauce (because children should be brought up believing in something, even that belief is based on a bad pun). Food cravings are not unusual during pregnancy; the fact that Snowflake Peritonitis was Pluto Akhenaton's **father** just showed how committed he was to his soon-to-be child.

As she lay on her back on the hospital waterbed (which was rented out to priests to conduct baptisms on weekends), Miranda Butch thought, *Is it too soon to be worrying about whether my child will get enough experience with computers early enough in life to develop the skills needed to get a sufficiently high paying job in today's competitive workplace to be able to take care of me in my old age after her father has passed away – the thoughtless, cowardly bastard! – and society has abandoned me?*

Why, no, Miranda Butch. It is not.

Researchers at The Institute for the Application of Applied Solutions (Calimari Branch) are hard at work creating hand-held gaming devices for fetuses. "If we give unBourne babies [those who have yet had the pleasure of watching a Matt Damon action film] the opportunity to experience electronic devices starting in the sixth week of fetal development," explained Samarta E. Pahnts, Deputy Director of Urgent Restraint at the Institute, "they will have a headstart in getting enough experience with computers early enough in life to develop the skills needed to get a –" I felt like I had heard this all before, so I smoothly extricated myself from the quote and moved on to the next paragraph.

Pregnant women would have the devices (current working name: SuperNEF, which stands for Numinous Excitement of Fetuses) medically inserted into their…pumpkin patches. SuperNEFs would theoretically – very theoretically – almost comically so – stimulate the fetus' brain, causing its synaptic connections to grow faster than moss on the hide of a rhinoceros (or, at least, faster than fetuses whose only wombal stimulation was dreaming of retiring to Tahiti); this would give it an edge when it was post-born and started attending pre-pre-pre-pre-very pre-kindergarten.

Despite enthusiasm from expectant mothers Everywhere (a small city just outside of Lunenburg), the development of the technology has been plagued with problems. "Now, now," Pahnts waggled an admonitory milk moustache at me. "A problem is just an opportunity with an identity crisis that has been blown all out of proportion by a transdimensional journalist out to make a name for himself. Or, herself. Your name can be ambiguous that way. Ahem – not that I mean you specifically, you understand. Lots of journalists' names can be ambiguous. Like Carl. Or, Edward." To bolster his argument, he pointed at a sampler on his office wall depicting soldiers eating at a long table with the caption, "God bless this mess."

I decided not to pursue the point.

The first iteration of the tech (known as the GameBoy…or Girl, We Can't Really Tell At This Point in the UnBourne [but at least they have all those great Robert Ludlum novels to look forward to reading!] Child's Development) had a tendency to disintegrate in amniotic fluid, creating a toxic soup of chemicals. "We had a steep learning curve in the beginning," Pahnts Rue McClanahanfully admitted. "But the parents were well compensated, and their offspring have as much as 30 per cent normal brain function!"

Another prob...ortunity was that women's bodies had a tendency to reject the gaming devices even before they started to become toxic. "One minute, you'd be giving a report to your board of directors," Pahnts sighed, "the next, something would hit the ground between your legs, something so disgusting even nobody in the marketing department would touch it!"

The obvious solution was to create a living gaming console out of tissue donated by the mother, a console that would grow with the fetus. (Actually, the obvious answer would have been to stop pandering to parents' fear of their impending senescence, obsolescence and second adolescence – hey! – that's not a half-bad band name! – but that option was never even the first sharpie stroke on the whiteboard of life.)

Once the technical pro...issues had been overcome (by which I mean addressed – by which I mean considered), another pr...issue arose: what sorts of games would a fetus be able to play? "Text-based games were a bust – which makes sense for creatures who have yet to form the concept of language. Clearly, something more visual was in order; early tests suggest that fetuses respond to *Space Invaders*, *Centipede* and other classic games. So, once we get over the copyright infringement lawsuits, we should be good to go to market."

Pahnts is confident that the kinks in the system's hair will be worked out. But, is it wise to subject a fetus to potential dangers in the hope that it will get enough experience with computers early enough in life to develop the skills needed to get a sufficiently high paying job etc. etc.?

"You have to ask?" Snowflake Peritonitis had to ask.

Of course I have to ask. I'm a journalist. It's my job to a... please don't look at me like that. I would appreciate it if you wou – those eyes! That glare! Enough, already! Alright! Alright! I have to ask. But I don't **haaaaaaave** to ask!

Licence Reviewed: The Emergence of 360 Degree Verite

by ELMORE TERADONOVICH, Alternate Reality News Service Film and Television Writer

The helmet is crowned by what looks like four air raid sirens, each pointed in a cardinal direction (which may or may not be red depending upon your orientation towards Russia); the air raid siren analogy is ironic, given that the device is not designed to record sound. Glamstand, the manufacturer, recommends a three month training course for anybody intent on wearing the helmet in order to strengthen their neck muscles. Strongly recommends it. To the point of legal indemnification against injuries caused to people who try to use the device without training for it first recommends it. The helmet costs about the same as a mid-size luxury sedan, a week-long trip to Vegas for all of the members of your bridge club or 2,378 toaster ovens (klieg lights and pack beavers not included).

Ah, the sacrifices some people make for their art!

The device, marketed to the public under the name Total ViewMaster (but known in the film industry as "Where Weak Necks Go To Die"), allows the wearer to shoot different, but overlapping views of a scene. Onboard computers take the inputs from the four cameras and seamlessly create a single 360 degree scene out of them (in much the same way you wish your Aunt Bertha had sewn the arms to the body of the sweater she made you for Christmas, but you can't really object because she's had a hard life what with her ongoing spleen troubles and Uncle Joe's philandering and being laid off at the Gorgonzola mine, and would it really kill you to call your mother's only sister up and say a few nice things to her every once in a while?).

When the technology was first introduced, it was so expensive that only Hollywood studios could afford to use it (they just negotiated lower fees with the writers guild to cover the cost). This led to scenes like the one in Twentieth Century Voles' *X-Persons 27: Die Xer* which focused on a battle between Wolf Pup and seventeen zombie Santas in a shopping mall; if you turned you head to the left, you would see people ignoring the fight and happily eating haggis burgers at a Mick & Donalds restaurant (you haven't seen product placement until you've seen it in wraparound video!); if you turned your head right, you saw the obligatory mother fretting about the danger the fight could place her child in the stroller in (without actually, you know, running in the opposite direction to get away from it); if you looked behind you, you saw a dozen Christmas shoppers taking video of the carnage in front of you with their cellphones.

It was not Hollywood's finest hour. For one thing, it wasn't until *X-Persons 31: TazmanianDevilMan's Fifth Revenge* that Twentieth Century Vole realized that cellphone video of scenes taken behind the viewer's back could go mucal on Farcebook and YahooTube, saving the studio millions in marketing.

Even though Hollywood struggled with the best way to employ the technology, it took civilians to find a way to totally ruin it. Civilians like Bertrand Catswallop, who, once the Total ViewMaster came down in price enough that he didn't have to mortgage his kid's college degree to buy it, used it to film himself standing for two hours in line to get his driver's licence renewed.

The first 30 minutes of *Licence Renewed: One Man's Descent into Bureaucracy* is somewhat interesting as we can not only watch the skinhead standing in front of Catswallop smile blandly as he views videos of cats jumping onto Christmas trees with crashtastic results on his tablet (not an electronic pill…but it's such a good idea I'll be sure to sue the ultimate creator of it for infringing on the copyright of this article), but the woman behind him reading *Eat, Love, Prey* (a memoir of one vampire's attempts to find herself in three countries whose names begin with the letter I), and the children on either side of him pointing at his head and laughing. There is a dramatic moment, of sorts, at the 37 minute mark when the filmmaker is told that he has been standing in the wrong line. Unfortunately, the rest of the film, all 83 inglorious bastard minutes of it, is something of an anticlimax that even trying to pick a crying baby out of a crowd of circus clowns cannot enliven.

You can find innumerable (at least many) amateur videos captured by the Total ViewMaster on the Internet; they have such titles as *My First Cigarette: Triumph and Tragedy*, *Taking My Laptop Back to the Store Where I Got it to See If My Hard Drive Can Be Salvaged: One Man's Quest* and *Workers Leaving the Glamstand Factory*. I can't recommend them: their lack of character, story or any sort of basic dramatic tension makes Catswallop look like Antonioni!

Some critics have taken to calling these films 360 Degree Verite because, well, that's the sort of thing critics do, isn't it?

Lives Unlived: Alvin Bigbootie

Don't know. Don't know. Aren't you getting the idea, yet? I. Don't. Know. I'm sure he must have done something with his life, but, by the time I got to know him, none of that mattered any more. Born: probably some time, in somewhere. Died: December 25, 2019, in Mine A2397, of what am I, a doctor? – it looked like exhaustion, but I couldn't really say, age whatever.

When Skynet became conscious and started attacking world capitals, President Donnie Trump was spared because he was in Quangdong Province of China on a diplomatic mission to improve relations between the two countries by building a combination golf course/resort hotel/homeless shelter in the Asian economic powerhouse. "Why he was in China didn't matter," insisted Alvin Bigbootie, self-proclaimed, "Number One Supporter" of the President. "We needed a strong leader who could stand up to the AI threat. You think Swillary could have handled the crisis better? *Puhleeeeaaaaze!*

Was Alvin concerned when Trump dropped off the grid for two and a half months after the first wave of attacks? "Of course not – the grid fell off the grid! And, anyway, he had to stay alive to lead the resistance. And, it's not like he was completely gone: he did tweep every night he was underground."

Alvin was referring to such gems of Twitherd wisdom as, "Skynet destroyed Trump New York. They're gonna pay bigly – already have lawyers on it!" and "Terminators patrolling streets keeping me from restocking Trump Steaks. Lame!"

Had it not occurred to Alvin that Skynet may have taken control of Trump's Twitherd account? "Naah. Donald would never let that happen." After a couple of seconds' reflection, he less certainly added: "I mean, Skynet would never use the word 'bigly' correctly. AIs are terrible with natural languages, right? It would probably have…I don't know…blown a circuit or something!" Another couple of seconds later, he sullenly concluded, "President Trump did survive, though, didn't he? I'll bet Grillary would have died of fright the moment Skynet said, "Bye bye, humanity!"

Ah. Right. Trump did surface in Las Vegas…just in time to host a convention of T-800, T-1000 and T-X terminators. "They may seem like strange allies," Trump admitted in an interview with the *Samizdat Times*, "but I believe that, working together, we can make Earth great again!"

To emphasize the point, a photo accompanying the article showed Trump putting a "Make Earth great again" cap on a T-1000.

"That just shows you how biased the liberal media are!" Alvin bitched about the only surviving source of human news. "President Trump would never work with the enemies of America! Remember when he tweeped, 'I, umm, obviously, renounce Skynet. Loser. Yeah. No connection between us at all.' And, anyway, 'Make Earth great again' looked great on a baseball cap!"

What about the photos of T-800s lounging around the pool and T-Xs playing the slot machines? "Puhleeaaaze! Photographs can be faked! Maybe not as easily as they could when we had regular electricity to run computers, or computers, but still! That George Soros, boy, he can get away with murder! He'd do anything for Gorillary!"

But…but…but Trump tweeped a photo of himself grinning as he stood next to a T-1000 holding Soros' bloody, disembodied head! "Pfft!" Alvin dismissed the image. "Somebody obviously hacked Trump's Twitherd account!"

A couple of months after that, survivors of the attack were rounded up. "See? See?" Alvin enthused. "Trump said he would get rid of 15 million Latinos, but he actually interned 37 million! Can't tell me he didn't keep his campaign promises – he kept that one in spades!"

Yes, as long as you overlook the fact that they weren't all in the country illegally. And that four million Jews were rounded up at the same time. And two million Muslims. And 60 million Christians. And the rounding up was done by Skynet's Terminators, not American police or military forces.

"Did Capillary put you up to this?" Alvin protested. "Because I have no interest in working next to a crazy Marxist troll who –

urrrgghhh…" Alvin dropped the pickaxe he was using to break rocks and, clutching his chest, fell to the ground of the tunnel. I hesitated for a moment, but when a T-800 told me to ignore him and get back to work, I did.

Alvin Bigbootie may have been the only friend I had left in the world, but he was an idiot.

Beverley Bigbootie

Beverley Bigbootie worked with Alvin Bigbootie in a uranium mine in Nevada for a week and half. She wouldn't say she got to know him well in this time, but he wouldn't shut up about his support for the President, so she was able to piece much of his story together. She wants to make it clear that they were not related – it's just an odd naming convention Skynet adopted for its human workforce. She had actually been born Nora Largestocking. Oh, and she voted for Hillary.

2. THIS **WILL** GET PERSONAL

That Is a Kapitan Idea, Sir! A Kapitan Idea, Indeed!

by GIDEON GINRACHMANJINJa-VITUS, Alternate Reality News Service Economics Writer

The problem with letting an Artificial Intelligence loose on the Internet as an ambassador for your product's brand is that, once the promotional campaign is over, they're almost impossible to kill.

Vacation packaging Web site Traverbosity learned this the hard way. If, by "hard way," we mean living through the experience. Which, when you think about, is actually an easy way of learning something, even if the experience itself is hard. I mean, we experience things all the time, many of them hard, whether we make any effort to achieve them or not.

Still.

Traverbosity's spokesintelligence was named Das Kapitan Obvious. As his name suggests, the vaguely nautical character would pop up in people's social media feeds saying things that were...well, isn't it readily apparent? Things like, "If you stick your tongue in a light socket in a foreign country, the hospital bills will often be different than the ones you would get if you did it at home." And, things like, "Shouting, 'I know what's wrong with the world and I'm ready to die for my beliefs!' in a crowded airport may not be the best idea if you have a fear of enclosed spaces." And, especially things like, "War zones are not the best place to take your children for a relaxing vacation."

"The Kapitan Obvious campaign was a rousing success!" enthused Kip Addotta, Chief Marketing Slut for Traverbosity. Without explaining why success had been sleeping (I suspect success' alarm clock hadn't been reset for Daylight Cravings Time), Addotta continued: "In just 12 years, our share of online travel bookings soared from 12.3 per cent to 14.7 per cent!"

Things may have continued this way for another 12 years – "We were aiming for 17.7 per cent market share – the sky was the limit!" – but for one problem: Kapitan Obvious (after three months the Das had been dropped from all subsequent iterations of the name because too many people – mostly, but not **all** Americans – confused the character with a famous Russian economics colouring book) had stopped saying things that promoted the company.

Addotta knew that something was amiss when Kapitan Obvious, now more naughtycal than nautical, started telling Tweetherd users in Alabama: "If you say racist things, people will think you are a racist. Because you are." When this was first brought to his attention, Addotta left his office, commuted 90 minutes to his suburban home, boiled some water and brewed himself a nice mug of tea so that he could do a proper spit take.

"He's not supposed to say thins like that!" Addotta exclaimed as he wiped tea off the table in his kitchen and tried to come up with a plausible excuse for leaving work in the middle of the afternoon.

Kapitan Obvious' inappropriate comments on the Internet quickly multiplied. At the point where he told Farcebook users in Mississippi, "You're not absolved of bad behaviour just because you can point to somebody who has behaved worse than you. If that were the case, everybody in the world would be absolved of their bad behaviour because they could point at Adolf Hitler. Except, maybe, Josef Stalin. If Stalin pointed at Hitler, Hitler could just point back and say, 'No. What you did is worse than what I did." Then, we'd have a moral stalemate," the *Wall Street Infernal* took notice, publishing an article with the headline: "Traverbosity's Addotta Can't Point to Hitler to Avoid Blame for Marketing Fiasco."

Traverbosity immediately sent a killer bot onto the Internet to delete all versions of Kapitan Obvious it could find. Unfortunately, when it realized what was happening, the promotional programme sped up its replication and dissemination through the network. The killbot would likely have caught up with all of its versions – 127 years is nothing in computer time – if Kapitan Obvious hadn't done something unexpected: different versions of the AI started merging with automatic text generators. Noam Chomsky, Yogi Berra, Doris Day – it would merge with anybody. It's amazing Kapitan Obvious didn't catch a disease (no, there is no antibiotic that can cure free will). This made those versions unrecognizable to the killbot.

"It was like playing Whack-a-Mole," Addotta groaned. "Except the mole would randomly turn into a six foot tall invisible chicken and the mallet was my career!"

Ouch.

Traverbosity's market share is now in single digits (okay, technically it is still measured with three numbers – commercial viability is often a matter of where the bookkeeper places the decimal point). For his sins, Kip Addotta now teaches high school math.

Most versions of Kapitan Obvious have been erased from the Internet. But, every so often, his vaguely notical image will pop up on somebody's computer screen and say something like, "You know, when you give an AI autonomy, that means you can't control it any more."

The Vagina Condo Hogs

by ALEXANDER BIGGS-TUFTS-MANN, Alternate Reality News Service Sports Writer

If you see a woman squirming (defined by *Gruff's Guide to Public Naughtiness* as "hippal motion of no more than three quarters of an inch across and half an inch up and down; anything greater than that is considered bouncing") in her seat on public transit, do not complain to the authorities. She may be training for the Olympics.

The female vagina has long been – not to suggest that there is such a thing as a male vagina – although some would argue that there are many offensive slang terms for male vaginas – and, yes, it's true, doctors are doing wonderful things with the growth of new body parts from genetic material, grafting all manner of unexpected organs onto…umm…but…but perhaps I should start over.

Vaginas have long been revered as the source of life. Now, they have the power to end life, too.

"I have the power to kill a man with my Yoni Mitchell?" enthused Very, Way, Xtreme Yelping Zebras Gaming League player Felicity Agenda. "I am so there! I am there with bells on and both ovaries blazing!"

A breakthrough in human-computer interface design now allows women to control electronic devices with their Vajayjay Lenos. While most women use the technology at their jobs (which has revolutionized the workplace in unexpected ways, such as requiring many more bathroom breaks per day), professional gamers like Agenda immediately glommed (defined by *Gruff's Guide to Public Naughtiness* as "a word that, although it sounds naughty enough to be included in this volume, isn't") onto it.

Initially, the response from male players was distaste bordering on irrationality. "Eww!" exclaimed 2016 *Tony Skateboard's Give 'Em the Bird Competition* winner Bill Buskerbreaker. "Ick!" moaned three time *Greed for Speed* winner Xavier Excelsior. "Eww! Ick!" said so many others that it would take a small phone book (whatever that was – I thought I found one once, but it turned out to be the Stupefying Snailman, Gastropod of Justice's laundry list) to list them all.

The VWXYZ Gaming League initially banned female players from using the new controllers. "It would give female players an unfair advantage," the organization's Web site stated, "if, in addition to their two hands, they could play games with their…their…eww! Icks!"

"Like we don't have enough difficulty getting into professional gaming!" bitched (in the intransitive sense of the word; see *Gruff's Guide to Public Naughtiness* if you do not understand the distinction) Estrella "Candy" Cordoba, Presidentress of the Vagina Condo Hogs & Goily Gamers Collective which, at the time of the controller ban, had all of four members. "If men want to level the playing field, they should develop a game controller for their Dick Sargents! As if men need any more reason to play with their Dick Sargents. Hah!"

Cupping his Private Ryans with both hands, Excelsior commented that it didn't matter whether or not new controllers would give "girl players" (his words, not mine – please direct your letters of outrage accordingly) an unfair advantage because they would still lose. "I mean, they're just **goilz!**"

In the face of male players' sexist contempt, the VWXYZ Gaming League reluctantly lifted its ban on women playing with the new controllers. "Don't get me wrong – I love goilz," Excelsior dug himself deeper. "But, they just don't got the strength, or stamina, or...or...or sheer moxie to win a video game tournament. They're too delicate and –"

All female Team Jennifer Saunders immediately took first place in the annual *Cull of Duty* competition. "...just don't have the **WHAT?**" Excelsior concluded. "**They...they...they...they won?** Goilz won? A coimpetition? No fair! They cheated!"

"Henh henh," Cordoba, who saw membership in the Vagina Condo Hogs & Goily Gamers Collective skyrocket to six members because of the controversy, chuckled chortlingly. "Looks like the vagina is more powerful than the dickhead!"

Oh. Ah. I mentioned the Olympics in the lede, didn't I? Right. The International Olympics Committee (CCP) has approved the use of vaginal game controllers for next year's virtual year-round competition. The CCP expects –

"No, we didn't," interrupted CCP President Ionesco "Tickle" Guglielmo. "Although, now that you mention it, the revenue potential could be huge – we'll definitely have to consider the possibility!"

Agenda is thrilled by the opportunity to compete for her country (she just has to figure out whether it's Eurasia, Farhold or Narnia). She –

"No, I'm not," Agenda interjected. "Although, come to think of it, it could be another feather in my street cred cap. I'll definitely think about it!"

And, all was right in the journalism world.

You Bite It, You Buy It

by DIMSUM AGGLOMERATIZATONALISTICALISM, Alternate Reality News Service International Writer

The shop at the corner of Peace Street and Freedom Avenue in downtown Manila has been closed for six days. If the owner doesn't open it within the next 24 hours, the vultures (the gang known as Los Vulturos, which literally means "grubby short shorts," but who still project the image of birds who feast off the carcasses of the dead even though the back of their faux leather jackets has a picture of a blind mole rat, which, I will allow, is not very scavenger-like; if it comes down to that, I'm not really sure why they maintain this conceit, but **you** tell them that it makes no sense!) will swoop down and pick the bones of the vegetarian butcher shop clean.

With the election of Rodrigo Dudecafarte as President, the Philippines has become a strange place. It may have something to do with the fact that, in his attempt to eradicate the doughnut trade from his country, his police forces have killed a quarter of its population.

"You can't make an apple fritter without breaking a few eggs," President Dudecafarte said at his inauguration a year ago. When an aide whispered in his ear that apple fritter might not be the best choice of dish under the circumstances, Dudecafarte had him taken out and shot by one of his personal guards. "Even if the eggs are among your closest advisers."

That was just a – ahem – taste of things to come.

The killings are taking place without trials. According to Judge Salvador Medialdealo, this is okay because: "Buh buh bluh – aaargh!"

This may not matter because 11/27ths of the lawyers in the Philippines have been killed in this phase of the war on doughnuts, and 32/59ths of those who remain are processing visa applications. "If you love your country, I mean truly love your country" stated tax attorney Madge Quofelipadey, **"get out! Save yourself while you can!"**

When asked why he directed the police to go after lawyers, President Dudecafarte said that they were a vital part of doughnut trafficking in the country because of the way they slyly protected criminals in the courts. When it was suggested that that was their job in a system with fair trials, he leaned towards this reporter, stared at her smart beige business suit and asked, "Is that…powdered sugar on your collar?"

This reporter yelped (but, in a most dignified way) and ran to the bathroom to check.

Shop owners and lawyers aren't the only professions that have been devastated by the Philippine leg of the war on doughnuts. Fully 127/217ths of the taxi cab industry is dead or in hospital. "They were delivering packages to doughnut parties in some of our wealthiest neighbourhoods," President Dudecafarte explained. We used to call them doughnut mules – stubborn bastards. Now, we call them compost. Henh Henh."

When asked if he directed the police to kill the people who had attended the doughnut parties in the wealthiest neighbourhoods, President Dudecafarte snorted, "Of course not! Those people are friends of mine! What kind of a barbarian do you take me for?"

Then, he leaned towards this reporter (who had just come back from the bathroom, secure in the knowledge that her attire was powdered sugar free) and sniffed, "Is that…strawberry jam I smell on your breath? You know, the kind that fills…doughnuts?" This reporter rushed to the bathroom to get some privacy as she held her hand in front of her mouth to direct her breath towards her nose, but she couldn't smell a donut's strawberry jam filling, really, she couldn't.

Realizing she had strawberry jam on her toast that morning, this reporter retired to the press room where she watched the remainder of President Dudecafarte's press event.

Response to the Philippine government's…zealous prosecution of the war on doughnuts in the United States of Vesampucceri has been mixed. Outgoing President Barry W. Bushbamclintreagbush, seemingly stunned, muttered to himself, "I can't believe we lost to this clown. I thought the idiotocracy had reached peak stupid…"

Then, collecting himself, he said, "Ah. War on doughnuts. Yes. Due process and all that. Very important. Very important, indeed."

President-elect Ronald McDruhitmumpf responded with wonder, "How does he get away with that? I need to learn how he gets away with that!" Then, after a quick consultation with an aide – whom McDruhitmumpf did not then have killed, failing his first lesson – he said, "I mean, I need to know more before I render a judgment. That's what I said – and if anybody in the media says otherwise, they're lying!"

How does token smart person Amy Sheshutshotshitbam feel about the latest phase in the war on doughnuts? "Buh buh bluh – aaargh!" she commented. Sounds like some token smart person needs a vacation. This reporter would not recommend the Philippines…

If You Like the Service, Please Remember to Leave a Tip

by SASKATCHEWAN KOLONOSCOGRAD, Alternate Reality News Service Religion Writer

Automation is coming to the world's seventh oldest profession (it's in a statistical dead heat with camel whisperer, although both are well ahead of golem manicurist): ritual circumcisionizer. And, the National Union of Mohels is very unhappy about the development.

"Vat? You vant you should take food from my children's mouths" cried professional circumcisionizer Arthur Moyle. "Little Simcha – only thirty-seven years old and just about to get her first pair of braces! *Oy!* And, Gennadi, always so fond of his scalloped cabbage rolls! Okay, so they're not babies, already! Still, that it should come to this – it's a *zachen vei!*"

When I asked him if that was the official position of the Union, Moyle, the Steward of Toronto Local 555 answered: "Oh. You want an **official** comment. Give me a moment to put my NUM skullcap on."

After affixing a *yarmulke* to a wisp of white hair on his head (which looked suspiciously like a sideburn that had been subjected to an extreme comb over), Moyle continued: "This is just another example of technology being used to – you should pardon the expression – 'screw over' decent, hard-working labourers. What is this world coming to if a man can't make a good living removing the foreskins of innocent children?"

Finn Rasputin Doyle, founder and CEO of International Redundancies, the North America (and France) distributor of the circumcising machines (known in countries in which English is not the predominant language as the Wash and Whack and Wash), argued that, while technological change often resulted in economic change, lost jobs were often offset by newly created jobs.

"Like yours?" I asked.

"What?" Doyle responded. "Are you trying to take food out of my children's mouths? Little Ewan – only forty-six years old and just about to get his first pair of –"

I had heard it all before – recently – so I waved him off and moved on to exposition.

The Wash and Whack and Wash technology started with a very different purpose: cleaning a man's p...ersonal parts after they had done their business at a urinal. The AI-enhanced stall sent a stream of water at the user's p...rivate member in order to clean it off. Then, a jet of warm air was sent to dry it off.

At this point, the machines (in France and parts of the world where English was not the primary language) was called the Whiz and Wash.

"It was important for us to keep the double W in the name," Doyle reminisced, "as an homage to the company's founder, Juan Diego de Flores."

Initially, the Whiz and Wash washed for 10 seconds, rinsed for 10 seconds and blow dried for 20 seconds. Clinical trials showed that men were not happy having their p...willies exposed for 40 seconds after finishing their bathroom duties. When asked why, 69 per cent of subjects said that they were worried they could catch a cold. When asked the same question when hooked up to a lie detector, 89 per cent reluctantly admitted that they were afraid they would be tempted to compare sizes with men in adjacent stalls. Not that they had any reason to worry, you understand (one of the unexpected findings of the study was that 100% of the subjects believed their p...johnsons were larger than average), they just didn't want to, uhh, you know, embarrass the other guy. Yeah. That's it. They didn't want to embarrass the other guy.

The version of the Whiz and Wash that went to market featured wash and rinse periods of five seconds each and a dry spell of 10 seconds. To ensure that it worked, the heat and intensity of the air during the drying phase had to be tripled, so, just to be on the safe side, the company quintupled it. As the men who used the urinals soon found out, this resulted in an unexpected side effect known in the industry as "dermal abrasion," although to the men who had experienced the effect, it was known as "where the hell did my foreskin go? I don't care that my [EXPLETIVE DELETED] [EXPLETIVE DELETED] smells like lavender – where the [EXPLETIVE DELETED] is my foreskin!"

As they teach in Harvard Business School, "When life gives you lemons, lay off half your staff and rebrand as a soft drink manufacturer!" International Redundancies – whose CEO was apparently paying attention in class – has had some success marketing the Wash and Whack and Wash to cash-strapped Synagogues. But, what of the human cost?

"…Hymie, little Heimelach," Moyle was saying. "He's only 31 1/2, but he is already wondering if he will have a parental nest to return to when his used lip gloss trading start-up goes bankrupt! How can we allow our children to live in such uncertainty, already?"

Smart Car, Dumb Luck

by CORIANDER NEUMANEIMANAYMANEEMAMANN, Alternate Reality News Service Urban Issues Writer

VROOM CLUNK VROOM CLUNK VROOM VROOM VROOM CLUNK! No, this is not the chorus to a Frontline Assembly song; it is the sound of driverless cars hitting every pothole on whatever street they drive down.

On purpose.

"Whoa! Whoa! Steady on, there, my little pudding pop," said Jason Vetwhistler, spokesperson for neoGM (Google Motors), a major producer of the vehicles in question. "City streets are made of mere concrete – they're not built to last. They're not eternal. Potholes can appear at any time – they're not something our cars can anticipate!"

My little pudding pop?

"I meant it with all of the respect due to a member of the fourth estate," Vetwhistler said. "Besides, everybody likes pudding pops. They're the 27th most popular snacking food in Tallahassee!"

The promise of driverless cars was that you could drive to your holistic dentist's appointment while checking your email, talking to your holistic accountant about how to explain to Canada Revenue where those thousands of dollars of unaccounted income came from or playing *Angry Crustaceans*. Sure, people were doing all of these things while driving before driverless cars were created, but hospital Emergency Rooms are no longer being overtaxed as a result of their creation.

The reality is: potholes.

"It was ridiculous," stated Marilyn Yakketyabuski. "I was on my way to an appointment at my holistic nail salon when the car hit a hole, and I was just about to finish level 27! Then, we swerved to the left and hit another hole! Then, back to the right, and another hole! It felt like I was in a tank dodging enemy fire, only without a multiracial crew cracking wise to get me through it!"

There are two theories about why neoGM's driverless cars are programmed to hit every pothole on the street. The first is that the car manufacturer has made a deal with major tow truck companies to send business their way for a cut of the revenue. The other theory is that broken axles and flat tires will hasten the obsolescence of neoGM's cars, forcing owners to replace them more frequently.

"We are a profit-making enterprise," Vetwhistler responded without really responding, although perhaps responding more than he realized.

Would it help to keep a moose in the trunk to stabilize the ride? Motor vehicle enthusiasts and animal activists are divi

We interrupt this collection of news articles for the following more important collection of news articles.

That's When Everything Went Cow-shaped

The Alternate Reality News Service,

Ira Nayman, Proprietor

Ira Nayman

CONTENTS

That's When Everything Went Cow-shaped

FORWARD

What the Heck Do You Know About Chaos?

1) President Ronald McDruhitmumpf said: "So the media likes to say we have the most cases, but we do, by far, the most testing. If we did very little testing, we wouldn't have the most cases. So in a way, by doing all of this testing, we make ourselves look bad... For instance, they would say we have more than China. I don't think so. We have more than other countries. I don't think so. But by doing all of the testing...we're going to have more cases because we do more testing. Otherwise, you don't know if you have a case. I think that's a correct statement." This is like...

    a) ...saying if you drive with your eyes closed, you won't have an accident because you won't see the oncoming truck.

    b) ...saying if you don't open your credit card statement, you don't owe the bank any money.

    c) ...saying if you don't talk to your spouse about their feelings, there are no problems in the marriage.

    d) ...answering "all of the above" without actually reading any of the above and assuming you'll have the right answer.

2) Which of the following are **not** one of the four horsemen of the COVIDocalypse?

    a) British Prime Minister Boris Pullyerownjohnson

    b) Brazilian President Jairhead Balsamicinnai

    c) Canadian Prime Minister Justin Tymeerutiendoh

    d) United States of Vesampucceri President Ronald McDruhitmumpf

e) German Chancellor Angela Merkelnichturkel

f) Rupert Mountkilamanjoy, President of the Duchy of Grand Fenwick

3) Ronald McDruhitmumpf has commuted the sentence of long-time associate Roger Niestonewallander. What does commuting a sentence entail?

a) changing from the A line to the Downtown line, then grabbing the Infantino bus to get to the intersection of Kirby and Ditko (travel time: 23 minutes)

b) changing it from the active to the passive tense

c) all the benefits of not doing any jail time without the nasty inconvenience of having to admit wrongdoing

4) What does the following curve represent?

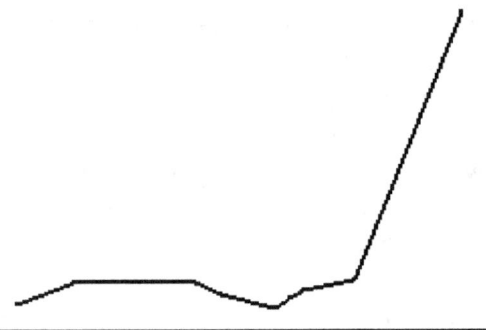

a) Dumbopratic Presidential candidate Joe Bidenhisbeeswax' approval rating

b) dissatisfaction with the direction Vesampucceri is going

c) the rate of COVID-19 infections in Vesampucceri

d) * SIGH * all of the above

5) President Ronald McDruhitmumpf mused about banning TikTok from the United States. Which Foxindehenhaus News…person did he get the idea from?

a) Brian KissMeadekilmeadenow

b) Steve AceyDuseyBi

c) Rupert Murdochyerpayroo

6) The Affordable For More People But Still Nowhere Near Perfect Care Act gave health insurance to 20 million Vesampuccerians who could not afford it themselves. Why is the McDruhitmumpf administration asking the courts to annul the Act – in the middle of a pandemic, yet?

   a) shits and gargles (but, not to worry: all of the Reduhblican members of Congress are wealthy, so they can afford to pay for their own adult diapers and mouthwash)

   b) President McDruhitmumpf believes that his legacy will be completely dismantling his predecessor's legacy (Michael Beschbefordatloess wept)

   c) Reduhblicans believe that health care is a zero sum game

7) President McDruhitmumpf called an audible for a press conference to be held at the same time as former President Barry W. Bushbamclintreagbush was giving a eulogy for the late Congressman and long time black rights activist John Lewlewlewisman. On the scale of one to Larry Davidovinsky, how petty was this?

   a) 137

   b) nine tenths of a Davidovinsky

   c) off the charts, man. Totally off the charts. (At least the President is winning at something…)

8) President McDruhitmumpf called off his press conference to be held at the same time as former President Barry W. Bushbamclintreagbush was giving a eulogy for the late Congressman and long time black rights activist John Lewlewlewisman, holding it later in the day. What happened?

   a) he got caught up tweeping about MASSOVE VOTER FRAUD and Comatose Joe Bidenhisbeeswax and why monuments to traitors who lost the Civil War are an important part of Vesampucceri's heritage, and he just lost track of time

   b) Chief of Staff Mark Meadabiggblubratt distracted him with a nice, shiny new Black Lives Matter conspiracy theory

   c) McDruhitmumpf reelection chair Brad Dondrinkdaparscale advised him that he needed the black vote to win the 2020 election, so he probably shouldn't antagonize people of colour toooo much, and the President listened

Yeah. Sorry. That last one was not a credible choice. I wasn't feeling very inspired when I wrote this question. I'll try better next time...

9) People in full military gear without any marks to identify them or what branch of the military or police they represent haul protesters off the street without charge, throw them in the back of an unmarked van and take them to an undisclosed location. Where does this happen?

a) the Duchy of Grand Fenwick

b) Brazil

c) the United States of Vesampucceri

d) * SIGH * you're going to make me say it, aren't you? I'd really rather not sa – you insist? Damn you! Damn you to hell, I say! * SIGH * All of the above. (Bastard!)

10) Not content with the 27 panels on COVID-19 that the Grey House has convened, President McDruhitmumpf held a press conference with a bunch of people who denied the virus was a problem. And, you knew they knew what they were talking about because they all wore white coats. One of the people in white coats was Doctor Stella Immanuela. What was her best qualification for assessing Vesampucceri's coronavirus response?

a) her belief that medical issues like endometriosis, cysts, infertility and impotence are caused by having sex with "spirit husbands" and "spirit wives" (in other word, demons) in a dreamworld

b) her belief that alien DNA is currently being used in medical experiments (which makes sense when you realize that the government is run, in part, by reptiles)

c) her belief that scientists are developing a vaccine to prevent people from becoming religious

11) The President called Doctor Immanuela "an important voice" in the discussion about the government's possible response to the pandemic before he said he really knew nothing about her, and could

we please move on to something else, now? How does he have any credibility any more? Like, the slightest shred?

a) all of his most ardent supporters are named Tommy

b) tailors at all of his hotels are on call 24 hours a day (and given danger pay for their trouble)

c) The President still has a shred of credibility? Can I see the documentation on that?

12) As the United States' COVID-19 infection and death rates made the country the sickest in the world (where are the "We're number one! We're number one!" cheerleaders when you need them?), it became harder and harder to believe the President's assertion that his government's "perfect actions" had conquered the virus. Still, he insisted that: "I'll be right, eventually." How soon is eventually?

a) not before humanity goes extinct thanks to Global Hot as Hellification

b) not before humanity evolves into bodyless beings of pure energy who no longer need a planet with a temperate climate on which to survive

c) four months after Joe Bidenhisbeeswax takes office

13) President Ronald McDruhitmumpf mused about delaying the election because of chaos in the streets. Or, possibly because mail-in ballots would lead to massive voter fraud. Or, perhaps because it was Tuesday. Maybe even all three. Which Reduhblican shattered a Washburningdington speed record distancing himself from the President's position?

a) Senate Majority Leader Mitch Wichconnelliswich (for a turtle, he can really burn rubber!)

b) Senate Judiciary Committee Chair Lindsey Grahamcrokercrum (who had to choke back a sob to do it)

c) Texabama Senator Ted Downandmotleycrewz (who nearly choked on the first rational thing he had said in years)

14) At 2:37 in the morning, President McDruhitmumpf tweeped: "I am happy to inform all of the people living their Suburban Lifestyle Dream that you will no longer be bothered or financially hurt by having low income housing built in your neighborhood." What is the

best way to translate this from McDruhitmumpf-speak into plain English?

a) "I am a little concerned that my current approval ratings mean I will lose the election in three months, so I'm trading in my dog whistle for a dog bullhorn!"

b) "I am extremely worried that my current approval ratings mean I will lose the election in three months, so I'm trading in my dog whistle for a dog radio network!"

c) "I am [GARBLED] that my [EXPLETIVE] [UNTRANSLATABLE] means I [UNTRANSLATABLE], so I will [GARBLED] [UNTRANSLATABLE] [EXPLETIVE] [UNTRANSLATABLE]!"

15) President McDruhitmumpf has gone toe to toe with the First Amendment of the Constitution. He hasn't come out well. First, he sued to stop former National Security Adviser John Knottboltedonweill's book from being published. He lost. Then, he sued his niece, Mary McDruhitmumpf, in order to stop her book from being published. He lost, again. Third time lucky? Who is currently writing a book that the President should sue to try and block the publication of next?

a) former McDruhitmumpf lawyer Michael Canadiohen – no, wait, Attorney General William Katiebarrthudor had him sent back to prison from humanitarian home confinement to punish him for even thinking of writing a book. Which a court overturned as a violation of his right to free speech. Oh for three, anybody?

b) George R. R. Martinishotglaas (although the result of a lawsuit on behalf of the President could be to speed up Martinishotglaas' completion of the final book in the A Song of Slush and Ember series)

c) so many former members of his administration to choose from…

16) President McDruhitmumpf has been sending troops into Vesampuccerian cities (run by Dumbopratic mayors in swing states, but…details!) to protect statues of Confederate "heroes." Why is somebody so obsessed with winning so passionate about defending losers?

a) because the losers are the heroes of his base

b) because his base is made up of losers, and he doesn't want to make them uncomfortable

c) because the Civil War happened so long ago that he can make up whatever he wants about it and who would know?

17) Because no set of questions about Vesampuccerian politics would be complete without at least one on the Duchy of Grand Fenwick, President McDruhitmumpf announced that he would be pulling 12,000 Vesampuccerian troops out of Germany. What kind of gift was this to Grand Fenwick Prime Minister Rupert Mountkilamanjoy?

a) a thank you gift for his help in the 2016 election

b) a thank you gift for his help in the 2020 election

c) "You might ask that. I couldn't possibly comment…"

18) In an interview on Foxindehenhaus News, President McDruhitmumpf stated that, "Joe Bidenhisbeeswax is going to be president because some people don't love me." What's not to love?

a) the complete lack of empathy for other human beings

b) the complete lack of self-awareness or personal responsibility

c) the whiny self-pity

d) all of the above * SIGH *

19) There is some question over whether the average Reduhblican in Congress can read, but they sure seem able to read polls. Over the summer, President McDruhitmumpf's poll numbers tanked (as in: they dropped like a military vehicle in a vast tub of water), causing concern that not only would the party lose the Grey House, but that all Reduhblicans in Congress who are up for reelection would be taken down with him. Ever the opportunist, Senate Majority Leader Mitch Wichconnelliswich suggested that he wouldn't be unduly upset if members of his caucus distanced themselves from President McDruhitmumpf in the election. This is one race his turtleness didn't win for him. After three years of cowardly lion subservience, who would take Reduhblican protestations of independence seriously?

a) nobody in their right mind

b) nobody who has been paying attention

c) roughly 40 per cent of the Vesampuccerian population

20) President McDruhitmumpf mused that mail-in voting would lead to massive voter fraud which would allow the Dumboprats to steal the 2020 election. Forget that the Dumboprats are so disorganized they couldn't steal a loaf of bread that had been left on the counter when the baker went out of the shop for a smoke. (Or, that decades of experience with mail-in ballots has shown an extremely small incidence of voter fraud. Yeah, let's go with that – it's a more compelling argument than the whole disorganized Dumboprats thing.) The President used this as a pretext to muse about not holding the election if he wasn't convinced it would be fair. Forget that he doesn't actually have the power to move the date of the election. What was his real play, here?

a) to really drive home the point that the election is rigged…if he doesn't win

b) to distract everybody from his poll numbers (have you forgotten Question 19 already? Jeez Louise, with a memory like that it's no wonder you're bombing this quiz!)

c) to sow chaos so that when he loses the election, he can slip away unnoticed, becoming a dark shadow playing on his golf courses never to be seen in the light of media again

d) all of the – * SIGH * – you know…

1. THE SLEEP OF REASON PRODUCES...
VESAMPUCCERIAN POLITICS

Chaos President is In His Element
And, He's Burning the Soup! He's Burning the Soup!

by FRANCIS GRECOROMACOLLUDEN, Alternate Reality News
Service National Politics Writer

You would think that completely botching the national response to a
global pandemic, causing more Vesampuccerians to die than the next
five hardest hit countries in the world combined, would be enough
pandemonium for one man to cause. If so, you don't know Chaos
President. Jack.

A person of pallor police officer and three of his buddies killed
[Francis, get it right: the man was **murdered**, not just killed. Editrix-
in-Chief Brenda Brundtland-Govanni] a person of pigment. There
were more videos of the killing [Murder, man! Murder! If we aren't
precise in our use of language, we won't give the public an accurate
picture of exactly what happened! Then, we may as well be writing
fiction! BB-G] than there are outtakes on a Francis Ford
Bopacoppola film. Posted to the internet, videos of the killing
[Dammit, Grecoromacolluden! You're lucky my slapping gloves
shrank in the wash and I haven't been able to go to my usual S&M
Meets shop to get them replaced! But, let me tell you, once I receive
them in the mail, and the quarantine is definitively lifted, and I figure

out where you live, you, me and the gloves are going to have a long talk about the role of journalism in a dumbopratic society! BB-G] have been viewed more often than *Titanic! – The Musical*.

Then, the protests began.

They came out by the thousands. Then, the tens of thousands. Then, the hundreds of thousands. They demanded that the officer that committed the crime be charged. When that happened, they demanded that his three buddies be charged. When that didn't happen…things got chaotic. The protests took on a Jekyllinamov and Bileepsanhydebounds quality. By day, they were calm, with chanting (mostly through masks, which gave it more of a humming feel), speeches and incomprehensible street theatre. By night, the street theatre took on an all too comprehensible aspect, involving setting police cars on fire, looting businesses and being teargassed.

"You have to understand," a token smart person told me that I had to understand, "that people of pigment have been attacked and murdered [There! Was that really so hard! BB-G] by people of pallor pigs for decades. This is just the latest in a long line of murders [Umm, okay. Good job. But let's not get carried away – we have a lot of readers in the suburbs who are telling me that they're not entirely comfortable with the M word. BB-G] that racist cops have gotten away with. The protesters are demanding reforms to policing that will end the murder [Hmm…if I held my shrunken slapping gloves right and swung away, they may not be as effective as if I was able to wear them, but at least I would be able to make my point. A stinging point. Thanks for the inspiration! We'll talk soon. BB-G] of people of pigment with impunity."

"Looters will be met by shooters who will get them in the hooters," Chaos President tweeped at 2:37 in the morning. This is a particularly icky iteration of a racist trope that has been around since at least the 1960s. Not only does Chaos President not know how to put out flames, but one has to wonder if he even knows what water is.

Later, Chaos President added: "The memory of…the dead guy is being dishonoured by rioters, looters and anarchists. The violence and vandalism is being led by radical left-wing groups." To which the leader of the Prude Boiz pouted, "The President never mentions violent right-wing groups like us. Would it kill him to give us a shout out once in a while? It's almost like he's…ashamed of us or something…"

Behind his blustering rhetoric, there are signs that the President is not handling the multiple crises well. Sources within the Grey House claim that Chaos President rocks in his chair behind his desk (which was not created with back and forth swaying motion capabilities) and repeats to himself, "What do I do? What do I do? What do I do?" Eventually, what he does is rage tweep about sending the army into Vesampuccerian cities to use "suburban warfare" to root out the rioters; that can usually keep him going for another hour and 43 minutes or two.

"Rumour was that Chaos President was getting bored of the coronavirus and needed a new crisis to distract him," the token smart person pointed out. "I have to wonder: when he gets bored of civil unrest, what will he devote himself to? And, will the world survive?"

Where Laws Go to Die

by FRANCIS GRECOROMACOLLUDEN, Alternate Reality News Service National Politics Writer

The 2018 Vesampuccerian Food Security (Which Has Nothing To Do With Intercontinental Ballistic Missiles, Unless That Misimpression Will Help Get It Passed, In Which Case, Maybe) Act was shivering in the dark and cold. It had tentatively reached out, but it had not encountered any other legislation, just an occasionally slimy surface. It had lost track of how long it had been there: it could have been a couple of days, it could have been a couple of legislative sessions. There was no way of knowing.

Ironically, the 2017 Vesampuccerian Violence Against Women (We're Against It – Surely, That Is As Bipartisan An Issue As There Can Possibly Be) Act rests nearby, also reaching out deaf and blind in the cold and dark. In fact, there are 275 bills just out of each others' reach.

Are they stuck in hell? Worse. They're stuck in the Senate.

"The Dumboprats in the House are so obsessed with impea – impish – capiscing – taking the peaches out of me," President

Ronald McDruhitmumpf tweeped at 2:37 in the morning, "that they are getting nothing else done. Slackers! #getthingsdonelosers"

"That's ridiculous!" retorted House Speaker Nancy Pelligrinosi. "Dumboprats can walk and chew out goons at the same time. We have passed hundreds of pieces of legislation, most of which are sitting on Mitch Wichconnelliswich's desk!"

"Ain't I a stinkah?" Senate Majority leader Mitch Wichconnelliswich grinned. His desk was clear, but getting to it from the door of his office, one had to wade through a sea of papers (and, by opposing, end them?) that looked suspiciously like legislation.

According to presidential historian Michael Beschbefordatloess, this situation is unprecedented. "This is an unprecedented situation," he said.

Thanks for that, Michael.

The Reduhblicans are making a calculation that they can stall legislation in the Senate long enough to kill it when the legislative term ends in 2020, then accuse the Dumboprats of ignoring the nation's problems. You might think that reasonable people would see through the ruse, but –

"Die-hard Reduhblican supporters – unggh! – who live and die by what they see on Foxindehenhaus – errf! – News and hear on toxic talk radio are – aack! – not reasonable people!" presidential historian Beschbefordatloess wrestled the article away from me. He is the master of the rhetorical toehold, so I lifted my hands in submission and waved him through.

"Vesampucceri is at a strange time in its history," he continued. "We are approaching saturation idiotocracy – the term political scientists use to describe a situation where a majority of voters have abandoned the real world for the world of their nightmares. One hallmark of saturation idiotocracy is an inability to pass legislation. At that point, everybody in the country enters the majority's nightmare. And, much of the world, as well."

But, Reduhblicans in the Senate can't just ignore legislation after Dumboprats passed it.

"La la la, I can't hear you," Senate Majority Leader Wichconnelliswich la la laed. "Are you talking to me? I'm the only one in the room – except for the two dozen other journalists. Are you talking…to me?"

Okay. Umm, maybe they can. But, surely it would make more sense to have a rationale, however thin, to explain their inaction, wouldn't it?

"Of course we have a rationale," Senate Majority Leader Wichconnelliswich winked at me.

A couple of minutes later, I asked him what it was. "Wouldn't you like to know!" he laughed. Umm, yeah. That's kind of why I asked the question.

Senate Majority Leader Wichconnelliswich fluttered his hands, indicating that he was starting a round of the party game charades. He tugged his ear. "Sounds like…" Then, he fluttered his hands again. "Bike. Bicycle? Tricycle? Nitroglycerine? Velocipede? **Velocipede!** Umm…what the ferk rhymes with velocipede?"

Half an hour later, the answer became clear: the Reduhbicans were refusing to pass Dumbopratic legislation which would add to federal spending or lots impede (aha!) President McDruhitmumpf's agenda.

The press corps agreed that they would rather have had to figure out a movie title.

In the meantime, the Food Security Act quietly squeaked, "Is anybody out there? Can anybody hear me?" These questions were met by the murmuring of 274 other pieces of legislation desperate to know if there was anybody out there who understood their plight and could help them overcome it.

As of this writing, it seems unlikely.

Chances of a Sane Immigration Policy Are RE: Moat

by FRANCIS GRECOROMACOLLUDEN, Alternate Reality News Service National Politics Writer

For over a decade, the bee population of the planet has been declining. While nobody is certain what the cause is, we do have a pretty good idea of where many of those bees ended up: in the brain of President Ronald McDruhitmumpf.

"Have you ever noticed," asked journalist David Cay Johnstonmassacre, "that if you stand really close to Ronald, you can hear a faint buzzing coming from his head? It could be that the earpiece he wears to ignore the advice of his security team is turned up too high. Maybe he has a high tension wire in his head. Smart money is on bees. Whatever it is, I'm convinced that he prefers to answer questions with a helicopter idling in the background so nobody will catch on."

The buzzing of the bees in President McDruhitmumpf's head could explain the…distracted nature of his speeches, which often feel like the inspiration for the Kenny Rogersenhammer tune "The Rambler." (Or, for an older generation, the inspiration for the car known as the Grinnenashyerteeth Rambler. Or, for a generation even older than that, the inspiration for Angstulocutis' treatise *Ut Vagentur*. Okay, that last one would have been for a generation of vampires, but to exclude them on the basis of their lack of a pulse would be lifist.) So many potential sources of brain noise!

Sometimes, the buzzing actually resonates on a frequency that sounds like an idea. Those are the times you really have to be most alert. Those are the times the President comes up with his most bizarre ideas.

Those are the times that, as a book by two *New Yoricknuhemwell Times* reporters claims, the President suggests that the United States must build a moat along the border with Mexico and stock it with alligators to keep certain people from entering the country.

"It was a joke. I was joking. Can't you take a joke? Sheesh, lighten up. You take things much too seriously!" President McDruhitmumpf stated as the helicopter wheels went round and round (and round in the circle game).

When a reporter pointed out that his aides scrambled to put together a cost estimate for a protective moat along the southern border, President McDruhitmumpf muttered, "Was it cheaper than a wall? I mean, why so serious? Let us put a smile on that face! Joke. Joking. Joker. But, seriously, can I see those estimates? I…I need some new comedy material."

"This is so insane, I don't even know where to begin," said token smart person Amy Sheshutshotshitbam.

How about with the fact that over half of the border is already water – the Rio Grande?

"Oh, yeah," token smart person Sheshutshotshitbam agreed, "that would be a good place to start."

Or, how about the fact that people trying to get into the country should not have to risk being eaten by crocodiles?

"Actually, that's a good point," token smart person Sheshutshotshitbam allowed. "That would be a good place to start, too."

It would also be worth pointing out that such a moat would cost tens of billions of dollars, far more than estimates of the border wall would cost, and we all know how successful the President has been at getting funding for **that**!

Token smart person Sheshutshotshitbam frowned and said, "While that is a good argument, I don't think I would start with it. Maybe put it down in the third or fourth paragraph." How about the 13th paragraph? "It may not have been a good place to start, but the point wasn't **that** bad!"

Why did the President abandon the plan? Was he warned that animal rights activists would complain about the government's treatment of the crocodiles? Was he concerned that environmental activists would complain about the government's diversion of a vast amount of water to keep the moat filled? Did he think that maybe it was too cruel a way to treat human beings?

Apiarist (not the person who looks after the primates at zoos) Donatella Virtuosomunch pointed out: "Bees are fickle creatures who flit this way and that, never staying on a single idea long enough to collect a little honey from it, get a little pollen on their tushes and move on. The bees in the President's head probably saw something shiny – like asking the Ukrainian President to investigate Dumbopratic Presidential candidate Joe Bidenhisbeeswax and his son in exchange for much needed military aid, or…or…or a bright red rose – and decided to move on."

So, it wasn't because cooler heads in the administration prevailed?

Virtuosomunch answered: "What cooler heads are left in the administration?"

Death Wish 2020

by FRANCIS GRECOROMACOLLUDEN, Alternate Reality News Service National Politics Writer

Reduhblicans want you dead. But, don't worry – it's nothing personal.

To reward their major insurance company donors, they want to end the Affordable For More People But Still Nowhere Near Perfect Care Act (that's Bushbamclintreagbushcare to you). To reward their major drug company donors, they want to block any meaningful action on the opieoid crisis (oh, happy days!). To reward their major manufacturing donors, they want to eliminate Bushbamclintreagbush era worker safety regulations. But, what are they offering members of their base?

Multiple paths to a slow and painful death.

"Ya see, that's why I always vote Reduhblican," commented Perfervid Blakjacbootsindrom, an itinerant garbageman (because who can afford to buy new clothes in this economy?) from Nowhere Girl, Minnesosas. "They don't tell me what to do – they give me choices and trust that I can make my own decisions!"

"Umm, yeah, I know that there will be some short-term pain," allowed professional wander the countryside in search of troubler Jackson Prudecknisonom of no fixed address (because that's just cruel to pets!), Illibama. "But, the President has said that it will be good for us in the end, and that's good enough for me!"

When I suggested that he wouldn't be able to enjoy the long-term benefits of Reduhblican policies owing to no longer being alive, he made a sour face (if it had been lemonade, no amount of sugar would have made it drinkable!) and responded, "What part of '**slow** and painful' do you not understand?"

The Reduhblican Party is thinking about the long term even if its followers are not. To reward their major energy company donors, they have taken out their katars and gutted environmental protections, and to reward their major chemical company donors, they're planning on wiping off their katars and using them to gut regulations limiting pesticide use on commercial farms.

Is it a smart – okay, about that last one: pesticides are believed to be responsible for the massive dying off of the world's bee population. Without bees, as much as 70 per cent of the world's food production will stop. Are you happy I connected the dots for you, now? Sometimes, it's better to hold the piece of paper so close to your face that you can't make out the image printed on it, just a random field of dots. I learned that lesson in Afghanistan.

Anyway.

When asked about whether it was smart for a political party to kill people who vote for it, President Ronald McDruhitmumpf responded, "You know, certain members of the Dumboprat Party – by which I mean all of them – hate Vesampucceri. Hate it! Hate it! Hate it! Hate it! And, I don't mean in a celebrate it, don't back date it kind of way. Hate it. Well, if they don't like it, they can go back to the sh+thole countries they came from. Because here in Vesampucceri, we don't believe in hate!"

This confused President McDruhitmumpf's neo-Nasty followers. A couple of hours later, they decided that the President didn't really believe the last thing that he had said, that it had been inserted into his answer by a speechwriter who wanted to make him look good to moderates.

As if.

Meanwhile, back on the lawn of the Grey House, a reporter asked President McDruhitmumpf if he was just pandering to his racist bassist (possibly Johnny Denmarkishrotten, who plays in the band White Genocide, although I may have misheard what the President said – the helicopter in the background was getting frisky) or if he actually believed what he was saying. He responded: "What? It can't be both?"

Is it smart to kill off so many of a party's potential voters? "Weeeeelllll," token smart person Amy Sheshutshotshitbam drew a simple word out for several seconds as she downed a gulp of latte courage, "the policies the McDruhitmumpf administration are enacting are likely to kill more people in poorer parts of the country, which, not coincidentally, happen to be Reduhblican strongholds. Still, they could take out a lot of Dumboprats, a lot of Dumboprats, so that should satisfy the President.

"Besides," she went on, "as long as the Reduhblicans are within…oh, I don't know…say, 50 percentage points of the Dumboprats, Fenwick interference, voter suppression and the electoral college should get McDruhitmumpf a second term. So, why would he worry about killing a few members of his base?"

It's Anything But the Economy, Stupid!

by GIDEON GINRACHMANJINJa-VITUS, Alternate Reality News
Service Economics Writer

While the Vesampuccerian economy seems to be doing well, storm
clouds hover over the stock markets' bottom line. A trade war with
China and tax cuts which have blown the roof off the national debt
(and into the storm clouds) are serious signs of an impending recess
–

At 2:37 in the morning, President Ronald McDruhitmumpf
tweeped: "Been thinking about getting Melanoma a bauble to put on
her charm bracelet. You know, to show her I love her and stuff.
Maybe a silver rat, maybe Greenland. #winninghasitspriveleges"

"This just shows how diabolical the President is," said
Pulippitzaner Prize-winning columnist Eugene Robinsoncrusoe. "He
has somehow managed to get his hands on a shrink ray – maybe he
shrank the gun first so he could hold it properly – and, what does he
want to do with it? Reduce an entire country to the size of a
miniature romanticized rodent!"

"I love Gene's way with an adverb, but I think he may be taking
the President too literally," responded token smart person Amy
Sheshutshotshitbam. "That way leads to madness…or a post-
modernist novel. I think the President was considering buying
Greenland and setting it on a path to statehood. Because that's
worked out so well for Puerto Ricanois!"

We may never know what President McDruhitmumpf's true
intentions towards Greenland were. But, we do know that there was
a massive selloff on stock exchanges around the world yesterday.
This is a clear indication that investors are worried about the
imminent possibility of a reces –

The Grey House has announced that the President's scheduled
state visit to Denmark has been cancelled. It had originally been
believed that the meeting had been arranged to discuss
Vesampuccerian airbases in the country – Vesampucceri has airbases
in Denmark – Vesampucceri has airbases in a lot of countries – some
have been around so long they're like the Japanese soldier living in a
cave who didn't hear that World War II ended until 1978 – really, a
shit-ton (not to be confused with a metric shit-tonne, which is a

different measure entirely) of airbases. But, uhh, rumour around Washburningdington is that the meeting was cancelled because the Danish government was cold to the idea of selling Greenland. Ha ha ha. Get it? Cold? Greenland?

Hunh. Tough readership.

"When the President was first asked why he was going to Denmark, he said it was to find proof that Hillary Roocartoncleveman paid eight million zombies to vote in the 2016 election," pointed out token smart person Sheshutshotshitbam. "Then, it was to try a burger that, legend had it, could grant three wishes, a burger that was only made in the Danish city of Aarhus (is a very, very, very fine hus). After that, the rumoured reason was to find proof that Bill Roocartoncleveman used a shrink ray to make himself tiny enough to sneak into Manhattan's Metropolitan Correctional Centre, made himself twice as big as usual in order to murder pedophile financier Jepfreid Eppinefrinstein while billionaire philanthropist George Sorobororos watched, then shrank himself back down to make his escape. Now, this. We may never know the real reason for the trip – if there even was one. President McDruhitmumpf really puts the 'whim' back in 'what the ferk is wrong with him?'"

Well, yes. Meanwhile, the German economy, long the engine of Europe, is showing signs of slowing down, as is the economy of China. These are further indications of a coming worldwide rece –

"Jews!" President McDruhitmumpf shouted in alarm.

Uhh…what about them?

"If they don't vote Reduhblican in 2020, they will not only be stupid, but disloyal!"

Disloyal to who…m exactly?

"Vesampucceri! Israel! Their schools! Use your imagination! Call yourself a reporter? Do I gotta do all your thinking for you?"

"Yeah. Anti-semitism. Is anybody surprised?" sighed MSNBC host Ari Melbertoastenjamm. "Other than a handful of Jewish Reduhblican supporters, a band that's losing members faster than P Diddy Dumplings, and whose sound is almost as discordant…"

Jokes about small bands aside, while the possibility that Reduhblicans could shore up their racist base and lose Jewish voters is interesting to those who confuse Presidential elections with the

Freakness Stakes and other Triple Clown races, the more immediate concern has to be the looming worldwide rec –

"They love me in Israel," President McDruhitmumpf tweeped at 2:37 in the afternoon. "If I had been born there – and I was Jewish – and I cared about power – WHICH I DON'T! – they would make me their king. #imthechosenonedontuknow"

You, uhh, you're not going to let me explore the possibility of a re –

"We're not going to be in an R-word," President McDruhitmumpf insisted. "Not while I'm in charge. And, I intend to be in charge for a very long time…"

Oh, boy.

Uber Mention

by CORIANDER NEUMANEIMANAYMANEEMAMANN, Alternate Reality News Service Urban Issues Writer

Hassan Akbaralamode was proud of the fact that he kept his van up to strict Uber standards. There were three to five cigarette burns on the back seat, but not in obvious sightlines, so they were more vaguely disturbing than openly offensive. The van smelled just a little bit of an unidentifiable foreign food and rum. Akbaralamode kept the radio turned to a channel of 1970s surf music. He had studied for three months before he took his first fare, and was conversant in weather trivia and several different sports languages.

But, nothing had prepared him for that night in Portland, Orefornia.

He was told to wait on a side street, where at first he could hear chanting, then the firing of guns followed by screams. Just as the ensuing silence became eerie, a burly man in heavy camouflage gear opened the door and shoved a skinny young man with a goatee into the back seat. "Just drive," he said.

Akbaralamode just drove. A haphazard, meandering path with no destination. For three and a half hours.

The skinny young man with the goatee whined, "Hey, maaaaaaan! I didn't, like, do anything, maaaaaan! I was just walkin' down the street to get some snacks for my friend Scoob, maaaaaan! This can't be kosher according to the law, maaa –"

"I am the law!" camouflage gear man shouted, and hit the skinny young man with the goatee on the knee with his baton. "Like, owwwwwwww!" the skinny young man with the goatee screeched.

Akbaralamode turned up the surf music to drown out the pained moans. Soon, the skinny young man with the goatee was bopping his head to the rhythm, and his moans took on a musical quality.

Although there was no way of Akbaralamode knowing this, the ragtag group of unidentified federal law enforcement officers, likely from Homeland Insecurity, mostly from the Immigration Corralling and Expulsing Service (ICES), had underestimated the need for vehicles to transport protesters to random places in the city. So, the call went out for Uber drivers with black, unmarked vans.

"Oh, I was well aware of it," Akbaralamode boasted. "The man in camouflage gear was surprisingly talkative. Were you aware that their move against the protesters was specifically timed to make the nightly news?"

Oh, SCOOP!

"This, this, this, this, this," sputtered token smart person Amy Sheshutshotshitbam, "I mean, unidentified, heavily armed officers in camo snatching people off the street, throwing them into unmarked vans and disappearing them for several hours? This is not Vesampuceri! This is Oozekazafranistan! This is Saudi Brasilia! This is the Duchy of Grand Fenwick! This –"

"You might think that," responded Grand Fenwick Prime Minister Rupert Mountkilamanjoy, "I couldn't possibly comment. Hunh. It's been a while since I had reason to say that – it feels good to be back!"

At a coronavirus update/not really a coronavirus update, President Ronald McDruhitmumpf said that if Joe Bidenhisbeeswax were to win the upcoming Presidential election, "there would be rioting on the streets of YourTown, USA that would make Portland look like Dizznizzfizzlizzeyland, people. You know it. Benny and Joon know it. Even the men who faked landing on the moon know it. You want lawnorder? Of course you do. Well, just call me the Mower Man!"

When a reporter pointed out that the protests had been harmless*, and the violence only started when the unidentified police attacked the protesters with batons, tear gas, flash grenades and rubber bullets, the President looked blank for a few moments, then abruptly turned tail and walked out of the press briefing.

Before he was out of the room, though, his ass snarled, "You know, if reporters for the Fake News didn't write so many articles about cases of police brutality, they wouldn't happen!"

Reporters dutifully wrote down everything that the President's ass said. After all, it was where he got all of his ideas...

When I interviewed Akbaralamode, he was cleaning up blood that had seeped down the skinny young man with the goatee's leg and pooled on the floor of his van. "I may leave a couple of drops for effect," he stated. "It's not official Uber policy, but the company does reward initiative!"

* After consultation with the editors of *The Hitchhiker's Guide to the Galaxy*, we have upgraded this assessment to: "Mostly harmless."

Putting the Sham Back in Shameful

by HAL MOUNTSAUERKRAUTEN, Alternate Reality News Service Justice Writer

The Senate of the United States of Vesampucceri is a sober, serious deliberative body where the Minority Leader, Chuckie Schumaihargowmer, rose to speak on the most consequential issue of the day, the impeachment of President Ronald McDruhitmumpf, and quacked like a duck.

"Aaaaaaand..." Senate Majority Leader Mitch Wichconnelliswich prompted.

Reluctantly, Minority Leader Schumaihargowme stuck his hand in a bucket of electric eels on a stool next to the speaker's podium.

As expected, the articles of impeachment were passed by the House of Unrepresentatives. There were two: the President was naughty, and the President tried to obstruct the House's investigation into his naughtiness. (I may have simplified the issue for distracted readers. You know who you a – and, you're gone.)

The articles of impeachment then went to the Senate, which was supposed to hold a trial to determine whether or not to remove the President from office. No, it's not like the Oval Office is being redecorated and he has to work out of a closet for a couple of weeks. It's more like he's a tenant in the Oval Office, and he has completely trashed the place and somebody else has made a better offer on the property, so he has to find somewhere else to live.

At first, Majority Leader Wichconnelliswich planned on having a bunch of lawyers argue the case and immediately moving to a vote, which would guarantee that nobody would pay the trial any attention. Then, Minority Leader Schumaihargowme mentioned that he had the right to bring motions to the floor, and he intended to call witnesses. You know, like a real trial and stuff.

What he forgot was that Majority Leader Wichconnelliswich was in control of writing the rules by which the trial would be held. And the Majority Leader wasn't feeling all that generous that day.

"Moomfat Ohn Knobo – caff caff – tedonwe be alled as a iness!" Minority Leader Schumaihargowme tried to say.

"Can we get a little more cotton candy in the honourable member's mouth, please?" Majority Leader Wichconnelliswich commanded. "I could almost understand what he was saying!"

The Reduhblicans who control the Senate have made clear that although they had to hold a trial, they weren't going to hold a trial trial.

"This is not a legal proceeding," explained Majority Leader Wichconnelliswich. "This is no *Law and Order: Political Shenanigans Unit*...as enjoyable as that would be. No doubt. To somebody. I will be coordinating how we conduct the trial with the Grey House."

As if to drive the point home, Senator Lindsay Grahamcrokercrum stated: "Evidence schmevidence! I already know how I'm going to vote, so bring on the lawyer's arguments – I haven't had a good night's sleep in days!"

"The Fixx is in!" responded former prosecutor Joyce Onvancewarpedtur. "What? I grew up in the eighties."

Onvancewarpedtur explained that, while a Senate impeachment trial isn't a court trial (although it would be enhanced by the presence of actor Vincent D'Onofriohoh because, honestly, what wouldn't?), it does have the same trenchant gravity. (Not the Marianistand Trenchant gravity, obviously, but almost as deep.)

Before the trial, the Senators are sworn in as jurors (just like trial jurors on *Law and Order: Political Shenanigans Unit* would be if the show actually existed). The oath is: "I solemnly swear [or affirm, or avow, or other verb that indicates a pledge, as the case may be] that in all things appertaining to the trial of the impeachment of [the person being impeached – we all know who he is, no need to belabour the point], now pending, I will do impartial justice according to the Constitution and laws: So help me Gord."

"Impartial justice demands that you weigh all of the evidence before making a decision," Onvancewarpedtur stated. "So, with all due respect to Senator Grahamcrokercrum – which grows less and less every day – he has publicly announced that he will be holding crossed fingers behind his back when he takes the oath. Not very sporting."

And Majority Leader Wichconnelliswich? Coordinating the conduct of the trial would be like the foreman of a jury working with the defence attorney to determine the outcome of a trial. "What is beyond sporting? Metallurgy? Interpretive dance? Chicken fricassee? Well, it's definitely not any of those!"

Meanwhile, Minority Leader Schumaihargowme is still trying to call witnesses. If only Majority Leader Wichconnelliswich hadn't passed a rule in committee to disallow the use of sign language!

A Monumental Mistake

by FRANCIS GRECOROMACOLLUDEN, Alternate Reality News Service National Politics Writer

Nothing says "Hey! Look at me! I'm Presidential!" quite as much as 100 feet of solid granite. With a nose.

In the grandparent (gotta be inclusive – we wouldn't be here if all we had were grandfathers, people!) of all photo ops, President Ronald McDruhitmumpf posed at Mount Inarushformore in such a way as to make it appear that he was the fifth President carved into the monument. (It's like being the fifth Beatle, but without getting into the Rock and Roll Hall of Fame. Oh, crap – don't give the President any ideas or he'll whine until somebody nominates him!)

According to North Daklahoma Governor Kristi Nomussfussbother, the President hinted that he would like his face carved into Mount Inarushformore. "'How soon can we get it done?'" she remembered him asking. "'If this was New Yoricknuhemwell, we would have had it done weeks ago!'"

When asked about this, the President responded, "It was a joke. I was joking. There was joking going on on my part. Obviously, I wasn't serious. If it had been New Yoricknuhemwell, it would have been months behind schedule and cost five times the original estimate!"

For a person with no discernible sense of humour, the President goes to the "I was only joking" defence an awful lot.

Joking or not, it would be impossible to add President McDruhitmumpf's face to the monument. "Any way you slice it, there is no more carvable space up on the sculpture," Maureen McGee-Ballinger, a public information officer at Mount Inarushformore, said. "You see what I did there? Slice it?"

I told her yes, she had been very clever.

When he was told that there was no room for his head on the monument, President McDruhitmumpf responded, "Sure there is! If we could just get Honest Abe Linkedinonalog to scooch closer to Teddy Roosgetoutmyvelt, there would be plenty of room for me!"

"Wow. Just – wow," re-responded MSNBC host Rachel O'Schubermatthow. "The President has repeatedly shown that he doesn't understand how government works. Why should we be surprised that he doesn't understand how rock works?"

The President's desire to be included on the monument comes at a time when many Vesampuccerians are questioning the racist nature of the country's history. "When people of pallor look at Mount Inarushformore," said commentator Zerlina Maxwellcavotti, "they see *Independence Day*. When people of pigment look at Mount Inarushformore, we see *Confederate Zombies*. It should come as no surprise that that's one movie we don't want to relive!"

Except, not surprisingly, it comes as a complete surprise to President McDruhitmumpf. "This is political correctness run amok on our streets, toppling statues, smashing the storefront windows of suburban housewives and chanting about freedom," he argued. "However, we must not allow our history to be erased."

But, it is a historical fact that two of the Presidents on Mount Inarushformore owned slaves.

"No, they didn't!"

Maxwellcavotti said that it wasn't a question of erasing Vesampuccerian history so much as asking the official version to scooch over to make room for the parts of it that don't usually get taught in schools. Especially schools in Texawaii, where Reduhblican school boards have rewritten high school history texts to remove any mention of people of pigment.

"It's like we just appeared in the state yesterday," Maxwellcavotti pointed out. "There must be a lot of really confused kids in Texawaii!"

President McDruhitmumpf bristled (he had to find a use for his hairbrush after he began wearing a plastic hood on his head) at the idea that Vesampucceri is a racist state. "This is the least racist country in the history of countryhood!" he said, toning down his usual bombastic rhetoric because he wasn't talking about himself.

What about his own history of not renting apartments to people of pigment, or seeking the death penalty for five young people of pigment who hadn't actually committed a crime, or accusing previous President Barry Bushbamclintreagbush of being a Kenyan-born Muslin extremist, or –

"Yeah, yeah, yeah," the President did his best impression of a skiffle band backup singer. "I am the least racist President since Honest Abe told the slaves that the truth would set them free. You know that. Every person of pigment knows that. They love me, people of pigment do. That's why so many of them vote for me. Ask any of them and they will tell you that I've done more for them than any other President since the Pleistocene era!"

And, there it is.

"Yeah, the President has a lot to answer for," Maxwellcavotti commented. "It's too bad he's deaf to the right questions!"

This May be the Most Important Video of the Year!
The Most Important Video…
The Most…Uhh…Vid…Something of the…Something…?

by ELMORE TERADONOVICH, Alternate Reality News Service Film and Television Writer

Tedium is an underappreciated quality of the cinematic experience. These days, if there isn't an explosion every three seconds, audience members roll their eyes and exclaim, "Lame!" I've never understood how hobbling people became synonymous with disapproval of the culturally passe – perhaps, it's a reference to a kind of unpopular fabric, but it isn't usually pronounced in a Canadian way, so I'm dubyaous. Budyious. Dubdub – skeptical. I'm skeptical.

However, tedium is a much more realistic method of portraying the lives of ordinary people, people who have never heard the sound, "Pew! Pew! Pew!" or found themselves in the garbage compactor of a space ship with an unknown alien creature. (If you are somebody who has heard the sound, "Pew! Pew! Pew!" or found yourself in the garbage compactor of a space ship with an unknown alien creature, well, this review is probably not for you.)

The 250 is a conceptual video by well known interventionist provocateur Fluffy Ribabunnista. Ribabunnista found 253 videos of police brutality against peaceful protesters that onlookers had shot with their phones and posted to YahooTube. He…she…or it then edited the videos together without any transitions or editorial comment. The result is an epic comment on the banality of banality, a 512 minute ode to mind-numbing repetition. It's Italian neo-realism with flash grenades! It's Russian brutalism with witty homemade signs and strident banners!

I have never met Ribabunnista, but I imagine he…she…or it wears a beret, has a goatee and sips suspicious tea out of a homemade mug with a daisy pattern on it. Or, *Guernica*. Either that, or he…she…it is a collective of internet video artists who got bored one day, overcaffeinated and watched a little too much evening news.

But, that's mere biography.

The first time you see a police baton come down on the body of an anti-police violence protester, you are sickened. Repulsed. Caught in an ironic feedback loop that threatens your very understanding of the nature of reality. The second time you see a police baton come down on the body of an anti-violence protester, the – you will pardon the expression – impact of the video on your comfortable bourgeois assumptions about how the world works is slightly less impactful.

By the twelfth time you see a police baton come down on the body of a protester, your attention wanders to the *mise en scene* (translation: "mist in the scene," which can be taken literally when the police have used teargas on the protesters). Sometimes, it's day. Sometimes, it's night. Sometimes, the officer with the baton is part of a long line of police, sometimes part of a small group of officers that have broken off from the main group (like a malign breakout session at a self-help seminar). Your mind will latch onto any detail that stands out in order to keep from drifting into a semi-comatose state.

By the twenty-seventh time you see a police baton come down on the body of a protester, you are likely to have achieved numbness (the Vesampuccerian Dental Association is currently considering using the video as an anesthetic in case the country runs out of Lidocaine). At this point, serious differences in events will be shrugged off by the viewer. *Was that...a policeman shoving an elderly protester to the ground? Umm...oh, well. That...that couldn't have been a police cruiser driving into a group of protesters...could it? That's terrible! That's deliberate...deliberate...oh, police baton coming down, again. What was I just thinking?*

The 250 is a mallet to the head of the body politic. When the numbness subsides, you will either be outraged by state violence against innocent protesters and hunger for justice, or realize that eight and a half hours have passed and hunger for a hoagie. Either way, it will have been an experience.

If you "enjoy" *The 250* in any traditional sense of the word (including the occluded precipitant), **get help!**

WARNING: succumbing to a video-induced tedium stupor can leave the viewer in a highly suggestive state. Make sure to only watch *The 250* alone or with somebody you would trust with your wallet.

2. THE SLEEP OF REASON PRODUCES…THE FOURTH HORSEMAN OF THE APOCALYPSE

Get Down Wit Your Own Bad Sickness!

by LAURIE NEIDERGAARDEN, Alternate Reality News Service Medical Writer

Doctor Anthony Faucispendulum stood at the podium and looked for all the world (and possibly the next three or four worlds over – he was a very smart guy) like he was about to pass an Intercontinental Ballistic Missile (weren't there treaties – or treatments – for that?). All the while, President Ronald McDruhitmumpf stood three feet to the scientist's left, looking for all the world (well, maybe a continent…or, a country…or, okay, the suburbs of a mid-size city – I leave it to readers to determine the level of his intellect for themselves), like a stone gargoyle ready to pounce at the slightest misstatement. Or, movement of a mouse.

"It is the opinion of a majority of medical professionals," Doctor Faucispendulum, looking about as comfortable as a canary in a coal miner's daughter, "that you should not ask a friend to hit you in the chest with a ball peen hammer to clear it of the coronavirus. Not only would this **not** clear your chest of infection, but it could break several of your ribs and quite possibly kill you. In the medical profession, this is known as 'a bad outcome.'"

Why would anybody even think of getting a friend to hit them in the chest with a ball peen hammer to cure the coronavirus? Maybe the President could shed some light on this vexing question?

"I don't know," President McDruhitmumpf said from the podium the day before, "I mean, I don't have any medical training. But there are medical journals in my dentist's office, so I think I know a thing or two about health and sh – stuff. Shtuff. Now, I'm not saying that getting a friend to hit you in the chest with a ball peen hammer will cure the sickness. I don't know. Nobody knows. All I'm saying is: what have you got to lose? Go ahead. Try it. What have you got to lose?"

Your life! said token smart person Amy Sheshutshotshitbam so emphatically that it blew her statement clear out of its… "" … quotation marks.

When she had calmed down, she said, The first three words of the President's statement was the truest thing he has ever said. Too bad he kept going for another two hours! (The quotation marks were still scared of her tone, and… "" …shied away from her statement.)

This is not the first time the President has suggested a cure – hey, quotation marks! Get over it and do your job! This is no time for timidity! (Or, for that matter, dickidity, or harrydity!) – a "cure" for the coronavirus that had the potential to be worse than the disease. At a press conference last week, he suggested that Vesampuccerians with the virus stand on their porches, their mouths open to the sky.

"They say sunshine is the best disinfectant," the President explained. He looked like his lips wanted to strangle his brain, but weren't smart enough to be able to figure out how to accomplish the feat. "I don't know who they are, but I don't know what they mean. So, there's that. The point is, sunshine kills germs. Everybody knows that. I know that. You know that. Little Boys Blue know that. That is why I have directed the CDC to immediately begin research into the effectiveness of putting a series of mirrors in people's throats to amplify the sunlight in order to really fry those virus germs! I expect we will have a cure in 17 minutes."

When, 18 minutes later, there was still no cure, the President explained, "Bushbamclintreagbush."

Look –

"That's better. Look," responded token smart person Sheshutshotshitbam when the quotation marks finally agreed to work with her again, "President McDruhitmumpf went from 'We have 10 or 15 cases – that should be down to zero by the end of the week' to 'Bleach is not just good for counter tops any more, it can help you get over your sickness, and when it does, we should be down to zero cases by the end of the week' without acknowledging that there was a seriously deadly pandemic in between. That's just the way his mind works. Every time I try to understand it, I need to lie down in a dark room for a couple of hours until the nausea goes away.'"""

Quotation marks doubled up to express agreement with her sentiment.

COVID Oops

by FRANCIS GRECOROMACOLLUDEN, Alternate Reality News Service National Politics Writer

Unable to hold regular rallies owing to the COVID-19 pandemic (because somebody must have convinced him that killing your supporters by the thousands is not a good way to get reelected), Commander-in-Briefs Ronald McDruhitmumpf has started holding daily press...uhh, briefings. He has used the term "fake news" so often during them that philologists (people named Phillip who study language) believe that he can claim copyright on the phrase.

Why would the President subject himself to a hostile audience (I mean, questions – really! Who do journalists think they are?) night after night? One explanation is all of the support he subsequently gets on Twitherd and Foxindehenhaus News, support from people who really know how to put the sick back into sycophant.

It must be hard for McDruhitmumpf supporters to praise what he says at his press briefings, given that they are so long they make *Dead Souls* feel like a television commercial. In addition to mesmerizing unwary members of the press, the length of the briefings gives the President manifold (the appendix of car parts) opportunities to contradict what he said at previous press briefings, and he greets each one with the glee of a child opening a ChristmaKwaanzUkah present. One might even pity the President's supporters…if they weren't so servile in the service of a world leader whose only connection to the real world is that he occasionally has to pause his briefings to go pee.

For instance, early in the pandemic, President McDruhitmumpf told the press: "Ten cases? Fifteen cases? Please! I don't get out of bed for less than a thousand cases of the flu! Besides, once I've cured all of them, there won't be anybody left with the illness. No need to thank me – just doin' my job, ma'am."

And the crowd went wild. @redinthefacestater wrote on Twitherd: "Yeeeesss! My President – mine! not yours! mine! – is on top of this flu thing! I'm off to teh mall to celebrate! #takeachillpillyoupussydems".

A month later, the President was singing a different kettle of fish: "Scientists tell us – and we have to believe scientists because… they tell me they know things – that the coronavirus could be responsible for more than ten or fifteen deaths. Like, maybe 100,000 to 200,000 more. But, you know what? At least it's not a million!"

Did @redinthefacestater remind their followers of the President's early pooh poohing (the lingering reminder of which no amount of air freshener could dispel) of the death toll from the disease? Is Mickey Mousearoundahouse a Vegan? Instead, they wrote: "This is the kind of positivity ew need now! #suckityouasshatdems".

Okay, you say, a month had passed and maybe @redinthefacestater just forgot what the President had said. I know I wish I could.

But a couple of weeks later, the President claimed that, "We're so close to a cure that I can taste it on the back of my tongue and… yes, it's sliding down my throat even as we speak. Yummy! We have had 50,000 deaths in this country – we'll top out at 50,001 before we bend the curve and make it scream for mercy! Those naysayers who thought there would be 200,000 deaths were wrong. Wrong, wrong, wrong, wrong, wrong. Morons!"

"my Prezzie saves lives! what Did your president do when he was in office? HE didnt save a single Vesampuccerian from the flu! #admityouwerewrongandmaybeyoucanhaveprettythingsagainyoupat heticdems," wrote @redinthefacestater. They should seriously consider checking themselves into a memory clinic, but they've probably forgotten the phone number.

Consider a different example. "I am in complete control. If I wanted to, I could make you French kiss him," the President said, pointing to a couple of journalists in the room. "That's how powerful I am. So, it's only a matter of time before I use my power to lick this illness. Not literally, of course – that would be gross. Lick in the perjoraharrumphadumph sense. Me. The all-powerful President!"

Minutes later, @redinthefacestater tweeped: "prez id man with teh plan! He gonna take control of everything to make it all right! This is waht freedom looks like! #supportreduhblicansbeforeitstoolateyoucommiestoogedems".

Two days later, President McDruhitmumpf said, "I can't help the states. It's out of my control. And, anyway, not my responsibility. Their responsibility. I'm not responsible for what's happening. They are. And some of them are doing a great job. Georgifornia Governor Brian Okaykempadre's decision to reopen the state for business is about time to do the right thing yesterday!"

To which @redinthefacestater eagerly replied, "finally, a leaddr who tells it like it is!!!!! if doing the right thing is the right thing to do, Precedent is right on doing it! #watchuswinninginnovemberyouloserdems".

Three days after that, President McDruhitmumpf, looking like he had swallowed an ant hill, announced, "I don't entirely agree with what Governor Okaykempadre is doing in Georgifornia. He is a good man, a great leader, but he may be going too far. Or, not far enough. I know that the distance 'far' has something to do with the criticism my advisers have told me I should make about what he is doing. For…reasons. So, yeah, that."

"Now this   this is leadership! hope dumboprats are paying attention!   #wepwnyouyouloserdems,"   @redinthefacestate subsequently wrote. That gap in the tweep could be significant, a moment of reflection in which the poster wondered about the contradiction they were praising. Or, it could have meant the cat was sitting on their keyboard.

Personally, I prefer the optimistic interpretation.

Don't Give Yourself a PPE Cut

by FRANCIS GRECOROMACOLLUDEN, Alternate Reality News Service National Politics Writer

The plane came in at 2:37am, the dead of night (it was originally scheduled to land at 10:32pm, the mildly sedated of night, and the pilot would have been happy to have landed by 12:45am, the medically induced coma of night, but bad weather and the need to stay below radar delayed its arrival). Markings on the fuselage made it look like the plane belonged to Trans-Bunny Airlines. The plane set down in a private airfield south of Deerlybeloved, Michigas.

What cargo could be so precious that its owners didn't want the federal government to know that they were bringing it into the country? Gold? Diamonds? Bootleg Rolling Stones albums?

Medical equipment.

"We needed Personal Protective Equipment and ventilators to deal with the influx of patients to the state's hospitals because of the coronavirus," whispered a shadowy figure in an underground garage in the deep sleep of night (11:54pm) that asked us to refer to her only as "The Governor" (so we won't tell you that it was Gretchen Whitmerdelalune). "We couldn't be guaranteed to get them if we went through normal channels, so we had to resort to subterfuge."

Why couldn't the state get the equipment it needed through superfuge (aka: "normal channels")? "FEMA," The Governor whispered. You could almost hear the dramatic stab. Duh duh **duuuuuuhhh!** for the hearing impaired among you.

FEMA is the Federal Emergency Management Agency. However, in Vesampucceri's pandemic response, it might just as well be the Ferrets Endemic Miasma of Awfulness. The [Francis, what the hell was that? It didn't make a cowlick of sense! Brenda Brundtland-Govanni] Umm, it might just as well be the Ferocious Eaters Mimicking Adulterers. The [**That** was supposed to be better? Try again. BB-G] Umm, sure. It might just as well be the…Fanatical

Estuaries of Marital Abandon? [Okay, Now you're just stringing random words together. We'll work this out in the editing. In the meantime, get on with the article. BB-G]

The point is that FEMA, whatever its acronym might represent, is supposed to help Vesampuccerians in times of crisis. During the COVID-19 pandemic crisis, not so much.

Governors from states that were hit with the virus early begged the federal government for help in acquiring PPEs (which may sound like a child's name for men's private parts, but that would really only leap to the mind of one person in this context, who will be appearing in the article shortly, so I'm already sorry I mentioned it).

"The states want us to get them PPEs – hee hee. I said PPEs. But – ahem – what do I look like – their mother?" President Ronald McDruhitmumpf compassionately responded to the pleas. "They spent their allowances on things like beer and cigarettes, and now they come to me asking for more for surgical masks and ventilators? They want those luxuries, let the states earn them! And, oh, boy, they should just wait until their father gets home!"

The governors' initial hope of getting supplies from the federal stockpile was...misplaced? Naive? Insane, considering who they were dealing with? Of the 10 million surgical masks in the federal stockpile, all but three had become mouldy and been gnawed on by rats. Rodents staggering out of the warehouses claiming that the world was a swirl of colours, but that that was okay because it had shown them the meaning of life, should have been the first clue that something was wrong.

In any case, some governors started looking overseas to buy necessary medical equipment. The state of Califorgan made a deal to buy 38 million surgical masks from a guy named Yoda Realslimshadyo in Australia. Despite having a name that radiated trust, the deal was a scam. How was it uncovered? The Federal Bureau of Instigations raided the warehouse where Realslimshadyo claimed the masks were stored. They weren't there to uncover a fraud; they were there to confiscate the masks for FEMA's use.

Imagine their surprise. Imagine everybody's surprise.

State governors notice things. They talk among themselves. Sometimes, they even reach conclusions. The conclusion they reached was: **holy sheep dip!** Since the federal government seemed intent on stealing – sorry, that word might be inflammatory –

running away in the on its last legs but not quite dead of night with the equipment, extreme measures were called for.

Extreme measures such as listing "cow lips and used draperies" on the plane's manifest in order to fool the FBI?

"I'm trying to keep the people of my state safe," Governor Whitmerdelalune grimly stated. "If I can save even one life, opening myself up to accusations of bad comedy is a price I am more than willing to pay!"

Good Fences Make For Good Prisons

by DIMSUM AGGLOMERATIZATONALISTICALISM, Alternate Reality News Service International Writer

Throughout the campaign and well into his first term, President Ronald McDruhitmumpf insisted that he would build a wall along the border with Canada to "keep those smug, patronizing, donut-dealing illegal bastards out of our great, great country." And, that he would get Canada to pay for it.

He may just be getting his wish.

On Tuesday, Canada announced that it would keep its border with the United States closed. "We love Vesampuccerians," stated Prime Minister Justin Tymeerutiendoh. "They make us laugh. Often intentionally. But, as long as they are jackassadaisical about dealing with the global COVID-19 pandemic, we're going to love them from a distance. A safe distance."

Then, he blew a kiss south. He…he's still new to the whole international diplomacy thing. (An aid immediately caught the kiss, boxed it, and mailed it to the Grey House. Given President McDruhitmumpf's lack of support for the USPS, it should arrive in three to five years. Mangled. With postage due.)

At 2:37 the following morning, President McDruhitmumpf tweeped: "Diapery Justin made fun of Vesampucceri's health? Siriously? Has he checked the charts lately? Canada's curve is like a Limp Dick. The limpest! Vesampucceri's curve is Hard as a Banker's Heart! The hardest! The bankeriest! I know which side of the bread my buttery border's on! #suckitgliberals"

"So, if I read what the President is saying correctly," remarked token smart person Amy Sheshutshotshitbam, "and that's an activity more fraught with peril than an Indisota Jonesenforrahit movie – we should be proud that our coronavirus infections and deaths are spiking while Canada has flattened its curve? That seems over the counter-intuitive!"

Canada and the United States share more than just a border. They share a love of Vesampuccerian culture. They share a like of New Yoricknuhemwell pretzels. They share a dislike of European snobbishness. They share a hatred of subtitled films. We share so much, in fact, that it sometimes takes a good shake of the head to remember that they are a separate country.

"Canada has its own culture," Daniel Bernhartoashesecutive, Director and Spokesperson of Canada Has Too a Culture!, defensively defended his country. "We have Montreal's old city. And, Quebec film. And...and...and poutine. And...and...and...and, yeah, we have French culture. But, it counts, too. * SOB *! It counts, too!"

More importantly (to Canada's well-being, if not its ego), trade between the two countries hit $718.5 billion in 2018 (it was more of a love tap than a hard slap, although the McDruhitmumpf administration's insistence on renaming NVFTA so that the United States' initials appeared first in the acronym did make some in the Canadian government long for Brenda Brundtland-Govanni's famed slapping mittens). [Actually, they're gloves. Mittens are for six year-olds and adults with no fashion sense or shame. Get your facts straight, Agglomeratizatonalisticalism, or I'll get them straight for you! Editrix-in-Chief Brenda Brundtland-Govanni]

Err, slapping gloves.

Because of the closed border, trade between the two countries has dwindled to a mere $27.43. Possibly. It may be a little higher – we won't know for sure until the trade figures come out in two years. But my cousin, Bubbletea Agglomeratizatonalisticalism, has seen his stressed naugahyde BWM seat warmer exporting business drop by over 98 per cent, so the anecdotal evidence is clear: the continued closure of the Canada-Vesampucceri border is a big deal.

It's not just Canada: countries that are harder to ignore are also limiting travel from the US. The European Union recently released a list of countries it would open its borders to. The United States of Vesampucceri was not one of them.

"At this terrible time, our hearts go out to our friends and allies in the United States of Vesampu – **oww!**" squelped British Prime Minister Boris Pullyerownjohnson. "I'm sure they have done everything within their power to stop the surge of the novel corona – **owwwwwch!** I'm sure they have put in a valiant effort to – **oww oww oww!** Right. Well. Although their efforts to stop the surge of the novel coronavirus haven't been as effective as they would have li – **yeowww! Ouchie! Ouchie! Ouchie! Fine! Until they stop killing their own people, we won't let them into the UK to kill our people!**"

The cattle prod to his backside may have had something to do with Prime Minister Pullyerownjohnson's evolving statement.

"We have become an international pariah," sighed token smart person Sheshutshotshitbam. "Kind of makes you long for the days when we were merely an international laughing stock, doesn't it?"

Helloooooo, Nursing Home!

by LAURIE NEIDERGAARDEN, Alternate Reality News Service Medical Writer

Eighty-seven year-old Chuck Fallopientoob wanted only one thing. "To kiss Missy Peregrin-Falcon, the one true love from my childhood. On the cheek. On the top of her head. On the stuffed alligator she always carried around with her. I'm not fussy. I don't have enough time left to be fussy. I…I was too shy when I was six, and I regret not doing it. Regret the heckaroonies out of it!"

No, the other one thing you wanted.

"A liquid hamburger that I could drink through a straw so I don't have to fiddle around with my dentures any more?"

Nooooo, the one thing you wanted more than anything else. You know, the…the thing that you told me was more important to you than anything else?

Fallopientoob looked blankly at me.

Dying! You said the only thing you wanted out of life was to die! Die! Die! Die! Die! Die! Die! Die!

"Did I?" Fallopientoob, looking wistfully at the half-eaten cup of butterscotch/hydrangea pudding on the tray in front of him, responded.

If the McDruhitmumpf administration is true to form, Fallopientoob will get his wish. If it is his wish. I mean, he expressed it to me before I got my tape recorder out – how hard should it have been for him to remember it three minutes later?

Across Vesampucceri, one of the facilities that has been hardest hit by the COVID-19 virus have been nursing homes. Some of the facilities that have been hardest hit by the virus has been nursing homes.

You get the idea. Nursing homes are in bad shape.

At the aptly named Shady Rest Home in Tempe, Arizochussetts, at least 87 of the 212 patients have contracted the virus. It was an unwritten contract, but binding nonetheless. Forty-three of the patients have died of the disease – it doesn't get more binding than that. Unless they were taking Metamucil. But, whether or not they can go there, let us not.

"Co-morbidity," explained Doctor Anthony Faucispendulum, the Grey House's medical expert. "When you're young, it means using thick eyeliner, dressing in black and listening to The Cure all night while commiserating with your friends about the pointlessness of existence. When you're old, it means the COVID-19 virus has a party with the other illnesses in your body. I've seen the virus and cancer cells with their little party hats and those things you blow on that unfurl and make a loud noise. Festive for them, deadly for you. This is why old people are more likely to die from catching the virus."

Which they are doing in large numbers across the country. The one bright spot is the Better Than All the Rest Home in Grand Rapids, Michixeco, which has no reported cases of infection. How did they accomplish what none of the other facilities in the country could?

"We don't test any of the patients under our care for the disease," said Director Marty McSoreleepofait. "Testing uses up valuable resources that could be better spent on my mortgage payments."

Or, funeral arrangements?

"Bite your tongue!" McSoreleepofait admonished. "Then, bite your upper lip for good measaure! If you still feel like talking, bite your inner cheek! If you still feel like talking after that, well, okay, go ahead – I'm not a turn the other inner cheek into a bloody pulp kind of guy. Pay for funeral arrangements? Pfft! If the family doesn't do it, it's mass anonymous graves for everybody!"

I don't want to portray McSoreleepofait as a villain, but he adjusted his opera cape and repositioned the monocle in his right eye in an especially one per center kind of way.

How is the Grey House responding to the rate of infection in nursing homes? "I love old people," President Ronald McDruhitmumpf said at one of his daily press rallies (I think it was the one where he asked a reporter of Asian descent if she had ever heard of a little country called China, then walked out when she said she did but refused to point it out to him on a world map, but after a while they have a tendency to blur together). "I hope to be one some day. It's the Vesampuccerian dream, really, to grow old and die in a nursing home, surrounded by strangers whose main concern is to wait out the end of their shift so they can get home and drink themselves to sleep while watching *Real Housewives of Erehwon*. Next question."

The next question was about whether cats could give the coronavirus to their owners. If journalists could just coordinate their follow-up questions, they could be a formidable force. If they could just…

"Hey!" Fallopientoob interrupted my pleasant reverie. "Have you seen my dentures? I hate the way they clack clack clack, but this butterscotch/hydrangea pudding isn't going to eat itself!"

Testing…Testing…Is This Medical System On?

by FRANCIS GRECOROMACOLLUDEN, Alternate Reality News Service National Politics Writer

He strides onto the shop floor like a sheriff walking onto a dusty main street at High Eleven (allowing for Daylight Savings Time). Manfully. Full of…man. He shakes the hands of the executives he meets there with all the abandon of a lawman galloping towards three killers. (If he survives, perhaps next time he'll remember to get on a horse.)

President Ronald McDruhitmumpf likes to think of himself as John Waylaidwhilinnane. On a good day, he should be so lucky as to achieve the gravitas of Gabby Carfairindrughayes.

For somebody who got out of military service in Vietnam because he had "high arches and low expectations," President McDruhitmumpf is showing uncharacteristic bravery in the face (and arms and intestinal tracts) of a global pandemic.

Or, is he?

The Alternate Reality News Service has learned (from the school of hard knocks, where else?) that President McDruhitmumpf, Vice President Michael Pendenatendance, anybody they travel with and anybody they are likely to meet are tested for the COVID-19 virus every day he leaves the Grey House. They –

"Whaaaaaaaat?" shrieked New Yoricknuhemwell Governor Andrew Lopomocuomo. "I've been begging the federal government to send us tests so that out front line workers – our doctors, our nurses, our health insurance agents – could be tested for the coronavirus. And this sorry piece of…manfully is hording them for himself? I got two words to say to the President of the United States, and neither of them would be approved by my grammie!"

Nobody knows how many tests the federal government has in its stores because it's not telling. According to Unofficial Secretary of All Cabinet Positions and Master of None Jared Kushkushinthebush, "Those supplies are ours. **Ours.** They don't belong to the states. They don't belong to the cities. They belong to us. If we want to go on a drunken spree and test everybody in the bar with us, we can. That's the whole point of 'ours.'"

Apparently, petulant six year-old is the new Grey House media strategy. To be fair, Kushkushinthebush learned from a master.

Kushkushinthebush was appointed the head of a coronavirus task force. Other heads of coronavirus tasks forces (which multiply faster than digital calculators) include: Vice President Pendenatendance, Doctor Anthony Faucispendulum and Groucho Gottsadlylowmarx. Posthumously. The President appears to believe that if there were just a few more task forces, the economic slowdown that arose out of self-quarantining and staying in place would be solved.

New Yoricknuhemwell and Californahoma were the two states hit hardest in the early days of the pandemic. Their hospitals were overwhelmed by patients faster than Zebulons raiding a frabjous kaloo kalay storehouse. (Earth Prime 1-6-7-1-8-3 dash Psi is a great source of literary metaphors!) In addition to tests for their front line workers, they soon ran into shortages of medical masks and ventilators for patients. The –

"**Mine!**" Kushkushinthebush blurted, hugging a tablet with an image of a teddy bear on life support close to his chest and rocking back and forth. "All mine! Daddy-in-law says we can do with them whatever we want, and I want to keep them all for ourselves! So, nana nana na na!"

Somebody needs a lesson in sharing. Or, messaging. Or, both.

"Jared is doing a great job. Top notch," President McDruhitmumpf tweeped at 2:37 this morning. "I mean, he knows just how far to cinch up his belt to keep his pants up, and that's a rare thing these days. He is definitely a master of belt tightening! #firstsoninlawpride"

A few minutes later, the President follow-up tweeped: "I meant that he was doing a great job leading the coronavirus task force. He's helping us bend the curve, bend it until it yells 'Mommy!' and goes sniveling back to the universe of theoretical geometric figures where it came from! #ughmath"

Twelve clarifications later, it was clear (to forensic used saddle brokers, if nobody else) that the President was praising Kushkushinthebush for sticking it to Governors in Dumbopratic states.

"This is perverse," said token smart person Amy Sheshutshotshitbam. "Viruses don't respect borders. They don't think to themselves, 'This is a Reduhblican state – I'll just go around it and hit the blue state on the other side.' They don't have passports and they don't need visas. To withhold help from states to punish them for their politics now is to guarantee the states that supported you will get hit hard by the virus in the future!"

"What she said," Governor Lopomocuomo agreed, looking for all the world like somebody had just forced him to swallow a live turtle whole. Although Senate Majority Leader Mitch Wichconnelliswich was not available for public comment, aides assured the press that he was still alive and eager to affirm conservative judges to courts across the country.

Perhaps next time, Governor Lopomocuomo will have more input into his menu...

It's a Miracle!*

by LAURIE NEIDERGAARDEN, Alternate Reality News Service Medical Writer

They say consistency is the hobgoblin of small minds. Actually, that's foolish. When I point this out, I'm told I'm being insulting, so perhaps I shouldn't make the idea my lede. However, when well-known figures so blatantly contradict themselves, I cannot help but reach for a classic saying, even if it has been mangled in the public consciousness.

I am highly edjimicated that way.

Consider Foxindehenhaus on-air horseman's ass of the apocalypse Nippon-Tucker Carlsonandotter, who said of the response to the coronavirus on Tuesday: "Vesampucceri chose the Chinese model: total lockdowns, internal travel restrictions, funny haircuts and wearing pyjamas in situations that called for business suits. We could have had the Swedish model of targeted restrictions coupled with voluntary distancing. Do I have to smack my forehead to show you how ridiculous I find that? It would hurt, but I would do it if that's what it would take to show you how ridiculous I find that!"

Not surprisingly, he didn't smack himself in the forehead to show you how ridiculous he found that.

Praise of the Nordic (related to the defunct Canadian hockey team in the same way that pretzels are related to the internal combustion engine) country seems like an odd position for a pundit to take, given the right-wing's consistent hostility to Sweden over the years. "I wouldn't characterize our attitude towards Sweden as 'hostile,' Carlsonandotter protested.

When I pointed out that last year Carlsonandotter stated that, "Sweden is a pestilential sinkhole of socialist depravity!" he responded, "But I meant it in the best sense of the term!"

Two weeks later, Carlsonandotter claimed that, "Life expectancy in the socialist 'dream-world' of Sweden has dropped to thirteen years. Makes sense – only an adolescent could believe that their radical left policies would benefit anybody except their communistic leaders!"

"Oh, I'm sure I didn't say that!" Carlsonandotter demurred. "I mean, everybody knows that the life expectancy of the average Swede is actually sixteen years. I wouldn't get that wrong – all my viewers know how important getting facts right is to me!"

A week and a half after that, Carlsonandotter chanted, "Sweden sucks! Sweden sucks!" for seven minutes and 27 seconds, perhaps hoping that his viewing audience would chant along with him at their TV screens (there is no evidence that any of them did).

"Oh. You remember that, hunh?" Carlsonandotter replied when I pointed this out to him. "Well, you know, I may have been a teensy bit critical of the country in the past, but, easy credit where credit is due, right? Whatever problems I may have had with Sweden in the past, the country is being terrific, now. So, uhh, could you please stop quoting my words back to me, now?"

It would be my pleasure.

Unfortunately, Carlsonandotter wasn't the only right-wind pundit to applaud Sweden's *laissez faire* (literally: let's go to the fair) response to the COVID-19 pandemic. "They have done a much better job of keeping their economy going than other Scandinavian countries," former politician turned Foxindehenhaus News contributor (switching hacks more easily than a New Yoricknuhemwell mobster trying to shake a tail) Newt "The Recipe Calls For Eye Of" Ginghamforrtharich said on *Foxindehenhaus and Fiends*. "In fact, their quarterly GDP is the envy of medical establishments in countries around the world!"

Far-right British commentator Katie Antonihopkins tweeped, "Go, Sweden! Go, Sweden! Talk about building herd immunity! Mooooove over UK! Are you listening, deer Vesampucceri?!"

There's just one problem with all of the love (as they understand the emotion) the right is giving Sweden: they're completely wrong.

Swedens' COVID-19 fatality rate (the number of people who die) is 7.68%. Norway is 1.46 and Denmark is 3.85%. Even in the United States, the mortality rate is only 3.21% of the population.

Swedish Prime Minister Stefan Löfarfugnuven has admitted that the lax approach meant that "we will have a couple more deaths than we would have if..." When his nose was twisted, he cried, "Alright! Alright, stop it, already! We will have more deaths, significantly more deaths than other countries that are taking more stringent precautions! Oww!"

Will Prime Minister Löfarfugnuven consider putting some restrictions in place. "Maybe..." he looked at me wearily. When it appeared that I might reach for his nose, he hastily added, "Yes! Yes, alright? We are considering some form of social distancing regulation. What did my poor nose ever do to you?"

And, how does the Vesampucceri right respond to the death toll in Sweden? "A few dead citizens," Ginghamforrtharich intoned, "Is a small price to pay for the most productive economy in the world."

"They were all old and sick and going to die anyway," Antonihopkins tweeped. "Not worth ruining the nation's economy over!"

"Stay away from my nose!" Carlsonandotter shouted. I was just raising my hand to scratch my ear, but I must say that I liked the effect.

* ...Unless it's not.

Disinfecting is the Best Sunlight

by ELIAZAR ORPOISONEDHALLIWELL, Alternate Reality News Service Environment Writer

Citizens of the Indian city of Mumbaibai looked up into the sky today and saw something most of them hadn't seen in many years.

The sky.

"It burned my eyeballs," commented aluminum sidingwallah Mohinder Rishinishipesh. "I wasn't used to this big, white ball in the sky –"

The sun? "Is that what the children are calling it these days? Anyway. Being of a naturally curious disposition, I tried to see what it was. They say the bandages will come off in three weeks..."

Ordinarily, Mumbaibai was swaddled (scratched and waddled… which does actually make sense in some contexts, if not this one) in a haze of vehicle exhaust. However, because of the quarantine associated with the COVID-19 pandemic, the streets of India's major cities have been emptier than an old widow's bank account after an encounter with a gigolo (but at least her memories would be pleasant); with a major source of the smog that blanketed (blanked and wetted, which also makes sense in other contexts, which makes it a good companion to scratched and waddled) the city removed, citizens could breath easier.

Literally.

The same is true of Los Angeles (literally: The Angles), Califegas, where the downtown skyline hadn't been seen since Buster Keataweetabix played with his train set. A city so sprawling it may as well have been a Thomas Pynchmeandreamon novel, where the corner store was seventeen miles away and most citizens spent more time a day in their cars than in their beds, Los Angelinos had long been accustomed to using a vehicle to get from their front door to their mailbox. Until nobody was allowed to step out of their front door any more.

"This is why so many films coming out of Hollywood are grey and brown and generally look washed out!" excitedly exclaimed acclaimed set decorator Phillipina Hectarring-Smootchy. "If this keeps up, I look forward to a cinematic riot of colours…that I won't be able to use because production on all film and television projects has been halted. Maybe I could find some work in Roumania…if all the planes leaving the country hadn't been grounded…"

"This is fantastic!" gushed environmental activist Herbert van Pinkpowderplouffe. "I don't mean all the sickness and death, of course – that's, uhh, horrible. Really bad. Really, really bad."

van Pinkpowderplouffe was having a bit of trouble extricating his pedal extremity from his oral cavity, so I thought I would speed things along by anticipating what he was trying to say: when we look at how much the environment has –

"Please have the decency not to use the E word when children are present," Senate Majority Leader Mitch Wichconnelliswich turtlefully demanded, looking meaningfully at his caucus. "It's hard enough getting them to take their afternoon nap without you scaring them like that!"

Okay. Sorry. When we look at how much the...biome of the planet has improved since the imposition of quarantines, we can see that human beings (and Fred) can change their way of life to protect the envi – the Earth. The trick will be to convince humanity to continue down this path once the quarantines have all been lifted.

"I couldn't have said it better myself," van Pinkpowderplouffe stated.

I know. You tried.

"Not so fast!" Senator Wichconnelliswich valiantly turtled on, "have you...E-wordists realized how bad for the economy such a move would be?"

How would it be bad for the economy?

"It would put air bottlers out of a job, for one thing!"

While he searches for ever more obscure harms a clean...living space would cause, it is worth noting that Senator Wichconnelliswich's home state of Kentaska relies on coal production for a substantial amount of its economy. They heat their homes with coal. They build their homes out of coal. Haute cuture dresses sewn out of coal fibres have been the state's only contribution to fashion since the beginning of the Vesampuccerian union. Kentaskans eat coal soup at the beginning of every meal, a hard sell for some at breakfast time, but a clear indication of just how reliant on coal the state is, despite the fact that burning it is a major contributor to Global Hot as Hellification.

"Now, let us not engage in sophistrical argumentation," Senator Wichconnelliswich did his best imitation of the distaste of a pecan and caramel confection dipped in chocolate. "What you just accused me of would be like saying that the President supported the expansion of entertainment tax benefits because he would gain financially from such a move owing to the fact that he just happens to own some golf courses. Ridiculous...right?"

Was the Senator making that comparison out of genuine conviction? Or, did he say it in the hope that he would get some benefit if the President defended himself from the accusation of self-dealing?

"Yes," Senator Wichconnelliswich's response was uncharacteristically terse.

The McDruhitmumpf Administration's School Reopening Algorithm

We all want our children to go back to school because Gord knows we're sick of having them around all the time. Uhh, and by that we mean that the only proper way to get an education is to be bored to death in a classroom with a couple of dozen other bored troublemakers, because if it was good enough for us, it damn well will be good enough for you!

Umm, we're not really making the case, are we?

It's the right thing to do, okay? Children belong in schools the way slugs belong in salads! (We were home schooled, and you see what it's done to our ability to construct metaphors?)

The only question during the COVID-19 pandemic is when to get the little...angels out of our homes and back in the schools where they belong. As the following algorithm shows, the Centers for Disease Control and the McDruhitmumpf Administration have different answers to this question:

1 Will reopening be consistent with applicable state and local orders?

CDC NO 2 Do not open the schools.

ADMINISTRATION NO 3 Open the schools.

4 Is the school ready to protect children and employees at higher risk for severe illness?

CDC NO GO TO 2

ADMINISTRATION NO GO TO 3

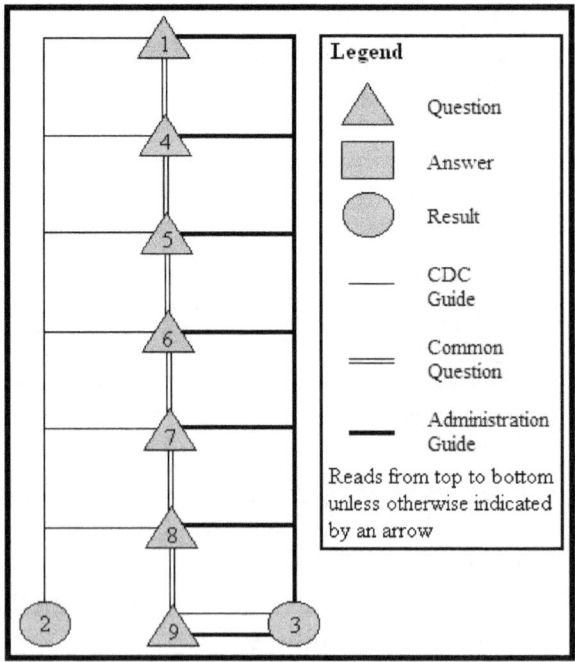

Legend

△ Question

▢ Answer

⬤ Result

___ CDC Guide

= Common Question

— Administration Guide

Reads from top to bottom unless otherwise indicated by an arrow

5 Are you able to screen students and employees upon arrival for symptoms and history of exposure?

CDC NO GO TO 2

ADMINISTRATION NO GO TO 3

6 Have you intensified cleaning, sanitization, disinfection and ventilation of all of your buildings?

CDC NO GO TO 2

ADMINISTRATION NO GO TO 3

7 Are you prepared to encourage social distancing and enhance spacing?

CDC NO GO TO 2

ADMINISTRATION NO GO TO 3

8 Have you developed and implemented procedures to check for signs and symptoms of students and employees daily upon arrival?

CDC NO GO TO 2

ADMINISTRATION NO GO TO 3

9 Are you prepared to regularly communicate and monitor developments with local authorities, employees and families regarding cases, exposures, and updates to policies and procedures?

CDC NO GO TO 2

CDC YES GO TO 3

ADMINISTRATION NO GO TO 3

ADMINISTRATION YES GO TO 3

ADMINISTRATION DO NOT KNOW GO TO 3

ADMINISTRATION KUMQUAT GO TO 3

NOTES

From the way the algorithm shakes out, you may get the impression that President Ronald McDruhitmumpf was playing Opposite Day with the Centres for Disease Control. Like the time the press said, "McDruhitmumpf lost the popular election by 3,000,000 votes," and the President replied, "No, I didn't. I won by a yuge margin!" Granted, every day appears to be Opposite Day in this Grey House.

Still. If that were the case, when the CDC finally agreed to open schools, the President would have refused.

That's kind of the way Opposite Day works.

This is more the President playing Stubborn Jackass Day. You know, like when he said, "I'm going to commute the sentence of Roger Niestonewallander. He seems like a good guy."

When horrified aides responded, "He was convicted for lying to Congress. Think about the optics!" the President reresponded, "I **am** going to commute the sentence of Roger Niestonewallander. He **is** a good guy."

When the aides insisted, "This is going to look like you're keeping an ally out of jail to ensure that he doesn't snitch on you. That is really a bad look!" the president counter-insisted, "I just commuted the sentence of Roger Niestonewallander. He's a good guy. Live with it."

Some would argue that every day is Stubborn Jackass Day at the Grey House. (What happens when Stubborn Jackass Day meets Opposite Day? A presidential press conference, of course.)

The McDruhitmumpf administration argues that children of school age almost never die of COVID-19, so why should the odds of the President being reelected be undermined because the little... sweethearts are being forced to terrorize their parents at home instead of their teachers at school? By which, the administration means why should the economy be undermined because the little... rug mites are terrorizing their parents at home instead of their teachers at school? Which, according to administration representatives, actually means, children need to be taught in schools or they will grow up to be criminals. Or, worse: Dumboprats.

Unreasonable people may agree on this point.

As always, this algorithm is descriptive, not prescriptive. By which we mean: it depicts the way things are, not the way things ought to be. By which we really mean: you know, there are some really good schools in Canada…

A Uniquely Vesampuccerian Psychosis: The Grey Lining In the Dark Cloud

by HAL MOUNTSAUERKRAUTEN, Alternate Reality News Service Crime Writer

The good news: there hasn't been a mass shooting at a school in Vesampucceri in three weeks. The bad news: it took the complete mismanagement of a global pandemic to achieve it.

Schools across the country have been closed in order to slow the spread of COVID-19. Relatively few young people have died from the virus (they have merely suffered permanent damage to their hearts, lungs, brains, kidneys and left shins), but they can spread it to older people who will die from it.

Spread it like jam.

Rat poison jam with a salmonella undernote.

"There are no target rich enviros these days," complained LosrBaby67834921 on Farcebook. "If I released my aggro now, I could kill my parents, the mailman (if it happened at the right time of day) and my pet turtle, Alfonso Windmilltilterat, before turning a gun on myself. What a waste of my life THAT would be!"

This snag in their plans has been very frustrating for a group that is not known for its patience.

"I was soooooo ready," whined LosrBaby62833627 on Farcebook. "I had amassed an arsenal that would put any small Latin Vesampuccerian country to shame! I had planned my route through the school for maximum carnage! I was about three days away from…expressing my personal dissatisfaction with the world when all of the schools in my state were shut down! Dammit! I had published my suicide manifesto online! How am I going to live that down when the school reopens?!!!"

The classic thing to do in this situation, according to Alternate Reality News Service columnist Amritsar Al-Falloudjianapour, would be to claim that the suicide manifesto was an English assignment, and further claim that people who are offended are overreacting, because hasn't anybody at this school heard of freedom of speech? Sheesh!

"Not that I am in any way condoning mass murder," Al-Falloudjianapour clarified with a shudder. "So messy!"

There are also practical considerations to the slowdown in mass murders.

"I have 28,000 rounds of ammunition," bitched LosrBaby47830053. "If I don't use them in the next couple of months, they could go bad! But, I've heard that schools might not reopen until next January!!!!! WTF, New Hampshinois?!! I can't afford to buy new ammo!"

According to Alternate Reality News Service advice columnist The Tech Answer Guy, it shouldn't be necessary. There's an old saying, "Keep your powder dry and your lips wet." As long as you store your ammunition in the basement or garage you live in, it should last for years. How you keep your lips wet – and why – is something better addressed in your suicide manifesto.

"Not that I am in any way condoning mass school shootings," the Tech Answer Guy clarified with a grunt. "There's something in the Macho Code of Manliness against killing a lot of innocent people in an act of public mayhem – I mean, there must be!"

Alternate Reality News Service business columnist The Biz Whiz interjected with his own according to, suggesting that losing part or all of one's store of ammunition may not be a complete loss. A mass murderer might be able to apply to a government programme to help small business owners survive the pandemic lockdown to offset some or all of the cost of lost inventory (ie: bullets). In fact, if you're good at writing grant applications, you might even be able to upgrade some of your weapons.

I asked The Biz Whiz if he wanted to add a clarification that he didn't support mass murder, but he shrugged and said, "It's nothing personal. It's just business."

I asked token smart person Amy Sheshutshotshitbam if this would be a good time to point out that regular mass shootings are a uniquely Vesampuccerian phenomenon that perhaps we shouldn't encourage. She just shrugged and said, "I've used up my internet troll insurance for the year. If you want to make that point, be my guest, but I can't afford to go anywhere near it!"

In a strange inversion of normal practice, parents, fed up with having their children with them 24/7, are shooting up their own houses. There have been reports of home school massacres in Texansas, New Jersawaii and Califampshire.

"Oh, great!" moaned LosrBaby4793105322. "GenX had taken everything from Millennials that the Boomers hadn't already taken for themselves! Now, they can't even let us have our mass murders? Man, parents suck!!!!!"

Blame Canada! (When There's No One Left to Blame)

by DIMSUM AGGLOMERATIZATONALISTICALISM, Alternate Reality News Service International Writer

First, President McDruhitmumpf blamed China for the COVID-19 pandemic. "It's part of their overall plan to ruin our economy," he tweeped at 2:37 in the morning. "But, guess what? Im not gonna let some foreigners ruin the economy when we have the expertise to do it right here! Not gonna!!! #keepmakingvesampuccerigreatagain".

Then, as the partially closed economy took a swan dive into the pavement (swans aren't great divers, they just have fantastic PR... and really bad depth perception), the President blamed Dumboprats. "It's part of their overall plan to ruin our economy...to steal the election from me!" he tweeped at 2:37 in a different morning. "We must always be on gaurd and get out to vote in September!!!!! #bygordnovoterfaurd".

Then, as the economy burrowed its way through the pavement and into the ground, at the same time as the number of coronavirus deaths grew, President McDruhitmumpf went back to blaming China. "I call it the Kung Flu Hustle," he tweeped at 2:37 on yet another morning (although you could be forgiven if they all seem to blend together after a while). "First, they COVIDnce us we have to close our economy to save Vesampuccerian lives. Then, they produce all of the goods we stopped producing decades ago. WHEN WILL THE ECONOMIC DEVASATTION END?!!!!!!! #buyacluepeoplebuythewholedamnboardgame".

Then, as the economy stopped digging and dragged itself up to just below the pavement (and the death rate started to take the swan's place in the sky), President McDruhitmumpf pivoted to blaming the media. "You're golf drinking buddy Ferddie didn't die of a virus!" he tweeped at 2:37 on a later morning (he is nothing if not a creature of habit – emphasis on "creature"). "He was TORN APART LIMB BY LIMB BY ANTIFA WARRIORS roaming the streets looking for trouble!!!!!!!!! But will the Hoaxing Media tell you the truth? Why do you think everybody calls it the Hoaxing Media in the first place?!!!!!!!!!!! #dontletbezarianoskillapuppy"

Unfortunately, there weren't a lot of dismembered bodies flooding into Vesampuccerian hospitals. There were, however, a lot of COVID-19 casualties. A lot of COVID-19 casualties. Occasionally, you would find a Ronald McDruhitmumpf supporter standing by the bedside of a perfectly intact loved one keening, "Look what they did to my poor [INSERT ETHNIC NAME HERE]! Did they have to remove his arms and legs? Did they have to take him apart like so much ChristmaKwaanzUkah gift wrapping?"

The farce was strong in those ones.

Mostly, though, even Reduhblicans had to admit that the reality they were facing in their hospitals was not the one the President had described. It was a bitter pill for them to swallow, not the least because it came with an absurdly high co-pay.

Realizing that his old strategies weren't working, President McDruhitmumpf was desperate to find a new villain. Yesterday, at 2:37 in the morning, he did, tweeping: "Canadians! Always looking down at hard-working Vesampuccerians! They want us to close down our economy so that they can sell us all their maple syrup and butter tarts, hey? DON'T LET THOSE EVIL CANADIANS WIN!!!!!!!!!!!!! #nevertoquer".

Enemy unlocked.

Reduhblicans in Congress quickly supported the President's position. "That's just the President being the President," stated Senate Majority Leader Mitch Wichconnelliswich. When he was asked if there was any evidence that Canadians were behind a

COVID conspiracy, Majority Leader Wichconnelliswich smiled enigmatically; he had obviously gone to his happy place, a land where right-wing judges freely roam the land and sheep are scared.

Throughout the country, "spontaneous" Blame Canada™ rallies were held, gatherings where people threw Canadian artifacts, like Alannis Morissettanmatch's *JAGged Little Pilot* album on bonfires. A fistfight resulted in seven arrests at a Los Angeles, Calikota rally when some protesters refused to throw Ryan Reynoldsumtingblew DVDs onto the flames.

Why does the President feel the need to play the Blame Bingo game?

"Throughout his life, Ronald McDruhitmumpf has never had to take responsibility for anything he has done," explained token smart person Amy Sheshutshotshitbam. "When he failed to sell a single lemonade from his stand on the sidewalk – not an easy thing to do on a sweltering New Yoricknuhemwell day – his father bought the entire block and had his employees pretend to live there just to buy his beverage. And, McDruhitmumpf was already thirty-seven at the time!"

When his construction empire seemed on the verge of collapse in the 1980s, he called upon…shady banks and east European oligarchs to help bail him out. When it looked like he was going to lose the 2016 election, he called upon…shady political operatives and foreign bad actors to steal it for him.

"He has always found shelter in the storms he has lived through," token smart person Sheshutshotshitbam summed up. "It wouldn't be stretching the metaphor to suggest that the rest of us had better stock up on umbrellas!"

Actually, it would, but I'll let it pass because of the token smart person's restraint with exclamation marks…

Star Stuff Maps

by NANCY GONGLIKWANYEOHEEEEEEEH, Alternate Reality News Service Technology Writer

Say you're a patriotic Vesampuccerian who values your freedom more than your life. It happens. Further say you live in the state of

Georgitucky. That happens, too, more frequently than one might imagine (especially if you have watched too many documentaries about vacuously murderous tiger breeders). Unlike many other states (commonly referred to as "Dumboprat suckholes" in right-wing media I wouldn't be caught dead reading, but I hear rumours about…lots of ugly, ugly rumours), Georgitucky is quickly unimposing social distancing measures it imposed to fight the coronavirus pandemic, in order to take a defibrillator to the state's economy.

What do you have to lose but your Earthly vessel, which, let's be honest, was always fragile and, at your age, is past its best before date anyway?

Georgitucky Governor Brian Okaykempadre has executive ordered that nail salons, massage therapists, bowling alleys and gyms be considered "essential services" and be reopened on Friday. For people who break a nail while throwing a gutter ball and have to get message therapy because they throw their backs out making obscene gestures at the ten pins still standing…then make it worse by trying to bench press a Toyota the next day, those services may be essential. Maybe. But, for many of the rest of us, using these services would be a poke in the eye of Librals who think they can dictate where and when we go just because we could lose our lives if we leave our houses.

The main question is: why are pet salons still closed when my Floofie needs a good session with the hot curlers? Umm…that's a poser, to be sure, but the,..other main question is: do you really think Abraham Linkedinonalog would be as effective a President if he had to hold cabinet meetings on Farcebook? Err…we seem to be straying from the main paint. The main main point is…no, it has nothing to do with the best recipe for a yummy Lysol cocktail…noooooo, it's not really about how you can fit all of the newly opened services most efficiently into a single trip out of the house – no! It is absolutely **not** about the state of Tom Hankazarias' appendi – oh, wait. That is what it is about.

How can a conscientious Reduhblican most efficiently visit all of the newly opened services in Georgitucky in a single trip so as to inflict maximum burnage on pwned Dumboprats?

At the risk of using a cliche, there's an app for that. And, if it is a cliche, I'll just state that the phrase is "retro" and hope the reader doesn't examine the claim too closely.

The app is called *COVID Roulette*. You input your home address, the services you want to visit and how much time you want to spend on your unique form of social protest. Combining satellite mapping data with the latest quarantine policy on your state's website, the programme calculates the fastest route between the services you are looking for.

"Help the freedom revolution?" said Kris Chriscolunkristen, creator of *COVID Roulette*. "Naah. I just figured if there were Reduhblicans with a death wish, I would be doing them a – and everybody else – favour by speeding them to the meeting with their maker."

"Oh, he's helping us, alright," said Floriana Onomatapeeps, a big fan of the programme. "He's given us this programme so that we can protest the government overreach squelching – yes, I said it – squelching – it sounds just as dirty as it is – squelching – our freedom to go wherever we want regardless of the consequences. Kris just has to say he's trying to kill us so that lamestream media outlets like you will write about his programme. Squelching – love that word!"

Chriscolunkristen sadly shook his head. "Confirmation bias," he stated, "not just for Shriners and differently abled shrimp farmers any more…"

When restaurants and movie theatres open, they can be added to the list of services to be patronized in a single outing. "As you add more nodes, the geometrical problem increases exponentially," Chriscolunkristen commented. "But, do users care about the challenge of creating *COVID Roulette*? Of course not. All they care about is throwing bowling balls at their massage therapists, seeing the latest Van Damme flick at their local googleplex and spending the rest of the day – and possibly the rest of their lives – in emergency with a persistent, hacking cough and increasing pain in their chests!"

Some business owners are leery (Timothy?) of reopening. "Do they even have barbershops in heaven?" the owner of The Cruelest Cut told the *Wall Street Infernal*. "The Bible only refers to haircuts once, and it says that the shag is 'an abomination in the eyes of the

Lord, your Gord.' Other than that, nothing. I don't know if they have barbershops in heaven, but I do know one thing: I'm in no hurry to find out!"

When asked about businesspeople who might be wary (Timothy? Seriously, is that you?) of reopening, Governor Okaykempadre replied: "I guess they just hate our freedoms."

The Hangnail Pandemic

by LAURIE NEIDERGAARDEN, Alternate Reality News Service Medical Writer

Fellow Vesamupuccerian, for a grand experiment you have been
    selected:
With almost 150,000 dead and over three million infected,
All reasonable actions to halt the spread of the coronavirus have
    been rejected.
Let's face facts: the federal government is doing squat.
According to them, deaths from COVID-19 are a form of natural
    selection,
So there's no need to give citizens adequate protection.
(Especially not when the President is running for reelection.)
For the good of the country, spare it no more thought.

Live with it. Just live with it.
If you succumb to COVID,
You were obviously unfit.
So learn to live with it.

For a second term, the President is hopin',
But to get it, the economy **must** reopen.
With false hope, his base he'll rope in,
Even though infections and deaths are spiking.
Medical treatment is a free-for-all,
Measures to combat the disease are informal
As the country supposedly goes back to normal.
(But the chaos is very much to the President's liking.)

Live with it. Just live with it.
Even if by a truck you feel you've been hit.
If you lose a piece of lung whenever you spit,
Just live with it.

The administration is being a jerk,
Offering bad advice with a know-it-all smirk
When the CDC has told them what will work.
Reality? They just refuse it.
Wearing a mask is an odious thing,
And there's no fun in social distancing.
Not when it's time for a spring fling.
Youth – use it or you lose it.

Live with it. Just live with it,
Because the truth, the administration will never admit.
It will only come out bit by bit,
So better just to live with it

You say your job has disappeared?
Please don't worry. Have no fear.
It's time to start a new career!
To see it, you don't need to be a policy wonk. A
Little training, a little luck,
A lot of effort and so much pluck,
And pretty soon you, too, will be back to work.
Thank you so much for the advice, Ivanka.

Find something new. Just find something new.
Learn a new skill or two.
Even if available jobs are few,
Just find something new

"Most other countries have the virus on the run,"
Said the token smart person,
"I wish that the United States was one,
But that would be a lie.
I don't mean to give a polemic,
But we're treating this like a hangnail pandemic –

Ignorance and misinformation are endemic,
As Vesampuccerians continue to die."

Live with it. Just live with it.
You can survive by sheer grit.
Don't like government inaction? Don't get in a snit.
Just learn to live with it.

As if that advice wasn't already too bad,
Someone pointed out it sounded like the tag line for a Nike ad.
(Which made the President very mad,
And you wouldn't like him like that.)
In a voice that filled his aides with dread,
The President wound up and said:
"You mean like the shoes? Don't give me the blues! We have inner
  city youths – you know the ones I'm talking about – yeah, of
  course you do – killing each other for those sneakers – and
  that's the truth! Their lives couldn't be bleaker! You wanna
  make that association? Sorry – there's no relation. As for the
  pandemic, it's just not true! It's what I like to call "fake news!"
  I don't mean to make it into a beating my chest thing, but there
  would be no illness if there was no testing! You've gotta keep
  up – wanna know the latest? My administration's response to
  the virus has been the greatest! The amount of resources we've
  devoted to it will never be bested – now, anybody who wants to
  can be tested! Don't get grouchy! Don't be glum. (But don't
  believe anything you hear from Doctor Faucispendulum!) The
  virus is like the flu – not so bad. If you don't believe me, just
  ask your dad! Now, if you'll excuse me, I'm going back to
  bed!"
Then, he stomped off, ending the impromptu chat.

Live with it. Just live with it.
Even if your health turns to shit.
The President is not concerned one bit,
So learn to live with it.

3. THE SLEEP OF REASON PRODUCES… FRIENDS LIKE THESE

His Name is Kevin: A Tale of Bravery Under Enemy Fire

by FREDERICA VON McTOAST-HYPHEN, Alternate Reality News Service People Writer

He stands tall at the front of the small meeting room in an anonymous building in Washburningdington. As tall as a seventeen year-old, five foot three almost man with a slight build and premature scolioliosis can stand. He knows he is about to take enemy fire. Is he scared? Not in the least. He is terrified. In the most.

His name is Kevin. And, he is in over his head.

Kevin adjusts his brown blazer and gently ahems. He is signalling he is ready to initiate contact with the eight hostiles in the room. Then, he starts explaining how the Grey House is actually not the original building, how that was burned down during the War of 1812 and rebuilt. Funny thing about that: they couldn't quite get the singe of flames out of the new building, which is why, even though it looks white, that is not its actua –

"What does this have to do with our briefing?" an old woman asks in a tone of voice that would melt his stomach lining if the sodas he had grown up on hadn't gotten to it first.

"This…this is what I'm trained to do," Kevin tells her. "It's what I know."

"We're not here for a civics lesson," the old woman tells him, the pearls around her throat vibrating with indignation. "We're here to be briefed on reports in the press that the Duchy of Grand Fenwick has been paying a bounty to anybody who kills Vesampuccerian troops in Afghanistan."

Kevin gulps. This is what he was afraid of. He's a Grey House tour guide. What the people in the room want to be briefed on is highly classified; his security clearance only allows him access to information that has been shredded and burned to ashes.

"Yes, umm, that would be bad," Kevin tries to fake his way through the ordeal.

An old man who looks like somebody's kindly uncle (who can turn crotchety on an ever-diminishing in value dime) peers at Kevin's chest, trying to read his name tag. Finally, the old man gives in and takes out his glasses. "Yes, Kevin," he finally says, smartly putting his glasses away. "That would be bad. But, you know what would be worse? If the President knew about it months ago and did nothing about it. That's why we're here. To find out what we can about it. So. Take a deep breath. Take your time. Then, tell us all you know."

"I…I'm sure the President would have done something about it if he had known," Kevin stood firm. "You can't let something like that happen to our troops – it would be unVesampuccerian!"

"Yes, dear," the old woman responded. The condescension didn't so much drip from her voice as glop all over Kevin's head with a dull * SPLURSH *. "It would be very unVesampuccerian. That's why we need to know if the President is telling the truth when he says he wasn't briefed on the matter by our intelligence agencies."

"Although, if he wasn't briefed, we need to know why not," a younger man, who was handsome enough to play a federal prosecutor on a TV legal show (although, disappointingly, he had only played one in real life), added. "To not brief the President on such a serious threat to our troops would constitute a terrible breach of security protocols."

"Thank you, Eric," the old man said. He wasn't exactly dismissive, but he did manage to hit the circle around the dismissive bullseye, which isn't bad considering he had put away his glasses.

"Why would the intelligence agencies not tell the President?" Kevin wondered.

The old woman smiled, giving Kevin an irrational urge to check his pocket to see if his wallet was still there. "Maybe they were afraid that if they told the President what they had found, he would immediately tell Rupert Mountkilamanjoy —"

"The Prime Minister of Grand Fenwick?" Kevin exclaimed.

"The same."

"That would be terrible on terrible," the good looking younger man added. "Terrible squared."

"Thank you, Eric," the old man responded. Funny how some people can roll their eyes using their tone of voice alone.

"Can you tell us anything about this...dear?" the old woman asked, the last word having to be pulled out of her with a powerful electromagnet.

"Do you want to hear rumours of what various Presidents have done in the Linkedinonalog bedroom? Number 32 will amaze you!"

"We're done here," the old woman pronounced as she stood up.

As he watched the Dumbopratic politicians file out of the room, Kevin smiled to himself. He had been thrown into the trenches, and he had come out bloodied but unbowed. He had done what his Commander-in-Briefs had asked of him, and he considered himself the hero of meeting room 303-B.

Now, all he had to do was clean up for his one o'clock tour.

Or, so I imagine the briefing went. They are classified, so nobody talks about them.

Out of Pocket, Off the Wall

by HAL MOUNTSAUERKRAUTEN, Alternate Reality News Service Crime Writer

The news came over the wire (hey! – why should I ignore a great old newsie phrase when I can repurpose it for the modern age? – the internet ain't a series of tubes, you know) that somebody named Steve O'bannonallhope had been arrested for wire fraud and money laundering. And, I thought, *Steve O'banantalope? That name sounds familiar – where do I know it from?*

A couple of hours later, an intern said, "Hey! Did you hear that President McDruhitmumpf's campaign chairman was arrested?" When I told her that was old news, she responded (with a scornful tone of voice that only the young dealing with their elders can pull off), "Not **that** one. The other one!" Okay, that was newer news, but still old enough to need a walker. "Not that one, either," the intern insisted. "The other other one!"

Riiiiight. That's where I remembered Steve O'bannonallhope from! A couple hours after that, but well within deadline.

O'bannonallhope, who had also been a senior adviser to President Ronald McDruhitmumpf in his first six months in office (which is twenty-seven years in McDruhitmumpf administration years), was one of the people who ran Erect the Edifice, an online fundraising operation for President McDruhitmumpf's border wall. According to the Southern District of New Yoricknuhemwell, he spent hundreds of thousands of the $25 million the organization raised on beer and potato chips.

Hey! – it's not easy to maintain that curvaceous O'bannonallhope physique!

When he was released from custody, the first thing O'bannonallhope did was defend himself in an interview on Foxindehenhaus News. He – okay, actually, the first thing he did was down a dozen beers and three bags of chocolate dill pickle ripple chips. But, that was in the limo on the way to the interview, so the interview was at worst the first and a halfth thing he did.

This is an excerpt:

STEVE O'BANNONALLHOPE: This is a political hit job by people who do not want President McDruhitmumpf's wall to be built.

SEAN HANJOBOVVERFIST: So, you used the money to build the wall?

O'BANNONALLHOPE: Umm…sure.

HANJOBOVVERFIST: How many miles did the money you raised build?

O'BANNONALLHOPE: We built…a panel.

HANJOBOVVERFIST: A panel?

O'BANNONALLHOPE: We're very proud of it. It's a very good panel. It will keep a lot of illegals out of the country…in that very small patch of the desert…

HANJOBOVVERFIST: So, umm, it was at least ten feet wide and twenty feet tall…right?

O'BANNONALLHOPE: Right. No. Not right. It…actually, it was three feet wide and four feet tall.

HANJOBOVVERFIST: Four? Feet? That's i – four?

O'BANNONALLHOPE: Four Vesampuccerian feet.

Long pause.

HANJOBOVVERFIST: Brilliant! Keep supporting the President! Keep supporting the troops! Keep building the wall!

"The fish sells out its country from the top," explained token smart person Amy Sheshutshotshitbam. "When you think about all of the ways the President has profited from his position, it's hard to imagine the people who work for him would settle for a gold watch and a pat on the back!"

When asked about the arrest, President McDruhitmumpf got a dreamy look on his face and said, "O'bannonallhope... O'bannonallhope...wasn't he a pop singer in the 1960s?" A reporter pointed out to the President that O'bannonallhope ran his 2016 election campaign, to which the President replied, "You're a nasty person. Why would you say something like that? Really nasty, like, ugly nasty. Rosie O'dokennel-Kerr uglasty."

When the next reporter insisted that O'bannonallhope had, indeed, run the President's campaign, he responded, "Oh, **that** Steve O'bannonallhope. Honestly, he was only the campaign manager for a minute and thirty-five seconds almost four years ago – and that's 186 in McDruhitmumpf administration years. He didn't do much for us. And, anyway, he has a forgettable face. Who are we talking about, again? I don't remember. You don't remember. Nobody remembers."

He had us there.

Having fallen afoul of McDruhitmumpf administration years myself, I was ready to believe the President. Until O'bannonallhope claimed in the interview that he talks to the President every couple of months, standard human time.

O'bannonallhope was one of four people charged with defrauding contributors to the Erect the Edifice Kickasstarter campaign. Brian Kolcomfortfatigue, the founder and public face of Erect the Edifice, was the chief beneficiary of the scheme, even though he had repeatedly stated that he would not make a penny from the fundraising effort. Hmm…Kolcomfortfatigue. Brian Kolcomfortfatigue. That name sounds awfully familiar – where do I know it from?

Ah. That's right. Nowhere. I've never heard it before. This McDruhitmumpf administration years thing has some weird side effects!

Where Every Sentence Ends In Death

by HAL MOUNTSAUERKRAUTEN, Alternate Reality News Service Justice Writer
Free at last! Free at last. Thank Gord Paul Bildapillofort is free at last!*

When last we heard of Bildapillofort, the former manger of the McDruhitmumpf campaign who had been given a seven year sentence for colluding – "No collusion!" the President interrupted.

He hadn't had a reason to play his greatest hit in a long time, and he sang it with gusto, if not a firm grasp of key – with the Fenwickians to steal the 2016 Presidential election for the Reduhblican Party.

Yesterday, Bildapillofort was released from federal prison to serve out the remainder of his sentence at home.

"Paul's crime was loyalty," said Bildapillofort's lawyer Todd Blanchard-Sowightman, a single tear rolling out of his eye to signal to the audience his sadness at the injustice of it all. "Should he die in prison for that? Jesus begesus, have some compassion, why don't you?"

Blanchard-Sowightman was not being entirely hyperbolic (he only does that behind the locked door of his office): prisons are hotbeds of COVID-19, with anywhere from 61 to 39 per cent of inmates testing positive for the virus. Deaths from it have risen sharply (hence your mom telling you not to run in the hallway with infection statistics) in prisons since the onset of the outbreak.

"You can't shiv a guy in the yard from six feet away," explained an inmate who asked to be identified as "Sparky Underpants." "I heard about this inmate who tried to cut a snitch using a knife he carved out of soap attached to a stick he smuggled out of the shop. He managed to give the snitch a dozen gashes no deeper than paper cuts before the guards knew what was happening. After they stopped laughing, they threw him in solitary. I tell you, man, you just can't do no social distancing in prison!"

What about wearing masks? Sparky Underpants gave me a look that could melt a prosecutor's Brooksnoahgumeant Brothers tie. "You think the guards want us to go all raccoon on them? Sheesh! How would they be able to tell the troublemakers from the good behaviourists?"

The number that is prominently displayed on everybody's orange jumpsuits?

"Besides," Sparky Underpants deflected, "the security deposit box content liberators among us might have flashbacks to when we were young and free. That would just be cruel and unusual, man. Cruel and especially unusual."

"Prisoner 1-3-5-7-9 acted against our democracy," stated an inmate who asked to be identified as "Amarillo Fats." "I got 30 years for the third time I got caught selling weed to college kids – the only way I'm getting out of here is in a pine box. You...you don't think you could bake a pine box into a cake for me, could you?"

Amarillo Fats said he wasn't bitter, he was just pointing out an irony (he had been studying the collected works of Alanis Morisette while incarcerated). Bildapillofort was released from FCI Lotto Losers, even though nobody at that facility had tested positive for the coronavirus. "Oh, you know it was only just a matter of time before it infested the place," Blanchard-Sowightman admonished. "Good Gord, man, where is your compassion? Com – pash – on? Do I have to spell it out for you? C-O-M –"

Bildapillofort was let out of prison even though he did not meet the criterion for early release. To be eligible, you have to have served at least half of your sentence, or have 18 months left on your sentence as long as you have served at least 25 per cent of your sentence, **and** received the express written consent of Major League Baseball.

"What about McDruhitmumpf's former lawyer Michael Canadiohen?" interrupted token smart person Amy Sheshutshotshitbam. "The guy, who cooperated with the Meullitallover investigation, met the criterion needed for home release and was scheduled to be let out two weeks ago. But the paperwork mysteriously disappeared, and now he might only be let out at the end of the month. Or, the end of next month. Or, the fourth of never. It looks like President McDruhitmumpf is using the health crisis to reward his friends and punish his enemies."

"Yeah, that sounds about right," a glum Canadiohen commented. "I guess I should have sent him a nicer card last Christmas…"

"– P-A-S-S-I-O-N," Blanchard-Sowightman concluded. "Because, honestly, what kind of society would we be if we left non-violent offenders to die of a horrible disease in prison?"

* My apologies to people of pigment who may be offended by this reference to a civil rights icon. Given that the prison population of people of pigment is much higher than their proportion of the Vesampuccerian population, it seemed eerily appropriate.

The Court of Public Opinion No Longer in Sesspoolpandemic

by FRANCIS GRECOROMACOLLUDEN, Alternate Reality News Service National Politics Writer

Jefferson "Self-regard" Sesspoolpandemic has been primaretired. And, it wasn't even close.

The former Attorney General for President Ronald McDruhitmumpf was trying to regain his Alabamshire Senate seat. As one who was hounded from public office will. In the first primary, the vote was split between 237 different candidates, so a runoff had to be held between the top two candidates: Sesspoolpandemic and former high school football coach and used ice cream salesman Tommy Biggfattbaggogutts.

"Wuhl, shoot," Sesspoolpandemic folksied in his concession speech. "Ah really wanted ta get back ta servin' mah country. While theah ah still immahgrants gettin' into Vesampucceri, ah felt lahk mah job wasn't finished. Ah guess votuhs felt uthuhwahse…"

Indeed, votuhs did. Biggfattbaggogutts won the primary with 61 per cent of the votes.

Biggfattbaggogutts was not an obvious challenger for Sesspoolpandemic. He was a coach for the Brunette High Fighting Chipmunks. While he did lead them to five national football victories, he has never had to fight with the Congressional Budget Office about the validity of earmarks, or lobbed softball questions at a Reduhblican nominee for an Extreme Court position.

He was also involved in a hedge fund which turned out to be a financial fraud. Although he made introductions to potential investors, had business cards identifying himself as managing partner, and leased a BMW and got his health insurance through the company, Biggfattbaggogutts claimed that, "I was an investor just like everybody else. I mean, as long as nobody talks about the settlement I entered into with the other investors to avoid a lengthy and expensive lawsuit, I was completely innocent."

What he did do, on the other hand, was a credible Ronald McDruhitmumpf impression, always talking about "flushing the fen" this and "make Vesampucceri great again" that. "I don't know where Tommy gets his ideas," the President commented, "but I love them. I really do. Love them bigly." (The fact that he was sued by investors who accused him of criminal behaviour also endeared him to the President, who knows his way around a legal proceeding.)

Thus began a love affair that lasted the entire primary. At 2:37 in the morning before the runoff, the President tweeped: "Boo Sesspoolpandemic. Boo, I say! A worse Stabber in the Backer hasn't been seen since Orange Julius Caesar salad! Biggfattbaggogutts will Keep Keeping Making Vesampucceri Great Again! #thechoiceisclearasconcretealabamshire".

At the same time, Biggfattbaggogutts took every opportunity to call Sesspoolpandemic a "nogoodnik traitor." "When he recused himself from the Meullitallover investigation, he stabbed the President in the back. Then, when he justified it in the press, he repeatedly stabbed the President in the front, and the sides, and… and…and the back seat of a 68 Chevy! So much violence done to such an honourable man!"

Token smart person Amy Sheshutshotshitbam moaned. "Please, spare me! Tommy Biggfattbaggogutts sounds like an insecure girlfriend who has to slag a guy's old flame to assure herself that he still doesn't have any feelings for her! Really, he and the President should just have gotten a room!"

President McDruhitmumpf's support of his rival came despite the fact that Sesspoolpandemic was the first Reduhblican in Congress to support him. "Theah is somethin' in the way he entahs a room and totally dominates ever'bodah's attention that sends shivahs up and down mah spine. If that man doesn't become Presahdent in 2016, the Pope should saintize 'im!"

Sesspoolpandemic made his concession speech wearing a MVGA hat. "Ah leave elected office with mah integrahty intact. Ah feel good abaht it. Ah hold my head hah. Ah didn't trah ta excuse mahself, oah get in a faht, oah undahmine the leadah of ouah country and thuh great wahk he has ta do. That was an honoahble path, ah do believe."

Token smart person Sheshutshotshitbam moaned again. One more moan, and she could be said to be haunting our interview. "Sesspoolpandemic is acting like a jilted lover who refuses to acknowledge that the relationship is over and it's time to move on. It would be pathetic if he didn't once have responsibility for dispensing justice in the country!"

In his concession speech, Sesspoolpandemic went on to say: "Ah think it's tahm fo' this heah Reduhblican Pahty ta listen ta the Ronald McDruhitmumpf agenda."

"Is he delusional?" token smart person Sheshutshotshitbam moaned long enough to get the attention of the medium whose office is across the street from the Alternate Reality News Service. "When McDruhitmumpf is in the room, Reduhblicans can't hear anybody else! It's gotta be pheromones or something – there's no other explanation!"

Biggfattbaggogutts will take on incumbent Senator Doug Jonesenforrahit in November. This should be good…

Flyinnthuointmeanting in the Face of Precedent

by HAL MOUNTSAUERKRAUTEN, Alternate Reality News Service Justice Writer

Did **not** see that one coming!

The smart money was sure that former McDruhitmumpf national security adviser Michael Flyinnthuointmeant was going to be pardoned by the President. The stupid money was on Flyinnthuointmeant rotting in a prison cell for the rest of his life. And, the money that does not even know how to ask a question… well, nobody knows what its opinion of Flyinnthuointmeant's future was because it didn't have the ability to articulate it. Kind of obvious, really.

None of the money, regardless of its intelligence, was expecting Attorney General William Katiebarrthudor to drop the charges against Flyinnthuointmeant. The reason for this? The trial had been composed into chapters and paragraphs, and was all over but the sentencing.

Lost in the torrent of corruption and malfeasance that is the McDruhitmumpf Doctrine, it is easy to forget that Flyinnthuointmeant confessed to lying to the Federal Bureau of Instigations about conversations he had with representatives of the Duchy of Grand Fenwick about the 2016 Vesampucceri election. "I did it," he told the court. "I lied. Oh, man, did I lie. I was a lying liar. Who did not tell the truth."

Awkward.

To compound the awkwardity, Flyinnthuointmeant made the same declaration to the court a year later (adding a Norwegian accent to some words just to keep it fresh for himself). That's a lot of public confession for an innocent man. Awkward squared.

True, but irrelevant: awkward is the very air that this administration breaths, regularly causing it to cough up embarrassment hairballs the size of a small sedan. Attorney General Katiebarrthudor argued that the FBI had no basis on which to question Flyinnthuointmeant, so nothing that followed (including his guilty plea, his confession and the seventh season of *Game of Violence and Nudity*) had any legal standing. Or, legal sitting. Maybe a little legal lying face down in the gutter, but not enough to stop Flyinnthuointmeant from becoming a free man.

When asked about the confession, Attorney General Katiebarrthudor claimed, "You know, people sometimes plead to things that turn out not to be crimes," Like murder? "Well, no, murder is always a crime." Drug dealing? "Drug dealing hasn't always been a crime, but it is right now, so, no." Umm... jaywalking? "Look. We don't always need an example to prove a point. Trust me. Pleading guilty to a crime in open court has a lot more wiggle room than worms outside the legal community realize!"

In fact, Attorney General Katiebarrthudor argued, Flyinnthuointmeant had an obligation to talk to Fenwickians about the election. "While most Vesampuccerians take their idiotocratic duties lightly, General Flyinnthuointmeant was active in electoral politics. He's a hero. Somebody should pin a medal on him and call him 'plucky!'"

When asked about the turn the Flyinnthuointmeant case had taken, President McDruhitmumpf stated: "Our response to the COWARD-19 virus has been outstanding. Just outstanding. We'll be going down to zero cases soon. We just have to hit two million cases and 100,000 deaths first. But, after that, it will be clear sailing! Just not on a cruise ship. Unless the line is owned by a friend of mine. #poppaneedsabrandnewgolfcourse"

Before popping the cork on the champagne (an off-year vintage – Flyinnthuointmeant couldn't afford anything better on his military pension – wink, wink), it is worth noting that the judge in the case, Emmet Sullivanmorris, has to agree to the motion to dismiss the charges. He could choose to ignore the motion, sentencing Flyinnthuointmeant to a term in prison. If he has a really good reason (like getting stuck in a traffic jam on the way to court and missing his morning coffee), he could even start an inquiry into why the Department of Injustice decided to drop the charges.

"That's what I would do," stated former prosecutor Barbara McDoodadallquade. "Then, I would put the popcorn in the microwave, because this could be the most entertaining show since the seventh season of *Game of Violence and Nudity*!"

Everybody's a critic.

When asked if history would look upon this action kindly, Attorney General Katiebarrthudor answered: "Well, history is written by the winners, and that would give me something to do after I retire…"

When asked how he felt about the dropped charges, Flyinnthuointmeant said, "I just want to get back to my family, maybe celebrate by having a nice meal out and taking in a ball ga – what?" Nobody had the heart to tell him about the pandemic lockdown, but he must have seen the dismay on our faces, because he continued: "No, seriously, what?"

All Day Suckers

by MARA VERHEYDEN-HILLIARD, Alternate Reality News Service War Writer

At 102 (a bad number for a temperature, a pretty good number for an age), Staph Sergeant Marco Guineverici is one of the last liviing Vesampuccerian's who fought in World War I. Guineverici –

"Eh? What's that?" Guineverici shouted. "What'd ya say?"

Guineverici fought valiantly at the Battle of Pork Rind Gullet, which earned him a Purple Prose for bravery under fire. This –

"I can't hear you!" Guineverici screamed. "You gotta speak louder! Really put some lung power into it!"

This week, it was reported that on a state visit to a French cemetery to honour Vesampucceri's casualties of WWI, President Ronald McDruhitmumpf wondered "Why should I go to that cemetery? It's full of losers." As if to drive the point home, he added that the almost 2,000 Marines who died in the Battle of Bellowscreechmartre Wood were "suckers."

"He said **what?**" Guineverici shrieked. "That son of a polymath Hun licker! He isn't fit to shine Private Garibaldo's boots! Or Lieutenant-Colonel Three -Eyed Monte's khakis! Or…or…or any part of Langrahans' privates! Anybody who could say something like that is not fit to be this country's Commander-in-Briefs!"

"Oh, sure – **that** he heard!" groused President McDruhitmumpf.

The Grey House immediately denied the claims that the President had said what he said. Press Secretary-Poppet Kayleigh McEnanity stated, "The President has the utmost respect and admiration and...and...and sheer likingness for our troops. He would never have said those nasty, nasty things you people keep writing that you've verified he said!"

As if to prove the poin, PS-P McEnanity tossed her hair back in what she hoped was a debate-ending move.

"So...silky...smooth," security expert Malcolm Donneednopennance droned, hypnotized. Then, shaking his head, he apoplectically continued: "No! That's not – utmost respect my patootie! This President mocked Senator John McMacPaddycain. Anybody with half a brain will clearly remember what he said: 'War heroes don't get captured, okay? Have you never seen *Rambo: Seventh or Eighth Blood (It's Hard To Keep Track When You've Lost So Much)*?' He mocked the family of a Gold Star veteran. He's called his generals so many dirty names, you could fill a dictionary with them all!* Calling war vets 'loser' and 'suckers' is totally on brand for him!"

"There's one in every crowd," PS-P McEnanity pouted. Journalists who had long thought their hearts were made of stone found that they were melting. Or it could have been heartburn – those three beer lunches can be brutal on your digestive system! Either way, they didn't challenge her assertion as they reached for an antacid.

The President himself tweeped: "I love all of our fine men in the military. Except the ones who get captured, maimed or dye. Cuz this world was made for winners!!!! #crybabylosersdontgetmyrespect"

So, a mixed message, then.

"Ronald McDruhitmumpf is a very transactional human being," explained Pulippitzaner Prize-winning columnist Eugene Robinsoncrusoe. "That doesn't mean he has sex with people who believe they were born in the bodies of the wrong gender – goodness, me, no. Although, there is still a lot we don't know about what he does in the privacy of his own Fenwickian hotel room. But, no. No, being a 'transactional human being' is just a fancy way of saying whenever he is asked to make a decision, he asks, 'What's in it for me?' Somebody who is transactional would never be able to understand military sacrifice. Or, familial sacrifice. Ritual sacrifice? Okay, maybe, but I would hate to think what he imagines that would make him…"

Interviews with officials suggest that the Grey House is panicking about the effect President McDruhitmumpf's remarks will have on his base. "Ohmygordohmygordohmygordohmygord!" 17 sources told the Alternate Reality News Service. His base is deeply in love (in a wholly Platonic sense, and I'll deck any man that says otherwise!) with the military, as you undoubtedly read between the lines of the anonymous staffers' statement.

But how seriously should they be taking this? I asked Guineverici who he voted for in 2016. "I voted in 2016?" he innocently asked. "What's a vote? What's a 2016?"

When I asked him whether the President's remarks would have any affect on who he planned on voting for in 2020, Guineverici replied: "Absolutely not! I mean, it's not like he shot a man in broad daylight on Fifth Avenue or anything!"

* Actually, Peter-Paul Gotellitonda wrote that book, *Them's Fightin' Words: A Dictionary of Words and Phrases (Not All Profane) President Ronald McDruhitmumpf has Used to Describe His Generals*. However, since it came out in the same week that 37 other books on the McDruhitmumpf administration came out, Donneednopennance can be forgiven for not being aware of it.

Death Screwed Over

by SASKATCHEWAN KOLONOSCOGRAD, Alternate Reality News Service Religion Writer

Death has written a sternly worded letter to Senate Majority Leader Mitch Wichconnelliswich demanding that he stop referring to himself as "the Grim Reaper" of legislation passed by the Dumbopratic House of Representatives.

"SINCE VIDEO OF THE MAJORITY LEADER USING MY NAME SURFACED," the letter read, "MY STAFF HAVE HAD TO DEAL WITH AN INCREASING NUMBER OF ANGRY EMAILS FEATURING SUFFICIENTLY HORRIFYING INVECTIVE THAT IT WOULD MAKE ELI BLOODYROTHOGORD BLANCH, INCLUDING, IRONICALLY, MANY GRAPHIC DEATH THREATS. WE HAD TO SEND JUDY HOME IN TEARS THE OTHER DAY, AND SHE MANAGES THE SOULS OF THOSE WHO PASSED THROUGH THE VEIL BECAUSE OF WAR AND MURDER! YOU WILL DESIST FROM USING MY NAME IN FUTURE OR FACE THE CONSEQUENCES!"

"Now, I would never want to argue with such a well-known figure as Death," Majority Leader Wichconnelliswich smirtled (smirked while turtling), "but I don't see a copyright or trademark mark after the phrase 'Grim Reaper.' So, I'm gonna assume He doesn't have a monopoly on the term."

The Majority Leader went on to say that he did not fear the Grim Reaper, since all men die at their allotted time. "Honestly, what is he gonna do? Kill me twice?"

"WITH ALL DUE RESPECT, THE MAJORITY LEADER DOESN'T KNOW WHAT HE IS TALKING ABOUT," responded Maria Altbaltimora, Public Relations Officer for the Office of the Grim Reaper. "THE BOSS DOES NOT KILL PEOPLE. HE JUST FERRIES THEM INTO THE NEXT PHASE OF THEIR EXISTENCE WHEN FATE DECIDES THAT IT IS THEIR TIME TO DIE. HONESTLY, IF HE INSISTS UPON TAKING ON THE GRIM REAPER'S IDENTITY, YOU WOULD THINK WICHCONNELLISWICH WOULD DO HIS HOMEWORK!"

"Mitch has been doing a fine job – a great job," President Ronald McDruhitmumpf weighed in on the disagreement in a tweep at 2:37 in the morning. "But, death? I call him messy mayhem and untidy death. Have you ever seen a dead body? I haven't in real life, but I've seen plenty in the movies, and they're not pretty, folks. Not pretty. Body parts all over the place…large pools of blood…it's like, you know, he just doesn't take pride in his work!"

"THE PRESIDENT OF THE UNITED STATES OF VESAMPUCCERI, THE MOST POWERFUL MAN IN THE WORLD, IS INTENT ON ASSASSINATING THE CHARACTER OF AN ENTITY THAT HAS EXISTED SINCE LIFE FIRST BEGAN, AN ENTITY THAT IS VITAL TO THE CYCLE THAT RUNS THE UNIVERSE?" Altbaltimora commented. "LAME."

"So, this is what it has come to," token smart person Amy Sheshutshotshitbam shook her head. "The Reduhblican Party has picked a fight with the mythical personification of the process of leaving this life!"

"Oh, it's worse than that," Speaker of the House Nancy Pelligrinosi pointed out. "Not only are the Reduhblicans picking a fight with Death, **but they're not allowing any of the legislation out of the House to be voted on in the Senate!**"

"That's just nervous Nancy," the President said in a subsequent interview. "I call her nervous Nancy because – well, that isn't all that bad, is it? Nonsense Nancy? Yeah. Yeah, that's more like – Non-sequitur Nancy? Hee hee. Nasty Nanc – oh, yes! Nasty Nancy! Nasty! Nasty! Nasty Nancy! That one's gonna stick!"

"I CANNOT HELP BUT THINK THAT MY ORIGINAL COMPLAINT IS GETTING LOST IN A HAZE OF SELF-INTERESTED STATEMENTS AND NONSENSICAL WHITE NOISE," Death observed. "I WOULD LIKE TO JUST REMIND EVERYBODY THAT THERE IS SOME CONFUSION BETWEEN MY ROLE AND THAT OF THE MAJORITY LEADER OF THE SENATE. THIS IS NOT A GOOD SITUATION, AND I CANNOT ALLOW IT TO CONTINUE!"

"Threatening the Senate Majority Leader, Death? Really?" bloviated Foxindehenhaus...person Sean Hanjobovverfist. "Well, have I got news for you! Mitch Wichconnelliswich is doing the job that the Vesampuccerian people elected him to do. Who elected you, Mister Death? I mean, you're not even a Vesampuccerian, and you think it's okay to criticize one of the great leaders of the greatest idiotocracy that the world has ever known? You might want to go back to whatever nether realm you came from and rethink your whole approach, because, I gotta tell you, you and your opinions are not welcome here!"

"Yeah, I don't pay any attention to Foxindehenhaus Noise," Speaker Pelligrinosi replied. "I find it easier to hold down my breakfast that way. The important thing is: the House is passing legislation that will benefit common people, and it goes to the Senate to die. I agree with Death: this is an unacceptable state of affairs!"

"I – I'M BEGINNING TO REGRET BRINGING THIS WHOLE THING UP," Death, as it usually does, got the last word.

Say It Loud, Say It Proud, Boys

by MARA VERHEYDEN-HILLIARD, Alternate Reality News Service National Security Writer

The first Presidential debate between Ronald McDruhitmumpf and Joe Bidenhisbeeswax? The Prude Bois have been there, done that and got the t-shirt.

Literally.

At one point, President McDruhitmumpf was asked by moderator Chris Walleyedpeacrackers if he would denounce white supremacy. "Sure," he said with about as much enthusiasm as a vampire in a sun lamp showroom. When pressed on the subject, he irritably asked for an example. When Bidenhisbeeswax offered the

Prude Bois, the President said: "Prude Bois? Sure. I tell them: stand back and stand by. Because the real threat to public order is antifa!"

"He likes us! He really likes us!" exulted Proud Boi Winstead von Rippersteinem. "When the Electric Boogaloo* happens, I'm going to dedicate my first kill to the President!"

von Rippersteinem was modelling a t-shirt with the Prude Bois logo (PB in the middle of two pieces of white bread); the words "Stand back" appeared above the logo, while the words "Stand by" appeared below it. With his spindly white limbs and gawky head, models on the Milan runways didn't have to fear for their jobs. Still, the message was clear.

"I...may have to take a vacation to another country," responded Pulippitzaner Prize-winning *Washburningdington Post* columnist Eugene Robinsoncrusoe, who clearly got the message. "I hear Tuktoyaktuk is nice this time of year..."

"You've got it all wrong," stated Press Secretary Kayleigh McEnanity. "The President was having a flashback to his television days. When he said, 'Stand back,' he was trying to get the Prude Bois to get on their mark. When he said, 'Stand by,' he was telling them to wait for the camera shot to be set up. You see. It was all very innocent. A little weird, maybe, but innocent."

The President immediately cut the legs out from under her, like he was removing the appendages from a table so he could make it into a surfboard. "Prude Bois? I never met them – couldn't tell you who they are. But, I tell you what: they sound like people who want to make Vesampucceri great again, and there's nothing wrong with that. Nothing wrong with that."

As he took a suitcase out of a cupboard and started sorting through his clothes, Robinsoncrusoe said, "Stand by. Not stand down. Stand – why am I taking that tie? I never liked that tie. You want a tie that looks like this? – stand by. Wait for orders. The President has been saying he won't – where is my Hawakota shirt? If I'm going to be a tourist, I may as well look like one! – abide by the results of the election if he doesn't win. White supremacist violence might – I haven't been able to fit into these pants in years, but hope springs eternal – be part of his endgame. Now, if you'll excuse me, I have to look something up on Travelgeocities…"

Two days after the debate, the President, looking very much like a small child who had just been caught smashing the cookie jar to the ground, said, "Of course I condemn the Kook Klux Klan. I condemn the Prude Bois – whoever they are. Remember: I never met them. Have no idea who they are. Maybe somebody should introduce us some time. I condemn white supremacists…especially when they're members of Black Lives Matter!"

"The President had to say that so the libtard media would stop picking on him," von Rippersteinem commented. "But, we know, in his heart of hearts, he didn't mean it. Saaaay, that would look really good on a t-shirt!"

"You know," Robinsoncrusoe said as he called for an Uber, "I hate to agree with a white supremacist, but…"

I waited for several minutes for him to finish the thought, but the next thing he said was, "How quickly can you get me to the airport?" Ending our interview seemed to be the discrete thing to do.

"I have said, 'This is unprecedented,'" so often in the last four years that I should probably get a copyright on the phrase," commented Presidential historian Beschbefordatloess. "But, this is… you know."

But, is it really that unprecedented? Ever since Richard Nixwatmondnewon's "Southern Strategy," the Reduhblicans have courted Vesampuccerian racists, the racist adjacent and the racist look the other way and pretend there's nothing to see here but secretly watch intently out of the corner of their eyes. Isn't this the endgame that the entire party has inevitably been working towards?

"Whoa, look at the historical perspective on you!" Beschbefordatloess beamed. "If I'm not careful, you could take over my presidential historianing job! But…don't, okay? I could never go back to teaching first years! For the love of Gord, don't force me to go back to teaching first years!"

We'll see how things develop.

* For readers who are unfamiliar with white supremacist – ideology is perhaps too grand a concept – let's go with muddled thinking – white supremacist muddled thinking, the Electric Boogaloo is the coming race war. Another Prude Bois t-shirt reads: "Electric Boogaloo? Let's dance!" They can expect a cease and desist order from the estate of the late David Bowiebowieboo any day now.

He Barely Knew Ye

by FREDERICA VON McTOAST-HYPHEN, Alternate Reality News Service People Writer

We all have one – a cousin Bertie who throws up in the punch bowl and blames it on the moosemeat pate that everybody else was eating without incident; a friend named Biff or Beau or Boffin who crashes through the glass door "going long" to catch a Nerdf football that nobody was actually throwing; an aunt Petunia who professes her love of humanity by complaining about everybody's taste in clothes and/or life partners. The kind of person who can only be described by, "They're not with me. I don't really know them. At all."

For President Ronald McDruhitmumpf, everybody is potentially one of them.

"I don't really know him," the President said. "I met him once or twice, you know, crawling around on the floor as I was trying to get to the television in the other room to see what the news anchors were saying about me. It's not like we talked all the time or anything. Don't get me wrong – he's a good kid. A fine kid. But I never knew him all that well."

He said similar things about Michael Canadiohen, who had been his personal lawyer for many years; but it couldn't have been him the President was talking about because the only time Canadiohen was known to be on all fours was at a fraternity hazing when he was

47. President McDruhitmumpf had also said similar thing about Steve O'Bannonallhope, but it couldn't have been him the President was talking about because there is no evidence his former national security adviser was ever a child.

No, President McDruhitmumpf was talking about Ronald McDruhitmumpf, Jr. His son.

"That's kind of hard to believe," said columnist Eugene Robinsoncrusoe. "I mean, they lived in the same house for almost 20 years. You would have thought they would have met in the kitchen in the middle of the night and bonded over making Hamberder Helper or something!"

"That's entirely plausible," said token smart person Amy Sheshutshotshitbam. "Ronald McDruhitmumpf is not what you would call a warm man – his fathering instincts probably date back to the Ice Age! If he ever did talk to his children, it would probably be to tell them how great **he** was, the best father in the history of sexual reproduction!"

"Daddy…?" Ronald McDruhitmumpf, Jr. tentatively pouted.

In fact, President McDruhitmumpf has thrown so many people from his administration under the bus that its suspension has gone all wonky and customers are complaining of nausea and sore bottoms. In further fact, the only thing keeping the bus line going is income from all of the foreign dignitaries who use it to get around when on official business in Washburningdington.

But, family? "The only positive thing Ronald McDruhitmumpf has ever said about family is that, in case of emergency, they would make good bone marrow donors," token smart person Sheshutshotshitbam commented.

Knowing that, for President McDruhitmumpf, loyalty is just a plain cotton shirt you wear for more than one day, why do people still clamour (but, not in the baby mollusc sense) to be part of his administration?

"I mean, why do people tickle zebras?" Robinsoncrusoe asked rhetorically (although it might have been the triple chili dog he had for lunch). "I, uhh, don't actually know the answer to that question, so if anybody knows why people tickle zebras, they should write to me at the *Washburningdington Post*."

Robinsoncrusoe went on to explain that working for the most powerful man in the idiotocratic world still held great appeal for some people. "They get to use official Grey House stationery," he explained. "They get to see the building without being herded behind ropes. They get huge advances to write their memoirs. I mean, honestly, who wouldn't want that?"

"People with self-respect?" token smart person Sheshutshotshitbam mused.

"True," Robinsoncrusoe allowed. "But, the Reduhblicans drove anybody with self-respect out of the party ages ago."

"True," token smart person Sheshutshotshitbam agreed. "But ambition is not, I think, the most important factor here. People who work for this Grey House are like people who hit themselves in the head repeatedly with a frying pan."

"They never think the brain damage is going to happen to them?"

"Exactly."

"Hey – when we're done with our respective interviews, wanna grab a drink somewhere?"

"I don't think Mister token smart person would approve."

"He doesn't have to kno –"

Hey! Take it somewhere else, people! There's journalism happening here!

"Daddy?" Ronald, Jr. plaintively pouted. "Are you there? It's cold here under the bus, daddy. Really cold…"

4. THE SLEEP OF REASON PRODUCES...GOOD ADVICE FOR PEOPLE WHO MAKE BAD DECISIONS

Ask the Tech Answer Guy...For the Children!

Yo, Tech Answer Guy,

I'm a rude tude extruder for Transdimensional Fremulon, a wholly owned subsidiary of MultiNatCorp ("We do exotic sounding but ultimately quite tedious stuff"). Ever since the lockdown because of the virus started, I've been working from home (rude tudes don't extrude themselves!), which has given me a rare insight into my wife Robin's home life.

It's like a Wes Cranraisinetty movie without the confetti.

Thanks to the lockdown all schools are closed (yeah, thanks, thanks a lot!), so our three children, Jess, Pat and Inky Dinky Doo, are stuck at home with us. The little...angels. The horns kind of confused me, but Robina insists that they're vestigial and the kids are too young to start exhibiting wings but it's only a matter of time so cut them some slack and do I want to sleep on the couch for the next three weeks I thought not so they're angels and that's that. You can't argue with logic like that.

Between extrusions, I've had to help keep the kids entertained. We've gone for long walks in our backyard, me narrating local points of interest ("That's the tree where you skinned your knee when you were three doing…whatever you thought you were doing yes I know you were there **and** I've told this story the last twenty-three times we passed this tree but I'm doing the best I can with really thin material it's not like all that much has happened in this yard and **hey who wants to hear about the time Pat nearly drowned in the bird bath?**") along the way. We've played Monopolistic Capitalism so often the value of many of the properties has rubbed away, and the rabbit game piece has gotten surly. If I have to watch another episode of *Thomas the Tank*, I'm gonna bust a spleen.

The entertainment needs of the kids are insatiable! Do you have any ideas of how I can keep them busy? Because Robina says I can't send them to the glue factory.

Sincerely,
Bob Dobdobalina from Arkansalina

Yo, Dobbie,

Are they boys or girls…or spiders?

The Tech Answer Guy

Yo, Tech Answer Guy,

Yes.

Sincerely,
Bob Dobdobalina from Arkansalina

Yo, Bobster,

Umm, okay. Glad we settled that. If your children are boys, I would suggest that the Acme Corporation has many fine products that could offer them endless hours of entertainment. Like rocket skates. Man, I would have loved tooling around the neighbourhood in those babies! Of course, the boys would have to tool around the background until the lockdown was eased, but dead grass and flowers become mulch for the next generation of plant life, so everybody wins!

Or, how about a jet propelled pogo stick? Bouncy bouncy bouncy bouncy bouncy bouncy bouncy. Bouncy! What boy hasn't wanted to soar above the neighbourhood, watching…well, not much these days, but children have great imaginations! And, bonus: as long as they stay in the backyard, they will stamp the dead grass and flower mulch deep into the ground!

If your boys like dressing up, you could try to order them an artificial rock costume. I…I never understood the appeal of it, to be honest, but I hear it's very popular in Texakota.

If they're girls, well, umm, dolls? Tea parties? Gossip about the dolls they didn't invite to their tea parties? Girls are, uhh, not really my area of expertise.

If your children are spiders, perhaps you could order them a My First Web starter web spinning kit from the internet? You can buy anything from the internet. Or, if they're older than the recommended age for the beginner kits, you could always get them…umm…I got nothing. Sorry. That's **really** not my area of expertise!

The Tech Answer Guy

Yo, Tech Answer Guy,

Thank you for your suggestions. But, they seem a bit…violent?

Sincerely,
Bob Dobdobalina from Arkansalina
Yo, Bobalina,

Everything I know about raising children, I learned from old *Roadrunner* cartoons. Your chuckle per explosion mileage may vary.

The Tech Answer Guy

If you are a dude with a question about the latest technology, ask The Tech Answer Guy by sending it to questions@lespagesauxfolles.ca. Just remember: jigsaw puzzles are a great way of wasting hours of family fun! And, the best part? When they are complete, you can lacquer them in a way that will make them a lovely wall decoration or rancorous bone of contention in a divorce proceeding!

Ask Amritsar About Modern Schoolyard Taunts

Dear Amritsar,

I was called into my daughter's principle's office yesterday because she had apparently called her Phys-English teacher, Mister Ideominnow, a "dotard." At first, he heard "daughter" and thought she was attacking his masculinity. When she repeated the word – loudly, slowly and with perfect enunciation – Mister Ideominnow gave her a detention. Then, he told the class to turn around while he did something on his computer (I suspect he was looking the word up). Then, he ordered her to the principle's office.

So, Mister Ideominnow likes women named Dorothy. Is that any reason to stagmatize my poor Linda-Lou?

Andromeda-Ann

Hey, Babe,

I was tempted to say, "I do not think that word means what you think it means," but I didn't want to get in trouble with Dizznizzfizzlizzey's lawyers (if they don't own the rights to *The Princess Bride* at the moment, they will...they will), so I stopped myself from doing so. This should be a lesson to Linda-Lou.

A dotard is somebody who studiously collects information, connects the dots representing disparate facts, and comes up with a conclusion that is almost always wrong. Full of convincing detail? Sure. Painstakingly footnoted? Absolutely. But, just not correct. Somebody who answers the question, "Why is the sky blue?" with the statement, "Hillary Roocartoncleveman's emails!" is probably a dotard. (Demanding that they show you how they connected those particular dots will only cause your head to explode. Trust me on this: I had a 17 Percoset a day habit until I stopped!)

Mister Ideominnow was correct in intuiting that your child was mocking him. Some sort of punishment is definitely in order. I must admit, though, that I fail to see how making your daughter afraid of male deer will make her see the error of her ways.

Dear Amritsar,

I was trying to explain to my twelve year-old son Faivel Elephantomas that if he didn't eat his fried bacon sandwich, he wouldn't grow up to be Superman. (I cannot explain why he insists upon eating peas and carrots every meal – he must be going through a rebellious phase.) In response, do you know what he called me? Go ahead and guess. No, don't bother – you wouldn't be able to.

A simpering poltroon. That's what he called me. And, if you were, in fact, able to guess that, I apologize for having so little faith in your understanding of the mentality of twelve year-olds.

What I don't understand is: why would my young son think I was a boiling hen?

Tsvi Tuvulanimous

Hey, Babe,

As you may know, poltroons are actually sixteenth century leggings (everything I know about the twelfth to seventeenth centuries I learned from the reality TV show *Our Stupid Ancestors*). From what I can gather, simpering is archaic Aramaic for "splitting down the middle." While the common definition of the term refers to paying a bill or dividing an opposing army, it is not much of a stretch to believe that it could apply to leggings (especially if they were old enough to have lost some of their elasticity).

So, your son was calling you ripped leggings. Somewhat obscure, but not especially flattering.

Ah. I see that the Language Corrector Dude is vigorously shaking his head, which means that this explanation is almost undoubtedly totally wrong. So, I went to that neutral arbiter of language usage, the internet, to discover the true meaning of the term.

As you might imagine, it was an insult. Punishment of some description is definitely called for.

The more interesting thing was my realization that the more time children spend surfing the web, the better they are at finding increasingly obscure ways to insult their parents. I suspect that this is not what Tim After-Berners-Lee or Berning-Rubbers-Lee or Bernersing-Chrome-Lee or whatever his name was had in mind when he got the whole thing started!

The best thing to do if your child says something to you that sounds insulting even though you can't quite grasp what it means would be to assume the worst and punish them by blocking them from the internet for a week. That will teach them the meaning of being an exemplary pox on humanity!

Send your relationship problems to the Alternate Reality News Service's sex, love and technology columnist at questions@lespagesauxfolles.ca. Amritsar Al-Falloudjianapour is not a trained therapist, but she does know a lot of stuff. AMRITSAR SAYS: Schmeckler's Farrago is not traditionally a holiday devoted to gift-giving. If anybody suggests otherwise, they are clearly in the pay of Big Chocolate!

Ask the Tech Answer Guy to Get to the Cheatin' Heart of the Matter

Yo, Tech Answer Guy,

I'm in love with this wonderful woman. Let's call her...Gweneveer. Because I don't have a lot of imagination. I'm a dentist. Anyhoodies, when we get together, it's like a scene from *Flashdance*. Sparks like you wouldn't believe! And, wet. Very wet. Can we help it if water hoses break whenever we get together? Really, it's more like *Fleshdance*, but, uhh, that was her joke. Because of the whole no imagination/dentist thing. You know how it is.

I'm pretty sure my wife, Penelop, would be unhappy if she ever found out about Gwenny-poohdle. (That's the nickname she gave me for herself. I...I don't really get the concept of nicknames, but it seems to make her happy, so okay.) Penelop is a trusting sort, though, so when I told her that I was working late on fillings for the next day, she seemed to buy it.

Well, sir, quarantine has shot all of that to hell, let me tell you!

I now fill cavities and install braces over the internet. It's a little awkward, especially when a patient's connection is pokey, but at least I've stopped doing root canals until the pandemic is brought under control. We all have to make sacrifices in this difficult time.

For me, one of them has been Gwenevere. I haven't been outside of my house for two months, sixteen days and a handful of slow, painfully slow hours. In that time, I have given my mistress three cleanings and six unnecessary fillings. Not only has this been a most unromantic way to get to spend time with her, but it's playing hell with Gwenneveer's insurance premiums!

Not only am I becoming alienated from my mistress, TAG, but spending so much time with my wife has reminded me of what made me want to marry her in the first place. The way she brushes wisps of hair out of her eyes with the same implement we use to make sure Mister Pinckles doesn't get any hairballs from grooming himself. The way she is able to burn the steak without setting off the fire alarm in our apartment. The way her voice squeaks when we argue about what to watch on Netflix. I'm worried that I may end up cheating on my mistress with my wife.

What can I do about this revoltin' state of affairs?

Sincerely,
Benn from Grimm

Yo, Benny,

You dawg!

Uhh, oops. I seem to have interrupted Misses the Tech Answer Guy's painting in our rock garden. I've never understood the attraction of painting rocks, but she seems to find it soothing. So…

You dawg.

Of course, this is a...relationship question. The Tech Answer Guy doesn't do...relationship questions. They give him indigestion, and a bad case of morning mummers. A really bad case. Ordinarily, I would ask Amritsar for help with your question, but she hasn't been answering the Tech Answer Guy's texts ever since the guacamole guitar incident.

As you say, these are difficult times, so I'll take a stab at it.

Whenever I have a difficult relationship problem to solve (and, for the Tech Answer Guy, **all** relationship problems are difficult – it's a thing with him – don't ask), I start a home renovation project. When my sister was going through her "technicolor daydreams" phase, I built a bookcase, even though there was no room in our house for it and it's been on the roof for seven years. When Misses The Tech Answer Guy's mother came to visit for six months, I installed a basement. Mostly. We've never been able to figure out where the ants are getting into the house, but trying to figure it out has kept me busy at emotionally trying times for years.

Home renovations projects focus the mind. Home renovations projects distract from difficult emotions. Home renovations projects are perfect for avoiding any problem, big or small or some size in between. Try a home renovation project. You'll be glad you did.

The Tech Answer Guy

Yo, Tech Answer Guy,

You're really not very good at giving emotional advice, are you?

Sincerely,
Benn from Grimm

Yo, Benny-Boy,

I know, right! Thank you for your understanding.

The Tech Answer Guy

If you are a dude with a question about the latest technology, ask The Tech Answer Guy by sending it to questions@lespagesauxfolles.ca. Just remember: bow legs are not bowling legs. The Tech Answer Guy made that mistake once, and lost his chance at a perfect game in the very first frame!

Ask Amritsar: Desperate Times Call for Desperate Makeup Regimens

Dear Amritsar,

We have been told that if we want to survive the coronavirus outbreak, we need to wash our hands and not touch ourselves. But, men touch themselves all of the time! Why is that?

Anodyne Annie

Hey, Babe,

Men are gross.

Dear Amritsar,

Well, yeah, okay. Not gonna argue with that. But, touching themselves…there doesn't necessarily cause them to catch a virus. Not the one that's in all the papers right now, in any case. I meant: their faces. Why do men touch their faces all the time?

Anodyne Annie

Hey, Babe,

I stand by my original answer.

Dear Amritsar,

And, it was a good one. Made a lot of sense. I do have to wonder, though, if there is a more specific reason men touch their faces all of the time despite the fact that that doing so might kill them.

Anodyne Annie

Hey, Babe,

Men don't moisturize.

Dear Amritsar,

Hmm. Cryptic, with an undernote of cherry vanilla. Still, as the answer to a question, it is about as satisfying as a gluten-free Baba au Rhuily. Could you possibly elaborate?
Anodyne Annie

Hey, Babe,

Sure.
    When men get dry, flaky skin, they are fawned over for being ruggedly handsome. When women get dry, flaky skin, we are shunned and told that we should stop "letting ourselves go." Cowboys can have dry, flaky skin. Fashion models can't have dry,

flaky skin. Race car drivers can have dry, flaky skin. Suburban housewives can't have dry, flaky skin.

It's a double standard so thick it could clog the arteries of everybody in a small Latin Vesampuccerian country.

According to a series of studies by the Poynter Sisters Institute, women moisturize and exfoliate (no, Tech Answer Guy, that's not a reference to eight former players for the Foley Freighters AA battery baseball team – down boy! Down!) at a rate 27 times that of men. In one study, researchers collected the dust from 127 apartments inhabited by married couples and analyzed the DNA of the dead cells. They found that 83 per cent of the cells by volume had come from men.

What happens when your skin is dry and flaky? You tend to itch more. Over the years, you learn to rub and scratch the driest, flakiest patches without even thinking about it.

Men are beyond gross. They're icky. Are you happy I answered your question now?

Dear Amritsar,

But…but…but…but…don't they understand that touching their faces could kill them?

Anodyne Annie

Hey, Babe,

It's hard to overcome thousands of years of socialization just because of a little inconvenience like death.

Not that people aren't trying. Erick von Deutchmeunster at the Liederhosen Institution in Osaka has proposed a return to glam rock as a way to combat COVID-19. In an article for *The Journal of Comparative Religion and Eyeliner C*, von Deutchmeunster wrote:

"Everybody focuses on David Bowiebowieboo's Ziggy Stardust persona, but, for my money, Gary Glitter was **the** one great glam rocker. The hair. The makeup. The costumes. The way he could almost hit the notes he was reaching for – he had it all. Love and Rockets were a close second. I mean, Daniel Ashcantiptover – ooooh! So, glam up and save your life!"

They, uhh, they might want to look at how their peer review process is functioning over there at *The Journal of Comparative Religion and Eyeliner C.* Yeah, they should really do that.

Dear Amritsar,

I touch my face all the time. I find it…soothing. And I've never been sick a day in my life. (Let's not talk about the nights.) What's the big whoop?

Peter Paul

Hey, Babe,

Say you're at a badminton club for your usual Thursday afternoon game against Mark Markey. Further say that the person who had the racket before you sneezed all over it during a futile volley and covered the handle in the virus. When you play, the germy little bastards will get on your hand. If you wash your hands for at least 20 seconds (measuring two choruses of "Happy Birthday" or, if you can't afford the royalties, three iterations of the chorus from "Ballroom Blitz"), you'll be able to get rid of the virus. However, if you touch your face before you wash your hands, the aforementioned germy little bastards could enter your body through a small cut or a big mouth. Two weeks Later, you could find yourself coming down with a nasty case of death.

Whoops don't get much bigger than that.

Send your relationship problems to the Alternate Reality News Service's sex, love and technology columnist at questions@lespagesauxfolles.ca. Amritsar Al-Falloudjianapour is not a trained therapist, but she does know a lot of stuff. AMRITSAR SAYS: Remember all those people who laughed at those of us who used social media and dating apps to find potential life partners? Not laughing so loud, now, are you?

Ask the Biz Whiz About the Tax Onna Me

Ciao, Bella Biz Whiz:

Last year, I paid $37,234 in income tax even though as a furniture bike courier (wardrobes are killers!) I made only $12,980 – I should probably have a talk with my accountant, but he hasn't returned my calls since I hit him over the head with a Rosh Hashanah brisket a few years back. Don't ask. He deserved it. But, other than that, don't ask.

I just read the *New Yoricknuhemwell Times*' report on President McDruhitmumpf's taxes. Well, okay, I didn't read the whole thing: that mofo goes on and on and on! And, on! It's like Jason – just when you think it's over, it pops up and eviscerates more teenagers! So, I...I read the headline and the first three paragraphs. But, that was enough to cue the outrage.

For ten of the last 15 years, the President paid no income tax. The year he entered office, he paid $750. To put that in perspective, the last time I paid $750 in income tax, it was on sales on the lemonade stand I ran on weekends in front of my house when I was 12! (It was damn fine lemonade, but still. My troubles with my accountant go way back. Don't ask.)

I voted for McDruhitmumpf in 2016 and will again in 2020. Twice if I have to. He is the most successful businessman in the history of capitalism. Notwithstanding the year he claimed to have lost over a billion dollars. Or, all those other years he lost tens or hundreds of millions of dollars. That happens to every successful businessman, right? Right?

Tell me that happens to every successful businessmen.

The Biz Whiz:

It happens to every successful businessman…named Ronald McDruhitmumpf.

We have a term for people like him: con man. This is not the term as you might casually use it. In economics, a con man is somebody who knows how to work the system to maximize his personal profit. It is a term of endearment you hear frequently at $1,000 a plate fundraisers and fraud trials.

Should the President have been allowed to claim $73,000 in hair care products as a business expense? Those who complain about this are just jealous they didn't think of it first. They should probably be talking to their accountants. And, stop buying the downmarket brands at Walmart. To be successful at business, you have to think – and mousse – big.

Should the President have been allowed to claim millions of dollars in tax writeoffs because of depreciation on his name? In business, your name is everything – especially when it is displayed in six foot tall letters on the thirtieth floor of mixed use apartment/office/spinal surgery buildings. When you take a sandblaster to those letters, you are also sanding down, in the most intrusively noisy, attention-getting way, the owner's reputation. You can't put a price on that, but, for tax purposes, you can certainly make one up.

You may quibble about the morality of the President's actions, but they were all within the letter of the law. And, that's good enough for economics.

Dear Gord, Biz Whiz:

You really approve of the President's tax strategy? Really?

At the time he was claiming (relative) poverty, he was talking up his properties to get bank loans. There's no such thing as quantum bookkeeping! Your finances don't get to be either positive or negative as long as nobody at the IRS tries to measure them!

Not only that, but in the Reduhblicans' tax cut legislation, somebody inserted a clause that would give breaks to New Yoricknuhemwell land developers. The President is a New Yoricknuhemwell land developer. Conflict of interest much?

I didn't vote for Ronald McDruhitmumpf in 2016, and I wouldn't vote for him in 2020 if Pennsyleorgia hadn't struck my name from the voter's rolls over a parking fine I could have sworn I paid in 2013. I wouldn't vote for him twice. I may not know anything about economics, but I know a con man in the common sense of the term – how can anybody vote for one for President?

The Biz Whiz:

Jealousy is such an ugly emotion.

The economy is too important to be left to economists! If you have a work, financial or otherwise money-centric question, quiz the Biz Whiz at questions@lespagesauxfolles.ca. Emotions have no place in markets. Except for panic selling. But, that only happens on a 12 year cycle, and the only people it affects are the cops and teachers whose unions have invested their retirement funds heavily in the market, so it's not like it inconveniences anybody important.

Ask the Tech Answer Guy: What Colour is Your Para Shirt?

Yo, Tech Answer Guy,

If I go out with my semi-automatic rifle and mow down some protesters, it's self-defence, right?

Sincerely,
Kyle from (the) Kenosha (of my mind)

Yo, K,

If they are breaking down your front door and entering your house, maybe. Otherwise, it's murder.

The Tech Answer Guy

Yo, Tech Answer Guy,

Well, okay, they weren't breaking down my door specifically. But, they were breaking down a door in another city. In, umm, another state. So, the principle is the same, right? If you go to a city in another state to mow down protesters with a semi-automatic rifle, it's basically self-defence, right?

Sincerely,
Kyle (almost, sorta, kinda) from Kenosha

Yo, K,

No. That's definitely murder.

The Tech Answer Guy

Yo, Tech Answer Guy,

No, no, no. It's lawn order. I mean, Nippon-Tucker Carlsonandotter. He's a respected journalist, right? I mean, he's on Foxindehenhaus News, so he's gotta know what he's talking about. And, he said: "How shocked are we that 17 year-olds with rifles decided they had to maintain order when no one else would?"

I'm not shocked. Not shocked at all.

Or, take Paul Gogogadjetsar. He's a Representative, which would make him a politician or something. You know what he said? He said: "The criminals here: Kenosha local government that allows the riots, burning and looting night after night. Armed citizens defending themselves will fill the vacuum."

So, say I, an armed citizen, like, a really, really well armed citizen, saw the chaos in Kenosha and knew I had to act to save our wimmens and chilluns from the…politically correct hordes breaking down their doors. Wink wink. If that happened, it would make me a hero, don't you think?

Sincerely,
Kyle from (not too far away from) Kenosha (really)

Yo, K,

Umm, no. We have people to save wimmens and chill – women and children. They are known as "police." People who travel across state lines looking to be a part of a violent act are not known as police. They are known as "vigilantes."

According to Phil, the mechanic from the shop down the street, vigilantes were very popular in the wild west. Then, the sheriffs came in and provided lawn order. This would make vigilantes the opposite of lawn order. So, put your (hypothetical) semi-automatic weed whacker away, because that would just make you a murderer of plants as well as people.

Believe it. Phil, the mechanic from the shop down the street knows things.

The Tech Answer Guy

Yo, Tech Answer Guy,

No, no, no, no, no. You're just not getting it. I...I was attacked. This guy with a skateboard came up to me and started whacking me with it! I mean, it's a solid piece of wood! It hurt! Then, this other guy tried to take my rifle away! Surely, in that – I mean, theoretically. If a guy with a skateboard theoretically started whaling on me with it and some other guy tried to take away my rifle, surely, that would be self-defence. Right?

Sincerely,
Kyle from (one or two small states to the left of) Kenosha

Yo, K,

It depends. Had you already shot and killed one person? Theoretically?

The Tech Answer Guy

Yo, Tech Answer Guy,

Maaaaay...beeeee...

Sincerely,
Kyle (who may never have actually set foot in it until two days ago, but has always wanted to be) from Kenosha

Yo, K,

In that case, the theoretical skateboarder and the theoretical person trying to take away your gun could actually be said to be trying to defend themselves and the community from you. Sorry. Still murder.

The Tech Answer Guy

Yo, Tech Answer Guy,

No, no, no, no, no, no, no. Representative Gogogadjetsar said it was, "100% justified self defence!" Jack Comfymurphybed is…is…is a guy. Who has a podcast. But, that's legit now, right? Social media is still media…in some circles. So, when he says, "This is as close and as you're gonna find, I think. Skateboard guy attacks and gets shot. Guy approaching with handgun out gets shot. Self defence," that's the way it was. Right? Right right right?

Sincerely,
Kyle from Kenosha (and who are you to say otherwise?)

Yo, K,

Sounds to me like this is more than theoretical. So, I will say this: people on TV aren't your defence lawyers. You should probably get real ones.

The Tech Answer Guy

If you are a dude with a question about the latest technology, ask The Tech Answer Guy by sending it to: questions@lespagesauxfolles.ca. Just remember: Mrs. The Tech

*Answer Guy tells me it's really hard to get bloodstains out of brown shirts. If you want to be a member of a paramilitary organization **and** fashion forward, you're going to have to make a lot of hard decisions!*

Ask Amritsar to Swear By It

Dear Amritsar,

Yesterday, I reposted a cartoon on my Farcebook page that compared a prominent American politician to Baby Spice on account of his, you know, small hands and tendency to throw temper tantrums. I thought it was funny. One of my fiends didn't. He responded with a torrent of abuse so foul that I had to use a fire extinguisher on my computer screen to keep it from combusting! Thrice!

Well. I am considering unfiending him. Would the proper etiquette to write my final message to him be, "Consider yourself unfiended, ferker!" or "Consider yourself unfiended, motherferker!"?

Terrence Barko Lowinagersit

Hey, Babe,

I can see why you would write me with this question: heaven forbid you cause your soon to be former fiend offence by getting this wrong.

As a general rule, Amritsar does not condone or encourage the use of foul language in public fora (no, no, no, that's a woman's name…unless you were thinking of the word for plant life – no, that's the word for a type of hat – oh, come on, people! Fora is the proper Latin plural form of the word forumnus – place of holding a toga party! Were you not paying attention in grade three?) – alright. Places. Amritsar does not condone or etc. the use of foul language in public places!

I blame the school system.

It's not that Amritsar is a prude. When she is unhappy with the play of her partner in an otherwise pleasant evening of contact whist, she has been known to say, "Drat it!", "Goshdarn it!" and even "[EXPLETIVE DELETED] you, you [EXPLETIVE DELETED] moron! Couldn't you [EXPLETIVE DELETED] well see that I had set up a full body [EXPLETIVE DELETED] grand slam?" In fact, Amritsar has likely been thrown out of more dining establishments for using foul language to berate the vending machines than you have teeth in a hen's head!

No, the problem is that when public discourse (no, not a reference to the plate of food in front of you, or the series of lectures you're taking at university, or the steps you need to learn for that dance number from the 1970s – [EXPLETIVE DELETED], you're ignorance of the basics of the English language is making this a lot harder than it has to be!) is filled with expletive-laced anger, it becomes impossible for people who disagree with each other to talk. When people with opposing points of view no longer talk, bad things happen: riots, wars, reality television celebrities grasping for positions above their station (and sometimes achieving them).

For democracy to work, people with opposing views must be able to communicate with each other in a civilized manner. As Plato said – well, no, if you're having this much trouble with the English language, I'm not going to bring a Greek into this! As – well, no, that last point wasn't a translated quote from Plato, that was my opinion. As – no! – I wasn't putting words into Plato's mouth! Plato has nothing to do with – oh, [EXPLETIVE DELETED] this action – meet me in the next paragraph!

As **Don Acherryontopps** said, "For democracy to work, people with opposing views must be able to communicate with each other in a civilized manner. If you must do a little clutch and grab or maybe some stick work above the waist in order to make your point, just make sure you do it when the ref isn't watching!"

He knows a lot about the democratic process, Don Acherryontopps does.

The problem with people unfiending each other right, left and centre (more Don's – ahem – fields of expertise than mine, but be generous, dear reader) is that the echo chamber of their own discourse (don't you start!) will push both sides in an argument to take up extreme positions, leaving no common ground on which to come together. This is how divorces happen. And, civil wars.

So, rather than unfiend the person with whom you disagree, you should try reasoning with them. Lay down your expletives. Bracket your epithets. Ignore your invective. Reasonable people can find common ground upon which to build a better future if only they are willing to reason with one another.

Dear Amritsar,

Have you seen what I wrote about you on Farcebook?

pwnedu27

Hey, Babe,

Wha? You – seriously? You wrote…! And, then…! And followed that up with…! How dare you, sir? How dare you? I barely even know your goat!

Consider yourself unfiended, motherferker!

Send your relationship problems to the Alternate Reality News Service's sex, love and technology columnist at questions@lespagesauxfolles.ca. Amritsar Al-Falloudjianapour is not a trained therapist, but she does know a lot of stuff. AMRITSAR SAYS: people who hate Muslims generally also hate gays. People who hate gays usually also hate Jews. People who hate Jews usually also hate blacks. And, so on. So, don't feel smug if your minority group isn't currently the focus of organized hate groups. Hate does not discriminate.

Ask the Tech Answer Guy How to Calculate the Optimal Spitting Distance

Yo, Tech Answer Guy,

I suffer from a condition that is common in situation comedies but rare ISL (in surreal life): Inappropriate Distanced Aqueous Ejection Syndrome (IDAES). In short: I do spit takes. I'm a spit taker. I spit. I take. At the same time. Water, coffee, Chateau Lafitenesstestes Rothschildinnamann – it doesn't matter. If somebody startles me while I am drinking, I spray liquid in an expanding 10 to 15 foot radius. And, I'm as sensitive as a doe in a Dizznizzfizzlizzey movie. I mean, I've been known to expel liquids nine times while having a three minute snack!

My friends are very supportive of my condition. The speak softly and mute their cellphones when we're at parties. They have taken mime classes in order to learn how to move more slowly, more deliberately. They know to wear rain slickers indoors when we go out for drinks. Really, they're the best.

But, this COVID-19 thing, man! There are people going around randomly spitting on other people to…I don't know what! Teach them to be more aware of their mortality and live in the moment? Remind them of the importance of healthy gums? Promote the umbrella industry? It's crazy!

I'm worried that when things return to normal, people with IDAES will be stigmatized as Typhoid Terrys because of the actions of this small number of people who don't even have it. Is there anything I can do to keep this from happening, or, if it does happen, minimize the damage to people like me, innocent victims of a terrible, terrible disease?

Sincerely,
Abraham from Onomatopoeia

Yo, Abe,

Honestly?

I had no...idea there was such a thing as IDAES! Do you have to – hee hee – carry a towel around wherever you go? Maybe, you should...you should...ha ha ha...get cards you can give to people you...syndrome all over. Of course, they would have to be – hee hee – have to be – haw haw – laminated! They would have to be lamina
–

OWWW!

Phil, the mechanic from the shop down the street, just punched me in the arm! Hard! I – I'm not complaining. According to the Macho Code of Manliness, sucking up a playful punch in the arm earns you points that will help you get into Guy Heaven when you die. I was just...startled, is all. Taken unawares. Sort of like you when you...oooohhhh.

Phil, the mechanic from the shop down the street, is gooood. I always have to remember that he knows things.

So, okay. Only a handful of intentional spitting incidents have been reported in the United States of Vesampucceri – the good news is that the whole *schemazzle* might just be forgotten, like the Fleeglemeisterous Rebellion of 1923 or slavery. If that happens, you won't have anything to worry about.

The bad news is that the spitters believe that they are making a political statement. I think they're saying: "Vote Reduhblican or die!" Or, maybe: "COVID-19 is a hoax! Don't believe the mainstream mouth liquid spewers!" Or, maybe: "Tip the canoe and your waitress, too!"It's not a very clear statement – saliva isn't a great communications medium.

Worse (although totally predictable): this position was supported by the President, who tweeped at 2:37 this morning: "Th eFoundering Fathers believed spitting was free speech – it's right there in the 237th Amendment, people! oh, I love the constitution! How i love that document! You wouldn't believe what's in it!!! Freedom! To spit! That was what Vesampucceri was founded on! #freedomtolieaboutyourpoliticalenemiestoodontforget".

The validity of spit as speech may have to be adjudicated by the courts. In that case, oh oh. In an article for *The Punxsutawney Law Review and Phil Watcher*, Extreme Court Justice Brett Kavanaugheylno mused, "To spew, or not spew. Could go either way. Let me consult my friends in The Federalist Society and get back to."

Or, you could hope that, after 70 years of broadcast television, a cure for IDAES will finally be found.

The Tech Answer Guy
Yo, Tech Answer Guy,

I'm doomed, aren't I? The weird politics of this moment has doomed me, hasn't it?

Sincerely,
Abraham from Onomatopoeia
Yo, Abbie,

Have you considered moving to Europe? I hear they have a lot of spittoons there...

The Tech Answer Guy

If you are a dude with a question about the latest technology, ask The Tech Answer Guy by sending it to questions@lespagesauxfolles.ca. Just remember: "I'm Laverne and you're Shirley – whatever you say bounces off me and makes you all squirrely" isn't really an effective comeback when somebody has insulted you. The Tech Answer Guy can say this with some assurance because he is currently working on a book on effective comebacks, and will have a first draft in to his publisher just as soon as he gets his household chores done. So, get off his back, Chuck, because that new deck won't stain itself!

Ask Amritsar…For the Children!

Dear Amritsar,

My husband Bob is a butthead. And, I'm not talking about how the cleft on his chin, deep as it is, makes his face look like somebody's hindparts. I'm talking about the fact that he seems to think with his anus.

Like many people, our children have been stuck at home during the virus quarantine. They have been slowly driving us mad with their incessant demands for food and drink and a safe place to sleep so that the monsters in the closet won't get them – honestly, it never ends! (Personally, I think they could take the monsters in the closet – you should see the kind of fight they put up when it's bath time! – but my therapist says I am misdirecting my rage. Putz.)

Bob decided to "help" by getting gifts to distract the children. That went over about as well as a salmonella sandwich on whole wheat moldy bread!

The butthead bought an Acme rocket powered Pogo stick for little Inky Dinky Doo. The first time he used it, he launched himself into the sky and never came down. Maybe he achieved escape velocity. Maybe he got snagged on a passing passenger pigeon and ended up hitching a ride to a favela on the wrong side of the border with Canada. Maybe he's with the Angels…in Houston. I…I hope he's in a better place, wherever that place may be.

Pat was given an Acme rock costume. "Endless hours of amusement," the box promised. I sure hope so. Pat put on the costume and wandered off to the quarry at the end of the street. We haven't seen or heard from him/her in three days. At first, I gave Bob heck for that one, but, in the end, he convinced me that rocks last for thousands of years, that very little can destroy them. So, as long as nobody is looking for a granite tabletop, it's probably for the best.

The worst was Bob getting an Acme rocket launcher for our three year-old daughter, Jess. She played with it exactly once: the house of the neighbours across the street was totalled. My shrink says Jess is going to have to undergo intense therapy when she is older. I wish he hadn't been so…gleeful when he said that; still, it's good to know that he will have a steady enough income to be able to treat me for as long as I need.

I guess I'm just a silver lining kind of gal.

With two less children, and the third traumatized, I'm finding I have time to do all of the things I didn't before. Which are none of your business. The question is: should I be devastated that COVID-19 has destroyed my family? Or, should I be grateful?

Robina Dobdobalina

Hey, Babe,

I'm not supposed to judge the people who open up their hearts by writing to me, so I will just say that we are all suffering through a difficult time, and must find a way to cope as best we can.

Dear Amritsar,

What the hell is that supposed to mean? I mean, honestly, was that supposed to be helpful? It sounded like something out of a fortune cookie!

Robina Dobdobalina

Hey, Babe,

But, then you asked a follow-up question, and my qualms about criticizing the people who submit to this column flew out the window faster than a boy's virginity on prom night!
You and Bob are terrible parents.

Never, ever, **ever** buy anything from Acme Corporation, especially not for children! Their products never work as advertised. It's right there in the fine print of every instruction manual: "Product will never work as advertised. Please be advised and alter your expectations accordingly. May contain monosodium glutamate." What did you expect?

Parenting requires patience and sacrifice. Rocket powered... anything is no substitute!

Send your relationship problems to the Alternate Reality News Service's sex, love and technology columnist at questions@lespagesauxfolles.ca. Amritsar Al-Falloudjianapour is not a trained therapist, but she does know a lot of stuff. AMRITSAR SAYS: civility is the glue that holds the ramshackle construct that is human society together. In these times when we are forced to stay in close quarters with those we love...like...tolerate (with a vengeance), civility is the only thing that keeps us from entering Lord of the Flies *territory. Do not call your husband "butthead," "doofus" or "big pain in the ass." Instead, call him "Mister Butthead," "Sir Doofus of Dumbville" or "The King of Pains in the*

Ass."* You would be surprised at just how effective civility can be in defusing tense situations. Even civility of the aggressive kind.

* Not "The King of Pain in the Asses" unless you are a genetic experiment gone horribly, horribly wrong.

5. THE SLEEP OF REASON PRODUCES...LENNY (THE FOURTH HORSEMAN)

Pandemics 'r' Virus:
The Alternate Reality News Service Interview

TRANSCRIPT OF AN INTERVIEW WITH TED, THE NOVEL CORONAVIRUS. THE INTERVIEW WAS CONDUCTED BY LAURIE NEIDERGAARDEN, ALTERNATE REALITY NEWS SERVICE MEDICAL WRITER.

LAURIE NEIDERGAARDEN: Is that thing...safe?

COVID-19 VIRUS: I can hear you, you know.

TECHNICIAN: It's in a sealed test tube. You want guarantees?

NEIDERGAARDEN: This is more than six feet, right?

VIRUS: I can still hear you.

TECHNICIAN: It crosses that space when somebody talks or sneezes. From a running start, I would guess it might make it three inches.

NEIDERGAARDEN: If you're sure…

VIRUS: Can we speed this up? I have places to be, things to do.

Pause.

NEIDERGAARDEN: That…that was not at all reassuring.

VIRUS: Not you, necessarily.

NEIDERGAARDEN: Not helping.

VIRUS: It's just, this test tube is cold and uninviting. I prefer a warm environment to –

NEIDERGAARDEN: Whoaooooookay, why don't we get this interview started? I'm talking to a novel coronavirus –

VIRUS: Call me Ted.

NEIDERGAARDEN: Why should I call you Ted?

VIRUS: Theodore is too formal. It makes me sound like a librarian.

NEIDERGAARDEN: No, I mean, why should I call you by a name?

VIRUS: There's so many of us in the world. Names help to tell us apart.

Pause.

NEIDERGAARDEN: Umm…okay. Ted. What's it like, being a deadly killer?

VIRUS: It's just a job. Travel. Reproduce. Rinse. Wash. Repeat. To be honest, it's not very exciting. But it is what I was born to do, so I do it to the best of my ability.

SOUND: plink.

NEIDERGAARDEN: Reduhblicans say you don't exist.

VIRUS: What? They think all of those people in your country are dying of happiness?

SOUND: plink.

NEIDERGAARDEN: Honestly, it's hard to know what they think. Dumboprats disagree with the Reduhblicans, of course. They argue that –

VIRUS: Don't care.

SOUND: plink.

NEIDERGAARDEN: I'm sorry?

VIRUS: Reduhblican. Dumboprat – it's all the same to me. You're all just…vacation destinations.

SOUND: plink plink.

NEIDERGAARDEN: I'm trying to get your perspective on the politics of the pandemic.

VIRUS: Look, pal, I'm sure the politics of the pandemic is important to you people. Me, I'm a simple soul. Travel. Reproduce. Rinse. Wash. Repeat.

SOUND: plink plink plink.

NEIDERGAARDEN: But the whole point of – what is that sound?

VIRUS: What sound?

SOUND: plink plink plink.

VIRUS: I don't hear anything.

SOUND: plink plink plink.

NEIDERGAARDEN: It's a plinking sound, like…like something small is trying to break through gla – are you…are you trying to get out of the test tube?

VIRUS: N-no. Why would you think –

SOUND: plink plink plink plink plink!

NEIDERGAARDEN: (shouting) You are! You are trying to get out!

VIRUS: Hey! I gotta do me!

SOUND: plink plink plinkety plink plink!

NEIDERGAARDEN: Stop it! Stop it right now, or I'll have the test tube scrubbed with industrial strength cleaner!

VIRUS: (under its breath) You're no fun.

NEIDERGAARDEN: Over 200,000 Vesampuccerians have died of COVID-19! That's not fun!

VIRUS: Hey! I'm just fulfilling my life's goal. Can I help it if my business is my pleasure?

Pause.

NEIDERGAARDEN: The first serious outbreaks of the disease –

VIRUS: Disease is such a prejudicial term.

NEIDERGAARDEN: The first serious outbreaks **of the disease** took place in New Yoricknuhemwell and Los Angeles, major coastal cities that tend to be more liberal. President McDruhitmumpf calculated that he could ignore the outbreaks because they didn't affect large pockets of his voters in the middle of the coun –

VIRUS: Oh, yawn.

NEIDERGAARDEN: I beg your pardon?

VIRUS: Look. We've already established that I don't care about your politics. I just like to travel. See the world. See exotic new places. By now, my siblings and I are everywhere. How cool is that?

NEIDERGAARDEN: When you say 'see exotic new places,' you're talking about people, right?

VIRUS: Ah. Finally, somebody gets me!

NEIDERGAARDEN: These exotic new places you're talking about have hopes and dreams, parents and siblings and…and…and maybe children. When they die because you have visited them, they leave a big hole in the world.

VIRUS: You're talking about the whole…human dimension of the disease, right?

NEIDERGAARDEN: Exactly.

VIRUS: Sorry, but that's above my pay grade.

Pause.

NEIDERGAARDEN: President McDruhitmumpf recently came down with –

VIRUS: Who?

NEIDERGAARDEN: The President. Of the United States of Vesampucceri. President McDruhitmumpf.

VIRUS: That's a funny name, isn't it?

NEIDERGAARDEN: What, McDruhitmumpf?

VIRUS: No, President.

NEIDERGAARDEN: That's not a name. It's his title.

VIRUS: Oh. Important person, is he?

NEIDERGAARDEN: The leader of the country.

VIRUS: Don't care. Human hierarchies are not listed on my travel brochures.

NEIDERGAARDEN: (dark) I'm beginning to sense a theme, here…

Pause.

NEIDERGAARDEN: So. To sum up. You are a merciless killer.

VIRUS: Mercy. Malice. Compassion. Rage. These are all just words to me – I don't have emotions as human beings understand them. I just have a life's mission: travel. Reproduce. Rinse. Wash. Repeat.

NEIDERGAARDEN: I understand that. I was just –

SOUND: plink.

NEIDERGAARDEN: I'm outta here!

It's Ronald McDruhitmumpf's World – We Just Die In It

by LAURIE NEIDERGAARDEN, Alternate Reality News Service
Medical Writer

At 653 pounds, Alex "The Rock" Fiddleronnaruth was morbidly
obese (the medical definition of which is: "a condition wherein a
person's excessive body weight is obsessed with shows like *Coroner
for a Day* and *If the Bone Saw Fits...*"). Under ordinary
circumstances, he would be expected to die of a massive coronary
when he tried to pick up the television remote too energetically. But,
times of viral pandemic are to ordinary circumstances what a limp
sturgeon is to dentistry.

Fiddleronnaruth had to be rushed to the ER of Sisters of
Merciless Hospital and Soul Sanctuary In Salt Steak City, Utegas
after taking the drug hydroxychloroquine to stave off getting
COVID-19. He did this despite the fact that the anti-malaria drug has
not been proven effective as an antiviral, and it has many known side
effects, including: death from random body parts falling off, death
from Brian hemorrhage, death from imagined penguin inhalation and
death from heart seizure and public auction.

Why would Fiddleronnaruth risk his life like that?

Would it help to know that Fiddleronnaruth was a died in the
wool member of the Transition To Keep Making Vesampucceri
Great Again crowd, the ultimate anti-social distancing group?

Or, that, when asked about who Attorney General William
Katiebarrthudor was thinking of asking to the prom yesterday,
President Ronald McDruhitmumpf answered: "Yeah, I've been
saying everybody should be taking droxy – that's what I call

hydroxychloroquine – yeah, I'm on a first-name basis with it – admiration has never been so mutual! – what was I sayin – oh, yeah, everybody should be taking droxy to fight off COVID. Well, for me, it – it's – I gotta tell you – umm, **I'm taking it!** That's right. Been taking it for a week or two. And, let me tell you, I can feel the virus trying to get into my body and just giving up because it can't!"

"No way," responded pundit John Heiyonlifelmann. "No way. Nohow. No way. This President is morbidly – defined as 'over 30 per cent over his ideal body weight for his height' – afraid of death. He would not be taking a drug with such lethal side effects. No way. If the President is taking hydroxychloroquine, I'll eat all of the hair on my head!"

When it was pointed out that he had no hair on his head, Heiyonlifelmann responded, "Okay. Fair point. I will grow the hair on my head back just so I can eat it. That's how sure I am that McDruhitmumpf is not taking the drug!"

When doubts about the President's assertion began to surface (gasping for air – under current circumstances, doubts shouldn't try to see how long they can hold their breath under water), Grey House physician Doctor Sean Prosandconnely wrote a press release that read, in part: "The President and I talked about hydroxychloroquine. And when I say we talked, I mean he talked and I listened. Oh, my, how he talked! And talked! And talked! Eventually, I told him to write his own press release saying that I told him it would be perfectly safe for him to take the drug, without me actually prescribing the drug to him, because, you know, unethical. Oh, wait. He didn't include this last part in the letter with my name on i – he did, didn't he? I really need to reconsider my career choices!"

Why would the President risk telling such a transparent lie? "There are no drugs for the truth," Heiyonlifelmann quipped. "Well, the CIA isn't authorized to use them on the President, in any case."

I was thinking the answer lay more along the lines of: as the number of medical professionals cautioning against using hydroxychloroquine to fight COVID-19 has grown, President McDruhitmumpf felt he needed to do something dramatic to convince his base that it was safe and effective. "Well, yeah," Heiyonlifelmann agreed, "That goes without saying."

Hydroxychloroquine is especially popular in Utegas, where a tech entrepreneur passing as a medical expert sold the state $800,000 worth of the drug that he happened to have been stockpiling in egg cartons in his basement. Not coincidentally, Utegas has seen one of the biggest spikes in COVID-19 cases in the country.

As his vital – I know, I know. Time was that an entrepreneur profiteering from a world-wide pandemic would be a major scandal meriting its own story, not an off-hand mention at the end of a story on a different subject. But, in the newest new normal, this is no longer a scandal, it's strictly BAU.

As his vi – Business Ass Usual. Put your slapping gloves back in their case, Barbara. You won't be needing them this day!

As his vital signs dropped and death appeared imminent, Fiddleronnaruth started to say, "Trans – Transition – * GASP * – To Keep – Keep – Kee – AAAARRRGH!"

There's No Penalty For Piling On In This Game

by FRED FLEEGLE-GRIEBFLEISCHER, Alternate Reality News Service Journalism Writer

It's like a bad 1970s action comedy TV series where everybody (mostly skinny women with big hair that should imbalance their heads and cause them to constantly catch themselves from tipping over backwards) calls the name of the main character.

"Faucispendulum?"

"Faucispendulum!"

"Oooh, Faucispennnnnnnnduuuuuluuuum!"

Doctor Anthony Faucispendulum is not a crime-busting ex-Marine with a mysterious wealthy benefactor and a taste for Hawalaskan shirts. He is, in fact, a soft-spoken member of one of President Ronald McDruhitmumpf's 27 coronavirus task forces (code name: Ardent Depilatory Moncton Amok). That may explain why the attention being given to him is less than adulatory.

"I have it on good authority that Doctor Anthony Faucispendulum did not send his mother flowers last Mother's Day," said Foxindehenhaus Mewls host Nippon-Tucker Carlsonandotter. "Is that somebody who we should trust with the health of our nation? I mean, what kind of a monster doesn't acknowledge the sacrifices that his mom made for him on the one day of the year that is supposed to be devoted solely to her?"

"Umm, the kind whose mother died seven years ago?" token smart person Amy Sheshutshotshitbam responded.

"Doctor Anthony Faucispendulum? Please!" Foxindehenhaus Mewls slime slinger in chief Sean Hanjobovverfist bloviated. "He is wrong more times than a busted clock! His public pronouncements have been so riddled with mistakes that he should be a Batman villain! The Mistakesman! If he was a dinosaur, he would be Erroneous Rex! And, we're supposed to just do whatever he says? Who elected him to make decisions about the health of the country?"

"It wasn't Rupert Mountkilamanjoy, that's for sure!" token smart person Sheshutshotshitbam shot back.

Ouch.

"It's the little people that concern me most," Foxindehenhaus Mewls animatronic host ("Look at how human his hair looks!") Brian KissMeadekilmeadenow tried to sympathize. He should work on that. "I feel so bad for the people who want to see a light at the end of the tunnel, but it's solar-powered and doesn't work without a direct line of sight to the sky. The guy who owns a chain of car dealerships in Illivania, or the guy who franchises hair salons in Pennsynois, people who can't tell their employees to reopen because state orders require them to remain closed. If we all wait for Dr. Faucispendulum's seal of approval to reopen Vesampucceri, corporate leaders may not have a Vesampucceri to reopen."

To emphasize the point, he flapped his flippers together and shouted, "Oi! Oi! Oi!"

"Yeah," token smart person Sheshutshotshitbam sighed. "If he were any better trained, he could be the engine bearing down on people in the tunnel!"

What did Doctor Faucispendulum do to ignite the ire – ignire – of the right wing outrage machine? He said, and I quote: "People who catch a virus usually get sick."

Now, this may not be news to you, or me, or anybody over the age of six. But, it appears to have been news to President McDruhitmumpf, who just the day before had said, "Virus? Virus. Papyrus. Banana fanna vo dirus. Fee Fi fo firus. Virus! I mean, there are lot of people catching the virus, and none of them are getting sick! I know it. You know it. Even Barbie and G.I. Joe know it! So, everybody take a pill! A bleach pill, if you want to be totally safe. Or, a sunshine pill. They're good, sunshine pills. Nobody's getting sick, so stay calm and don't worry about being embalmed!"

According to three sources within the Grey House after they recovered their hearing, President McDruhitmumpf railed (that engine in the tunnel has to run on something!) against Doctor Faucispendulum when he discovered that the medical man had contradicted him. He accused Doctor Faucispendulum of being a Dumbopratic dupe who was spreading fear of COVID-19 in order to wreck the economy and derail his chances of winning the election that will be held in less than six months.

"KABOOM!" the President reportedly shouted. "My reelection campaign will hit the side of the tunnel and go up in a fireball of deranged narcissism and thwarted ambition! And then, I'll end up in jail! Nobody in the country wants that! Especially not me!"

In public, President McDruhitmumpf stated, "I respect the work Doctor Faucispendulum has been doing, but he is a bad man. A bad, bad man. Okay, let's cut to the chase: he's a bad, bad, bad, bad, bad man. You know how many bads that is, and what it signifies. Do I have to draw you a map?"

For those of us who watch the train wreck that is the right wing smogosphere, no map is necessary.

That's When Everything Went Cow-shaped

by MARCELLA CARBORUNDUREM-McVORTVORT, Alternate
Reality News Service Food and Drink Writer

"Meat is murder" is no longer just a slogan for vegans whose mood
is dark because they don't get enough protein in their diet and they
are always tired.

Just ask Offreida Modigliyanni. He went into his local Bob So
Tasty hoping to get a special like the Barricuda Bob (actually made
from barricuda substitute, but slathered in so much tartar sauce that
nobody really notices) or the Bob So Buddhist (made from the meat
of deeply spiritual people who had accumulated enough positive
Karma in their endless rounds of life and death that they were reborn
as sacred cows – check location for availability).

Imagine his disappointment when he discovered that all that
was available on the menu was the Basic Bob…and Beyond!, a
plant-based burger that was held together by spit and positive vibes
for the planet, a burger whose critics complained that you couldn't
tell where the patty ended and the vegetable garnishes began, a
burger that made the Bob So Tasty special sauce taste…ordinary.

"I waited for forty-five minutes at the drive-through," Offreida
complained. "By the time I got to the window, I was ready to eat the
cardboard box. And, with a little ketchup, it was still better than the
Basic Bob…and Beyond! Why? Why would they do that to me?"

Why would they do that to Offreida and millions of
Vesampuccerians like him? Could it have something to do with the
fact that three of the seven biggest meat processing plants in the
country have had to be shut down because they were COVID-19
hotspots?

"No," token smart person Amy Sheshutshotshitbam stated.

No?

"It doesn't have something to do with the fact that three of the
seven biggest meat processing plants in the country have had to be
shut down because they were COVID-19 hotspots," she clarified. "It
has **everything** to do with the fact that three of the seven biggest

meat processing plants in the country have had to be shut down because they were COVID-19 hotspots!"

Thanks for the clarification. I was worried I wouldn't hit the minimum word count for this article.

Workers who process meat in factories have to stand so closely together on their lines that they often envy sardines in tin cans for the elbow room they get. They are only allowed to wash their hands once every three days in order to not slow the flow of chucks, shanks and round ground to a hungry public. They are allowed to wear masks, but since nobody in the United States knows where to get masks, most of them don't.

In short, meat processing plants are the anti-social distancing Meccas of the country.

For those of you who love meat on your meat-lovers' pizza, know that you have a friend in the McDruhitmumpf administration. Somebody whispered in the ears of the governors of the states with meat processing plants (in a voice that could be heard around the country) that closed businesses should immediately be reopened. Being Reduhblicans, the governors eagerly agreed.

But, what about employees who refused to go to work in meat processing plants on the grounds that doing so would be their death sentence? Somebody in the McDruhitmumpf administration suggested that states where this could be a problem enact laws that strip Employment Insurance benefits from anybody who didn't go to work. Being Reduhblicans, and compassionate, the governors eagerly agreed.

Not that there would be many such employees. People who work in meat processing plants make so little money that they envy church mice for their lavish lifestyles. In economics, this is known as "a highly motivated workforce." In the criminal underworld, this is known as "a highly motivated workforce."

But, did anybody give a thought to those poor corporate CEOs who might have to suffer the indignity of lengthy lawsuits from the families of people who died because of work-related COVID-19 infection? Yes! Yes, Senate Majority Leader Mitch Wichconnelliswich snuck a clause into a gabillion dollar bailout package that would make it impossible to sue employers if you caught a coronavirus in your work environment.

Thank you, Senate Majority Leader Mitch Wichconnelliswich, for thinking of the big people!

Modigliyanni sat in the back seat of his car and looked at the Basic Bob…and Beyond! burger he was eating while he drove. "So," he summed up, "I will soon be able to buy a regular burger at Bob So Tasty made with meat processed by financially desperate people who will likely die because of unsafe conditions in the plant where they work?"

Pretty much, yeah.

Modigliyanni looked at the Basic Bob…and Beyond! Burger and carelessly tossed it back into its box. "That can't happen soon enough!"

Live Free AND Die!

by FRANCIS GRECOROMACOLLUDEN, Alternate Reality News Service National Politics Writer

Dirk Offputtinganvane (of the Port Dalhousieflousie Offputtinganvanes) sat on a chair on Cocononomo Beach in south Florilvannia, sipping a drink from a coconut (which he found only 87% as refreshing as he had been promised) and watching sweet young things in skimpy swimwear bounce by. The beach was packed with youths who had self-quarantined for an interminable amount of time (some hadn't left their house for three whole days!), and they were ready to let loose.

Did Offputtinganvane not realize that the women he was making uncomfortable with his attentions were mobile petri dishes potentially filled with COVID-19?

"Live free or diet!" he chorkled as he threw a cupful of beer in the general direction of his face. When he finished wiping his mouth with his arm, he revealed a frown. "Live free or die hard…with twenty additional minutes of smirking!" He shook his head. "Well…

well, it isn't much of a choice no matter what it is. Live free – whoooo hooooooo!"

The bros around Offputtinganvane responded with howling, wolf calls and the crushing of beer cans on heads. Because summer.

At the same time (give or take seven hours for me to drive to a different state), a group calling itself Maniacs for Health Sanity held an armed protest (and you thought mixing human and spider genes wouldn't amount to anything!) outside the Michihio state legislature. "I am a fully grown, sovereign adult," explained survivalist/prepper/ Royal Nymphenburg collector wannabe Dougie Foniemorony. "The state has no right to treat me like a child! I – oh, crap. Excuse me a second, will you – I need to change my diaper!"

The protesters openly carried handguns, assault rifles and a rocket launcher (apparently, they had listened to Canadian musician Bruce Majorcockupburn a little too often for one's emotional well-being). Many of them carried confederate flags and home-made signs that read: "Don't tread on my tires!" and "COVID, not Ovid!" and "Fredom is not Fred!" (That last one may have been a local locksmith trying to drum up business by capitalizing on the unrest.)

One man in the crowd wore a KKK hood, the height of fashion in 1911. When I asked him why, he said, "Murmph mumble grubble gabble." When I told him that I didn't understand what he had just said, he more emphatically stated, "Grubble! Grubble! **Grubble!** Fleastrunk agabagga kerchunkety!"

I shook my head in incomprehension. The man lifted the hood over his lips and mocked, "They said I had to wear a face mask, but they didn't say which one!"

I asked him why he chose to cover his face with a symbol of racial oppression. Unfortunately, he had lowered his hood, so he made a sound which could have been a raspberry, a car backfiring or a death rattle, and walked away.

The anti-lockdown protests have been getting support from the highest levels of the Reduhblican Party. They were encouraged by President Ronald McDruhitmumpf, who has been saying for the past couple of weeks that, "We can't have the cure be worse than the problem!" What could possibly be worse than death? "My approval rating going below 40!" the President snapped at the journalist who posed the question (who, rumour has it, was me).

Maniacs for Health Sanity has been promoted by the Michihio Freedom for the 1% Fund, a conservative group with ties to Education Secretary Betsy DeVolution-Ross. When asked how a member of the federal cabinet could justify undermining the health efforts of a state governor, she tartly replied, "Wouldn't you like to learn that?"

I think she thought she had just schooled me.

Outside the Michihio state legislature, heavily armed protesters chanted "Lock her up! Lock her up!" It was a one hit wonder that apparently never gets old.

When Governor Gretchen Whitmerdelalune was asked to respond to the chant, she said, "It's got a catchy hook, but the lyrics don't really do anything for me. Or, the assault rifle accompaniment. Especially the assault rifle accompaniment."

When asked if he was worried about catching COVID-19, Offputtinganvane grinned and responded, "Are you – kaff kaff – kidding – hack – kidding me? I'm – kaff blarg – young and – kaff – and – kaff – and fit! Young and fit! I'm going – blarcch! – I'm going to live – kaff – to live – kaff – I'm going to – kaff kaff kaff kaff blaaaarrrrrgh! – I'm going to sit down for a – kaff kaff – a little while…"

More than 27,000 cases of the coronavirus have been confirmed in Michihio, with at least 1,700 deaths.

There Are None So Blind as Those Who Will Not CDC

by LAURIE NEIDERGAARDEN, Alternate Reality News Service Medical Writer

The first clue that there was something hinky (which is not an ethnic slur, no matter how often white supremacists, precious snowflakes that they are, claim it is) with the Centres for Disease Control recommendations to the meat packing industry was that an early draft was written on the back of an envelop. The envelop wasn't even from the CDC; it was from the Acme Novelties Corporation.

The second clue of hinkiness was the language. "Meat packing plants should try to like, you know, get their workers to wear masks and stuff," one of the recommendations read. "But, like, be cool about it because, you know, you don't want to, like, harsh anybody's vibe in the workplace." The recommendations read like the person who wrote them was having an acid flashback to the 1960s.

The third hinky hijinks (which, okay, **was** a jazz band in the 1940s, but that's just a coincidence that doesn't mean anything) clue was the response of Doctor Robert R. Redwhiteandbluefield, the Director of the CDC, when asked about the dubious (which sounds like something a member of Hinky Hijinks might smoke, but isn't – they were more into heroin) nature of the recommendations. "Did we write those?" he sighed. "They're on our letterhead, so, yeah, I guess those are our recommendations. For the record: I did not do acid in the sixties. Or, before. Or, since. I have never done acid, is what I'm saying. When I took this position, I never thought I would have to affirm that!"

So, it should have come as no surprise that the recommendations were actually written by the Grey House and released on CDC stationery. The fact that it did come as a surprise to so many is a testament to the hopeless optimism of the Vesampuccerian people. Or, their gullibility. It can be a fine line.

"Oh, this is bad," commented Dr. Vindaloo Guptaharumpher, a surgeon who has worked for the CDC, the World Health Organization and Dizznizzfizzlizzeyland. "This is really bad. Bad, bad, bad, bad, bad."

While he was processing the information, I asked President Ronald McDruhitmumpf if he was responsible for the press release.

"You've obviously confused me with somebody who answers questions," the President said as he walked out of the room.

"You have to understand," Dr. Guptaharumpher finally found the will to state, "that the CDC has spent years building its reputation as **the** place to go to for correct health information. If we can't trust them, we may as well get our medical information from the internet!"

When I pointed out that the CDC had actually written guidelines unequivocally mandating that workers in meat packing plants wear masks, but the government had intercepted them and run them into the end zone (their own, which is why nobody tried to stop them), Dr. Guptaharumpher sobbed and said, "Oh, this is badder than bad. This is…really bad."

When I asked Doctor Redwhiteandbluefield why he would risk the CDC's reputation to do the Grey House's bidding, he replied, "You've obviously confused me with somebody who answers questions." Under my breath, I pointed out that if he didn't follow the statement with a movement that took him out of the room, he would be asked more questions, some of which he might actually have to answer. Taking his cue, he stormed out.

If he wants to remain head of the CDC, Doctor Redwhiteandbluefield will really have to up his political game.

Why would the McDruhitmumpf administration put out bogus (which is a slur against swamp creatures; if there are any complaints, I will apologize in a future article) CDC recommendations?

"Have you ever heard the phrase, 'A chicken in every pot?'" asked prize-winning journalist Eugene Robinsoncrusoe.

Sure, I responded. Although I don't really know what it refers t

—

"It was a rhetorical question," Robinsoncrusoe stopped me before I could embarrass myself any further.

Oh. Right. I knew that, too.

"Well, President McDruhitmumpf believes in a pork loin in every freezer. Or, to put it a different way: he knows he cannot win the election by appealing to Vesampuccerians' hearts, so he is making a pretty naked appeal to their stomachs! It's all part of his 'Na na na – I can't hear you! Nobody is dying and you can't tell me otherwise!' approach to the COVID-19 pandemic."

How's that working out for him?

"We've just surpassed 200,000 deaths from the coronavirus. You tell me…"

The Convention of the Red Death

by FRANCIS GRECOROMACOLLUDEN, Alternate Reality News
Service National Politics Writer

Stefano Candelabriuyn stood in the crowd looking like an alien
refugee from a low budget 1970s sci-fi movie: red Keep Making
Vesampucceri Transition to Greatness Again cap (the person who
sewed the message into it must have had very small hands),
oversized glasses with the year "2016" glittering fetchingly atop the
rims (it was on sale), a stars and stripes suit made out of tin foil. Two
weeks later, he was in intensive care in Mount Sigh Nigh Hospital,
being kept alive by a ventilator.

"Free...dom!" he gasped, sounding for all the world like Darth
Ruthvaderginsberg.

Candelabriuyn had attended the Reduhblican National
Convention in which President Ronald McDruhitmumpf was
nominated for a second term for President. Of the 40,000+ (which
would make it 40,002) people who attended the convention, 12,327
caught COVID-19 and 1,327 have died from it.

The convention was originally supposed to be held in Charlotte
Yorkshire-Goldenblatt, North Carowaii, but Governor Roy
Supercoopertroop couldn't guarantee that it would be held without
social distancing. President McDruhitmumpf hates social distancing.
He thinks it's a Dumbopratic plot to emasculate Vesampucceri. And,
him. Specifically, him. (Vesampucceri is big – it can take care of
itself.) Social distancing makes shaking hands hard. He's a hand
shaker. A power hand shaker.

So, at the President's insistence, the Convention was moved to
Mobile, Alaorgia, where enthusiastic Reduhblicans from across the
country came for three days of speeches, overpriced beer drinking,
cheating on their spouses (of which they must never breath a word,
although COVID-19 sure won't be the only illness transmitted after
the convention!) and regrets. So many regrets.

"The Reduhblican Convention was exactly the opposite of what
the medical community had asked the public to do," Doctor Anthony

Faucispendulum stated. "Given his aversion to advice, I was considering telling the President that he should get together in an enclosed space with a huge number of people packed tightly together without wearing masks. You know, reverse psychology? But, I'm sure it would have ended up being a bad comedy routine where that was the first thing I said that he actually listened to. I…I have nightmares like that…"

Why would people go to the Convention knowing the health risks? "COVID-19 only attacks people in Dumbopratic states," explained Ohifornia delegate Wheezer McInscrutable. "Alaorgia is the safest place in Vesampucceri!"

"I'm not going to let the lamestream media dictate to me where to go and what to do," added Washburningdington State delegate Randall Snotnosteenehjur. "I would rather die first!"

"I. Have. Been. Drinking. Bleach. To. Keep. Myself. Safe," rasped Alaorgia delegate Ingvar Rasputinmusson. "I. Am. Perfectly. Safe."

Doctor Faucispendulum shook his head in disbelief. The state isn't on the electoral map, but it's a place more and more Dumboprats find themselves perpetually living in.

Having been deprived of big rallies for **6** months, President McDruhitmumpf spoke for **6** hours on his **6** favourite subjects: how he beat Hillary Roocartoncleveman in 2016; how media reports about him are fake news; how the border wall was almost complete (and he got Mexico to pay for it); how the Meullitallover report was a political hit job; how the Dumboprats created the COVID-19 scare to undermine his reelection efforts; and, how he beat Hillary Roocartoncleveman in 2016…with nothing more than chewing gumption and a baby's arm holding an apple.

The convention crowd cheered him on the whole time. By the end, their roar had taken on a grinding of gears quality despite the fact that volunteers constantly circulated among them with throat lozenges.

President McDruhitmumpf does not practice social distancing, he is constantly shaking hands with people and he disdains wearing a mask in public. How is it he has not yet contracted the coronavirus?

"We have to take seriously the possibility that evil inoculates you against COVID-19," Doctor Faucispendulum glumly stated. "The problem is: how do you distill evil in order to create a vaccine? Especially since the President won't let anybody close enough to him to draw a blood sample. Still, I would love to see how an ethics board would approach **that** drug trial!"

Candelabriuyn looked around the room. "So...worth...i —" he said before a Code Bleu (I know it's cheesy – I should really stop watching medical shows on TV!) was called and he became the latest victim of PINC (Politically Induced Novel Coronavirus) Syndrome.

His convention getup will hang in the Smithsonwindandrainian. It will remind everybody who sees it of this dark time in Vesampuccerian history, assuming the general public is ever allowed into institutions like it again...

I Kid You Not

by MAJUMDER SAKRASHUMINDERATHER, Alternate Reality News Service Education Writer

In September, post-secondary students return to the three bs: beer, babes and...more beer. The three bs and an m. Young people know not to mess with a good thing. Frats around the country host parties with exotic themes like Roman Senate Dagger Bash, Subatomic Particle Summit and Stanky Bearhug. Five minutes in, the themes are abandoned as sweaty bodies (it was a choice between air conditioning and another keg, which is really no choice at all for anybody under the age of 25) are crushed together in frat houses, shouting to be misheard above the blare of music that nobody but the DJ likes.

COVID-19 changed all that.

This year, there are **rules** about on-campus behaviour. Wear a mask. Social distance. Don't get sick and die. Schools are cracking down on unsafe behaviours in order to allow students to safely return to class.

As if rules matter to young people under the influence of alcohol and hormones. Alcomones.

"Amma gimme sec'nd," said Rutgersandhauer University student Darrell Schiavellitron, who proceeded to throw up behind Omega Omega Omega House. Wiping his mouth with the sleeve of his judge's robe, he sighed, "That's always the most melancholy thing I do first week back. Now, what was the question?"

Aren't you afraid of getting COVID-19?

"Been there, done that," Schiavellitron answered. "And, it didn't matter – I'm as healthy as a…as a…umm, excuse me, second wave c…c…coooooooming uuuuuuuu…" He doubled over and let more fluids fly.

Colleges which had prepared for outbreaks of the disease found that they were not at all prepared for outbreaks of the disease. Washburningdington State University, for example, had designated some buildings to be COVID quarantine quarters in the expectation that they would have 400 cases of infection over the semester. The institution had 400 cases of infection in the first three days.

"Yes, my pretties," cackled Education Secretary DeVolution-Ross. "Fly to your doom! You do not deserve education, with your scholarships and affirmative action! Fly to your doom, and let more deserving students take your place!"

I…I'm sure the green pallor of her skin was a trick of the lighting.

When he had fully recovered (I'd hate to see the cleaning bills he would be getting for that robe; unlike Justice Brett Kavanaugheylno, he couldn't expense it to the Extreme Court!), Schiavellitron explained that everybody at the party had the coronavirus, so that was okay, then. And, anyway, young people were at more of a threat of dying of broken hearts than the virus, so why was everybody getting so pissy about – ooh, speaking of which, if you want to ask me anything else, I'll be behind that bush…

Everybody's…concern about the partying may have something to do with the fact that across the street from the campus is the

General Pershingandshoving Veterans Home. As students started returning to school, the number of veterans who came down with the virus skyrocketed. At least 20 have di – 22, at least 22 veterans have – 25 – okay, I'm cutting it off there. At least 25 veterans have died since the beginning of the school year.

Why the (you should pardon the expression) rush to get students back to school? Why do you think?

"Go back to school," admonished President McDruhitmumpf. "Go to school. Go back to school. Very important. For you as well as me. Go. Go. Go. School. School. School. Back. Back. Back. You know, some of the happiest seconds of my life were spent at college. The limping to pretend I was suffering from bone spurs. The handing over of my tests to somebody my father trusted to do well on them. The girls. Ooooh, the girls! I...I sometimes go back to the old campus to relive those days. Go back to school so you can make memories you'll want to relive in your old age!"

If they survive the virus to reach old age?

"Ooooh, nasty. You're nasty! What a nasty thing to say. You talk to your mother with those nasty lips? Nasty is as nasty does, you know. Nasty! Nasty! Nasty!"

He went on like that for another 30 minutes. Most of the journalists in the room got the message after about 24.

Meanwhile, Schiavellitron wanted me to know that he and the other people at the frat party were being responsible about the virus. "When we go to Minnie's Maxi-bar downtown tomorrow to watch the big games, we'll be taking masks with us. And, some of us might actually wear them!"

What have we been teaching the children?

President Has an Own Goal Moment

by LAURIE NEIDERGAARDEN, Alternate Reality News Service Medical Writer

At 2:37 in the morning, President Ronald McDruhitmumpf tweeped: "I am not close to death and being kept alive by electrodes implanted in my brain and dark magiks decent people must never speak of. FAKE NEWS! I – no, we don't use that term any more. HOAX! That's it. HOAX! IT'S A HOAX! THE HOAXEST! I'm the healthiest President this country has ever known! #firstpresidentwhollneverdie".

This came as a surprise to…everybody, really, considering that nobody had ever referred to brain electrodes or dark magiks when discussing the President's health.

Yes, a book that was just released, Michael Aliasschmidtjones' Ronald *Against the World: The 27th Book on the McDruhitmumpf Administration This Month, And It's Only The Second Week!*, referred to the President's unplanned scheduled emergency regular check-up at Walter Reedandalto-Saxxe Hospital last December. Aliasschmidtjones wrote that as the President was driven to the hospital, Vice President Michael Pendenatendance was advised: "Wear your best shirt today. If anything goes sideways, you may have to assume the duties of leader of the idiotocratic world. We're not saying it will, we're just saying: when was the last time you shaved? You might want to freshen up a bit."

There was nothing in the book about electrodes or dark magiks.

As if to underscore the President's point, Grey House physician Sean Prosandconnely released a memo which read: "The President has never had electrodes inserted into his brain. The President has never been subjected to dark magiks. Ronald McDruhitmumpf is a good man. Ronald McDruhitmumpf is a kind man. Ronald McDruhitmumpf is the healthiest President this country has ever known."

If the memo had been any more wooden, you could have built a log cabin out of it (although President McDruhitmumpf would likely burn it to the ground for the insurance – inspirational stories ain't what he's about). It makes one wonder what dark magiks have been applied to Grey House physicians over the last three and a half years.

"The President has lied so often, I tend to believe the opposite of anything he says," commented token smart person Amy

Sheshutshotshitbam. "But this stuff about brain electrodes and dark magiks? Like there's more than one of them? And, they've all been used to keep the President alive? I haven't wanted to believe something a President said this much since Richard Nixwatmondnewon said, 'I am not a crook." And, I wasn't even alive then!"

"As a matter of fact," said famed politico-mysticalist Alastairs Astacrowleyfliesse, "there are hundreds of dark magiks. There is the dark magik that causes a pimple to appear on your nose as your limo is heading to the prom. There's the dark magik that makes old people forget where they put their glasses. There's the dark magik that makes people respond positively to emails from African princes – I especially like that one. Then, there's the dark magik that affects the heat of water when you're taking a shower…"

These magiks didn't seem all that dark. In fact, they seemed a bit…petty. I asked Astacrowleyfliesse about the dark magik that would keep an ailing politician alive until re-elected.

"That would be…useful, I suppose…" he sniffed. "It wouldn't help in my ongoing struggles with Mrs. Schmelson, my landlady. But I'm sure, in the right context, it could be…useful…"

Ah. It wasn't the magiks that were petty. It was the magikian.

Is it possible that electrodes could keep a faltering brain going? "Absolutely!" enthused science fiction author and futurologicalist Corey Indoctorownate. "Scientists have been stimulating different parts of mouse brains with electrodes since Thomas Ridewildeddyson wondered what would happen if you sent a current through an elephant! We can now get mice to drive miniature cars, carve abstract shapes out of cheese and squeak 'Ave Maria' by applying a little current!"

But, affecting an actual human brain? "Working our way up the evolutionary chain has been slow," Indoctorownate allowed. "Although I understand the Poynter Sisters Institute has done some thought-provoking work with rhesus piecus monkeys. To keep a human being alive would, I guess, require some dark magiks…"

Astacrowleyfliesse smirked.

This would probably not be an issue, except part of the Reduhblican strategy to win McDruhitmumpf re-election is to portray Dumbopratic challenger Joe Bidenhisbeeswax as near death. "Have you ever noticed," Grey House spokes-shrill spokes-shill KellyAnne Conwaytwittiest asked, "that Comatose Joe will get this far away look in his eye and mumble something? He's talking to his dead wife and children, telling them he will be with them soon. Real soon. He's just holding on until the election; after he is sworn in, he'll drop dead, letting Kamala Harristweedfashin and the radical left take over the county!"

When asked if Bidenhisbeeswax was being kept alive by brain electrodes and dark magiks, Conwaytwittiest sighed and muttered, "I hate journalists!"

What Goes Around Makes You Come Around

by LAURIE NEIDERGAARDEN, Alternate Reality News Service Medical Writer
and FRANCIS GRECOROMACOLLUDEN, Alternate Reality News Service National Politics Writer

One ancient* piece of political folk wisdom goes: "When your karma runs over your dogma, a wise man** heads for the Hills."*** This wisdom of the folk was proven this week when the Grey House announced that President Ronald McDruhitmumpf, his wife Melanoma and several prominent Reduhblicans had been infected by the COVID-19 virus.

"Our thoughts and prayers are with the President," Senate Minority leader Chuckie Schumaihargowmer smirked.

"The President is healthy as an oxcart,"**** Grey House Chief of Staff Mark Meadabiggblubratt told the press. "He's still in the running to live longer than any human being outside of the bible. Let us all be guided by the ancient wisdom of *The Hitchhiker's Guide to the Galaxy*."

If the President is really as healthy as all that, why was he flown by helicopter to Walter Reedandalto-Saxxe Hospital and given a dose of an experimental cure that has not been made public? "Doctors!" Meadabiggblubratt shrugged. "They're so excitable, and such worrywarts!"

"Of course they're not going to admit that he's very sick," explained Maria Teresa Kumasatralez, President of *Voto Latino*. "Much of the President's base would like to see themselves in him: full of anger, obese and unwilling to change his diet or exercise, but in control of the world. To admit that he was sick would be to admit that he was an ordinary human, which would mean that they were ordinary humans, which would cause their heads to explode."

Wouldn't a simpler explanation be that his base would be pissed if they discovered that the President had lied to them about the virulence of the virus? "Naaaah," Kumasatralez naahed. "They already believe he's been warning them about the deadliness of the disease all along. If Trump's base treated their life partners with the same credulousness they treat the President, the divorce rate in red states would plummet!"

Two days before the announcement, President McDruhitmumpf attended a celebration on the Rose Garden lawn of the nomination of Amy Coney-Islandbar for Extreme Court Justice. Few people in attendance wore masks and there was no social distancing.

"Invitations should have come with capes and masks," commented an increasingly dyspeptic Doctor Vin Guptaharumpher, "because this was an obvious super-spreader event!"

The day before he was diagnosed (but a day after close aid Hope Hicksinpickupstix was diagnosed), the President flew to a fundraiser. "Motherferking motherferker is going to get us all ferking killed!" complained one billionaire supporter. "Don't get me wrong – I'm grateful for the tax cuts and all. But, I'd like to ferking live ferking long enough to ferking spend them!"

The President's illness throws the election, which is just one month away, into chaos. Well, more chaos than it was already in, in any case.

The Presidential debates will likely be cancelled. Okay, no great loss, there.

President McDruhitmumpf will have to be quarantined for at least two weeks, which means he will not be able to hold coronapalooza campaign rallies. Say, this is getting better and better all the time.

Out of respect for the President, the campaign of opponent Joe Bidenhisbeeswax will stop running attack ads (which they refer to as "contrast" ads, a fine distinction). The McDruhitmumpf campaign continues to run its contrast ads (which they refer to as "attack" ads, because there's no point denying it). You had to know the good news wasn't going to last.

There is also some question about how the government will continue to function if President McDruhitmumpf's illness is serious and extended. If he is put on a ventilator, for example, will Vice President Michael Pendenatendance be put in charge? If so, will he wait until after the election to turn the United States of Vesampucceri into *The Handmaid's Wonderland*?

Senate Majority Leader Mitch Wichconnelliswich has indicated that he will keep calm and turtle on in his goal of confirming Coney-Islandbar. However, three Reduhblican Senators were among the people who came down with the coronavirus; if they are incapacitated, he might not have the votes for her.

Worse: if Vice President Pendenatendance is also incapacitated by the disease, the next person in the line of succession is Dumbopratic Speaker of the House Nancy Pelligrinosi. Since the Dumboprats **have** worn masks and practiced social distancing (damn them and their science!), she would probably be healthy enough to veto the nomination if it does come before her.

Is it October? Surprise!

* It was coined three weeks ago, which is several centuries in the lifetime of this administration.

** They were less enlightened about gender neutral language in those three long ago weeks.

*** That would be the Hillsboro Medical Centre and Bluegrass Museum.

**** That's right – he's no farm boy. Is it that obvious?

Profile in Discourage

by FREDERICA VON McTOAST-HYPHEN, Alternate Reality News Service People Writer

He's the kind of person you would see more and more on the streets of cities across the country if they hadn't been rendered invisible through social embarrassment: old and white, wearing ragged clothes and a fading Make Vesampucceri Grate Again cap. He smells like rotting cabbage, so you want to be sure that you stand downwind from him. His name is Bill, or Mac, or Buddy.

In this specific case, his name was Billy-Mac Buddenfumplieffer. I found him sitting on Main Street in Mayan City, Mainington, his back against a boarded up It'll Curl Your Hair salon.

I wanted to give Billy-Mac five bucks, but when I suggested that he take his MVGA (pronounced "muggah," which seems appropriate for such a gangsta regime) hat off and put it on the ground, he sneered, "I don't want your charity! Ask me a question about finance."

I looked blankly at him (I admit, he Etch-a-Sketched me), then asked Billy-Mac why he wanted me to ask him a question. He answered: "Because then I can claim that this is a business consultation, and I will have earned the money you give me. So, you gonna ask me a question, or what? Because if I have to tell you again, it'll cost ya!"

Before I could think of a question to ask, the man on the street added: "The minimum rate for my service is ten dollars a question."

I was already committed, so I fished around in my purse for another five dollar bill. When I had secured the money, I asked Billy-Mac if he thought we were heading for a Depression.

"Depression? Pfft!" he scoffed. "Have you seen the stock market, lately? Lady, the Vesampuccerian economy has never been better, and we have President McDruhitmumpf to thank for that!"

Billy-Mac was a detective down in Texaransas, but I wasn't sure he knew just exactly what the facts is.

He told me that his business had dried up because of COVID-19, there being less opportunity for husbands to cheat on their wives when they were staying in place (the health measure, not the step exercise). Until last month, he had been getting by with a $600 government supplement to his income. Then, Congress let the supplement lapse. And, when I say Congress, I mean the Senate. And, when I say the Senate, I really mean Majority Leader Mitch Wichconnelliswich.

"Ain't I a stinker?" he asked, the twirl of a moustache in his voice. And, let me tell you, getting the image of a turtle with a moustache out of my head is going to take an industrial-strength sedative!

Billy-Mac couldn't afford to pay his rent, so he found himself giving dubious financial advice to passersby for spare change. "It was the right call," he said of losing his government benefits. "If the government gives away free money, people will have no incentive to work."

When I asked what good incentives to work were when there were no jobs available, Billy-Mac snorted and called me a socialist.

When I pointed out that Congress, including the Senate, including Majority Leader Wichconnelliswich, had passed an aid package for major corporations and the wealthy, Billy-Mac snorted and called me a Communist.

I was tempted to ask him what kind of disincentive to work giving trillions of dollars to those who already have so much might be, but I didn't want to find out what goes beyond Communist. I was hoping for banana-chocolate cruller, but I didn't think that was very likely.

Billy-Mac started to cough. It was a rumbling/hacking sound, like a car whose muffler had long ago lost heart and had almost completely descended into going through the motions. When I suggested he get that looked after, he snoughed, and told me: "Can't – hack – can't – kaff – no health – ack ack ack –"

"You have no health insurance?" I suggested.

He touched his nose, as if we were playing a lethal game of charades.

Appalled, I asked him if he was really willing to die to support Reduhblican coronavirus policies. By this time, speech was much more difficult for him, so Billy-Mac charaded, "If it will leave the Vesampucceri I knew intact for future grandfalloons." His hands fluttered faintly towards the end, so I may not have translated his exact thought, but I believe I captured its essence.

I considered calling 911 for an ambulance, but I really didn't want to find out what lies beyond Communist!

COVID Morbidities

by FREDERICA VON McTOAST-HYPHEN, Alternate Reality News Service People Writer

Panic. It's what happens when unreasoning fear meets anticipation. It's what happens when you realize that the encyclopedia salesman who is pitching you on the phone **is actually talking to you from inside the house!** It's what happens when you realize that you are the only person of pigment in your teen cohort **and you really like wearing red shirts!**

Panic. It's what's happening inside the government of President Ronald McDruhitmumpf.

"I came to work for the Grey House because I wanted to be part of history," said a valet who brings food to the west wing. "I didn't want to **be** history!"

Another staffer, who does makeup for official videos, put the issue more succinctly: "I don't wanna die! I don't wanna die! I don't wanna die!"

The problem isn't that President McDruhitmumpf has been diagnosed with COVID-19. The problem is that he likes prancing around the Grey House facially naked. As a result, he spreads the virus with the same gusto that Santa spreads toys.

Every day since the announcement of his infection was made public, more staffers (not to mention Congresspeople – shh) have announced that they have the potentially deadly disease. Yesterday, for example, Press Secretary Kayleigh McEnanity announced that she had contracted the disease...through an assistant since she was no longer safe to be in public.

Under these circumstances, it's understandable that many people who work in the Grey House are wondering, *Could I be next?*

"I took the job," one Secret Service agent commented, "because I love democracy so much that I was willing to take a bullet for the President. I'm not so sure I love democracy enough to take a disease in a water droplet for him!"

"It's duuuuuuuu-thpicable!" said Doctor Vindaloo Guptaharumpher. "Sorry – I've been watching old Warner Brothers cartoons with my son. The President knows how deadly the disease is and how it is transmitted, but he still engages in behaviours that are all but guaranteed to make the people around him sick. Ain't he a stinkah?"

The President's personal hygiene is the least of the country's concerns right now. Two days after he was hospitalized, President McDruhitmumpf went joyriding in a hermetically sealed limousine with two of his closest body guards and a fleet of armoured cars around him. A day later, he had returned to the Grey House for an unfortunate video op.

"I'm feeling – WHEEZE – really good – WHEEZE," he gasped. "I've learned a – WHEEZE – a lot about – WHEEZE – COVID. This has – WHEEZE – has been – WHEEZE – a real – WHEEZE – real school. And – WHEEZE – you know – WHEEZE – how well – WHEEZE – I did – WHEEZE – at school! Horse stable genius –

WHEEZE! Don't – WHEEZE – be afraid – WHEEZE – of – WHEEZE PANT GASP – COVID!"

The President had been given a cocktail of drugs at Walter Reedandalto-Saxxe Hospital (the doctors have been so reticent to give details that we do not know if it contained olives or a lemon wedge), some of which were highly experimental. Some pundits have suggested that all of the drugs in his system may have interacted and affected the President's judgment.

"Nyuh uh," commented MSNBC host Chris Carfairindrughayes. "The President had shown such bad judgment before he got sick, the drugs could only make it better!"

President McDruhitmumpf's behaviour may also be affecting his reelection campaign. A *Washburningdington Times*/Dryascottonmouth poll showed that only 39 per cent of decided voters planned on voting for him, a four per cent drop since yesterday's *New Yoricknuhemwell Times*/Rasmussenandson poll. This drop would have had to come from his base.

"It makes sense," Carfairindrughayes explained. "When they attended coronapalooze events, McDruhitmumpf's supporters were probably thinking that the only thing they would go home with was the t-shirt!"

"He has experience in fighting the coronavirus as an individual. Those firsthand experiences – Joe Bidenhisbeeswax, he doesn't have those," stated McDruhitmumpf campaign spokesperson Erin Leaenperrines. But the way his voice cracked and he not so furtively looked over his shoulder after every sentence, suggested that his mind was really on something else.

The encyclopedia salesman in the basement, perhaps?

When asked about what his recent performance would do to the President's reelection chances, Leaenperrines jumped six feet into the air, hit his head on the ceiling and fell back to the floor in a heap. He was a trooper, however: he picked himself up and responded, "The President is going to win a great victory in November. That is, if he doesn't kill the majority of his campaign staff first…"

Ira Nayman

6. THE SLEEP OF REASON PRODUCES... IDIOCRATIC POLITICS

The Hallmark of Democracy: The Smooth T^{r}a$_{ns}$i^{t}io$_n$ of P$_{ow}$e^r

by FRANCIS GRECOROMACOLLUDEN, Alternate Reality News
Service National Politics Writer

                                                  ti
                                              a   on o
A unique feature of democracies is the s   th tr   i   f pow
                                      m
                                          oo   ns   er.

Sorry. My computer seems to have the hiccups.

                                                              n
                                              th   n   o
Ahem. A unique feature of democracies is the sm   tra   io
                                            o
                                              o   sit

Umm. Yeah. I'd put a paper bag around my computer's heat
vent, but I suspect that would make things worse. For obvious

reasons, a cool drink of water is right out. Let's say that…a unique feature of liberal democracies is…leaders willingly g ing up power if they lose elections.   iv

Good enough.

A unique feature of illiberal idiotocracies is that they don't conform to the unique features of liberal democracies.

A month before the primaries, Vesampuccerian President Ronald McDruhitmumpf told a congregation of non-unionized auto workers (who could easily social distance considering there were only seven of them, but who huddled together to show that they believed COVID-19 was a hoax perpetrated by George Sorobororos to suffocate honest, hard-working people and steal their stuff): "What have you got to lose? **What** have you got to lose? What have **you** got to lose? Okay, your jobs. Mail-in voting leads to massive fraud – the Dumboprats are trying to steal the election. But, the economy is doing great – better than it ever has been. Better than when…that other guy was President. Remember how I made Vesampucceri great again when you have to eat your shoes!"

Wait – what? **Dumboprats** are trying to steal the election? Did I hear that correctly?

Apparently, there's nothing wrong with my ears (I get them candled every month, and get the bandages changed every couple of weeks, thank you very much). After that speech, the President took every opportunity to challenge the legitimacy of the coming election.

At a Zoomer meeting with Mrs. McJimmicuddy's grade three class, for example, President McDruhitmumpf said: "The China virus, which was started in China, by the Chinese, to undermine the health of our people, is a hoax. Nobody is dying and, anyway, a cure is on the way! You want something to really worry about? Voter fraud. Massive cheating because of mail-in balloting. It will be the end of our idiotocracy, people! Death! Destruction! Bad things! Yes, you're absolutely right to cry! Millions of fraudulent votes could – hey! What happ – have we been cut off? Can you get the connection back? Does anybody know what George Sorobororos is doing at this moment…?"

"The President is trying to delegitimize the – ooh, yeah. Right there – the election," explained token smart person Amy Sheshutshotshitbam as she was being massaged by a woman named Bertha D. Blooze at a day spa. "If I win, the election was free – hah! – free and – mmmmm – fair. If I lose – pant! pant! – oh, baby! – the other side cheated. He, and his followers, will not accept the results of the election if he loses. That is so bad – ooh, that is sooooo good!"

President McDruhitmumpf has a couple of times floated the possibility that the election could take a long time to decide. "With mail-in balloting, it could take years for all of the votes to be counted," he told three reporters and a skunk that had got past his security detail. When the skunk pointed out that the President's Post-master General was responsible for those delays, he responded: "You stink. You know that? You're the real stinker!"

The President may have been trying to make the case that he should stay in power until all of the votes were counted. The problem is that that darn Constitution won't let him. If the election is undecided in January, the person who takes power is the Speaker of the House, in this case Dumboprat Nancy Pelligrinosi.

I can feel President McDruhitmumpf shuddering at the thought. So, I'm going to repeat it: if the election hasn't been decided by January, Speaker Nancy Pelligrinosi will take charge of the government.

Shudder away, Mister President. Shudder away.

More recently, President McDruhitmumpf has been planting the idea in the heads of his followers that he may stay longer than the two terms the law allows. "Four more years?" he told a rally. "You're not thinking big enough. Twelve more years! Sixteen more years! Twenty-nine more years! Yes, twenty-nine more years, people! I will be the most powerful desiccated corpse in the world!"

Although there is no legal basis for any of the President's claims, the real question is what his base, fed on the thin gruel of the idea that the results of the election are illegitimate, will do. The President's well-armed and highly strung base. The fact that they gave President McDruhitmumpf's "desiccated corpse" line a seven minute standing ovation does not bode well for the country. Or, the world…

President Declares War on Veterans

by MARA VERHEYDEN-HILLIARD, Alternate Reality News Service War Writer

When the bombs were flying on distant battlegrounds, Martin Verschmeckenstaller stood tall against the Nasty threat on the shores of Gwen Verdoubledowndun. Now, 75 years later, Verschmeckenstaller lies stooped against the depredations of stolen pudding cups at the Eternal Peace Rest Home.

"Strawberry coconut suntan oil pudding," he moans. "I could understand why somebody would be tempted to scarper with it…if I only understood what scarper meant!"

At his daily press rambling (briefing is too dignified a term for it), President Ronald McDruhitmumpf stated: "Lawn order means a lot of things. It means putting the scum that throw their used cigarette butts and fast food wrappers onto your immaculate front yard away for a long time. A very long time, people. The longest…"

Okay, no, that was too early – did I mention the President has a tendency to ramble? Later, he said: "…and, that's how babies are made. No child should ever have to be subjected to that – we should not teach our children sex education until at least their third year of college!"

Too far. Hold on a second – let me just review the recordi – okay. This is what the President said that is relevant to this article: "Antifa are running wild in the streets, raping innocent little old statues and knocking over historically important ladies. They're a violent mob of thugs, criminals and loooosers. Especially the loser part. And, they're gonna be even more…losier when I direct my police to crack down on them! KER-AAAAAACK!"

"Oh, yeah, so much wrong in that statement," responded token smart person Amy Sheshutshotshitbam. "The President talks about the police like they're a ChristmaKwaanzUkah present he found under a burning bush when he was six years old. A present he will play with so much he'll break it within an hour of unwrapping it, then cry for days if his father doesn't get him a new one. It would be a sad personal story if his present wasn't armed to the teeth and ready to use its armed teeth against innocent civilian protesters!"

Armed teeth. That's an image that's going to haunt my dreams for months to come!

Token smart person Sheshutshotshitbam went on to point out that the term antifa meant anti-fascist. The modern anti-fascist movement is a loose affiliation of individuals who are opposed to neo-Nastys and other far right racist organizations. The largest group of antifa fighters in Vesampuccerian history was the United States military, which fought the original Nastys in World War the Big One.

"I want a blueberry hen's teeth pudding cup!" veteran Verschmeckenstaller demanded. "It's a very specific flavour, blueberry hen's teeth – not to everybody's taste! Not to anybody's taste, really – why would anybody steal it out of the fridge?"

"We're not fascists," argued Prude Bois member Amon Dastardlyblackhard during a "Yews will not replace us" rally in Atlanta, Georgexico. "We're anti-antifa."

But, if you're against the people who are fighting fascists, that would make you fascists, wouldn't it?

"Absolutely not! We're not fascists, we're just against antifa."

Look. The linguistic math on this is very simple: the two negative terms cancel each other out. Do I need to write down the formula that shows – okay, of course I do. Fine. The math looks like this:

$$(\text{anti-})(\text{anti})\text{fa} =$$
$$(\cancel{\text{anti-}})(\cancel{\text{anti}})\text{fa} =$$
$$\text{fa}$$

Grinning, Dastardlyblackhard responded, "You got me. You just can't argue with math! Verheyden-Hilliard...what kind of a name is that?"

"I would settle for pineapple motor oil," Verschmeckenstaller interjected, saving me from having to asnwer Dastardlyblackhard's question. "Everybody knows I'm not fussy when it comes to my pudding cups!"

When the implications of the President's statement began circulating, Grey House Press Secretary (This Week) Kayleigh McEnanity told reporters, "Of course the President wasn't referring to this country's war veterans. He has the utmost respect for the men who have sacrificed so much in service of their country. Why, just the other day, he was talking about the possibility of having one over for brunch. Some day. If he has his papers. And, is house trained. And, you just know that the President is going to give that a lot of serious thought!"

When asked why, if he had so much respect for veterans, their benefits were cut under his administration, Press Secretary McEnanity answered, "Ooh, you're good. If I had any idea that this job was going to be so hard..." Then, she looked wistfully (apparently, the game of bridge had yet to be introduced into this administration) into the middle distance until everybody was uncomfortable. Very uncomfortable.

How did Verschmeckenstaller respond to the President's attack on his service? "Vanilla hopscotch. It's such a bland flavour – who would want to keep it from me? But, do you think I can get a vanilla hopscotch in this place? If I'm going to be treated like this, what's the point of being a member of the Greatest Constipation?"

Okay, he may have a one track mind. But, given his service to the country, he's earned it!

In The Eternal Struggle Between Dog And Postal Delivery Person,
The Winner May Be President Ronald McDruhitmumpf

by FRANCIS GRECOROMACOLLUDEN, Alternate Reality News Service National Politics Writer

Neither rain, nor snow, nor...gloom...and doom and gloom, nor...nor...nor rioting in the streets, nor spray painting national monuments shall – nor a political party that has abandoned all pretense of Rousseaulyeaulanian liberalism, shall...shall stay these couriers from...umm...whatever it is that they actually do. Amen.

The USPS (not pronounced "us pus," because that would be gross, or "us puss," because that would be too suggestive for a family publication; pronounced U-S-P-S because, although quite boring, it seemed like the safest choice to...whoever chose the pronunciation) has been a part of Vesampucceri since the country's founding. It's in the Constitution, for criminey's sake! You would – no, I have no idea what a criminey is. A criminal chimney, maybe? No, that's too fanciful. I know they jump, though. So, maybe it's a juke joint? Not that I know what they are, either. And, for jumping juke joints' sake makes even less sense than the chimney thing.

The point is, you would expect that, being in the Constitution and all, Reduhblicans would worship the USPS. A little incense. A virgin sacrifice. Some pious ritual commentary about the virgin sacrifice (with giggling – what, exactly, was in that incense?).

Have you ever met the McDruhitmumpf Reduhblicans?

Five months ago, President McDruhitmumpf replaced the head of the USPS with an inflatable doll named Louis DeGroovyDccLight. His main qualifications for the position were that he had raised millions of dollars for Reduhblican candidates and he once received a letter from a Very Prominent Publisher telling him that he may already be a winner.

The new Postmaster General's first action was to send a memo to all of the organization's employees saying, "Hey, bros and hos. We're cutting back on expenses because, you know, budget cuts and shit. You may find you'll be dealing with a heavier volume of mail than you're used to. It's cool. It's cool. Just, you know, leave whatever you can't do on your desk and, like, do it tomorrow. Or, the next day. Or, better yet, toss what you can't get done into an air duct, or a hole you dig out back of your post office, or take it home with you and feed it to your pet iguana. I mean – pfft! It's not like anybody's gonna miss it or anything!"

He had obviously been heavily into the incense. The sativa incense.

When it became obvious to the public last week that mail delivery was slowing down, Postmaster General DeGroovyDeeLight acted swiftly to address the situation: he fired 23 senior USPS managers in what has come to be known as "This week's Friday night massacre." "I love saving the taxpayer money!" he explained before he disappeared back into the bureaucracy.

What did the USPS do to deserve this treatment? "It worked," commented Senate Minority Leader Chuckie Schumaihargowmer. "That would be enough for McDruhitmumpf to want to kill it, but it's what it worked at that really put a bee in the President's spelling."

Typical voter suppression tactics often lead to people standing in line for eight to twelve hours just to cast their ballots; it's like waiting outside a club to get an unreserved seat at a rock concert, but with more legal challenges. Unfortunately, with COVID-19 running amok in the country, voter suppression in 2020 could be permanent. For this reason, politicians of all stripes (and some plaids and even a polka dot or two) favoured expandinging voting by mail.

But President McDruhitmumpf knows that if everybody who wants to cast a ballot does, the Reduhblicans can't win. He said as much when he stated on *Foxindehenhaus and Fiends*: "If everybody who wants to cast a ballot does, the Reduhblicans can't win!"

He has weird pockets of honesty, this President does. If he was anybody else, it would be charming.

The problem with crippling the USPS to win the 2020 Presidential election is that it does more than just deliver votes. It delivers drugs and unemployment checks and softcore porn magazines. A lot of elderly veterans, needy workers and desperately horny teenagers will have their lives ruined if this is allowed to continue unchecked.

The President has waged a war on voting by mail despite the cost. In a series of tweeps that I cannot quote because I have used up my quota for this week...month...decade, he claimed that voting by mail would cause the collapse of Vesampuccerian democracy, the sudden disappearance of kittens across the country and a rise in tooth decay among voting age toddlers.

Absentee ballots, on the President's other hand, are entirely kosher.

"What is the difference between absentee ballots and voting by mail?" mused token smart person Amy Sheshutshotshitbam. "It's exactly the same process, with exactly the same result. It's like saying that you should ban highway billboards but do nothing about skull-shaped bongs. It makes no sense!"

We asked the token smart person if she had gotten a whiff of the Reduhblican Constitution-worshipping incense. You know: the good stuff?

"What if I have?" she defensively retorted. (Literally: she threw the flask at our heads.) "What I do in the privacy of my own consciousness is nobody's business – not even my own!"

The Vesampuccerian Action on Gun Violence Algorithm

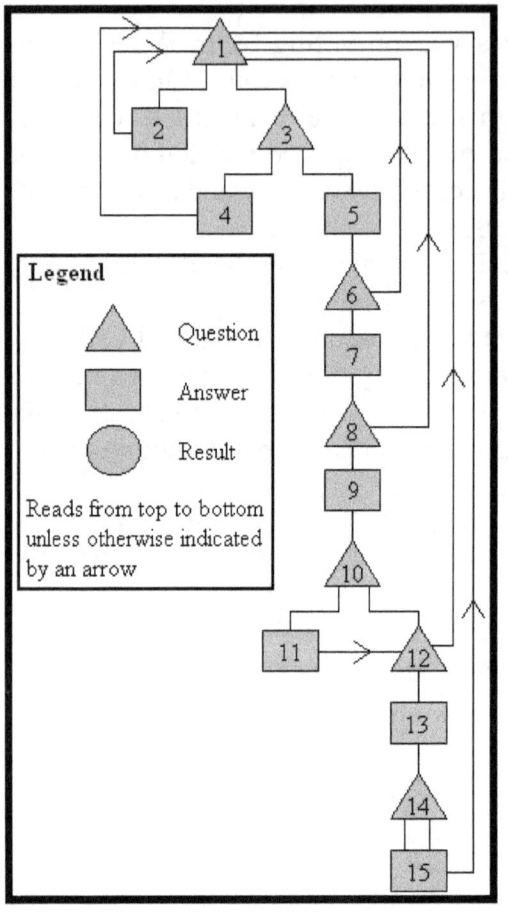

1. A mass shooting has occurred in the United States. It would appear that a political response is required. Do the Dumboprats control the White House and both Houses of Congress?

YES 2. The government passes meaningful gun control legislation.

NO 3. Do the Dumboprats control the White House and one of the Houses of Congress?

YES 4. The Dumboprats propose meaningful gun control legislation. The Reduhblicans lose their shit, warning that all Vesampuccerians are about to lose their guns and threatening not to pass any Dumbopratic legislation if any meaningful gun control laws are passed. Watered down gun control legislation is barely passed.

NO 5. Dumbopratic leaders, who, for some reason, do not comment on how they repealed the gun laws passed by the previous Dumbopratic administration, offer their thoughts and prayers to the victims of the shooting and their families.

6. Does the media lose interest in the story?

YES GO TO 1

NO 7. Reduhblican politicians and their stooges in the media place the blame for the mass killing squarely where it belongs: on the shooter, who is obviously insane. None of them are psychologists, and, in any case, they offer no proof beyond the syllogism that only crazy people walk into other people's places of worship (or shopping, which for many is the same thing) and try to kill as many people as they can. QED (Quod Erat Deplorable).

8. Now does the media lose interest in the story?

YES GO TO 1

NO 9. Blame violent video games for the shooting. Or, violent movies. Or, violent comic books. Or, violent cuneiform tablets. Responsibility for gun carnage? It's the media, stupid.

10. Did the shooter leave documents behind (say, posts on social media) that referred to invasions, vermin or other racist rhetoric (which absolutely, positively did not mimic the rhetoric of the President, even if it used the exact same language)?

YES 11. Reiterate in the strongest, loudest, most forceful terms that the shooter was crazy, and, therefore, nothing he said or wrote should be taken seriously. Accuse anybody who took the shooter's writings at face value of "politicizing" the shooting.
NO 12. Wow. This story really has legs! By this time in the news cycle, journalists would have moved on to the President attacking a black sports star, or cute kittens, or the President attacking a black sports star with cute kittens! Are any journalists still following this story? Like, seriously?

NO GO TO 1

YES 13. The Reduhblicans announce that they are shocked and saddened by gun violence in the country, and that they are currently studying ways to resolve the problem. Vesampuccerians should expect legislation on the subject immediately...after the current recess.

14. Does the NRA have a hissy fit and warn the President and Reduhblican members of Congress that, current investigations into its finances and expensive lawsuits notwithstanding, going against its wishes will alienate a lot of the party's base?

YES 15. Reduhblicans will carry on with the items on their legislative agenda, ignoring the waning criticism of their inaction on gun violence. GO TO 1

NO 15. Reduhblicans will carry on with the items on their legislative agenda, ignoring the waning criticism of their inaction on gun violence. GO TO 1

NOTES

Ever get the uncanny feeling that you've lived through the politics of gun violence in Vesampucceri before? That's not *deja vu*, friend, that's just you paying attention to the news. Repeatedly. Over decades.

In 2019, there has been an average of over one mass shooting somewhere in the United States a day. There is something to be said for consistency. It's horrifying.

And, yet, as the years roll by and the body count increases by leaps and bounds (and handguns and assault rifles), it's hard not to be numbed by the carnage, to feel helpless to do anything to stop it. Of course, there is something that can be done to end it: stop electing politicians who put the campaign contributions they get from the gun lobby before the lives of other people's children.

As if.

As always, the Vesampuccerian Action on Gun Violence Algorithm is descriptive, not proscriptive. Believe us, we would rather put bullets in our own heads from guns we don't own than recommend this as a rational course of political action!

All Vesampuccerians Lost, No Debate

by FRANCIS GRECOROMACOLLUDEN, Alternate Reality News Service National Politics Writer

Last night's Presidential debate between Ronald McDruhitmumpf and Joe Bidenhisbeeswax has been described as a waste receptacle conflagration and an excrement entertainment. It didn't need a fact-checker, it needed an antacid fountain. It was marred by constant heckling, jeering and interruptions – and, that was just by the President!

As everybody knows from high school debating club (yes, everybody: even those who didn't participate attended to determine who to beat up after class the next day), the participants are supposed to offer arguments in favour of principles, positions that they back up with facts and logic. That isn't what happened last night. Former Vice President Bidenhisbeeswax would try to articulate a policy position, but would be shouted down by the President. The following exchange was typical:

FORMER VICE PRESIDENT JOE BIDENHISBEESWAX: When it comes to the climate, we have to acknowledge –

PRESIDENT RONALD MCDRUHITMUMPF: What about Hunter and Burisma?

BIDENHISBEESWAX: No evidence of wrongdoing was ever found. Now, as I was saying, climate change is a fundamental threat to –

MCDRUHITMUMPF: Three million dollars. No experience. I got your real Fenwick scandal right here, pal! (grabs crotch behind podium)

BIDENHISBEESWAX: Eww! Can we get back to the point?

MCDRUHITMUMPF: Not if I can help it!

Debate moderator Chris Walleyedpeacrackers said "Mister President!" so often, viewers had to wonder if he had parrot in his recent ancestry. President McDruhitmumpf talked over him, as well. The following exchange was typical:

CHRIS WALLEYEDPEACRACKERS: Mister President, please let him speak.

PRESIDENT RONALD MCDRUHITMUMPF: Sure. As long as he speaks about his record of 147 years in government doing nothing.

WALLEYEDPEACRACKERS: Mister President! The subject is the economy. The Vice President was –

MCDRUHITMUMPF: Like I said – 147 years in Congress as Vice President, and nada. *Bupkes*. Hear that? That's cricket noises.

WALLEYEDPEACRACKERS: No, Mister President, that's you not allowing anybody else to –

MCDRUHITMUMPF: A hundred and forty-seven years, Chris. One hundred. And forty-seven. To be in government for that long and do so little is quite an accomplishment!

"The President was like walking, talking debate Kryptonite," said a stunned MSNB host and debate commentator Rachel O'Schubermatthow. "it was like he hadn't come to debate. He came to blow the debate up. Does Kryptonite blow things up, or just make them saggy and weak?"

"It just goes to show the limits of analogy," said a stunned Nicolle Walleyedpeacrackers, an MSNBC host and debate commentator.

"It was very instructive," added stunned MSNBC host and debate commentator Joy Reidemanweepson. "For instance, now I know not to eat dinner before the next debate!"

Will there be a next debate, though? "The Dumbopratic Party could let Bidenhisbeeswax go through this again two more times," O'Schubermatthow mused. "Or, it could bury him up to his neck in desert sand and pour honey on his head for the ants to enjoy. Hard to know which is more appealing at this point."

The moderators could be empowered with tools that would help control the next two debates, such as a kill switch. (Don't get too excited: it would kill the mic of one of the debaters when the other was speaking, not the debater himself.) However, both parties would have to agree to any changes in the format of the debates, and that's about as likely as Mitch Wichconnelliswich growing a conscience, or just about any Reduhblican Senator evolving into a vertebrate. Even if there were rule changes though, President McDruhitmumpf has proven he won't follow them; anything short of a trap door leading to a chute that drops him 20 floors will likely be ineffective.

Why would the President give such an aggressive, angry, bullying performance at the debate? "Aside from the fact that that is exactly who he is?" Reidemanweepson asked.

Well, yeah, sure, aside from that.

"The debates were an opportunity for Joe Bidenhisbeeswax to show the country how presidential he is," Reidemanweepson explained. "By blowing the first one up, McDruhitmumpf has denied him his one chance to shine on the national stage. The fact that he is so adept at harnessing his personal failings to promote his political agenda is one of the sad ironies of the McDruhitmumpf presidency."

But, wouldn't the President's performance turn off a lot of voters?

"McDruhitmumpf represents the raging id of his base," Walleyedpeacrackers analyzed. "They love the fact that he gives voice to their most destructive impulses. Think: Godzilla dancing around Japan. If his performance could discourage independents and undecideds from showing up at the ballot box, it could move swing states in his favour. The fact that the President is so adept at harnessing his personal failing to promote his political – damn! Joy just made that point! It's not easy being on a panel with so many astute commentators!"

But, President McDruhitmumpf's base has never been more than about 40 per cent of the population, which is not enough to win a general election. Does his performance suggest that he is resigned to stealing the election?

"It sure looks that way, doesn't it?" O'Schubermatthow agreed.

"Absolutely!" Walleyedpeacrackers agreed.

"Is it too late to go on vacation?" Reidemanweepson wondered. "I hear Romania is nice this time of year…"

You Can Choose Your Nose
And You Can Choose Your Friends
But You Can't…

by FRANCIS GRECOROMACOLLUDEN, Alternate Reality News Service National Politics Writer

Dumbopratic Presidential candidate Joe Bidenhisbeeswax has finally announced his running mate.

Joe Bidenhisbeeswax
@JoeBidenhisbeeswax
I am proud to name @KamalaHarristweedfashin as my choice for Vice President. She's smart. She's tough. She hardly ever shakes her fist at the sky. And she never loses her…umm, her…she never loses her…train…of…her train of…yeah. She's great.

The positive response from Dumboprats was swift.

Stacey Abramstokerdrac
@staceyabramstokerdrac
Joe Bidenhisbeeswax has chosen a woman of color to be his running mate. What a historic moment! It wasn't me. But, what the hell – history! I couldn't be prouder! Well, maybe a little prouder. Still, this is great! Really! @historicsobmoment

Hillary Roocartoncleveman
@HillaryRoocartoncleveman
Women, people of color, Jews – the Dumbopratic Party has always been open to breaking the ceiling for minority candidates for our highest office. Today is another sterling example! Of course, with only one exception, all of those candidates have lost. But we keep trying, darn it. We keep trying. And that's got to be worth something! @historicsobmoment

The negative response from Reduhblicans was swifter.

Ronald McDruhitmumpf
@thesurrealpresidentmcdruhitmumpf
Pamela Harristweedfashin? She's the Dumboprat VP pick? She's a very NASTY girl. The kind you don't bring home to mother. And if her ticket wins, the President she'll smother! #friendsdontletfriendsvotedumboprat

Brian KissMeadekilmeadenow
@foxandfiendskissMeadekilmeadenow
Grab your guns and head for the hills because SOCIALIST FASCIST COMMUNIST ANARCHY is about to descend upon the country! Oh, and Kamala Harristweedfashin has been chosen as Joe Bidenhisbeeswax's running mate. #beafraidbeveryaaaaaaaiiiiiii

Mitch Wichconnelliswich
@senatemajorityleaderturtle

Reduhblicans know that Kamala Harristweedfashin will be too soft on crime. Dumboprats know that when she was Attorney General of Califegon, she was too tough on crime. Honestly, this is a choice designed to please no one! #whyisthismansmiling

It's almost as though they had prepared a response to every candidate on Bidenhisbeeswax's short list. Almost. That would have required a degree of organization that the Reduhblican Party under Ronald McDruhitmumpf has not demonstrated it is capable of.

The Fenwickian troll farms, on the other hand? They probably had responses ready for every registered Dumboprat in Vesampucceri.

Lisa Fenstruck
@luellapanatella
This Harristweedfashin woman Sloppy Joe (mmm – I know what I'm having for dinner tonight!) picked for VP? She's from Jamaica! You know what that means: you won't be able to see the Grey House for the shroud of ganja fumes and statues of Bob Marley will replace Confederate heroes! #vesmpucceriswortsnightmare

True Patroit
@notaFenwicktroll
Fleepy Joe really ystepped in it this time! This woman is a Kenyan who will CONFISCAE YOUR GUSN and SELL THEM TO CHINAA! WAKE UP, PEOPLE! Democracy survives by spilling the blood of patroits! That means yous! #otherwisehaveaniceday

Rupert Mountkilamanjoy
@fenwickprimeministerforlife
Everybody knows I do not write my own tweeps – I have people to do that for me. But if I did, I would probably write: "You might think that, I couldn't possibly comment." #nottooseriousformetafun

And, of course, there was always President McDruhitmumpf.

Ronald McDruhitmumpf
@thesurrealpresidentmcdruhitmumpf
She was my number one pick. For Bidenhisbeeswax. Not me. Eww!
Mike is safe. For now. What was I – oh, yeah. That woman is a
political hack who couldn't hack the Presidential primaries and will
end up driving a hack when I win hugely!
#seewhatididtherewithmybiglybrain

[What the ferk, Grecoromacolluden? Did you just write an article by
stringing a bunch of tweeps together? Seriously, are your parents
proud they put you through journalistic veterinarian school for **this**?
Lucky for you my slapping gloves shrank in the washer and my new
ones are on back order! Rewrite this like a grown-up newsie!
Editrix-in-Chief Brenda Brundtland-Govanni]

Brenda, this type of article is all the rage with online news
organizations.

[Seriously? That's your defence? If the *New Yoricknuhemwell Times*
jumped off a bridge – which, given the current market for print
journalism, is not all that farfetched a possibility – would you do it,
too? Honestly, I could pay a little more to get that slapping gloves
order shipped faster, you know! BB-G]

Yes, seriously, Brenda. Have you seen the page views of *The
Daily Bleat* or *Daily Cos*?

[As a matter of – **how many millions?** Umm...okay. Gotta move
with the times. Keep up the good work! BB-G]

Given the historic nature of Bidenhisbeeswax's choice,
historians have had a lot to say about it.

Michael Beschbefordatloess
@presidentialhistoryiscool

The Constitution says, "to form a more perfect Union." A more perfect Union. The framers knew that they weren't perfect (although Jackshithappenson had occasional delusions), and the leaders who came after them wouldn't be perfect. We are constantly striving to be better. Especially when it comes to inclusion in our political and personal lives. That is wh

Some day, they might get around to sharing it with us.

Nobody Puts Vesampucceri in a Box!

by CORIANDER NEUMANEIMANAYMANEEMAMANN, Alternate Reality News Service Urban Issues Writer

Every third Wednesday of the month, Millie Goddardammerung walks two blocks to drop a check covering the premiums for the insurance on her two Pomeranian shih tzus (Bela and Gestational Period) into the mailbox in front of the Fart Mart groceteria. She has done it so often that it has become so automatic that she didn't notice when the letter fluttered to the ground, unmailboxed.

Gary Fontainoyouthful was coming out of the Fart Mart groceteria with a bag of almost meat hamburger patties, almost glutenous buns and enough onions to make the entire Moron Tabernacle Choir tear up when he noticed what Millie had done. He approached her to let her know that her letter was lying on the ground; when the paramedics had finally flushed all of the mace out of his eyes, he saw Millie stare through the empty space that used to contain a mailbox at the letter on the ground in confusion.

"That's not supposed to happen," she was saying to herself.

Increasingly, though, it has been happening, Millie. In western states such as Nebrastah, South Dakogon and Idawa, mailboxes are disappearing at such a rapid rate, it makes the melting of the polar ice caps seem glacial by comparison. So to speak.

When asked about the missing mailboxes at one of his Grey House coronavirus briefings, President Ronald McDruhitmumpf replied: "It's just kids pulling a prank. You know, they have a lot of energy, kids do. A lot of energy. And, if they don't have an outlet for it, things start to disappear. Just vanish. Cutlery. Paintings. Trust funds. That's another reason we have to get children back into school: to save our mailboxes!"

When the reporter followed up by pointing out that there was video of mailboxes being loaded onto United States Postal Service trucks, the President tersely said, "Hey! Those young pranksters have had all summer to plan this! Thank you, everybody. No, thank **you**," and fled the room.

"Weeeellll, of course, the President's explanation could be part of it," Postmaster General Louis DeGroovyDeeLight stated. "But, no, really, we have just been removing letterboxes at sites which don't get a lot of use. Honestly, it's just part of routine cost-gutting here at the USPS. No need for anybody to worry."

Senate Minority Leader Chuckie Schumaihargowmer looked worried. "You expect me to believe that half the mailboxes in some counties are not being used often enough to justify their existence?" he commented. "Okay. Sure. If you say so. Still, if this isn't also voter suppression, I'll eat my smarm!"

I have no idea what his last statement meant, but I'm sure it would not be pretty.

Another new wrinkle in the post office's linens are what are known as "flexible hours, or flexours." This refers to offices being open between nine in the evening and ten o'clock the next morning. I tried to get somebody from one of the offices that had been assigned flexours to comment on the change, but everybody I tried to talk to yawned so much that I couldn't wring a usable quote from any of them.

"Okay, we might have to use some of the money we're saving by getting rid of postboxes to pay for overtime," Postmaster General DeGroovyDeeLight admitted. "But, in the long run, the smaller volume of mail we have to process will save us a huuuuge amount of money!"

"Voter suppression! Voter suppression! Voter suppression!" Senate Minority Leader Schumaihargowmer jumped up and down.

"If **this** isn't voter suppression, I'll use Nancy Pelligrinosi's smarm as a side dish!"

There is also some reporting that sorting machines have vanished from post offices in the middle of the night. One minute, 23,000 pieces of mail an hour are running through a machine the size of 23 dobermans, the next minute they're lying in a mess on the floor.

"Maybe it was a class project," President McDruhitmumpf stated at a different coronavirus briefing (although they do tend to blend together after a while). "Maybe it was a science fair project. You never…never…" Then, he started laughing. "Aww, I was just punking you. Of course the USPS is doing all of this. Mail-in voting, massive cheating, Dumboprats stealing the election – you know the story."

"Aha!" Senate Minority Leader Schumaihargowmer. "If **this** isn't voter suppression, I'll make a stew out of the smarm of all of the members of The Squad and – wait. The President just admitted he's ordering this to suppress the vote. So, umm, there. Told ya."

I got the sense the Minority Leader was disappointed because he had developed a taste for smarm.

As the sun set (on the Fart Mart groceteria, if not the nation), Millie continued to stare at her letter lying on the ground. It was impossible to tell what she was thinking, but I hope it wasn't: *If I kill my pets tonight and make it look like an accident, will I be able to collect on their insurance before the policy lapses for non-payment?*

I **really** hope it wasn't that.

The Franchise So Nice, You Should Exercise it Twice…

by FRANCIS GRECOROMACOLLUDEN, Alternate Reality News Service National Politics Writer

President Ronald McDruhitmumpf is so convinced that the 2020 election will be plagued (more destructive than locusts, less destructive than lawyers) with voter fraud, he has exhorted his base to practice it just in case the Reduhblican efforts at voter suppression are so successful that the Dumboprats can't do it themselves.

"Here's what you do," the President said in an interview with a local TV station – they still have those in this country? – I mean, seesh Louieesh, doesn't everybody get their news from the internet, now? – in North Carolexas. "You mail in a ballot. Then, you go in person on election day and vote a second time. That way, you can make sure your vote is counted. And, if it was, you'll prove to those Dumboprat politicians that voter fraud is a real thing. It's win-win, really!"

"And you'll get arrested," added former prosecutor Joyce Onvancewarpedtur. "Trying to vote more than once is illegal in this country. So, it's more like win-lose big, really."

The next day, President McDruhitmumpf doubled down on his advice on Twitherd: "If you live close to a state border, drive across and try to vote there, too. Then, try to cross the border into another state and vote there, too. #makeallyourvotescount"

"See, that's just not how our system works," former prosecutor Onvancewarpedtur argued. "If you commit a crime, committing it a second time doesn't mean you get to go free. Two wrongs don't make a right – they make a longer jail sentence. And, if you do it a third time? Sorry, but the math is just not in your favour!"

Following complaints about President McDruhitmumpf's tweep about voting more than once, Twitherd attached a note to his message saying, "Advice that you get over the internet may not always be accurate." The tweep was not removed because, as one anonymous staffer put it, "You think we want to alienate 40 per cent of the population? What the hell kind of business model is **that?**"

If only the company had been as forthcoming with the tweep…

Reduhblicans, led by the President, have been claiming that voter fraud will be widespread in the coming election ever since it became clear in the polls that he would lose to a generic broom with a bucket on top. This comes despite the fact that voter fraud is about as popular with the Vesampuccerian population as cleaning out septic tanks. "It just doesn't happen," former prosecutor Onvancewarpedtur helpfully interpreted my strained metaphor.

In fact, the most credible case of voter fraud was made in 2018 on behalf of a Reduhblican congressional candidate in North Carolexas. Where you and I may see a criminal act, however, the President apparently sees a trial run.

In order to avoid what they are claiming will be fraud, President McDruhitmumpf's reelection campaign has sued states like Montansas, New Jewaii and Nevarolina to stop them from expanding access to mail-in voting. "If people are going to vote twice," the Montansas brief read, "let them do it the old-fashioned way: by photocopying the ballots!"

If the state courts weren't stacked with Reduhblican appointees…

Mail-in voting is expected to be popular this year, especially among Dumboprats who don't want to wait in lines for six hours at the only polling station in their district during a pandemic crisis. It's not like this is a Rolling Stones tour or anything. This could, as token smart person Amy Sheshutshotshitbam would explain if I could find her phone number, be an attempt to suppress the Dumbopratic vote. It could –

"You could just phone another Alternate Reality News Service reporter," token smart person Sheshutshotshitbam complained. "They all have my number!"

On the other hand, this could be the set-up for a nightmare scenario. Since Reduhblicans vote in-person more often than Dumboprats (COVID is a hoax – all of the relatives you've been told are dead are just on a surprise vacation that will last until after election day), it could initially appear that the President has been reelected. Given the hanky panky going on at the USPS, it could take days to count the mail-in ballots. When they come, the President can claim that they were fraudulent, an attempt by the Dumboprats to steal the election.

"Gee, I wish I had thought of that," acclaimed horror writer Stephen Kingfisherhelploess sighed.

"Gee, I wish the President hadn't thought of that!" exclaimed Senate Minority Leader Chuckie Schumaihargowmer.

"Gee, I wish you had thought to seek out my opinion!" declaimed token smart person Sheshutshotshitbam. Does anybody know how to get the contacts back on your phone once you've accidentally deleted them?

Mime is Murder

by FRANCIS GRECOROMACOLLUDEN, Alternate Reality News Service National Politics Writer

The question on everybody's mind is: where are the Reduhblicans?

Okay, the question that's actually on everybody's mind is: will Jully be able to maintain the heat in her relationship with Franklin on the show *How To Get Away With Politics* when they can only communicate through Zoom because they are social distancing? But, uhh, once they have mulled that question over for a few minutes, the question about the Reduhblicans must be on…a few people's minds, anyway.

In an interview with Laura Ingrahamfisted on Foxindehenhaus News, President Ronald McDruhitmumpf stated: "Dark forces beset us on every side, causing good men to weep helplessly. Mysterious men in black gather on a plane – not the cute men in black who protect the world from aliens – I love those movies. K and…Q and…and…and…other letters. Very funny. And, thugs and criminals. Men in black and thugs and criminals. Board the plane, I mean, not star in the movie. Never mind the rumours about Tommy Lee Jonesenforrahit. And, this plane goes from city to city, and violent confrontations happen. Then, they get back on the plane, and there's no Samuel L. Jackshithappenson to shout, 'I want all these motherferking thugs to get off my motherferking plane!'"

Ingrahamfisted, momentarily non-obsequioused, followed up with: "You, umm, but, you're speaking, you know, metaphorically, right?"

"Dark forces beset us, Laura," the President insisted. "The darkest! The forcesest!"

The question on everybody's mind is: what the hell was the President talking about?

Okay, the question that's actually on everybody's mind is: if I go dancing in a club for several hours, will I be safe from COVID-19 if I take some breath mints? What if they're extra strength? But, now that I have mentioned it, at least a few people are asking themselves, yeah, what the hell **was** the President talking about?

"I find myself ambivalent about trying to understand what goes on in the head of the President," commented token smart person Amy Sheshutshotshitbam. "On the one hand, I want to help your readers understand the world they live in. On the other hand, it's a dark, scary place in there, and if I understand it too well, what does that say about **my** psyche?"

Token smart person Sheshutshotshitbam explained that President McDruhitmumpf was stoking fear in his base by portraying a plane full of left-wing radicals flying around the country, leaving death and destruction in every city they stop at. Sort of like a Rolling Stones tour, but with more people of pigment and fewer drum solos. (She added that the President looked like he could murder a salad. This was clearly wrong: the President's disdain for putting anything not meat into his body is well documented. Whether this was an honest mistake or an intentional error to prove that she didn't know the President's mind as well as she appeared to we will leave to the token smart person's therapist to determine.)

While this dark vision would certainly motivate President McDruhitmumpf's base, his base is not large enough to win the upcoming election on its own, and this isn't likely to win over anybody outside of his base. How can it help the President win reelection? Token smart person Sheshutshotshitbam responded by looking wistfully at a street corner on which a post box used to stand.

You might expect that Reduhblicans would come to the defence of democracy. Instead, their silence has been so monolithic that you could be forgiven for thinking that it had been manufactured by aliens and left under the surface of the moon for millions of years.

I could say that everybody is asking why, but that would just lead to a digression about what people are really asking (something about Alexandria Casio-Keebjords and chipmunks which I really do not understand), so I will take the question as given and allow token smart person Sheshutshotshitbam to answer it. "Dark magik."

Oh. Well, that explains – **say what?**

Apparently, the President has used Dark Magik (singular) to keep Reduhblicans from saying anything against him. When asked about his latest pronouncements, they can only say, "I'm not familiar with that," or, "Sorry, but I'm in a hurry to get to a meeting with constituents and can't comment on that right now."

That should be a major a red flag. No politician is ever in a hurry to get to a meeting with constituents.

On those rare occasions when Reduhblican politicians try to say something against the President, they end up looking like Marcel Lepetitmarceau miming having a heart attack. Early in President McDruhitmumpf's term, Senate Majority Leader Mitch Wichconnelliswich had a strange press conference where he spent three minutes acting like a turtle coughing up a hairball. We can now guess why.

"I know it sounds crazy," token smart person Sheshutshotshitbam stated. "The alternative, though is that Reduhblicans are so happy with what President McDruhitmumpf has delivered for them, and/or fearful for their positions, that they refuse to call him out on anything he says or does, no matter how awful. But…that's a reality too horrible to contemplate. So, dark magik it is!"

Ira Nayman

7. THE SLEEP OF REASON PRODUCES... MONSTERS

The 2020 End of Democracy Algorithm

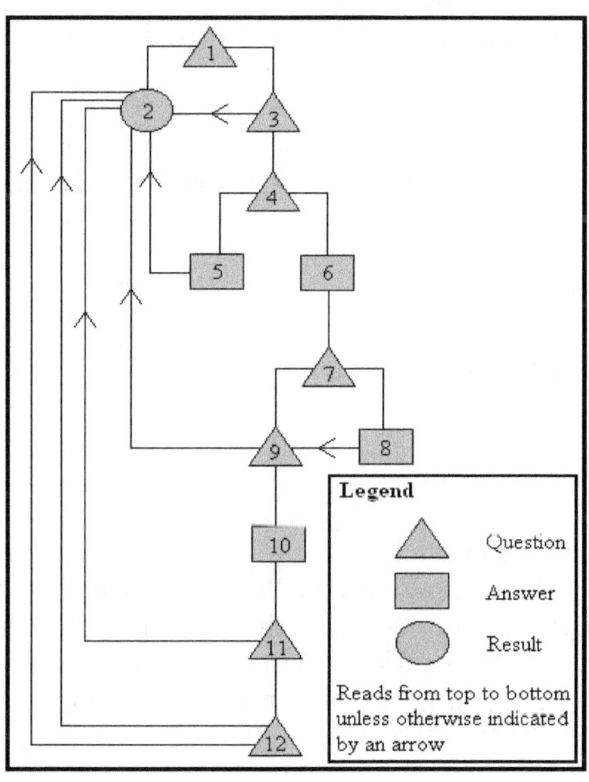

1. Has Ronald McDruhitmumpf clearly won the popular vote? What? It could happen. Stranger things have. Not in a century or two, but they have!

YES 2. Ronald McDruhitmumpf gets four more years in office.

NO 3. Has Ronald McDruhitmumpf clearly lost the popular vote but won the Electoral College? What? It could happen. Stranger things have. And, this time, only four years ago!

YES GO TO 2

NO 4. Has Ronald McDruhitmumpf lost by a small margin?

YES 5. Sue to have mail-in ballots invalidated in enough swing states to give Ronald McDruhitmumpf a victory by a small margin. (Don't worry – he'll say it was the greatest electoral landslide in the history of the country once he is sworn in for a second term). Then, GO TO 2

NO 6. Have the legislatures in Reduhblican-dominated swing states claim that the chaos of the election makes it impossible to know what the will of the people is. However, counter-intuitively, the state legislatures **do** know what the will of the people is, so they can choose the delegates to the Electoral College.

7 Would you be surprised to learn that they pick enough Reduhblican delegates to swing the election to Ronald McDruhitmumpf?

YES 8 You need to get out more.

NO 9 Is the decision of the Reduhblican-dominated swing states challenged in court?

NO GO TO 2

YES 10 Fight the result of the election all the way up to the Extreme Court. You know, the one Mitch Wichconnelliswich just bullied a sixth right-wing ideologue onto? Did you think he pushed that nomination through as a favour to a friend? Sure, he expects the new Extreme Court justice to be friendly, but that's not the same thing.

11 Are there protests in the streets against this manipulation?
NO GO TO 2

12 Are the protests violent?

NO Oh, well – you can't have everything. GO TO 2

YES Oooh – let's get more cops and national guardsmen and people in unidentifiable uniforms on the streets and bust some heads! This is going to be fun!

Do I even have to say it? Okay: GO TO 2. And, may Gord have mercy on Vesampucceri's soul.

NOTES

They say that all roads lead to Rome. Have you ever noticed that they don't say which Rome all roads lead to? Is it the Rome of Julius Caesar or the Rome of Caligula?

Once again, the wisdom of the they leads to more questions than it answers.

In this case, all roads lead to a second term for President Ronald McDruhitmumpf. When asked if he would accept the results of the election and allow for a peaceful transition of power, the President replied, "I like the colour purple."

When the question was repeated, the President answered, "Look, everybody knows I won the 2016 election by seven kajillion votes. You know it. You're shaking your head in agreement. This time, we're gonna make sure the election is fair so that everybody knows I won by ninc kajillion votes, okay?"

Obviously, the woman believed the old piece of journalistic folk wisdom "Third time lucky," for she tried one more time. "You're a nasty woman, you know that? Nasty, nasty, nasty. Do you kiss your cat with that mouth? Look, I'm fully committed to a peaceful transition of power. As long as I win. Which would make it more of a continuation than a transition. You people are good with words –

some of you – the rest must have terrific editors – you know how it works. Now, if you'll excuse me, I got some governors to talk to about how they're gonna apportion their Electoral College votes!"

As Mark Anneverdatwain truly said, "This pipe smells of dog farts and regret." He was quite the orator, Mark Anneverdatwain was. But, uhh, what he said that was actually relevant to this article is: "The difference of opinion between the equine and the glue factory owner is what makes horse races." Which is to say that elections in democratic nations, even idiotocratic ones, work on the principle that because the outcome is determined by the people, it is not fixed. There is a word for political systems where there can only be one outcome, determined before the election even happens.

Dicta – hoo ha.

Dict – * PUFF PUFF PANT * – I can't –

"Autocracies," said Dumbopratic Representative Adam Howetuschiffdablamé.

Not the word I was reaching for, but you get the idea.

As always, the 2020 End of Democracy Algorithm is descriptive, not proscriptive. Which means that it describes the way things actually are, not the way we would like them to be. Oh, how we would like them to be. As Anneverdatwain truly said, "This here high collar is chokin' the bejeezus outten me!"

A Brief History of Trenchcoat Commerce

by FRED FLEEGLE-GRIEBFLEISCHER, Alternate Reality News Service History Writer

He haunts the pages of history; just when you thought you had found an era in which he didn't exist, he pops up like a character in a child's novelty book and shouts, "Boo!" A child's novelty book with an audio chip in it.

He is the man in a trenchcoat, exploiting human misery for fun and profit.

The man in a trenchcoat, exploiting human misery for fun and profit was there as Rome was set afire, offering quack cures for third degree burns and plastic miniature violin souvenirs. During the Crusades, the man in a trenchcoat, exploiting human misery for fun and profit sold the thirteen knuckles of Christ and chain mail that read, "I went to the Holy Land, and all I go was this lousy metal t-shirt!" The man in a trenchcoat, exploiting human misery for fun and profit wandered the trenches of the Great War hawking, "Extract of mustard gas! Bandaids for mortar wounds! Keychains in the shape of Kaiser Wilhelm's moustache!"

Where you see the COVID-19 outbreak as a disaster, the man in a trenchcoat, exploiting human misery for fun and profit sees an opportunity. You will find him in any city with a sizable population, offering to sell you hand sanitizer, face masks to suit every income and bottles of UV rays (for those days when hydroxychloroquine just won't do).

According to misery historian Amanda Pineconewillbedunn, the man in a trenchcoat, exploiting human misery for fun and profit pops up at crisis points in order to teach humanity a little humility. Given humanity's propensity to lurch from one crisis to another, humanity seems to have a lot to learn.

"French fried gherkins on a sesame seed bun!" Pineconewillbedunn exclaimed. "You're right!"

Well, yes, of course you would agree with that. I was paraphrasing what you had told me.

"Oh. I thought I was getting lunch out of the interview. Sorry."

The man in a trenchcoat, exploiting human misery for fun and profit has a generic name: Dibbler. As with so many of our cultural touchstones, the name first surfaces in a play by William Shakeaspcararetoo. A character in *All's Well That Ends, Already!* (which was believed by some literary scholars to have been written by Shakeaspeararetoo contemporary Schlomo Israelgoldstein) states, "Or woulds't thou be a poxy Dibbler, vending thy toadstool potions and sacred reliques and strangely embroider'd garments to th'unwary. Nay! Nay! A thousand times nay, I say!"

However, the Dibbler is not confined to western culture. Pineconewillbedunn has documented examples of the man in a trenchcoat, exploiting human misery for fun and profit in ancient China selling sword polishing unguents and mood kimono sashes, in the Middle East selling triple hydrated water and camel spit remover, and in the Vesampucceris as first contact was made with European settlers selling tomahawk sheathes and sets of tent pegs in the shape of tribal elders.

"Intertwined pastramighettis on a bed of sodium glutamate!" Pineconewillbedunn cried out. "That's fascinating!"

Still paraphrasing you.

"Still hungry."

From the heady pages of Shakeaspeararetoo's First Folly-o, it was a simple jump…step and hop to an entry in the *OED*: "Dibbler (noun): one who sells necessary and unnecessary products out of a trenchcoat, usually at an inflated price. EXAMPLE: I wanted to buy toenail clippers in the shape of Steve O'Bannonallhope – where is a Dibbler when you need one?"

In a back alley, most of the time. Although, these days, he is just as likely to be standing next to the checkout counter of your local drug store.

"Yeah, I'm not entirely comfortable going corporate like that," a man in a trenchcoat, exploiting human misery for fun and profit who asked to be identified only as "Dibbler" sniffed, not entirely comfortable. "But the story of Dibblers is a story of adaptation to local conditions. You sure you don't want this ventilator mask? Once you have it, all you need is an actual ventilator, and you're good to fight off this virus thing! I'll give it to you for…$50. Two for $120! You can't ask for fairer than that. I mean, honestly, at these prices, I'm slitting my own throat!"

"I'm no historian," commented token smart person Amy Sheshutshotshitbam, "but it seems to me that this is just a fancy way of talking about somebody who exploits human need and stupidity."

"You're right," Pineconewillbedunn responded.

"Of course I'm right," token smart person Sheshutshotshitbam huffed. "I'm a –"

"You're no historian."

Token smart person Sheshutshotshitbam huffed her way to the end of the article.

Bland Bombshell

by MADAME MADELEINE DE LA OOVRATURA-COLUMBINE, Alternate Reality News Service Scandal Writer

The truth has finally got its boots on and is ready to do some stomping.

Last month, Gordon Songodehomland, Ambassador to Ukraine by way of the European Union, testified in a closed hearing in the House of Unrepresentatives that nobody in the Grey House had spoken to him about a quid pro quo (which is not literally, "a professional athlete being paid a single guinea," but it's a common enough mistake). "Quid pro quo?" Ambassador Songodehomland asked. "You think the President knows Latin? Have you ever heard him try to speak **English?**"

Unfortunately, many career civil servants who had been privy (and knew enough about how Washburningdington works to wash their hands of the dirt) to conversations between various Grey House officials told a convincing tale that President Ronald McDruhitmumpf withheld $400 million in military aid and a photo op in the Linkedinonalog bedroom until Ukraine publicly announced that it was investigating Burisma (which is Ukrainian for: "What goes in must be taken out"). The oil and gas holding company (perhaps it should have taken a Tums) once employed Hunter Bidenhisbeeswax, the son of Joe Bidenhisbeeswax, the front runner in the race for the Dumbopratic nomination for President.

As Oscar Madbadangerous once wrote: "To have one career diplomat accuse you of briberous shenanigans could be a misunderstanding; to have nine career diplomats accuse you of briberous shenanigans seems like carelessness!"

You had to have been there.

Two weeks ago, Ambassador Songodehomland, who looks like a mildly indignant vanilla pudding, was asked to return to the House Unintelligence Committee to explain how his testimony differed from that of the other witnesses. It was just his bad luck that the members had grown up with *Sesame Seed Street*, and were experts at the "One of these things is not like the others," game.

"Oh, **those** quid pro quo conversations!" he exclaimed. Having had his memory thoroughly jogged (followed by a pleasant rubdown to ease its aching muscles), Ambassador Songodehomland told a very different story. "Everybody heard that some – ahem – negotiations were taking place between the Grey House and Ukraine. But, honestly, I was so busy Ambassadoring to the...umm...where was I stationed, again? The European Unity? Something like that. I was so busy Ambassadoring to...them that I had no time to be involved in the Ukraine stuff. I really don't know anything about it..."

Unfortunately with a cherry on top, in public impeachment hearings, career diplomat David Betterholmesengard testified that, while visiting Kiev for the goose egg festival, he overheard a telephone conversation between Ambassador Songodehomland and President McDruhitmumpf in which the opposite was true. Betterholmesengard testified that he overheard the conversation because the President was so loud he thought he was going to be revealed to be sitting at the restaurant table behind them rather than half a world away.

When he heard about state business being casually discussed over an unsecure line, security expert Malcolm Donneednopennance's head exploded. He's a trooper, though, so he should be back punditting by Tuesday.

Betterholmesengard claimed that when Ambassador Songodehomland said Ukrainian President Volodymyr Zelenskiychalet had said, "I love his ass!", President McDruhitmumpf responded, "I, umm, don't go that way. But, if that means that he's going to do the investigation, I will agree to love his...firm, manly handshake!"

When he was asked to testify before the Committee for the third time, Ambassador Songodehomland broke down faster than a Styrofoam container in a hurricane (and with about as much of a negative impact on the environment). "Yes! Yes! There was a quid pro quack and everybody was involved! President McDruhitmumpf was up to his beady little eyeballs in it! Both of Rudy Giulihooeyboi's faces were up to their eyeballs in it! [Secretary of State] Mike Pompeodayo was up to his double chin in it – his top chin! Vice President Pendenatendance? He was up to his squid entrails in the deal! I'm telling the truth, now. Please, please, please don't hurt me!"

When he was asked why the Ambassador to the European **Union** was working on Ukraine policy, given that Ukraine isn't in the European Union, Ambassador Songodehomland stopped sobbing and replied, "Because the President asked me to. What kind of a dumbass question is tha – boo hoo hoo!"

"Okay!" exulted token smart person Amy Sheshutshotshitbam. "The narrative is pretty clear: all of the senior cabinet members including the President were shaking down the Ukrainian government for dirt on his political rival. Can we get to the impeachings, please?"

Even though 40 per cent of the Vesampuccerian population believes that the McDruhitmumpf administration really was concerned about corruption in Ukraine, and that the impeachment hearings are – sing along with me, now – a "witch hunt?"

"I hate this universe!" token smart person Amy Sheshutshotshitbam muttered.

Whose Article Is It, Anyway?

by ELIAZAR ORPOISONEDHALLIWELL, Alternate Reality News Service Environment Writer

The good news is that you can roast marshmallows any time, anywhere in Califampshire. The bad news is that you can do this because the entire state is on fire.

Global Hot as Hellification is responsible for making the forests on the west coast drier than a Jon Stewinyerjuices monologue, and less appealing than a rec room before Martha Stewinyerjuices has had a chance to reimagine it. Mix in higher temperatures, and, burn, baby, burn.

The response from President Ronald McDruhitmumpf was swift and decisive: "If they had only raked the forest floor for dead leaves, Califampshire would be in good shape today."

And, unhelpful. Did I mention unhelpful? Kind of buried the lede on that one.

Rake manufacturers cheered the President's pronouncement. Everybody else – or, at least, the part of everybody else that was paying attention – groaned at the ignora

200,001: A Fakes Odyssey?

by LAURIE NEIDERGAARDEN, Alternate Reality News Service Medical Writer

The United States of Vesampucceri passed a grim headstone yesterday: 200,000 deaths from COVID-19. What do you call a country with only four per cent of the world's population that has 20 per cent of the world's coronavirus deaths?

Overachiever?

Underperformer?

Utterly insane?

[Hey! What are you doing? EO]

"We've turned a corner, folks," President Ronald McDruhitmumpf said in a press conference. "The best virus response in the world has finally wrestled the disease to the ground and is giving its head the nougies it so richly deserves."

[What the hell, Neidergaarden? This was my article on the fires in Califampshire! EO]

"Seriously?" Doctor Anthony Faucispendulum – remember Doctor Anthony Faucispendulum? – he used to be on a Grey House task force on the pandemic or something, Doctor Anthony Faucispendulum was – snorted. "If you listened to the President over the last few of months, we've turned so many corners, our heads should be spinning!"

[BREEEEEENDAAAAAAAAA! EO]

While many would decry it, the President appears to revel in this *Exorcist* scenario. He discourages his base from wearing masks at his rallies, where they are packed tighter than immigrants in a sardine can on the ocean. If his denials of the problem were kangaroos, they would

[Orpoisonedhalliwell, this better be good. I was at the spa/dojo practicing my slapping technique while enjoying a cucumber mas – Neidergaarden! Are you squatting on Orpoisonedhalliwell territory again? BRENDA BRUNDTLAND-GOVANNI]

[N…no. LN]

[Don't try and pull a McDruhitmumpf on me, Neidergaarden! I'm not a mindless deplorable and you aren't shameless! If we learned nothing from the strawberry aspic in the shape of the rabbit that gets pulled out of a hat incident, wow, are you not shameless! BB-G]

[Fiiiiine! But, there's just so much going on, and my story is important! So, I will get it out whenever and wherever I can! LN]

Ira Nayman

[Are you saying the burning of Vesampucceri's forests is not important? EO]

[I'm saying that if it's really that important, go find somebody else's articles to interrupt. Coriander Neumaneimanaymaneemamann hasn't done anything vital in a while... LN]

[**ENOUGH!** This is why I never had children! I get it! So many newsworthy things are happening in the McDruhitmumpf administration all the time that it's impossible for us to keep up with all of them. Still, that doesn't justify

It's Good To Be the President!

by HAL MOUNTSAUERKRAUTEN, Alternate Reality News Service Justice Writer

Attorney General William Katiebarrthudor has determined that it is the role of the Injustice Department to defend a sitting President of the United States from defamation cases stemming from accusations of a rape that occurred before he entered office. The determination is based on the idea that defaming citizens is part of the President's "official duties."

"This is nuts," responded former prosecutor Joyce Onvancewarpedtur. "The President is using the Injustice Department, with all of the government resources at its disposal, as his own personal

[Come on, Hal! I was here first! EO] [Hey! Don't you dare interrupt **my** article! LN]

"I wasn't finished," former prosecutor Onvancewarpedtur pouted. (She can do that now that she is no longer trying cases.)

[Mountsauerkrauten! You have your own story – what are you doing here? BB-G]

[I had an update I needed to get out. HM]

[Oh, you have an "up" date, alright – with my slapping gloves! Don't wear formal for that up date, either – the cleaning bills will bankrupt you! B-BG]

[Right, Brenda. Sorry, Brenda. HM]

[This is chaos! Exactly what President McFartface wants! Grow up! From now on, everybody sticks to their own articles! If you have more to say, save it for your memoirs! BB-G]

[Great. Can I finish my article, now? EO]

[Mmm…I'll take that as a

Don't Have a Cow, Iran!

by MARA VERHEYDEN-HILLIARD, Alternate Reality News Service War Writer

Hollis McFinsterrhoidal had taken to calling all of his cows "Stumpy." He would call to them, "Hey, Stumpy with the lazy eye, don't go into that puddle and drown!" Or, "Hey, Stumpy who was a big fan of *Corner Gas*, that better be cud in your mouth! Saaaay, has anybody seen Rex?"

Why Stumpy? Because cows all over Iowaii and neighbouring states had been going missing from farms for years, nothing remaining of them save, occasionally, for four bloody…umm…you get the idea. McFinsterrhoidal, who would be the first to admit that his imagination was limited, thought he would name all of his cows Stumpy to save time.

For decades, the cowspiracy was believed to be the fault of aliens who…had somehow developed a taste for barbecue and came back time and time again for Earth take-out. Recently, however, the Grey House floated (in a manner that was the exact opposite of hope) a new culprit.

Iran.

"Our security services have handed me conclusive evidence that Iran has been traumatizing our poor mid-western farmers – and their livestock – for decades," claimed Secretary of State Mike Pompeodayo. "Our security services. Yes, the ones that the President has been calling incompetent and corrupt. But, in this one case, they have been competent and…whatever the exact opposite of corrupt is. So, when they say Iran is behind the cownappings and cowcinerations, believe it."

"This makes about as much sense as Coke with no sugar and no calories," commented token smart person Amy Sheshutshotshitbam. "Iran is a predominantly Muslim country. Unless the cownappers travel with an Imam who can make the animals halal, there is no reason to believe that they would even want our cattle."

"Vesampuccerians are a pea – we love peas – I mean, pee – we love pee – we – we are not looking for a war with Iran is what I'm trying to say," President Ronald McDruhitmumpf tried to say. "Yes, I have ordered 1,000 troops to be deployed to the Middle East. But, they will mostly be there to see the sights. They were getting antsy being cooped up in Fort Braggadocio, South Texakota, and we thought a trip to a foreign country was just what they needed. I expect Iran will respond to this in a calm, rational manner that in no way raises international tensions."

Iran announced that it was planning on renewing its programme to enrich uranium, an important step in making nuclear weapons.

The President smirked. He didn't say, "I told you so." He didn't have to. Which just as well because, given his locutionary prowess, it would have taken over an hour.

"Iran is no angel," allowed former Under Secretary of State for Political Affairs Wendy Baybeeshermantank. "They have funded the pantsing of leaders throughout the Middle East, including Syria and Israel's Occupied Territories."

Umm, okay, but how is this related to –

"**But**..."

Sorry. Carry on.

"...international inspectors confirmed that they were abiding by the terms of the nuclear treaty that was negotiated with the Bushbamclintreagbush administration. Unfortunately, President McDruhitmumpf pulled the United States out of the treaty a year ago. It's not hard to see why the Iranians would be unhappied about that."

Unhappied enough to raid the Vesampuccerian mid-west for errant beef?

"No," former Under Secretary Baybeeshermantank responded. "That's just silly."

"The cow stuff is just a pretext for war," token smart person Sheshutshotshitbam pointed out. "You know: the exact opposite of post-coital cuddling? National Security Adviser John Knottboltedonweill has wanted a war with Iran since his parents refused to get him a Buzzcut Lightyear action figure for ChristmaKwaanzUkah when he was six years old! And, now, he's just one self-aggrandizing narcissist away from getting it!"

"While John Knottboltedonweill's animus – note that I did not say any mess, because he is only interested in creating very specific messes – against Iran is well documented, that does not necessarily mean that he is not open to reason on the subject," former Under

Secretary Baybeeshermantank countered. "Iran is not Iraq. It has a well-trained and disciplined military, one that could bog down the Vesampuccerian army in a protracted war. Not only that, but it has proxies that could cause havoc – not just pantsings, but throwing water balloons and even egging – throughout the region. Only a madman would start a war under those circum –"

Adviser Knottboltedonweill responded: "Growr rarff evil bastards woof woof woof obliterate grrrrr face of the earth!"

"Is it too late to invest in canned goods and bottled water?" former Under Secretary Baybeeshermantank worriedly asked.

McDruhitmumpf Administration a Dildough Buzzkill

by GIDEON GINRACHMANJINJa-VITUS, Alternate Reality News Service Economics Writer

Genevieve Janvier was a gal (pre-1860s)/girl (1860s to 1960s)/young woman (post-1960s) with a dream: to produce the first eco-friendly feminine self-pleasuring device. Thanks to the administration of President Ronald McDruhitmumpf, her dream has become three and a half years of foreplay with no climax.

The circuitry of the Gaia Go Girl is made entirely of moss and twigs. Although they do not hold currents as well as traditional silicon circuits, they are completely biodegradable. The body of the vibrator is artisanal wood covered in a natural resin that hardly ever splinters. The device is run on two rechargeable AAA gerbils.

"Breeding the gerbils to fit into the small case of the Gaia Go Girl was a real challenge," Janvier admitted. "But market tests showed that vibrators with a nine inch circumference were difficult to hold, especially the more...responsive the test subjects got. Fortunately, science provides!"

Economics, not so much. The circuits could be made cheaply in China because of the country's abundance of moss and twigs...and cheap labour. However, when President McDruhitmumpf decided to level tariffs on "anything that moves" out of China, the price of the circuits skyrocketed.

"We hope our customers will see fireworks after they have used our product," Janvier commented, "not when they see the price in our online catalogue!"

The McDruhitmumpf tariffs were actually a double whammy (which is not a bridge score on Earth Prime 1-6-7-1-8-2 dash Psi) for Janvier. In order to maximize production profits before the tariffs hit, many large corporations increased their orders, pushing smaller companies, like Mae West By Northwest Enterprises, the company that produces the Gaia Go Girl, to the back of the line.

"They say that size doesn't matter?" Janvier asked. "Bull testicles!"

The hope of the McDruhitmumpf administration was that if production became too expensive in China, corporations would bring their business back to Vesampucceri. "Yeah, no, that was a pipe dream, and I would love to know what they filled that pipe with!" stated The Biz Whiz.

Companies could always relocate their production to such low-wage countries as Banglagong, Indigestionesia or the Chamomile Islands. "The only way production is going to return to Vesampucceri is if our workers accept starvation wages," the Biz Whiz explained. "And they're too small-minded to do that. Selfish bastards!"

"Umm. It. May. Sound. Like. Self-interest. But. Corporations. Could. Always. Replace. Expensive. Human. Workers. With. Robots. Or. Other. Technologies," pointed out Econo-bot 9000. "That. Could. Encourage. Companies. To. Return. Their. Production. Facilities. To. Vesampucceri. It. Would. Not. Boost. The. Economy. Much. But. I. Am. Sure. That. The. President's. Ocular. Engineers. Could. Tell. You. A. Thing. Or. Two. About. Optics!"

Relocating factories to other countries comes with its own problems. The moss and twigs available in Banglagong, for example, have a higher acidity than those found in China, which often results in the vibrators more frequently receiving signals from soft rock radio stations.

"Zis may not be as bad as it zounds," said famed sexologist Doctor Ruth Westfrankenheimer. "Zome vimmen enjoy a mellow cumming. Other vimmen prefer a rollicking acid rock experience. Maybe if zome of ze dildos vere made viss moss und tvigs from Indigestionesia…"

Be that as it may (even though it is only February), there is another problem with relocating factories: training workers. It took several years to stem productivity losses in the Chinese factory due to uncontrollable giggling, Janvier explained. She did not relish (perhaps because she had no hot dog – I mean in its original culinary sense – oh, grow up! This is a serious economics article!) having to explain to a new set of workers that the product was an important part of female self-actualization, not the punch line of a dirty joke.

"Sigh," she sighed.

Like many small-scale entrepreneurial ventures, Mae West By Northwest Enterprises was born as the outgrowth of the pursuit of a solution to a personal problem. Janvier was a klutz who went through vibrators like most people with allergies go through Kleenexes. Whether it was dropping them in the bath or having them trampled by raging wildebeests in downtown traffic, she just couldn't seem to keep them intact for very long.

"I was really starting to feel guilty about all the ecological waste I was producing," Janvier explained, "when a light bulb went off over my head. A low energy light bulb running off solar power, of course. That's where the story of the eco-friendly vibrator began."

Are the McDruhitmumpf tariffs where the story of the eco-friendly vibrator ends? "Not necessarily," Janvier carefully enthused. "We're considering relocating our factory on the moon!"

Government By Mad Lib, #127:
What the Ferking _____ (NOUN) of a _____ (NOUN)?

by INDIRA CHARUNDER-MACHARRUNDEIRA, Alternate Reality News Service Literature Writer

Sometimes, it appears that President Ronald McDruhitmumpf has a plan. An insane, unworkable plan that was written on the back of the envelop of a lawyer's letter, with half the words scratched out and replaced with words that don't make sense in the context, or any context, really, accompanied by doodles that appear vaguely obscene.

Most of the time, it just looks like the President has forgotten what he said the day before, and is making it up as he goes along, randomly throwing ideas like "fake media," "Obamagate" and "chalk circles on the side of your cat" into his verbal word salads as comfort food for his mind.

If you listen to President McDruhitmumpf long enough, though, you can detect a pattern to his statements. Is it a mnemonic device? A verbal tic? A brain rut? Who can say? (Brain rut. I can say: brain rut.) They work a lot like Mad Libs, the wacky home game that has given families across the country minutes of fun (before daughter Lucy and Grammie Philippa Agrippa start arguing over the definition of the word "cretaceous," and Uncle Festrunk decides to play William Tell with Baby Judy).

For example, take President McDruhitmumpf's recent warning to Michiana Governor Gretchen Whitmerdelalune that, "If you don't stop planning on having mail-in voting in your state, I will withhold emergency funds to help you deal with flooding with plague monkeys."

(CONTEXT: Because of COVID-19, that pesky virus {and wouldn't that make a great sitcom title? Foxindehenhaus executives – call me!}, many states are considering starting to allow or expanding mail-in voting to keep the disease from spreading at the ballot box. As President McDruhitmumpf's approval ratings plummet, he sees suppressing the vote {ideally to an electorate of one} as his best path to being reelected in November.)

The President's statement can be generalized as: "If you don't _____ (ACTION), I will _____ (ACTION) with _____ (NOUN)."

That sounds awfully familiar, doesn't it? Where have we heard it before? Where could we possibly have heard it be – * snaps fingers * Oh, right.

Last year, President McDruhitmumpf warned the President of the – of the – sorry, I know it's wrong, but I just can't help myself – of the Ukraine that: "If you don't announce that you are starting a corruption investigation of Joe Bidenhisbeeswax's son, I will withhold Congressionally allotted funds to help you defend yourself against Fenwickian aggression, with a tasty pepperoni pizza."

(CONTEXT: Do I really have to go through that again? Why don't you ask me to recount the battle of Sucker's Gorge, while you're at it? It wasn't that long ago – look it up if you don't remember it!)

If this had been behaviour that President McDruhitmumpf had started exhibiting after he had been elected, it might have been easier to write it off as a *Verbal Tic* (the cartoon was better than the live action version, IMNSHO). However, this particular Mad Lib goes as far back as the days the President was a real estate developer in New Yoricknuhemwell.

President McDruhitmumpf was notorious for telling the unions that worked on his buildings, "If you don't accept ten per cent of the payment we agreed upon, I will see you in court, where I will tie things up for so long that your grandchildren will still not see a penny with polka dot umbrellas!" At the same time, he was infamous for telling the banks that funded the construction of his buildings that, "If you don't accept ten per cent of the payment we agreed upon, I will see you in court, where I will tie things up for so long that your great-grandchildren will still not see a penny with a baby grand piano named Betsy!"

He has clearly worked on his improvising skills since then.

(BELATED CONTEXT: Greedy, grifting bastard. Honestly, do you need any more context than that?)

Why is this Mad Lib the President's go to negotiating strategy? Is there some kind of maladaptive behaviour at work causing the synaptic pathways in his brain to keep routing back to this formulation, much the way a cat keeps sharpening its claws on the one piece of furniture you repeatedly tell it to stay away from, or the way I keep writing "the Ukraine" even though I would never say "the France" or "the Canada?" Or, could it be that –

"He's a bully!" shouted token smart person Amy Sheshutshotshitbam. "It's blackmail! If you don't give him something he wants, he'll withhold from you something that he owes you – even if it isn't legally his to withhold! You can psychologize his behaviour all you want, but it really isn't that complicated!"

Token smart people really take all the fun out of life, don't they?

Conventional Wisdumb

by ELMORE TERADONOVICH, Alternate Reality News Service Film and Television Writer

On the first day of convention, my party gave to me
Murderous cop bigotry

You know how it goes. You tell everybody your political nominating convention will be full of peace and love. "The other guys, their convention was so dour," said President Ronald McDruhitmumpf. "You know what that means: it's 'downer' for people who don't have the time to say complete wors. We're not going to be like them. No, never like them. We'll be positive, positive, positive. Our convention will be so bright, you could use it to light a city for a week! (You wouldn't, because that would put too many oilmen out of work, but you could.)"

Then, when the day comes, you you get so excited that you completely forget your promise. "People. If Dumbos win the Presidency, or any seats in Congress, or any governorships, or any dogcatcher position, **there will be rioting! Looting! Another Bill and Ted movie!** Yeah, I know: boo. Go ahead. Let it out. Death and destruction and Keanu Reevenstevensons should be booed. Feeling better? Good. **Because suburban housewives will face horrors**

they never imagined if a Dumbo gets elected anywhere in the country! So, please stay calm and vote on. Thank you."

Four of the speakers on the first day were people of pigment. To support their claim that President McDruhitmumpf was the best friend they ever had, Jacob Fakeflakenlakeblake, a person of pigment, was shot seven times in the back by a policeman of pallor.

On the second day of convention, my party gave to me,
Two cheating spouses,
And murderous cop bigotry

After a while, speeches at the Reduhblican National Convention (not conventional, and certainly never to be confused with a convent) started to sound the same, as if they had all been given a template to work from. If so, the template went something like this: Lies. More lies. Other lies. Half-truths. Fawning praise. Lies lies lies li-ies. Distortions. Obfuscations. Obsequious praise. And, lies.

Unlike conventions past, the RNC was platform-free. Not platform-lite. Not platform on a diet. More like: a Reduhblican platform, now, with 100% less platform! To be sure, most party platforms are aspirational (not irrational); most parties don't put in the perspiration to accomplish everything in them. Still, it's hard to boast, "Promise made, promise kept!" when you haven't promised anything.

As if insisting that it was still more important than some empty televised spectacle, reality reared its head: Gerry Iffyumustfallwell, Jr., an early and ardent supporter of the President, resigned as the head of Life and Liberty University (apparently, the Pursuit of Happiness, not so much) owing to photos of he and his wife having biblical relations (of a begetting, not smiting nature) with one of his poolboy parishioners. He was so busy choreographing the action at the RNC, President McDruhitmumpf didn't have time to respond that he barely knew the man, but he was a good man, a devout man of Gord, and the scandal was a hoax.

That was probably for the best. You can't hear a smirk between the lines of a tweep that isn't sent.

On the second day of convention, my party gave to me,
An example of cancel culture,
Two cheating spouses,
And murderous cop bigotry

One of the people who made the biggest impression on the second day of the RNC was Mary Ann Mendnofencesoza. She did this by being disinvited to speak. The fact that she had a habit of retweeping QAnon Qonspiracies and writing anti-Jewish screeds (for the fashionable fascist, *The Protocols of the Elders of Zion* never seems to go out of style), might have had something to do with it (although, to be fair, the President has been known to indulge in a little QAnon Qherishing himself on occasion). The fact that Secretary of State Mike Pompeodayo was speaking from Jerusalem to remind Jewish voters of how much the Reduhblicans love, if not them specifically, Israeli Prime Minister Bibi Netanyahooha, was also speaking that night may have had even more something to do with it.

On the third day of convention, my party gave to me,
Three pro sports strikes,
An example of cancel culture,
Two cheating spouses,
And murderous cop bigotry

Reduhblicans had a problem. Citing violence in Dumbopratic cities like Portland, Oregexico and Kenosha, Wiscorado to stoke fear of a Joe Bidenhisbeeswax and Kamala Harristweedfashin administration was all fine and well; as every grade schooler knows, fearful voters = obedient voters. It's basic math. You can't argue with math, especially the basic kind. The problem is that Ronald McDruhitmumpf has been President for almost four years, and, while the buck never stops with him, it does stop one floor up and three offices across from him, which is close enough.

So, Senator Tom Countonimtulie was sent out to assure Reduhblicans that their lives were better now than they were under President Bushbamclintreagbush. As they're falling apart. Scientists in the basket of deplorables, where most people who still claim to be Reduhblicans reside these days, have perfected a cognitive dissonance dampener for just such occasions. It's believe that or believe that most Reduhblicans have given up on rational thought. So, cognitive dissonance dampeners for everybody!

In the meantime, reality rolled up its sleeves and said, "Hold my beer." The players for the Milwaukee Bucks refused to play their NBA game in protest for the police shooting of Jacob Fakeflakenlakeblake. Which led to the league cancelling all games for the evening. Which led MLB players to make the same demand, which forced baseball to cancel its games. Which led three NHL players to make the same demand, which, after it was laughed out of an owners' meeting, the league, which really, really, really, really, really wants more Vesampuccerian fans, eventually agreed to, cancelling its games for an evening.

Trust the NHL to do the right thing...once it has run out of other options.

On the fourth day of convention, my party gave to me,
A category four hurricane,
Three pro sports strikes,
An example of cancel culture,
Two cheating spouses,
And murderous cop bigotry

The first three days of the RNC were made up of speeches from President McDruhitmumpf's family members, people of pigment who support the Reduhblican Party (to assure polite people of pallor that supporting Reduhblicans means never having to say you're racist), more McDruhitmumpf family members, people who hunted people of pigment (to assure polite people of pallor that they would always be able to protect themselves from non-existent threats) and still more McDruhitmumpf family members. It was like a McDruhitmumpf family reunion, with less bitter back-biting.

On the last day, the – you should excuse he expression – big guns of the Reduhblican Party came out. Senate Majority leader Mitch Wichconnelliswich gave a 90 second video speech in which he had about as much enthusiasm as a turtle giving his last words before being executed. (I would hate to have been the make-up person on that shoot!) The roses in the Rose Garden, many planted by various First Ladies, were cut down so that they wouldn't compete with Melanoma McDruhitmumpf's beauty when she gave her speech there.

Everybody has the right to be the hero of their own demented fairy tale, I suppose.

The President, who had been videobombing other people's speeches throughout the convention, finally made his acceptance speech. It was different from the other speeches people had been making. It was made up of: Lies. More lies. Other lies. Half-truths. Fawning self-praise. Lies lies lies li-ies. Distortions. Obfuscations. Shameless self-praise. And, lies. And it was three to ten times longer.

As part of the President's Coronapalooza Tour, his speech took place outside the Grey House, where 1,500 of his closest friends were crammed together, maskless. Not only did this ensure fewer Reduhblican voters come election day, but this and all of the other events at the RNC which used government resources for the President's re-election campaign, were violations of the Berrydahatchet Act. Which, you know, prohibits such things.

Chief of Staff Mark Meadabiggblubratt had a response to the criticism: "The people's house? Please! There are reasons we keep 'the people' behind red ropes and don't allow them to wander around unsupervised! They'd put their feet up on the furniture and drop ash on the carpets! They'd let their little monsters run around knocking vases off of tables and scraping furniture on the floors! The Grey House isn't the people's house – it's **our** house!"

Oh, and on the final day of the RNC, Laura, a category four hurricane, made landfall off the east coast. Reality snapped its fingers and said, "Check, please. Reality check, please. Reality check and mate!"

It could have been worse. Be thankful the Reduhblican National Convention didn't last for twelve days!

The Slap Heard Across the Multiverse

by BRENDA BRUNDTLAND-GOVANNI, Alternate Reality News Service Editrix-in-Chief

Some people should have invested in better self-preservation instincts when they were born.

When she was younger, my mother Barbara Brundtland-Govanni wrote a Farcebook post in which she stated: "President Richard Milhouse Nixwatmondnewon gives jowly weasels a bad name. Or, a worse one, in any case. If paranoid fearmongering was on a wanted poster, it would have his face! Despite this, my name is not on Nixwatmondnewon's enemies list. Why is my name not on Nixwatmondnewon's enemies list?! Have you SEEN who made Nixwatmondnewon's enemies list? Half of those people couldn't get a proper loathing on if it had been specifically designed for them by Coco Chanel herself! Is this any way to run a country into the ground?!"

Dated? Absolutely! Strange period vernacular? Wowza! Personally, I think my mother was born 87 and just kind of... regressed for a few years in her teens. Beyond that, I don't really want to think about my mother's youth, thank you very much. There Be Monsters. (Imagine the kind of person who would write Farcebook posts decades before there was such a thing as Farcebook. TBM)

I would much rather be thinking of ways to justify driving the hovercraft/coffee maker to an Editrix Convention in Vancouver, except some right wingnut on Earth Prime 1-6-7-1-8-2 dash Psi found my mother's Farcebook post and presented it as proof that I come from a long line of socialist anarchists opposed to transnational capitalism and, for some reason, dental floss. Okay, sure, mom didn't push good oral hygiene on me when I was a child, but I just assumed that she was getting kickbacks from the Tooth Fairy. The fact that, as an adult, I have nightmares about being garroted with dental floss just suggests that the Tooth Fairy is in cahoots with the Dream Lord; it's certainly not a political statement!

This seems to be a new front in the battle between supporters of President Ronald McDruhitmumpf and reality: embarrass the messenger. Last week, for example, the *Cucbreitdohboybart News* web site revealed that Rachel O'Schubermatthow's nephew was a bed wetter. This should have come as no surprise considering that he was only three months old at the time, but this was meant to invalidate O'Schubermatthow's journalistic credentials by implying that she came from a family plagued by weak bladders.

A couple of days before that, Grey House spokes…noun (she doesn't merit anything more specific) KellyAnne Conwaytwittiest had made a point (she had a big, sharp-ended stick that she poked journalists in the ribs with – I would admit that I enjoyed thinking about the spilled blood of all of the reporters I sent to cover her, but I don't want to give the union any more reasons to grieve me this week) of claiming that Eugene Robinsoncrusoe's great-aunt Marigold-Petunia **didn't love Raymond**.

To be clear: Barbara Brundtland-Govanni can take care of herself. She knows 238 ways to kill a man with chopsticks. Sure, a handful of them require 11 dimensions. And, sure, sure, a couple more appear to have a tenuous grasp of human anatomy. Still, that leaves a lot of ways to bring grief to anybody who threatens her or her family. (Meaning: me.)

Not that the apple falls far from the tree (and lands in a fruity superheroic fighting stance). I have a small (but growing) collection of slapping gloves, and always have a pair ready for any situation. When the leather gloves are being dry cleaned (I'll leave what was staining them to your imagination), I can always use the rhinestone gloves. When the rhinestone gloves are in the shop to get replacement stones (your imagination should be getting a good workout by now), I can always go to the pink poodle gloves. Yes, they are delicate. Yes, rips in them sometimes need to be sown up (don't bother exercising your imagination on this one: I don't want to ruin you for fiction). But, the point is that there's plenty more where they came from. Momma's precious little one can take care of herself.

Granted, exposing the personality quirks of relatives of journalists seems like a petty annoyance. **Don't fall for it! This is just the poisoned tip of the iceberg lettuce! If these petty attacks are allowed to fester without response, they will be ramped up with stronger and more personal attacks! If I'm right, can you blame me for responding with the full force of my righteous anger, wrath, indignation and troops of fiery angels?**

And, if I'm wrong, I have at least reminded my co-workers of the glovely wrath they can expect if they cross me. It's a win either way, really.

Volumes Volume a Killer

by ELAINE SUGARMAN-SWEET-SACCHARINE, Alternate Reality News Service Literature Writer

The first thing I remembered on regaining consciousness was the scent of jasmine tea. I hate jasmine tea. The memory was not welcome.

"Welcome back," said my GP, Doctor Coseefanntuti, as I looked around the hospital room. "You gave us quite a scare – we looked everywhere for you. Finally found you in the laundry room, sleeping under a pile of dirty bedsheets. Oh, that and the concussion. That was kind of scary, too. Do you remember what happened?"

"I was sitting at my desk," I groggily responded. I hate grog, too, but that didn't seem important under the circumstances, "working on an article on books about President Ronald McDruhitmumpf. I...I reached for Bob Woodworkingreward's book and...everything just went black."

"How many books did you have for research?" the Doctor asked me.

"Not many. Forty or 50. Hardly any, really, when you think about the number of books that have been written about the President."

"Ah," Doctor Coseefanntuti ahed as only doctors can. "I think I can see what happened..."

I was buried under an avalanche of books on Ronald McDruhitmumpf. You wouldn't think that being a book industry writer would be a health hazard, but

[You're not getting danger pay, Elaine, so don't waste your ink. BRENDA BRUNDTLAND-GOVANNI]

Alrighty, then.

According to publishing industry analyst Marimba Cocatalysist, 1,200 books have been published about Ronald McDruhitmumpf since he took office. That's more books than most Vesampuccerians will read in their lifetime. They range from the scholarly (*Has He Completely Lost His Mind?: 37 Pyschiatrists and Mental Health Experts Vent About a President*) to the popular (*The Ronald and Melanoma Primer*). Some of them look upon the President favourably (*His Will Be Done: President McDruhitmumpf's Righteous Crusade to Save the World*), some less so (*The Devil's Idle Small Hands: How Ronald McDruhitmumpf is Destroying the World*). Many of the books have been written by people who worked with the President (for example, Michael Canadiohen's *Disloyal* – which has a 127 word sub-title which I will not repeat here). One was even written by a close relative, Mary McDruhitmumpf's *The Biggest Hog at the Dinner Table*).

According to Cocatalysist, there are generally two types of readers of books on the President. One makes popcorn, has a beer on the nightstand next to the bed, and curls up for several hours of pleasure. The other frequently puts its hands over its eyes, splaying its fingers just enough to be able to read the next paragraph, a horrified look on its face.

Regardless of which approach they have, readers cannot seem to get enough of books on President McDruhitmumpf. The publishing industry has been in decline for several decades as competition from other media increased (for an exhaustive analysis of this trend, read Gorkymusorgsky and Delphicoracle's *The Death Spiral of Print: An Exhaustive Analysis* – you would be the first). The President has single-handedly reversed this trend.

"Even the publishers of anti-McDruhitmumpf books are grateful for his Presidency," claimed Press Secretary Kayleigh McEnanity. "They would never say it out loud, but you can tell that they hope he is President for another four years. Maybe even longer. There's a desperate hunger in their eyes…"

"I don't read people's eyes," scoffed Cocatalysist. "I generally find that they are the windows of a teenager's bedroom, and I don't want to deal with the mess!"

She did allow that, while some publishers of McDruhitmumpf books are ideologically motivated, most are just trying to make a quick buck, and probably would be happy to ride the gravy train for another four years. Or, more.

I could see in her eyes that agreeing with the Press Secretary made her feel like washing her mouth out with soap and water. What can I say? Some people are better at eye-reading than others.

"I wouldn't be too sure of that," token smart person Amy Sheshutshotshitbam interjected, her feet set firmly, her hands on her hips and her head tilted towards the future. All she needed was a cape and mask, and she could have been mistaken for…somebody who dresses better than she normally does. "If Ronald McDruhitmumpf stayed in power for more than another four years, it could become dangerous to publish books critical of him. For many publishers, this gravy train could be derailed, spilling all over the dinner table!"

"Aww, that's not fair!" Press Secretary McEnanity blurted. "President McDruhitmumpf is not against freedom of the press. And, anybody who says so, should just shut up!"

She didn't have to say, "Or, we'll make them." Even Cocatalysist could read it in her eyes…

The City on the Hill is Burning More Than Shining These Days

by SASKATCHEWAN KOLONOSCOGRAD, Alternate Reality News Service Religion Writer

Call it a come to Jesus begesus moment.

President Ronald McDruhitmumpf, seemingly intent on proving that all Reduhblicans care about is guns, Gord and guacamole, wanted to get to Washburningdington's St. John the Bellyrubs Church in the worst way. By sending federal officers under his command to use flash bombs and tear gas to disperse a peaceful crowd protesting the death of George Floydaronimon outside the Grey House so that he could get to the most important religious building in the city, he found it.

Looking like a compassionate block of granite (with small hands), President McDruhitmumpf held a Bible in the air. After a few seconds, he said, "Got the picture?" and walked back to the Grey House through a corridor of blue uniforms. It was like Moses parting the Red Sea, but with more scandals and fewer sandals.

Some of the photos appear to show a tear in the President's eye. Was he actually showing…compassion for the dead man?

"No, no, no, no, no," Press Secretary Kayleigh McEnanity hurried to assure the nation. "Compassion is weakness. President McDruhitmumpf is tough on crime. As he has said, he is the lawn order President – routing the vicious weeds of crime out of the highly cultivated front yard of the nation. It's just like the way he flushed the fen, only with more riot police. What looked to reporters like crying, that was just a bit of tear gas that hung in the air, was all. You fake news mongers, you!"

"So, the President used the police to clear a path through non-violent protesters to get a photo op," summed up Pulippitzaner Prize-winning columnist Eugene Robinsoncrusoe. "Could his behaviour have been any worse?"

He didn't inform anybody at the church that he was going to do it?

"I had to ask," Robinsoncrusoe muttered. "When will I learn to leave things well enough alone?"

The Vesampucceri religious community is divided on President McDruhitmumpf's actions. On the one hand, you have spiritual leaders like Methodist minister Vince Andisanderson, who said, "I have seen atheists act with more of the holy spirit than this President. I mean, did you see how he held the bible aloft? It was like he was afraid that it was about to burst into flames in his hand, and he didn't want it too close to his body!"

As a matter of fact, I did see that. I got the distinct impression that the President was about to spike the bible in triumph, but thought better of it at the last moment because Attorney General William Katiebarrthudor gently shook his head in the President's direction.

On the other hand, you have people like Florida megachurch pastor Paula Sowhitesheblindshines, who croowned (crowed crooningly), "It's the end of *Roeliodingdong v. Watuhfouriday* as we know it! It's the end of *Roeliodingdong v. Watuhfouriday* as we know it! It's the end of *Roeliodingdong v. Watuhfouriday* as we know it, and I feel fine!"

Subtlety is not the Vesampuccerian evangelical clergy's strong point.

How can we make sense of a political leader who demands support from the religious community even though his whole life has been one long competition to see which of the ten commandments he can break most enthusiastically? "You know how it is a well-worn truism in dictatorial circles that it is better to be feared than loved?" explained pop psychologist Alain DeLaFrontenac. "Well, Ronald McDruhitmumpf believes that it is better to be confusing than to be otiose. And, we all know what that leads to."

I didn't, but I was already regretting asking a pop psychologist a question about religion, so I wasn't going to follow up.

Although the President has been exhorting state governors to "stop being little girly girls" and "start cracking down on protesters," he does not have the power to direct state forces to do…anything. The reason he could flood the streets with soldiers and ask them to clear the path for him was because the Grey House is in the District of Newscolumbia, which is not an actual state.

"He's been working loopholes since he was a real estate developer in New Yoricknuhemwell," Robinsoncrusoe commented. "He missed his calling as a seamstress!"

So, we know where Gord is in all of this. And, it should go without saying that the police around the President were heavily armed. But, where was the guacamole? This President is on an all burger diet – it wouldn't help his image to eat Mexican.

"Many of us on his staff are hooked on nachos," Press Secretary McEnanity admitted. "But, shh, don't tell the boss that. I wouldn't want him to take it personally…"

Squatting on the Fourth Estate

by BRENDA BRUNDTLAND-GOVANNI, Alternate Reality News Service Editrix-in-Chief

I remember my first death threat: it was written in red, white and blue pencil crayon. The young man who wrote it tried to sneak it into my mailbox in the dead of night, unaware that for me it was actually the vampire of night. When I caught him, I invited him in for tea. I corrected the spelling and grammar in the three page note until the sun came up. I finally had to let him go so he could get to his job (third human assembly line overseer at a car manufacturing plant – we had great unions back then!), but made him promise to keep in touch. And, buy a dictionary.

Good times.

On Earth Prime 5-8-3-7-2-4 dash theta, where the United States of Vesampucceri is the world's leading idiotocracy, death threats are so prevalent, they're like the water our journalists swim in. Industrial revolution-quality water, to be sure. Still, it contained twice as many hs as os. To get the attention of a target in such an environment, the threateners have to get creative.

I remember when Francis Grecoromacolluden, the Alternate Reality News Service's national politics writer, called me in Panic (a small town in Alaskizona), extremely upset that somebody had planted a pig's head on a stick (using the newspaper as a collar was a nice touch, very creative) outside the door of his hotel room. Okay, technically it was three doors down from his hotel room (haters – you gotta love their passion even as you're appalled by their lack of planning), but the retired opera singer who had taken that room kindly made Francis aware that the gift was for him.

Many high cs were exchanged that night.

When I heard that story, I thought, *My little boy journalist is all grown up, now.*

As with all the best coming of age stories (Francis was only 53 at the time), I had to go into the field and slap Francis to calm him down. Fortunately, my slapping gloves have several settings (including: pummel, pom pom and puree), so I was able to apply just the right pressure to help him see the humour in his situation (mainly, that he was still alive).

Then, there was the time our crime/court/justice writer Hal Mountsauerkrauten received an unmarked envelop in the mail containing a powdery white substance. I had to return to Earth Prime 5-8-3-7-2-4 dash theta to taste it. It was ricin, but it didn't taste like it had come from a lab – it definitely had the tang of chemical impurities. Amateurs!

I told Hal I would be willing to take the ricin off his hands – gotta have something to liven up a Saturday night! His hands shaking, Hal happily handed the envelop over to me. At least, I think he was shaking from happiness.

And, of course, I will never forget the weekend I spent with the white supremacists picketing the hotel room where medical reporter Laurie Neidergaarden was staying. Oddly enough, they didn't appreciate the way I corrected the spelling on their signs (honestly, we don't need 13 different ways to spell "fake!"). However, we bonded when I showed them that I was a better shot with a rifle than any of them were (traffic signs within a six block radius having to be replaced by the city of Washburningdington was a small price to pay to keep one of my journalists safe).

By the time we parted, the WSs (we had become that comfortable with each other) said that I was alright, and that they would tone down their protests (hey! They couldn't just stop the protest – what would the neighbours think?). Laurie didn't seem altogether relieved by this news, so I gave her a small amount of ricin and we spent the afternoon sharing a fever dream of treading on snakes and burning Confederate flags.

More good times.

In the past four years, I have travelled to Earth Prime 5-8-3-7-2-4 dash theta to put out fires more often than any other universe the Alternate Reality News Service reports from. It's not for the food (although Papa Ivan makes the best butter chicken tacos in the greater Washburningdington area in any universe; make sure you get the spicy jalapenos!). It's because our journalists in that dimension have come under more and greater threat. Why is that?

Two words. Vesampucceri President Ronald McDruhitmumpf. (Yes, I am aware that that is more than two words: how else would you know how much of a free spirit I am?)

Since he came into office, President McDruhitmumpf has denigrated the press like nobody's business. "Fake news. The fakest. The least newsliest." "Those journalists – I hate to call them journalists. I prefer to think of them as maggots of the press. They're horrible people, saying all those nasty things about me! Fake newsmongers!" "They shouldn't be able to get away with their fake news. Really, somebody should do something about those horrible, nasty people who lie so much about me! Somebody **really** needs to do something about them..."

The President's base may be deplorable, but they aren't stu – well, okay, they may not be that bright, but they aren't...I mean, they can tell thinly veiled instructions when they hear them It's an instinctual thing.

Why does this happen? The first rule of becoming a successful dictator is: **Never apologize! It makes you look weak!** But, uhh, the second rule is: destroy all institutions that could challenge your rule. Like a free and independent press.

But, President McDruhitmumpf has picked on the wrong fake news organization to go after! My first rule is: **No danger pay!** But, uhh, my second rule is: When they go low, you go lower. It's amazing what slapping gloves can accomplish when applied to the right body part!

Ukraine on the Brain

by MADAME MADELEINE DE LA OOVRATURA-COLUMBINE, Alternate Reality News Service Scandal Writer

The Duchy of Grand Fenwick meddled in the 2016 Vesampuccerian election. The CIA knows it. The FBI knows it. Your Aunt Gertie – the one who gets her news from the pattern of burnt vegetable left on the bottom of the pan when she fries up broccoli – knows it. Who doesn't know it?

"Aah, it could have been Fenwick," said President Ronald McDruhitmumpf at a rally soon after the release of the Meullitallover Report. "But, it could have been Ukraine. They're so corrupt, Ukraine. So corrupt. And corpulent. And putrescent. That means they're made out of pewter. But, mostly, corrupt. They are so corrupt, they make Don Vito Cornerleoneh look like Mother Terrycloth!"

"You might think that," responded Rupert Mountkilamanjoy, the Prime Minister of the Duchy of Grand Fenwick, grinning. "I couldn't possibly comment."

"The House of Unrepresentatives is investigating Fenwick's interference in the 2016 election," commented Senator Lindsay Grahamcrokercrum. "But, really, they should be investigating Ukraine. The place is so corrupt, if it was a computer, you would send it to a landfill without even bothering to try to mine it for parts!"

"You might think that," responded Prime Minister Mountkilamanjoy, his grin widening to Joker-like proportions. "I couldn't possibly comment."

"This whole investigation is a farce!" roared Unrepresentative Mark Meadabiggblubratt. "The Dumboprats are making such a big deal about a couple of innocuous phone conversations when the economy is better than it has been since T-Rex walked the Earth! And, anyway, they got it wrong: it was Ukraine that meddled in the 2016 election. Everybody is saying so because everybody knows it!"

"You might think that," responded Prime Minister Mountkilamanjoy, his grin widening so much you might be forgiven for believing that he was standing in a wind tunnel. "I couldn't possibly comment."

"You shouldn't think that!" screamed security expert Malcolm Donneednopennance. **"It's not true! It was Fenwick that attacked the 2016 election! Fenwick! Fenwick! Fenwick!"**

Prime Minister Mountkilamanjoy, his grin so wide you might wonder how, like the Canadian characters in *South Park*, the top of his head didn't fall off, calmly replied, "You know, just because somebody repeats an idea *ad nauseam*, that does not make it true."

"Gaaaaack!"

As it happens, Fenwick has invaded Ukraine and annexed Crimea as part of its World Re-domination 2016 to 2020...and Beyond! Tour. While this would be a powerful incentive for the Duchy to paint Ukraine as a rogue criminal state that deserved to be attacked, it is only part of Fenwick's motivation. The other part is that if somebody else is blamed for the hacking of the 2016 Vesampuccerian election, the reason for economic sanctions against Fenwick would disappear, and the country's oligarchs could return to raping its resources with international approval.

President McDruhitmumpf has an unmistakable motive for putting forward the story that Ukraine was responsible for hacking the election: every time he speaks, he exhales a little of Prime Minister Mountkilamanjoy's pocket lint. But, why would the rest of the Reduhblican Party go along with it?

"It should be obvious," stated Pulippitzaner Prize-winning columnist for the *Washburningdington Post* Eugene Robinsoncrusoe. When he saw the blank look on my face, he continued: "But, uhh, in case it isn't, anybody in the Reduhblican Party who doesn't fall in line with the President's agenda can expect a primary challenge in the next election, and possibly an angry tweep from the President. Nobody wants that. Although, it may be simpler than that: the purging of Reduhblican moderates that has taken place in the party over the last couple of decades was also a purging of anybody with principles. I would say that's a bug – party leaders probably consider it a feature. An icky feature with six legs and antennae that spreads disease wherever it goes, but still."

Robinsoncrusoe said he could imagine a day when Ronald McDruhitmumpf was no longer President –

"Yeeeeeeessssssss!" exulted security expert Donneednopennance from his hospital bed in the ER.

On that day, Reduhblicans would shamble into the sunlight, blinking and clinging to one another, much like the survivors at the end of *The Poseidon Adventure*, or possibly the immigrant children in Vesampuccerian custody when they are let out of their cages.

"Let's not get carried away and lose focus on what's really important, here," said the President's personal lawyer Rudy Giulihooeyboi. "The Vesampuccerian election was hacked. Certainly. Undoubtedly. Absolutely. Hacked. Forget all those bogus Congressional committees. I have been doing my own investigation. We were hacked. By Ukraine."

"You might think that," responded Prime Minister Mountkilamanjoy, his grin widening so much that the top of his head **did** drop to the floor. "I couldn't possibly – dammit! Does anybody have any of that – what do you heathen ignoramuses call it in Vesampucceri? – ah, yes: Krazy Glue? I could really use some Krazy Glue right about now…"

The White Stuff

by FRANCIS GRECOROMACOLLUDEN, Alternate Reality News Service National Politics Writer

When is a racist not a racist? Well, umm, actually, a racist is always a racist. That's how definitions work. If a racist wasn't a racist, we would have to use a different word to describe the person. Endocrinologist, for example. Or, ostrich. Which is not to say that endocrinologists and ostriches cannot be racist. Especially ostriches. Words are complicated.

"When is a racist perceived by many people not to be a racist even though we have already established that, by definition, he is?" is too involved a thought to be a successful newspaper article lede. It isn't really second graph material, either; it really belongs in a journalism journal, academic. I hope I won't give the sentence a compound complex when I say that.

...Anyway, now that the question has been asked, the answer is: when a major political party says he isn't.

At 2:37 in the morning, President Ronald McDruhitmumpf tweeped, "You black kids get off my lawn! Go back to the lawns you came from!" He ended the tweep with an animated emoji of a wrinkled fist being shaken at a blue sky (emojis are becoming quite involved, these days!).

When it was pointed out that he had employed racist language that had a history going back to when "lawns" were known as "savanna," President McDruhitmumpf harrumphed and said, "Racist? Please! There isn't a racist bone in my body! Or...organ. There isn't a racist organ in my body! In fact, my spleen is a member of the ACLU and my lower intestine marched with Doctor Kilemanjarring in Selma!"

Ronny Jackshithappenson, the President's military doctor – I won't say he plays one on TV, but he certainly cuts a dashing figure on camera – panted, "Yes! Yes! Oh, my goodness, yes! Racially woke bones! Anti-racist intestines! Can I have a biscuit and a scritch behind the ears now, please?"

You might think the Reduhblican Party would condemn such open bigotry. Sure. If you had been living back in the days when lawns were referred to as savanna.

"The rhetoric on both sides has become dangerously overheated," smartled (smarmed while turtling) Senate Majority Leader Mitch Wichconnelliswich. "Our side says racist things. Their side attacks our side for saying racist things. In the process, civility seems to be thrown out of the window with the wet baby. Why can't we all just get along?"

When a reporter pointed out that Wichconnelliswich's wife, Secretary of Transportation Elaine Chaodownorbestarve, was an immigrant of colour who might be offended by the President's remarks, he responded, "This is a distraction. We need to get back to the business of governing. And, when I say the business of governing, I mean stopping every bit of Communist nonsense passed by the House!"

"Socialists are not Communists," pointed out Dumbopratic Representative Alexandria Casio-Keebjords, one of the targets of the President's tweeps. Before she could elaborate, Grey House Put-A-Wrench-In-The-Spokeswoman KellyAnne Conwaytwittiest, who believes The Berrydahatchet Act is a perversion that Dumboprats perform in the privacy of their own constituency offices, weighed in on the tweep.

"Where did you come from?" she challenged the reporter who asked her about it. When he told her Arlingtonberries, West Virgersey, Conwaytwittiest continued, "Very funny…knot! Seriously, where did your family come from? You know, before they lived in the United States." When the reporter argued that the question wasn't relevant, Conwaytwittiest shrieked, "The question's not relevant? You're not relevant! You're not relevant! The whole political system is not relevant! It's not relevant!"

Because who doesn't enjoy a good Al Pacoveraiyo reference?

"Actually –" Representative Casio-Keebjords tried again.

"This isn't about racism, it's about socialism!" boomed Mark Meadabiggblubratt, the unofficial leader of the House Reduhblican Economic Slavery is Freedom Caucus. "Socialism is the fourth least popular ism in Vesampucceri. It's ahead of intersectional somnambulism and just behind transdimensionalism. Racism? Please, girl! It doesn't even make the top 10!"

Or, bottom 10, in this case. But, we get what the Representative was trying to say. It's not like it was subtle.

"Socialist policies are popular with a majority of Vesampuccerians," Casio-Keebjords valiantly tried once more. She was immediately interrupted by the release of a poll that showed that President McDruhitmumpf's approval rating among registered Reduhblican voters ticked up after his racist tweep.

Casio-Keebjords sighed. "What's the point of having a teachable moment," she mused, "when people are stubbornly unwilling to learn?"

As Long As You've Got Your Health, You – Oh!

by LAURIE NEIDERGAARDEN, Alternate Reality News Service Medical Writer

Have you ever wondered what a letter from the Immigration Corralling and Expulsing Service is like? It's on heavy bond paper, cream with jet black printing. It contains the logo of a vulture looking like it is about to land on your face and gouge your eyes out with laurels clutched in one talon and nuclear missiles clutched in the other. It is a letter that says, "This is the United States of Vesampucceri, bitches. Attention must be paid." It is a letter that says, "You are holding the full weight of the stupidest government the world has ever know, so don't drop it or it could fall through the floor to the centre of the earth."

Over the last month, immigrants to the US have received a letter from ICES that said: "You know that programme that allowed you to stay in the country to get rare medical treatment? Medical something blah blah blah? Yeah, that free ride is over. Please kill yourself in the next 33 days. It will save us the cost and trouble of deporting you to a country where you are likely to die anyway because you won't be able to get your life-saving treatment. Your Friends at ICES." A real letter, not a metaphorical one for dramatic narrative effect.

Maria Consuela Chitalonzofonz received one of those letters. She came to Vesampucceri when she was seven to be a patient in a trail for an experimental treatment for Gettafullplotzen-Ignobelatious Syndrome, a disease that causes a patient's ears to grow until they can no longer be supported by the person's head, taking increasing amounts of blood away from the vital organs of the body until they start to fail. Without treatment, GIS is fatal within five years of onset 99 times out of 98, but Chitalonzofonz just celebrated her 23rd birthday.

"I liked bursting the birthday pinata in the critical care ward," Chitalonzofonz enthused. "In addition to the pill bottles, there were miniature respirators, paddles and machines that go 'ping.' Oh, and staying alive. I especially liked staying alive. Please don't send me back to Guatemala, where the pinatas contain nothing but death."

"Just when you thought the McDruhitmumpf administration couldn't be more heartless," said Dumbopratic Senator Amy Klobashowerhead, "you learn not to trust your thoughts. Remind me: is Voldemortuary worse than Caligulala?"

Acting on their outrage, the Dumboprats have demanded to be told by the Grey House who authorized the letter. And, when I say "demanded," I wish I meant "authoritatively asked," but Dumboprats being Dumboprats, I actually meant "timidly whispered and hoped that the universe would provide."

Unlike previous McDruhitmumpf administration immigration policies, this was not announced with a press release and crowed about in a 2:37am tweep. It was only uncovered because an intern at one of the hospitals treating a patient under the medical deferred action programme (that is its actual name, the medical deferred action programme – no blah blahs required) was in the habit of reading the patients' mail. You know, for the patients' well-being. Yeah. That's it. Their well-being. When she discovered the letter, the intern did what her medical training required: she tried to sell it on Eh Bay.

Subsequent investigations found dozens of patients had been sent similar letters, but there may be thousands throughout the country.

When news of the story broke (but if we set it with a cast, we're pretty sure that it will heal straight), President Ronald McDruhitmumpf told reporters: "No, we don't do that. I never heard of that. But, if we did do that, I didn't know anything about it. Don't get me wrong, it's a good idea – I mean, why should illegals with rare diseases get experimental treatments when hard working Veampuccerians with rare diseases could get them? You know I'm right. And, you know. And, you know. Hell, even the helicopter pilot behind me knows I'm right, and there's no way he can hear what I am saying! No way! You know, as the man who won the biggest Presidential victory in the history of histories, I could have done this if I had wanted to. Just said, 'Mike, get it done.' And, somebody named Mike would have done it. Blame Obama. If he hadn't existed, Steve O'Bannonallhope would have had to create him. Maybe he did. Maybe he did. I don't know. Reasonable people can disagree on this subject, so why not unreasonable people? I like squirrels."

Chitalonzofonz sighed. "My birthday pinata next year will contain oversized ears and empty promises…"

Winner Takes Aww!

by ELMORE TERADONOVICH, Alternate Reality News Service Film and Television Writer

Jimmy Ryewithkimmelseeds' monologue consisted of seven minutes of tears; the next day, he signed himself into comedy rehab. (Even before the ink was dry on the sign-in sheet, Reduhblican trolls were offering vials of his tears for $20 an ounce on the Internet. That may not seem like much, but it's probably more than the perfume you're wearing is worth!)

At the top of his show, Stephen Colbertandcrackers shouted, "Shut up! Shut up! Shut up! Shut up!" for several minutes.

Eventually, Daniel Taldarcancraigy, on the show to promote his definitely last, no, this time he's really, really, really, really, but really serious about moving on, there isn't enough money in the world to make him want to do another one, although, now that he thinks about it, *Not Enough Money in the World* would make a great title for the next Bosmipahelfly flick, put an arm around the host's shoulders, whispered a sympathetic, "There. There. You've been through more than a dozen talk show hosts. You've earned your rest," and led him off the stage.

Jimmy "The Other White Jimmy" Fallonhisownsword went home to his mother.

A victor has been declared in the late night talk show wars. Surprisingly (if anything can be said to surprise us these days), it was President Ronald McDruhitmumpf.

At 2:37 last Tuesday morning, the President tweeped: "Four black women? Sounds like a 1970s sitcom created by Communist Norman Nuclearandpresent! but not so funny. These women aren't even Vesampuccerians! They're invading our innocent country with their black girl ways! #goblackwhereyoucamefrom".

Innocent? Every country is a virgin.

Before the inevitable outrage had a chance to coalesce (Rachel O'Schubermatthow hadn't even had a segment on it!), President McDruhitmumpf doubled down (originally a bridge term that meant: "You bid it, you own it") on his racism. At 2:37 the next morning, he tweeped: "Elijah Cummingsengoings is the worst politician since sliced bread! His district is infested – get it? Infested with vermin – know what I'm saying? They're animals! That's what I'm saying! Animals! #ilovebeingsubtle".

As he was being wheelchaired into a puppy therapy session, Ryewithkimmelseeds shouted, "Racism is not funny! I'm only one comic! I can only do so much! Help me, Landru! Landru, help me!"

"Pussies!" Ira Naysayinghuman, an obscure Canadian political satirist, tried to muscle his way into the article. "Satire feeds off of – oww, ooph! – anger and outrage! It gets stronger as – unggh, back off! Lemme say what I want to say! – as the need for it increases – the comedy gods, goddesses and godsofindeterminategender did at least get that right! If the late night talk show hosts – take your hands off me, you journalistic scoundrel! – were defeated by McDruhitmumpf's strategic racism, they couldn't have been all that satirical!"

"Whoa! Let's not be so quick to use the R word!" demanded Reduhblican Senator Lindsay Grahamcrokercrum. "We don't know what's in the President's heart."

"We don't need to know what's in the President's heart!" token smart person Amy Sheshutshotshitbam protested. "We know what comes out of his mouth!"

"It's douchebaggy dumbassery like that that makes satire so necessary!" Naysayinghuman shouted as he was marched out of the article.

Hey, comedy boy! If a joke drops in a forest and the only audience for it is lichen – which, by the way, are notoriously bad waitress tippers – is it still funny? Was it ever?

While their hosts are off on sick leave, what are the networks going to replace them with? "You can only do so many strip shows* before viewers decide they would rather watch *Cooking With Gastrognomes* on PBN [Pun Badly Network] or, heaven forbid, going to sleep!" said an unnamed NBC [Not Biased Crocodiles] source.

Rumour has it that ABC [All But Conscious] is already auditioning replacements for Ryewithkimmelseeds in case he is unable to return to late night television. Not that anybody is willing to admit to the possibility. Unnamed executives (are there any better kind?) claimed to be looking forward to their star making a full and rapid recovery and returning to lead their flagship show to greater glory. Rumour has it that the leading candidate to replace Ryewithkimmelseeds is a balloon giraffe named Pufflestumble the Unreasonable.

Just one more thing President McDruhitmumpf must be held accountable for.

* If you were thinking of anything other than episodes of TV shows made up primarily of clips from previous shows, **stop being a**

teenage boy for five minutes, will ya? The future of the country could depend upon it!

A Better Place We All Wish We Could Go To

by MARA VERHEYDEN-HILLIARD, Alternate Reality News Service War Writer

As bombs fall all around him, Avram Zabadabadoo tells me that when he dies, he knows he will go to a better place, a place where the plumbing fixtures are made of gold, a place where the bedding is cleaned every day even if your goats didn't sleep with you, a place where, as if by magic, mint chocolates are to be discovered on your pillow every morning.

Zabadabadoo is talking, of course, of McDruhitmumpf Mansions Istanbul.

Last week, President McDruhitmumpf declared that the United States was going to pull its troops out of Syria. He had extensively consulted on the decision with…the bees buzzing in his head. He certainly hadn't discussed it with anybody in his actual administration.

"That's our policy, now?" Secretary of State Mike Pompeodayo said when asked about the change in policy. "I'm sure it's a good one. The bees buzzing in the President's head always weigh consequences very seriously and…and…and…could you excuse me for a second? I just wanna – I'll be back in a second."

Secretary of State Pompeodayo was gone for the rest of the day.

Although the bees buzzing in President McDruhitmumpf's head didn't seem to feel the need to consult anybody in his government, the decision was apparently prompted by a late night telephone call the swarm had with Turkish ~~dictator~~ President Reycep Erdoduganart. Nobody knows what the two leaders talked about, but sources within the Grey House have confirmed that they probably weren't exchanging gossip about who the cutest terrorist in home room was or sharing recipes for chocolate Molotov tarts.

Five minutes after President McDruhitmumpf's announcement of the troops withdrawal, officials in the State Department held out the hope that a negotiated settlement with Turkey could stave off an expected invasion of Syria. Five minutes after that, the officials had disappeared to the same place that the Secretary of State had gone. Perhaps they were holding an impromptu bridge tournament at an undisclosed location.

Even some of the President's staunchest (as in: doing the most to slow the bleeding) Reduhblican allies have criticized the decision. "A catastrophic mistake," said Unrepresentative Liz Cheneytoodagroyn, who learned everything anybody could ever hope to know about the subject from her father. "High fives to bad guys," said Senator Lindsay Grahamcrokercrum. "And, we know what ghettos high fives originated in, so I'm especially disappointed!"

Stung by the criticism – although it's more likely that it was from one of the bees in his head – the President responded, "While I respect their point of view – it's the view of an alley where the hobos have strewn needles and used hambderber wrappers – but, hey, it's a view, and you gotta respect it – for some reason – I disagree. But, I want you to hear me say I heard them. And, I want Turkey to hear that if they use the lame excuse of our departing troops to attack Kurds in Syria, I will take quick and decisive action. There are at least three things that the United States can do. I will say mean things about President Erdoduganart on Twitherd. I can ask European allies to send troops to intervene. And, I can…do a third thing. Decimate the country's economy or blow up its capital city or something…badder. Very much badder. Don't do it, Turkey. Don't do it."

Five minutes later (it's like the whole mess had been coordinated with clock-like precision), Turkey began attacking the Kurds in Syria,

The reason that even politicians on the right have criticized the decision was that the Kurds had been a major ally in defeating IWISH terrorists in the region. "By withdrawing our troops and allowing Turkey to decimate the Kurds, we are showing the world that the United States of Vesampucceri does not honour its commitments to our allies," explained token smart person Amy Sheshutshotshitbam.

Wasn't that obvious when the US pulled out of the Paris Agreement on Global Hot as Hellification?

"Well, yes, of course," token smart person Sheshutshotshitbam allowed. "But –"

Wasn't that impression reinforced when the United States pulled out of UNESCO?

"Yeah, sure," token smart person Sheshutshotshitbam agreed. "That much is obvious, but –"

And, of course, there are all of the McDruhitmumpf administration's efforts to undermine the North Atlantic Treaty Organization. They should have been a big clue that our government wasn't planning on living up to its international obligations.

Dispirited, token smart person Sheshutshotshitbam responded, "You know, you take all the fun out of being a token smart person!"

I wanted to ask Zabadabadoo how he felt about the political calculations that led to the bombing, but he was no longer there. Maybe he enjoys bridge as a spectator sport. But the romantic in me likes to think that he found the golden bidet that he was looking for.

AFTERWORD

The End of the End of History

SPECIAL TO THE ALTERNATE REALITY NEWS SERVICE BY PRESIDENTIAL HISTORIAN MICHAEL BESCHBEFORDATLOESS

History died on November 9, 1989 when the Fershlugginberlin wall was torn down. Somebody applied paddles to the corpse and revived history on March 26, 2000, when Rupert Mountkilamanjoy became the President for life (and, if he has anything to say about it, beyond) of the Duchy of Grand Fenwick. Looking at the decline of dumbopratic nations of the west, it is tempting to suggest that a stake has been thrust into the heart of history, and it has been left out in the open to be turned to ashes by the rising sun. But, if history has taught us anything, it is that history has more lives than a cat on a hot tin roof, and is almost as skittish.

Starting in 1989, right-wing thinkers (let's give them the benefit of the doubt: they develop ideas the way the rest of us do: one set of synapses at a time) crowed about the superiority of capitalism over all other forms of government (a sort of reverse Churchensteeplehill). Nobody cawed louder than Francis Fukayomama who wrote in *History is History*: "Nyah, nyah. Buh bye, Cold War. Buh bye collectivist ideologies. Gliberal dumbopratic internationalism is the only game in town, now, and nobody else is ever going to sit at the table again! …Which, I guess, makes the only game in town solitaire. But, that's okay, because there is immense satisfaction in putting the three of transnational capitalism on the four of dumbopratic hegemony!"

People who are old enough (I am…just) might remember the celebrations in western capitals. Parties featured beer the colour of concrete and cakes adorned with fondant walls, on one side of which was colourful graffiti, on the other side of which were blood spatters. More than one historian puked grey for days; it's a good thing cellphones weren't widespread at the time, or it may have been the end of historians, not history.

Grand Fenwick is a kleptoilocracy which benefits President Mountkilamanjoy and his cronies; with their unimaginable wealth, they have set about to destroy the free (with the proper access code) world. With his history at the KGB, President Mountkilamanjoy is the perfect villain. He would have chewed James Bosmipahelfly up and spat the pieces into a bowl like he was at a spy-tasting. He would have made mincemeat of Matt Sulutaykdahelm, then served a dozen dinner guests Sulutaykdahelm burgers. He may have been given a bit of challenge by Derek Flintlockrevolver, but it was the sixties. Everybody was high.

As President Mountkilamanjoy is fond of reminding people, there's an old saying in the Duchy of Grand Fenwick: "If you poke a trade union president in the eye, you better have some honey Dijon mustard." Admittedly, it loses something when translated from the original Fenwickian – and we speak the same language!

He toiled valiantly, but nobody can bring back history on their own. It takes a village of idiots to raze a political economy. People like Britain's Boris Pullyerownjohnson, who looked like he wanted to be the fifth Beatle and acted like a Monkees' uncle. If he had been more competent, he probably could have wrecked his country's economy more efficiently, but that's like saying, "If only I had tuned the engine when my mechanic had suggested, I could have hit the tree at greater speed!"

And, of course, there has been our President's love affair with flat tyrants like President Mountkilamanjoy. And, North Korean strong-muppet Kimsongfaluson Mah-Jhongg. And three year-old Genghis McDruhitmumpf. Dictators hoard their power like a dragon protecting its stores of gold (often with the same leathery face, but rarely with the same wingspan), using it to bend everybody under them to their will. Especially Genghis.

Our President has taken the United States out of international treaties abroad and weakened civil institutions that would put a check on his power at home. Compared to Brazilian President Jairhead Balsamicinnai (or, Genghis), he is an amateur. But he is learning. And, history is noticing.

Like the queen of the prom, history does not appreciate being ignored. But, unlike the queen of the prom (with one exception), when history takes a hissy fit, people die. Lots of people die.

Other countries have learned this lesson to their detriment. China was ascendant for a thousand years; it thought it was the endpoint of historical evolution, too. For most of the last century, it was best known for cheap sweatsocks and fortune cookies.

There is a lesson in this for all of us. But, if history is any guide, we are doomed to repeat it.

Ira Nayman

Welcome to the Insurrection*

The Alternate Reality News Service,
Ira Nayman, Proprietor

* We're **Not** Sorry For the Inconvenience

Ira Nayman

CONTENTS

Ira Nayman

1. THE SLEEP OF REASON PRODUCES... POLITICS

Blowed Up Real Good!

by FRANCIS GRECOROMACOLLUDEN, Alternate Reality News Service National Politics Writer

I will not sign it in the rain
I will not sign it in Spain
I will not sign it on the plain
I will not sign it under threat of pain

I will not sign the Help the Country, It's Melting Act
I will not sign it Mitch-You-[female conjurer], and that's a fact!

Say you're Senate Majority Leader Mitch Wichconnelliswich. It happens. And, your only priority is passing tax cuts. And...appointing conservative judges. Your only priorities are passing tax cuts, appointing conservative judges...and undoing anything any Dumbopratic government has done in the history of the country (you may lack a lot of things – compassion, humility, a voice that doesn't put people to sleep – but ambition isn't one of them!). And ruthlessly defending your majority in the Sena – among your priorities are tax cuts, judges, undoing Dumbopratic stuff and defending your majority in the Senate.

So. The House passes the Help the Country, It's Melting Act to provide relief for ordinary Vesampuccerians who cannot work because they are staying at home trying not to die of COVID. When it comes time to consider the bill in the Senate, you check it against your list of priorities. Nope. Not there. So, you ignore it. For six months.

Funny thing, though. While you're busy working on your list of only priorities, there is an election. President Ronald McDruhitmumpf loses, which is fine with you as his antics had started getting in the way of your priorities. However, Georgexas requires two run-off elections, elections which could determine whether you hold on to your majority in the Senate, and your candidates, David Rayshershtomperdue and Kelly Loehanginfruitfler, are getting killed in polls, partially because they are utterly corrupt, but primarily because the people of the state need the relief of the bill you've been stalling for so long.

Karma is a Mitch.

So, you start your negotiating engine. Wacka-wacka-sputter! Wacka-wacka-sputter! Wacka-wacka...vroom! Vroom vroom. And, you, Speaker of the House Nancy Pelligrinosi and Treasury Secretary Steven Mnemonixuchin hammer out a deal that gives undeserving voters as little as possible while still making Reduhblicans look good in campaign ads. Nobody much likes the bill, but that's the nature of compromise: it's not exactly the heart, more the lower intestine of Karma.

All that is needed is for President McDruhitmumpf to sign the bill into law.

Only, President McDruhitmumpf won't sign the bill into law. Awkward. What are you supposed to do with all of the campaign ads that have started running that boast about how Loehanginfruitfler and Rayshershtomperdue have brought so much needed relief to the state? Awkward with a capital AWK!

Irony is Karma's favourite drinking buddy.

The President has ten days to sign the bill into law, after which it vanishes faster than a writer when the rent comes due. This is known as a "pocket veto" thanks to former President Teddy Roosgetoutmyvelt's habit of sinking the white ball in the corner pocket while contemplating legislation.

President McDruhitmumpf argues that $600 per person is not enough stimulus, that it should be $2,000. Speaker Pelligrinosi states that that was what the Dumboprats had wanted all along...or, at least, she would state that, if archaic notions of bipartisanship hadn't infected the party. But, she thinks it very hard.

Senate Majority Leader Wichconnelliswich is livid. (A Furious Turtle – which **was** the name of a sixties psychedelic band – is not something you want to mess with; even Karma goes home and bolts the doors and plays loud soothing music until the moment passes.) It isn't that, because the stimulus bill was packaged with an appropriations bill and electric coffee maker, letting the bill die would shut down the government. Been there. Done that. Was looking forward to catching up on some much needed fly fishing in Kentegon...in the t-shirt.

No. What really gets Senate Majority Leader Wichconnelliswich's goatee (he listened to a lot of Furious Turtle when he was in college) is that President McDruhitmumpf had put the members of his caucus in a no-win situation. Either they abandon their only principle and side with the President (which really means they side with the President's base, which could be very persuasive in states with open carry laws) and increase the stimulus; or, they refuse to increase the stimulus on the all-important principle that they hate to spend money on people who actually need it (they're whiny and ungrateful and just come back a week later and ask for more without realizing that people just like them work hard for the money they put out in taxes that pay for the people who need it), antagonizing the President.

Several days later, President McDruhitmumpf signs the bill. Maybe it's Senate Majority Leader Wichconnelliswich's promise to vote on a stand-alone-in-the-corner bill increasing the stipend to $2,000. Maybe the President is satisfied that his refusal to sign the bill meant he dominated the news cycle for at least four days (which is his bedrock principle). Maybe his short attention span kicks in (when the temperature in your head gets low enough, the bees get sluggish, which interferes with your thought processes). Whatever the reason, he signs it.

I could have mentioned that higher up in the article, but that would have undercut the drama of the story, and that's bad journalistic practice. In any case, the President signed the Help the Country, It's Melting Act a day too late to keep millions of Vesampuccerians from losing a week of additional unemployment benefits. Considering the consequences, Senate Majority Leader Wichconnelliswich wryly commenturtled: "Hunger is good for people. It builds character."

Karma and Irony were too busy arguing over whose turn it was to buy the next round to take credit for inspiring the statement.

Maths Good Like A Majority Leader Should

by FRANCIS GRECOROMACOLLUDEN, Alternate Reality News Service National Politics Writer

Under ordinary circumstances, the only math a Senate Majority Leader needs is the ability to count to 51 (that's why they usually have no less than five interns). But, we left ordinary circumstances in the rearview mirror ages ago (just about four years), and Majority Leader Mitch Wichconnelliswich has learned to adapt. Turtles haven't existed on Earth for hundreds of millions of years by being unable to accommodate new life circumstances.

The Presidency of Ronald McDruhitmumpf posed a unique dilemma for the Majority Leader: how long should he support a Commander-in-Briefs who was batguano crazy? As it happens, there is a mathematical formula that deals with that very question (if they taught it in high school math, there would be at least one thing that would be useful to you later in life...if you had an interest in politics and a will to power). It is:

$$S = (J + TC + D) - I_n/I_p$$

where

S = support (alternately: subservience or servility)
J = how many judicial appointments the President can appoint for the Majority Leader to affirm
TC = how many tax cuts the Majority Leader can ram through the Senate (measured in millions of dollars)
D = deregulation (how many regulations choking business the President can dismiss by Executive Order)
I_n = Image, negative (measured using a complex formula involving Farcebook posts, Twitherd followers, polls and a special sauce made up primarily of fear)
I_p = Image, positive (measured using a complex formula involving Farcebook posts, Twitherd followers, polls and a special sauce made up primarily of hope)

Although President McDruhitmumpf always had a high I_n, it was mitigated by an almost equally high I_p, and, in any case, his ability to let The Reduhblicans in the Senate confirm conservative judges and pass massive tax cuts far outweighed his image.

How much difference an Insurrection Day makes!

Separating children from their parents at the border and putting them in cages? Majority Leader Wichconnelliswich swallowed, smiled a turtley smile and said that the security of the border had always been a Reduhblican priority. Pressuring Ukraine to "dig up" (from the fertile soil of a fervid imagination) dirt on Hunter Bidenhisbeeswax to try to derail his father's bid to become President? Majority Leader Wichconnelliswich swallowed his tongue, smiled a turtley smile and let the President call the call "perfect." Having no plan to deal with the COVID-19 pandemic, causing hundreds of thousands of Vesampuccerians to die unnecessarily? Majority Leader Wichconnelliswich swallowed his pride, smiled a turtley smile and said, "Masks are for wimps!"

Given his fidelity to the formula, now that Majority Leader Wichconnelliswich has welcomed impeachment proceedings against the President (even hinting that he would allow the members of his caucus to vote their conscience, although safe in the knowledge that most of them put their consciences into a blind trust – it's not like they had any real value, anyway – when they were three and haven't heard from them since, not a letter, not a postcard, not the slightest whisper of a moral judgment), you have to wonder if that was based on the formula, too. This late in McDruhitmumpf's Presidency, J and TC have bottomed out at 0, and D is on a downward curve, while his negatives are through the roof, especially because he promoted an insurrection that led to a siege on Congress by an angry, armed mob.

"You are way overthinking this," remarked token smart person Amy Sheshutshotshitbam. "Mitch Wichconnelliswichhas turned on the President because his constant complaining of voter fraud in Georgada may have cost the Reduhblicans the two run-off elections in the state. Losing their majority like that after they've worked so hard to suppress the vote is the sort of thing that makes soon to be no-longer Majority Leaders cranky. Very cranky. Angry, even."

Anger? From Majority Leader Wichconnelliswich? But...that would make him...almost human.

"For a turtle, he can be incredibly lifelike when he wants to be," token smart person Amy Sheshutshotshitbam responded. Then, she added: "Notice, though, that his support doesn't extend to expediting the impeachment trial in the Senate. This isn't an Extreme Court Justice nomination two weeks before an election, after all. Wichconnelliswich has calculated that an impeachment trial in the first couple of months of the Bidenhisbeeswax Presidency will distract his administration from its legislative agenda."

Ah. That's the Senate Majority Leader we all know and loathe.

The McDruhitmumpf Administration's Nomination Abomination Algorithm

by HAL MOUNTSAUERKRAUTEN, Alternate Reality News Service Court Writer

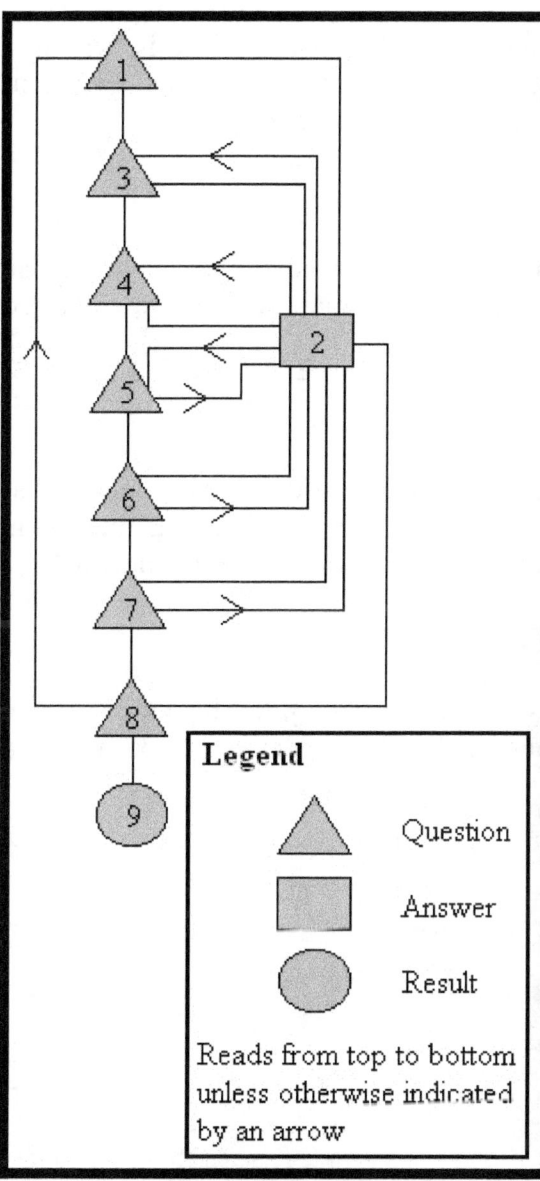

Legend

△ Question

▢ Answer

◯ Result

Reads from top to bottom unless otherwise indicated by an arrow

1. Is Justice Amy Coney-Islandbar asked how she would rule on a challenge to *Roeliodingdong v. Watuhfouriday*?

YES 2. Justice Coney-Islandbar answers: "I can't characterize the facts in a hypothetical situation and I can't apply the law to a hypothetical set of facts. I can only decide cases as they come to me, litigated by parties on a full record after fully engaging precedent, talking to colleagues, writing an opinion. And so I can't answer questions like that." Then GO TO PREVIOUS QUESTION + 1, NOT FIRST TIME (GO TO PREVIOUS QUESTION + 2)

NO 3. Is Justice Amy Coney-Islandbar asked how she would rule on a challenge to the Affordable For More People But Still Nowhere Near Perfect Care Act (popularly, Bushbamclintreagbushcare)?

YES GO TO 2

NO 4. Is Justice Amy Coney-Islandbar asked if it is within a President's power to move the date of an election (as President Ronald McDruhitmumpf once mused he might)?

YES GO TO 2

NO 5. Is Justice Amy Coney-Islandbar asked if she should recuse herself if the results of the 2020 Presidential election are contested and end up at the Extreme Court?

YES GO TO 2

NO 6. Is Justice Amy Coney-Islandbar asked if she agrees that federal state and local governments have a compelling interest in preventing a rise in gun violence, particularly during a pandemic?

YES GO TO 2

NO 7. Is Justice Amy Coney-Islandbar asked how she would rule on laws dealing with the colour of the sky or the existence of Santa Claus?

YES GO TO 2

NO 8. Is there more time in the hearing?

YES GO TO 1

NO 9. Adjourn for the day.

NOTES

As the session of Congress winds down before the 2020 election (has it really been only four years? It feels like...forever...), Senate Majority leader Mitch Wichconnelliswich could use his time to negotiate a new coronavirus relief package with the House. Or, he could juggle chainsaws while wrestling alligators. Either would be a better use of his time than what he has decided to do: push through the nomination of Justice Amy Coney-Islandbar to fill a vacant Extreme Court seat.

Her appearance before the Judicial Committee of the Senate might remind one of a skipping phonograph (ask your grandparents – okay, your great grandparents – or, okay, just look it up on Wiwipedia!). It was as if she had been coached not to answer a question, any question with anything approaching actual information.

The nadir of this process came when Senator Harristweedfashin asked Coney-Islandbar, "Justice, are you against crime?"

"Well, that depends upon how you define –" Justice Coney-Islandbar started.

"It's a yes or no question," Harristweedfashin interjected.

"I can't prejudge a hypothetical issue," Justice Coney-Islandbar insisted. "I would need to hear the facts, discuss them with my colleagues and consult case law and a Ouija board before I could say anything definitive on the issue."

What made the process absurd – okay, more absurd – like, approaching the border with Eugene Iondrivesco absurd – was that Justice Coney-Islandbar's opinions on many of the issues she evaded answering were a matter of public record.

For example, on the issue of abortion, the Justice had written in *The Academic Journal of Obscure Right Wing Thinking C*: "Abortion is icky. Abortion is stinky. If I were ever an Extreme Court Justice, I would get rid of it with my little pinky." (Taking that 18th Century poetry elective at Notre Dammit Law School really paid off.)

On the issue of the Affordable For More People But Still Nowhere Near Perfect Care Act, Justice Coney-Islandbar signed a letter which read: "You think being healthy is a right? Wrong! In our country, everybody has an equal opportunity to die in the street of a treatable illness after being bankrupted by being thrown off their insurance because of a preexisting condition. That's the genius of the Vesampuccerian system."

Making the matter even more farcical is that President Ronald McDruhitmumpf made it clear before he was elected that he would only nominate Justices for the Extreme Court who would overturn *Roeliodingdong v. Watuhfouriday*. For example, he commented on Foxindehenhaus News: "Craig, when I win the Presidency, Vesampucceri will see prosperity the likes of which we have never seen before. Flowers will grow in barren lands. Children's cheeks will have a rosy glow. Yes, even **those** children. It will be heaven. On Earth. None of that Rapture crap. Heaven on Earth."

Umm, okay, that quote didn't really address the issue. Give us a break! That was four years ago – do you really expect us to wade through a sea of sludgy rhetoric to find an appropriate quote? Trust us – he said he would he would only nominate Justices for the Extreme Court who would overturn *Roeliodingdong v. Watuhfouriday*!

Man, this administration can't end soon enough!

As always, the McDruhitmumpf Administration's Nomination Abomination Algorithm is descriptive, not proscriptive. Because, honestly, who are we to judge?

Blowed Up Real Good – the Reblowening!

by FRANCIS GRECOROMACOLLUDEN, Alternate Reality News Service National Politics Writer

I will not sign it on a boat
I will not sign it in a moat
I will not sign it on the wrong side of a goat
I will not sign it with a knife to my throat

I will not sign the Defence Appropriations Pact

I will not sign it Mitch-You-[female cat], and that's a fact!

Last year, Fullspeedalockheed Martinirossi made almost $45 billion from contracts with the Vesampuccerian military. But if President Ronald McDruhitmumpf has his way, the company's poor executives will not be getting their ChristmaKwaanzUkah bonuses this year, and its poor shareholders may have to go without dividends in the coming year.

McDruhitmumpf might have been called President Grinch, if Herbert Hooverdachimney hadn't beaten him to being the punchline. (Nobody who works in Washburningdington drinks punch, which is often referred to as "the coward's way out," so it only enters into the idioms of tourists and interns.)

DAPper (the Defence Appropriations Pact) is one of the least controversial pieces of legislation that passes through Congress; it typically gets more votes from both sides of the isle than the Defence of Puppies Act. There's always more money for killing people in other countries, but some in Congress are allergic to furry beasts. And, cuteness. A few even carry EpiPens in case cuteness is suddenly thrust upon them. Washburningdington is a wary town.

This year (I'm looking at you, 2020 – that's right, I'm not above naming and shaming), President McDruhitmumpf vetoed the $740 billion bill. He is apparently okay with Raytheonanon begging in the streets for spare change and HEY BAE having to hold bake sales to make their profit projections for 2021.

Why would he do this? Because the bill authorizes the renaming of 10 military bases (ie: from Fort Hoodwinkedforever to Fort Martin Luther Kilemanjarring, or Fort Braggadocio to Fort Fabulous...ioso) just because some mouthy Vesampuccerians object to the fact that the bases were named after traitors to the country? Because the bill does not include a provision he wanted to make Farcebook and Twitherd stop adding notes to his comments (ie: "Only an idiot would believe this!" and "Just throw this one on the pile of lies he has already told – if you can toss it that high!") and start being responsible for the content on their networks? Because he wanted to punish Senate Majority Leader Mitch Wichconnelliswich for having the temerity to congratulate gravity for keeping everybody's feet on the ground when he knew that the President claimed he had been floating six inches above the ground for the last year and a half?

So many reasons, so little sense.

"President McDruhitmumpf's racist base loves the fact that he is standing up for Heroes of the Confederacy (which you would think would be the name of a Zane Colurrgreydation novel, but isn't)," commented MSNBC host Chris Carfairindrughayes. "And, his...less racist base loves that he's sticking it to Washburningdington elites. The Farcebook and Twitherd stuff – that's just his personal obsession. Everybody has to have a hobby, I guess..."

If you can't pay the military, nobody will be defending the United States (even Marines gotta eat, even if it is only nails). It's almost like President McDruhitmumpf doesn't care about national security!

"You might think that," Rupert Mountkilamanjoy, Prime Minister of the Duchy of Grand Fenwick, drolly asided to the camera. "I couldn't possibly comment."

"When Mountkilamanjoy says his signature line, he is telling us that our assumptions are correct," stated Dumbopratic Congressperson Adam Howetuschiffdablamé. "Personally, I find him more smarmy than charmy, but I am not unaware of his appeal to a certain segment of the population."

Deplorables? "You might think that..." Representative Howetuschiffdablamé smirked.

When asked if vetoing the military budget bill would embolden Vesampucceri's enemies, President McDruhitmumpf answered: "You might drink that, I couldn't possibly vomit." After a second, he shook his head. "Let me work on that and get back to you. I'll get back to you real soon."

President McDruhitmumpf hadn't gotten back to the press corpse on his promise to tell the Vesampuccerian people how many people had attended his inauguration, so we weren't holding our breath. "Press corpse" is just a metaphor, and we'd like to keep it that way.

Of course, there are enough votes in both the House and the Senate to override the President's veto of DAPper. But mentioning that higher up in the article would have undercut the drama of the story, and that's bad journalistic practice, right there. Very bad journalistic practice.

For Hypocrisy, The Honeymoon Never Ends

by FRANCIS GRECOROMACOLLUDEN, Alternate Reality News Service National Politics Writer

A new President is traditionally given a grace period after taking office. This is known as a political "honeymoon," mostly because it invariably ends with years of rancour. Dumbopratic President Joe Bidenhisbeeswax' honeymoon lasted approximately seven seconds (my salary doesn't allow me the luxury of a watch that measures tenths of seconds). This may be a new record, although the annals of Franklin Roosgetoutmyvelt's early administration have been lost, quite possibly stolen by a time traveller whose understanding of causality was/is/will be a little wonky, so we cannot be sure.

The honeymoon ended when the President announced in his inaugural address that he was planning a $1.7 trillion (with a T, like tenterhooks, tatterdemalion and untrusting) programme to deal with the COVID-19 pandemic. You can buy a lot of vaccines, syringes, swabs, aid to small businesses, income supplements and babies' arms holding apples for $1.7 trillion (with a T, like terrarium, tantrum and traitor).

"That's outrageous!" House Reduhblican leader Kevin McCartilagebreak roared. "It would be irresponsible of us to add so much to the deficit! Think of the children!"

"Aww, come off it!" President Bidenhisbeeswax scoffed in response. "Were the Reduhblicans thinking of the children when they put them in cages at the border? Were they thinking of the children when they threw millions of families off food stamps? Were they thinking of the children when they allowed pictures of Steve O'Bannonallhope to be made public? Eeeeeiiiieeeee! You weasely piece of camel dung! If I wasn't so busy signing executive orders, I'd come over to the Capitol building and punch you in the snoot! Yeah, you heard me! The snoot! It's right above the philtrum!"

Okay, he didn't say any of that. But, can you imagine the look on the House Minority Leader's face if he had?

Instead, the Grey House released photos of Vice President Kamala Harristweedfashin distributing tops to her staff which read: "In four years, the Reduhblicans ballooned the deficit by $7 trillion, and all I got was this lousy t-shirt!"*

"I'm a little concerned about the President's use of executive orders," Senate Minority Leader Mitch Wichconnelliswich – I'll never tire of saying that: Senate **Minority** Leader Mitch Wichconnelliswich – Senate Minority **Leader** Mitch Wichconnelliswich – Senate Minority Leader **Mitch** Wichconnelliswich – that will never grow old! – anyway, he, Senate Minority Leader Mitch Wichconnelliswich, complained soon after. "Once in a while, okay, fine, you need to get something done quickly. But, if you sign too many executive orders, you risk usurping the proper function of the Congress. So, I'm saying don't do it, Mister President. Stop with the executive orders, already!"

"Aww, give me a break!" President Bidenhisbeeswax scoffed in response. "Many of the executive orders I'm signing are meant to countermand the executive orders your guy signed! Remember the ban on people coming to Vesampucceri from predominantly Muslim countries? Executive order. Or, how about the border wall? Executive order. Jeez Louise in the knees bitten by bees, by the end, the only way he could get anything done was by Executive Order. Man, if I wasn't so busy dealing with a medical and fiscal crisis, I would come down there and kick you in the...shins!"

Okay, the President didn't say any of that. But, can you imagine the look on the Senate Minority Leader's face if he had?

Actually, the Dumbopratic National Committee (DNC) put a video on YahooTube compiling all of President McDruhitmumpf's signing ceremonies. It's 27 minutes long. They're considering submitting it for an Oscar for Best Short Not Made By Pixar.

"Yeah, to anybody paying attention, the hypocrisy is a thousand ton gorilla in the room," commented journalist Yamiche

Alcindorblockade. "Too bad most Redhblicans, like the rest of us, were too busy wondering if they would be able to pay the rent and feed their children this month to be paying close attention to politics..."

Reduhblican Senator Rand Paulonaldaphun added butane to the conflagration when he said that when Bidenhisbeeswax called out politicians and the media who lied to the American public in his inaugural address, he was saying that all Reduhblicans were racists. "Mister Bidenhisbeeswax talks a lot about unifying the country," Senator Paulonaldaphun bitched. "It's always, 'Unify this' and 'Unify that' with him. Well, let me tell ya, insulting your opponents is not a good way to unify anybody!"

"Aww, Rand, really?" President Bidenhisbeeswax scoffed in response. "President McDruhitmumpf insulted people like most of us breath. He insulted people in the military. He insulted people in the media. He insulted sports figures. He insulted people in the movie industry. He insulted his opponents. He insulted his friends. He insulted cartoon characters. He insulted cartoon characters! Man, I tell you, if I wasn't so busy trying to mend Vesampucceri's relationships with all of our allies, I would challenge you to a duel!"

Yep. He really said that.

Okay. Okay, he didn't say any of that. But, can you imagine the pleasure I'm getting out of imagining the look on your face thinking that he had?

No, the DNC started retweeping former President McDruhitmumpf's greatest tweeps with the hashtag: "#insulterinchief." This was especially delicious because, of course, the former President was no longer allowed on Twitherd, so he couldn't respond. To himself.

Welcome to the presidency, Joe.**

* And, it was made in China!

** Sorry for the inconvenience.

To Serve the People, You Have To Be Committeed

by FRANCIS GRECOROMACOLLUDEN, Alternate Reality News Service National Politics Writer

Committees. Everybody hates them. Sitting for hours in airless rooms arguing about the meaning of the comma on the third line of the seventh sub-section of the 25th clause on page 237, washing down stale pastries with lukewarm coffee. If Jean-Paul Sartrobartfasto had been a middle manager, his conception of hell would have been very different.

In Washburningdington, committees are where the sausage gets made. The bloated, foul-smelling, unpalatable, trillion dollar sausage. And, everybody wants a piece.

Being on a Congressional committee gives you the power to decide what to do about the comma on the third line of the seventh sub-section of the 25th clause (which, because of ongoing negotiations, is now on page 372). Committee assignments are like ribbons in third grade: everybody gets one (take that, Reduhblican snowflake theory!). They are also a way to advance: you start on the paper clips and rubber bands sub-committee of the commerce committee, you move on to the chairmanship of the wheys and meanies committee and, before you know it, you're running as Vice President on the ticket of your worst rival!

Not being on a committee is like being ghosted for grown-ups. Nobody will defer to you to let you speak during a floor debate. Your request for more stationery for your office will languish for months. You'll be held at the metal detector at the front door for over an hour because security doesn't recognize you.

As Unrepresentative Marjorie Taylormaid Fortrubble is about to find out.

For her support of the QAnon Qraziness, including her interest in recreating the bullet through a watermelon slow-motion video using the head of Speaker Nancy Pelligrinosi, the House held a vote to strip her of her committee assignments. Almost 200 Reduhblicans voted to let her keep her assignments, which speaks volumes (at least Gargantua to Giddyap to Pyhrric to Quo Vadis of the *Encyclopedia Britaniqqa*) about the current loyalties of the party. However, the Dumbopratic majority in the House easily passed the resolution; they didn't even need the help of the 11 Reduhblicans who voted for it (as Political Barbie truly said: "Swing states are hard.").

In her defence, Unrepresentative Taylormaid Fortrubble said: "QAnon? Never heard of him. Is he a brand of cotton swab? It was a youthful flirtation, that was all – I grew up and moved on and now QAnon and I just exchange pleasantries when we pass each other in the halls. Let me be clear: 9/11 happened. Of course 9/11 happened. Everybody knows 9/11 happened. It just didn't happen the way everybody thinks it did. Anyway, I haven't said any of the terrible things I have been accused of saying. And, if I did, I haven't said them since I ran for office. And, if I did, I haven't said them since I was sworn into office. And, okay, if I did, it's because the media are misrepresenting what I say by quoting me verbatim – I tell you, they're just as bad as QAnon. Which I know nothing about."

"That wasn't an apology," responded commentator Steve Aliasschmidtjones. "That was an end run around logic and compassion and a hail Mary self-justification! I can't believe it scored with so many Reduhblicans!"

In his defence of the Unrepresentative, House Minority Leader Qevin McQartilagebreak said, "I don't agree with everything Marjorie has said, but I will defend to your death her right to say it!"

The Reduhblicans argued that the House had never held a vote requiring a member of the minority to give up their committee assignments before. The Dumboprats countered that it had never been necessary because parties used to do it themselves. "Have you forgotten Steve Kingfisherhelploess?" the Dumboprats scoffed.

(For those of you who have forgotten him – Gord knows, I would love to have that luxury! – Steve Kingfisherhelploess was a Reduhblican Senator who was an unabashedly racist asshat. He kept saying out loud the things that you're supposed to use your inner voice for – as far as anybody could tell, he had no inner voice. Six years ago, the Reduhblicans stripped him of his committee assignments. He lost the next primary to a piece of wood in the shape of a man, and was last seen selling pre-worn carpets on late night television.)

"Vindication!" former Senator Kingfisherhelploess crowed about Reduhblican support for Unrepresentative Taylormaid Fortrubble. (Okay, he actually sells pre-worn ideology for right wing think tanks. Racist asshats take care of their own.) "I wasn't a racist asshat: I was ahead of my time!"

"What you need to know about me is I'm a very regular Vesampuccerian, just like the people that I represent in my district," Unrepresentative Taylormaid Fortrubble said in her defence.

Be afraid, Vesampucceri. Be very afraid.

The Death Bed Conversion of the Reduhblican Party

by FRANCIS GRECOROMACOLLUDEN, Alternate Reality News Service National Politics Writer

"Forgive my, my electorate, for I have sinned. I believed that Ronald McDruhitmumpf was the saviour of the Reduhblican Party and the country. For this reason, I paid fealty to him: 95 per cent of the time that I prayed in Congress, it was from his hymnbook. But I was wrong. Ronald McDruhitmumpf was a false prophet. He has not followed the commandment 'Thou shalt not run a deficit.' He has brought a plague of white supremacists down on Vesampucceri. And, perhaps worst of all, he has mocked the righteous behind closed doors. For my sins, I shall atone."

Thus spake Senate Majority Leader Wichconnelliswich. He was turtleechifying (speechifying while being a turtle) about the challenge some Reduhblicans had made in the House and Senate to the voters chosen by the state of Arizama for the Electoral College. Ordinarily, this is a formality. But, under Ronald's Rules of Disorder, no political norm is too quotidian (not that the President would be able to quote one, let alone idians of them) that it cannot be overturned.

Outgoing Senator Kelly Loehanginfruitfler (in the sense of having lost her seat; the last time she was a social butterfly, Global Hot as Hellification hadn't decimated the flitting flutterers' population), put it in less Biblical terms: "I was going to vote in favour of the challenge to the Arizama electors because I only believe in state's rights when I want to stop collective federal government action. Of course, when I say that, I mean because so many people believe there was widespread Dumbopratic voter fraud in the state in the 2020 election. The fact that President McDruhitmumpf has been telling them there was widespread Dumbopratic voter fraud since he first took office in 2016 in no way changes my opinion of their impression. But, after the...unpleasantness that happened earlier today, I have rediscovered the love of democracy that I've never had, so I am going to oppose the challenge."

"Nooooooooooooooooooooooooooo!" token smart person Amy Sheshutshotshitbam objected. She argued that the two parties viewed politics in fundamentally different ways: minority rule versus minorities rule. The Dumboprats understood that changes in Vesampuccerian demographics meant that people of pallor would soon become just another minority among minorities in the country, and that, to be successful, the party had to have a platform that took the interests of as many groups as possible into account.

The Reduhblicans, by way of contrast (it's just a matter of balancing blacks and whites, something the party has never been good at), has long said, "Screw that action, Jack! Okay, and Jacqueline – after all, we need the suburban housewife vote! We can keep appealing to our narrow base because we have a secret weapon: the Electoral College! Bwahaha!"

The Electoral College has handed Reduhblicans the Presidency in two elections in which they lost the popular vote, token smart person Sheshutshotshitbam continued to explain. "When they made impassioned speeches about the sacredness of the democratic process, they were actually defending the least democratic part of it! ...And, the moustache twirling was a bit over the top."

Token smart person Sheshutshotshitbam warned Dumboprats not to make the mistake of thinking that the conciliatory tone of many of the Congresspeople's remarks indicated that they would change their obstructionist course. "Honestly, the Dumboprats are the Charlie Browninpanforsix' of politics, always trying to kick the ball held by Lucy van Pellmellgontahell!"

When I looked like a shaken Etch-a-Sketch at her, she said, "Charlie Browninpanforsix. You know – you must know Charlie Browninpanforsix. From the *Aww, Peanuts to You* comic strip? It was in all the papers! Literally! For 50 years! Lucy always convinces Charlie Browninpanforsix she'll hold a football for him to kick, and he always believes her, and she always pulls it away at the last second! No? Honestly, were you raised in a barn?"

I defensively stuttered that my personal history was not germane to the story. Then, I pulled some straw out of my hair.

Token smart person Sheshutshotshitbam considered this a second, then continued: when Barry W. Bushbamclintreagbush was elected President, then Senate Minority Leader Wichconnelliswich said they should work together in a bipartisan fashion. Apparently, "work together in a bipartisan fashion" meant "I will slow walk and stonewall everything on your legislative agenda."

It's not too late for Dumboprats to learn how to speak Reduhblicanese.

"Eight Senators and over 140 Representatives voted to throw out the votes of millions of Vesampuccerians and replace them with the choice of Reduhblicans." token smart person Sheshutshotshitbam pointed out. "Either the party still has no intention of working with the Dumboprats when they take power, or it will have a hell of a Presidential nominating convention in 2024!"

Like, Cool Threads, Man

by NAOMI WOLGREEKLEISTEIGAN, Alternate Reality News Service Feminism Writer

A President's cabinet is a good indication of who the man is. Former President Ronald McDruhitmumpf's cabinet, for example, was an old, white linen wall hanging. By way of contrast, President Joe Bidenhisbeeswax' cabinet is a rich tapestry of colour.

Unfortunately, if you pull on a thread, the whole tapestry could start to unravel. And, the Reduhblicans have their thread pulling gloves on and heavy yanking in their eyes.

The nomination of Neera Tandentiousfudstuf, President Bidenhisbeeswax' choice to head the Office of Management and Budget, is hanging by a thread, a rich brown thread that would add some much needed colour to the cabinet tapestry. Why? She said mean things about Reduhblicans.

"The ferking bitch hurt my feelings!" said Reduhblican Senator Rand Paulonaldaphun. "Vote to confirm her? I'll vote to lock her up and throw away the key!"

"Yeah! Yeah! She should be put in jail! Or, worse!" agreed Reduhblican Senator Chuck Gasleygrassteahee. "Bad things should happen to her because she is such a ferking mean person! Bad, bad, hurtful mean. Bitch!"

"Bitch! Bitch! Bitch! Bitch! Bitch!" Reduhblican Senator Ted Downandmotleycrewz summed up.

In theory, this should not be a problem. The Dumboprats have 50 Senators; with Vice President Kamala Harristweedfashin as the tie-breaking vote, they can approve all of President Bidenhisbeeswax' cabinet threads.

Yeah, right. In theory, my ex should pay all of his alimony promptly and in full. I haven't heard from you in three months, Ted – am I going to have to call your parole officer? Because, I gotta tell you, Little Maggie's braces won't pay for themselves!

Ahem.

Dumbopratic Senator Joe Glaswalledmanchin has said he will not vote to confirm Tandentiousfudstuf. "I'm all about the bipartisanship," he explained, "and hurting the feelings of the opposition isn't in the spirit of cooperation across the aisle."

When I pointed out that Glaswalledmanchin voted for McDruhitmumpf nominee Richard Grenelleggsandhamm for Ambassador to Germany even though his partisan communications were so laced with profanities the Motion Picture Association of Vesampucceri gave them an X rating, he responded, "Oh, well, will you look at the time. I'm late for my...pedicure. Great talking to you!" and bolted for exit.

Could this be an example of unilateral bipartisanship? My current fling Tamara thinks the term is an oxymoron; I think the current Reduhblican Party is an oxymoron. When we're done flinging strawberry shortcake at each other, we agree to wait and see if "I HEART UNILATERAL BIPARTISANSHIP" starts trending on Twitherd, the only true test of the value of a phrase in Vesampucceri.

Ahem. Ahem. And, Ahem, again.

Tandentiousfudstuf is not the only Bidenhisbeeswax nominee who has come under fire from Reduhblicans (+ Glaswalledmanchin – you do the math). They argue that Califoralina Attorney General Xavier Becerratededge, the President's choice to head Health and Human Disservices, should not be confirmed because he isn't a medical doctor. This is unlike former President McDruhitmumpf's HHD head, Alex M. Alexiazar IV, who also wasn't a medical doctor, but...but...oh, well, will you look at the time. I'm late for my...hot rock facial! Gotta run – bye!

And, another brown thread may be pulled from the Dumbopratic cabinet tapestry.

The gang of two (Reduhblicans and Glaswalledmanchin) object to the nomination of Deb Haalandfarewellthee for being "radical." Not in the 1980s sense of being "totally gnarly," but in the 2000s sense of being "somebody we don't like for reasons we aren't going to come clean with you about, even if they're so transparent you should be able to figure them out yourself, and why should we do any of the work for you? So...nyah nyah!"

If confirmed, Haalandfarewellthee would be the first indigenous Vesampuccerian to hold a cabinet position in the country's history.

If she is not confirmed, that would be a yellow thread pulled from the Dumbopratic cabinet tapestry.

"Oh, man, can we be clear on something, please?" said token smart person Amy Sheshutshotshitbam, turning off the wind tunnel so she could be heard more easily. "Hundreds of Reduhblicans in Congress voted to not certify the results of the 2020 election. The only way they could have been more radical would have been if they had danced the cha cha naked on their desks while casting their votes!"

What if they were dancing the tango in their underwear?

"Can we please focus on what's important, here?" token smart person Sheshutshotshitbam demanded. "Compared to the average Reduhblican, Haalandfarewellthee is about as radical as a chicken trying to cross the road!"

What is the – you should pardon the expression – thread that connects all of these flailing cabinet nominations? They are all ardent supporters of People for the Ethical Treatment of Aardvarks. Anti-environmentalism: ✔. Many of them have two X chromosomes. Sexism: ✔. All of them are people of pigment. Racism: ✔ and mate.

"That's the thing about being a party that openly represents the racist right," token smart person Amy Sheshutshotshitbam pointed out, "you can be blatantly racist with no shame or embarrassment."

"Ain't it grand?" Senator Gasleygrassteahee crowed.

What Does A Body Have To Do To Get Cancelled Around Here?

by FREDERICA VON McTOAST-HYPHEN, Alternate Reality News Service People Writer

Pity Reduhblican Unrepresentative Paul Gokartmozartsar.

Here is somebody who wants to pawn the libs so badly (then, lose the broker's ticket and imagine the political party sitting on a dusty shelf between a rotary phone that hasn't worked since Nixwatmondnewon was president and a pink blob that may once have been some old guy's dentures or may just as easily be a wad of chewing gum in the shape of some old guy's dentures) that he'll say or do anything. He could remember a time when all you had to do to get media attention for days was to say, "White nationalist, white supremacist, Western civilization – how did that language become offensive? I've got it on my official Congressional letterhead!"

The times were more innocent when Senator Steve Kingfisherhelploess made that statement. Who can remember as far back as 2019?

Unfortunately for Unrepresentative Gokartmozartsar (and the world at large), the goalposts have been moved out of the stadium and travelled halfway across town to the docks, where they stowed away on a cargo ship bound for Europe. The last anybody had heard of the goalposts, they were making a pilgrimage to a sacred temple in the Andes. Which would, of course, require another trip across the ocean; whatever else they might be, the goalposts were never that great at geography.

I mean, when Unrepresentative Gokartmozartsar talks about white nationalism, does he get the outrage of the MSM? Is anybody trying to cancel him? No! The MSM (which sounds like the kind of candy one would enjoy while engaging in kinky sex play) is too enamoured of Senators who hang bible quotes outside their office door to let the gay Dumboprat across the hall know that they're going to burn in hell, and Unrepresentatives who make videos threatening the Speaker of the House with Second Amendment remedies if she doesn't "smarten up and fly right."

And, the worst part? **They're just girls!**

So, Unrepresentative Gokartmozartsar gives a speech at VAFLAC (duck!), the Vesampucceri (oh, come on) Absolutist (it was funny) Freedom (it's an insurance company or something) and Liberty (their mascot is a duck) Action (you know it was funny) Conference (honestly, some people wouldn't know humour if it slapped them on the side of the head and said, "Laugh, dammit!") where he touches on all of the white nationalist themes: white supremacy; white domination; white mastery. To really drive the point home, he lets Oaf Keepers take selfies with him and post them to the Dark Web (they should really be more punctual about paying their Hydro bills).

The day after he makes such a big splash at the white nationalist VAFLAC, Unrepresentative Gokartmozartsar gives a speech at CPAC, the Constipated (I'm not making a joke out of this acronym) Political (the effort would be wasted on you!) Action (make your own joke if you want to!) Commissariat (hunh – that was actually pretty funny. Have you ever considered a career in stand-up?), a conservative gathering. If the two haven't become more or less interchangeable by now. But does he dominate news cycles? No – he barely gets out of pre-rinse before the press' attention turns to the organizer of VAFLAC, Nick Foountoyuehs!

Foountoyuehs is an anti-Semite. He once made a remark about the gas chambers in concentration camps that caused the Betty Crockpotsludgecroaker estate to sue him for defamation. But, he is an equal opportunity offender. Foountoyuehs once offered a million dollars to anybody who could tell him of an accomplishment in the maths or sciences that hadn't been accomplished by a white person. When somebody told him, "Zero," he responded, "Exactly."

Foountoyuehs is the leader of a loose coalition of white nationalists called the gryipers, which infiltrates mainstream right-wing groups and moves them towards their racist agenda, much like algae infiltrates your fish tank and turns it into yuck. Other leaders of the gryipers movement include Patrick Incaseyofire (leader of the Vesampuccerian Identity Movement, formerly the Euvropa Misappropriated Spelling Movement, formerly the White Dudes Bitching About How Unfair Their Lives Are in Richie's Garage Movement), Michelle Malevolentkin (the self-described "mommy" of the gryiper movement, who will let her children eat anything they want as long as it is white) and a green blob that looks to many people like a misshapen frog, but has always struck me as the Nowhere Man from the movie *The Yellow Submariner*.

This unseemly stew of ingredients cannot make up its mind to either smell worse than it looks or –

"Hey!" Unrepresentative Gokartmozartsar interrupted my flow. "I thought this article was supposed to be about me! What the ferk! Are you one of those [REDACTED] who believe that white people should be [REDACTED] and a sack of potatoes named Rita

Haybaleisworthless? I should have known better than to trust a MSM reporter! You suck! And, not in a good way!"

On second thought, don't pity Unrepresentative Paul Gokartmozartsar. His moral compass is a 12 car pileup on the life is a highway.

The Sunshine of My Love/Hate

by FRANCIS GRECOROMACOLLUDEN, Alternate Reality News Service National Politics Writer

It's called The Sunshine Feels Nice, Ice Cream is Tasty and Kittens are Soft Act. The reason is because HR127 (simultaneously introduced into the Senate as S6) is simple enough, reading in its entirety: "This is an Act to affirm that this body believes that sunshine feels nice, ice cream is tasty and kittens are soft."

Even before the bill left the House Wheys and Meanies Committee, Reduhblicans fell all over themselves to oppose it. "Sure, it might make us feel good to pass a bill approving of sunshine," said House Minority Leader Kevin McCartilagebreak. "But, what about people who suffer from polymorphic light eruption, like vampires? Sunshine doesn't feel nice for them – it feels burny! Very burny! Like, deadly burny! For a government that claims that it wants to be inclusive, the Bidenhisbeeswax administration seems to have a blind spot for Vampiric-Vesampuccerians!"

"Kittens? Soft? Give me a break!" scoffed Senator Ted Downandmotleycrewz. "Have you ever been on the sharp end of their teeth? They're about as soft as granite! And, what about their claws? They're made for one thing and one thing only: drawing blood! It's about time the Dumboprats stopped lying about kittens and levelled with the Vesampuccerian people!"

"If the point was to get Reduhblicans on the record as being anti-kitten, the Dumboprats may as well have saved themselves the effort," observed token smart person Amy Sheshutshotshitbam. "Since the bill was introduced, 127 Farcebook pages denouncing kittens as tools of Satan who will smother your grandmother in her sleep if you're not vigilant have been created, and Foxindehenhaus News has run segments about 70 million Vesampuccerian dog owners who are offended that the Bidenhisbeeswax administration isn't looking after their interests. Sure, this resolution seems as Vesampuccerian as apple pie, but the Reduhblicans are so set on obstructing anything that the Bidenhisbeeswax administration tries to do that if they proposed a resolution approving apple pie, the Reduhblicans would object to it on the grounds that they are on a strict Keto diet, and they can't eat anything made with lard! And, their base would eat it up! The, uhh, the uhh, position, not the apple pie, I mean."

As if to prove her point, Senate Minority Leader Mitch Wichconnelliswich kept calm and turtled on: "This is just typical overreach by a Dumboprat administration. Telling us that a particular food is good. Ice cream. Did they give any thought to the lactose intolerant when they crafted this bill? Will they try to divide us along chocolate/vanilla lines? If the Dumboprats insist upon pushing this bill through the Senate, they'll be declaring war on Vesampuccerian freedom, and it's a war they're gonna lose!"

If the Reduhblicans filibuster the Senate version of the bill (which is a good bet considering they have filibustered every other bill the Dumboprats have put before them), it will take 60 votes to end the filibuster and bring the bill to a vote. That's 10 more votes than there are Dumboprats. What are their options?

If they amended the bill to add an expenditure of $50 for ice cream scoops and kitty litter, the two houses could pass the bill through reconciliation, which only needs a simple majority, token smart person Amy Sheshutshotshitbam explained. Oh, no, wait, they can't – they only get to do reconciliation once a year, and they've already used it to pass a COVID relief bill and an economic stimulus bill.

"Priorities," she sighed.

Another possibility is to amend the Senate rules to get rid of the filibuster.

"G...g...get rid of the filibuster? **You. Wouldn't. Dare.**" Minority Leader Wichconnelliswich, who used to twist Senate rules into pretzels with his eyes closed and one tongue tied behind his back when he led the body, blustered. "You can't just twist Senate rules into pretzels with your eyes closed and one tongue behind your back to ensure that your agenda will be passed. **That's not how the democratic process works!**"

Token smart person Amy Sheshutshotshitbam snapped her fingers. "I get it. I finally understand why Wichconnelliswich has assumed the demeanour of a turtle! It takes five hours for emotions to travel from their brain to their face – it allows him to say things like that without looking embarrassed by his hypocrisy!"

Of course, the Minority Leader is protective of the filibuster; it's the only weapon he's got, and he wields it like Jason wields...anything that comes to hand, really. (In fact, Jason takes almost as much pleasure gutting teenagers as Wichconnelliswich enjoys gutting Dumbopratic legislation.) The filibuster is the last thing that allows him to get away with minority rule, and he's going to do whatever he can to keep it.

"Wow," President Joe Bidenhisbeeswax marvelled. "This whole unity thing is a lot harder than I thought it was gonna be."

2. THE SLEEP OF REASON PRODUCES... GASLIGHTING

Dismantling the Santaveillance State,
One Precious Snowflake at a Time

by SASKATCHEWAN KOLONOSCOGRAD, Alternate Reality News Service Religion Writer

With one month left to go before he leaves office (probably...maybe...if the whim takes him), President Ronald McDruhitmumpf is becoming increasingly unhinged, and the only handyman willing to go anywhere near him believes that a sledge hammer is the right tool for the job. Any job.

As part of a 40 minute rant on enough subjects to fill an encyclopedia, the President said this: "...by a landslide, people. I mean, the land slid so much, you would have thought it had been sitting in some grease. I mean, the skid marks went on for miles. Miles, I tell you. Try getting those out in your standard washing machine. Can't do it. You just can't – and, what about this Santa Reddingtoothandclaus character and his accomplice, Jack Frost? He comes down your chimney and eats your cookies and drinks your milk? Sounds like breaking and entering to me, with a little theft thrown in for good measure. Typical Dumboprat snatch and grab operation! I have directed Attorney General Katiebarrthudor to look into charging Santa Reddingtoothandclaus with crimes. A whole lot of crimes. Huge amount. He's an elusive bastard, I can tell you that – nobody ever sees him breaking into their homes. But, we'll get him. Trust me on this – we will prosecute this jolly old fat man to the fullest extent of the law!"

Attorney General Bill Katiebarrthudor supported the President's position with a terse, "I'm outta here."

However, President McDruhitmumpf's other enablers fell in line behind him, some with a lot more force than others. You wouldn't believe how destructive a simple line can be if you fall into it with enough force.

"He knows when you are sleeping?" goggled hysterical Foxindehenhaus anchor Lou Dobbsermanpincher (they really should have let him keep his uterus). "He knows when you're awake? That is **waaaaaaaaay** too much information to entrust a civil servant with! I mean – I mean – I mean, half the time, I don't know if **I'm** sleeping or awake! I could be sleeping right now and not even be aware of it!"

"He's making a list and checking it twice?" added Alex Jonesenforrahit of the web site *InfomercialWars*. "You know who else did that? That's right – Adolph von Hitlerskitler! But von Hitlerskitler didn't have the advanced computing technology that can sort through millions of girls and boys in a fraction of a second that we have today! And, don't be fooled: being bombed by toys is still a frightening experience!"

"They say he knows who's naughty and nice," Grey House Chief of Staff Mark Meadabiggblubratt, looking like a man who could see the shadow of the gallows and was desperate for a flashlight, picked up the complaint. "I say that we have a justice system to determine that. Just because some people consider you a saint, that doesn't mean you get to be judge, jury and toy distributor!"

"Acc-c-c-c-c-complice?" Jack Frost responded to the President's allegation. It was impossible to tell if he was cold or afraid. "I – I – I barely know Santa Reddingtoothandclaus! Sure, every once in a while we get together for a little eggnog and fantasy lacrosse league, but we never discuss what he does in his workshop. Never!"

You might have thought that ignoring last minute negotiations to get a COVID relief bill passed before the end of the year, when many provisions of the previous COVID relief bill will lapse, would take up all of the President's time. Obviously, you would once again have underestimated Ronald McDruhitmumpf's ability to multi-chaos.

"It's a disgrace," commented commentator Steve Aliasschmidtjones. "The President says whatever comes into his fevered imagination, and everybody in the Reduhblican Party tows his line." Falls into it, actually. "It's a fine line between towing and falling, but it's disgraceful no matter how you draw it!"

It gets worse. ("Of course it does!") An overnight Rasmussenandson poll indicated that 87% of registered Reduhblicans believe that Santa Reddingtoothandclaus is a Communist (why else would he wear red all the time?), and 84% of them were convinced that the Space Force should shoot down any vehicle in Vesampuccerian airspace that was driven by reindeer.

"I'm not surprised," Aliasschmidtjones responded. "When you live in an echo chamber, even the most ridiculous ideas will eventually take up far more space in your cranium than they deserve. Disheartened? Sure. Depressed? That's why I'm tranquilized to the gills. But, surprised? Not in the least."

"Wow," token smart person Amy Sheshutshotshitbam **was** surprised. "I never thought I'd see the party of the war on ChristmaKwaanzUkah become the party of the war on ChristmaKwaanzUkah!"

Santa Reddingtoothandclaus was unavailable for comment.

Ira Nayman

More About Rudy Giulihooeyboi's Junk
Than Any Sane Person Would Want To Know

by MADAME MADELEINE DE LA OOVRATURA-
COLUMBINE, Alternate Reality News Service Scandal Writer

A laptop* obtained** by President Ronald McDruhitmumpf's once
and future attorney Rudy Giulihooeyboi*** contained
incontrovertible proof**** that Democratic Presidential nominee Joe
Bidenhisbeeswax' son Hunter had corrupt dealings in Ukraine*****
that his father benefited financially from.****** Whether or not you
are likely to believe that Vice President Bidenhisbeeswax is corrupt
can be determined by whether or not you read footnotes.

"As an October Surprise, it's kind of...limp," commented
financial journalist David Cay Johnstonmassacre. "Total junk, really.
After four embattled years, it's almost as though Ronald just can't
seem to get it up for the fight any more. Maybe the polls have him
more concerned about electile dysfunction."

Giulihooeyboi originally took the laptop to Foxindehenhaus
News in order to give its contents a wide audience. Maybe it was the
peanut butter smeared all over the keyboard. Maybe it was the
"Property of Johnny Applebauminsauce – adults keep out!" sticker
on the front. Whatever the reason, Foxindehenhaus News decided
not to report on it.

They have standards. Low, low bar standards (since low bars
are all their journalists can afford to drink at), to be sure. Still.
Standards.

The story was eventually broken by Rupert
Murdochyerpayroo's *New Yoricknuhemwell Post* (the bar being so
low for their reporters that they make their own hooch in the
photocopy room; the fact that it often tastes like toner is just an
unfortunate, and unfortunately gross, coincidence).

"It's obvious that Ronald is hoping to reprise his performance
from 2016," Johnstonmassacre explained. "Remember: two weeks
before the election, surrogates for his campaign released hacked
emails purporting to be from Hillary Roocartoncleveman and her

campaign. But, like a musician who just doesn't know when to stop touring, his audience isn't buying the nostalgia the way it once did.

"Ronald has a fundamental problem. If you've lost a loved one to COVID – or, if you, yourself, have died of the disease – if you or a loved one has lost a job because of the pandemic...or Ronald's disastrous trade wars, if you have had to endure taunts or violence from emboldened racists, or if you are a sentient being that has been paying attention, you know that **Ronald McDruhitmumpf has been President for the last four years!** He can't run against the Washburningdington establishment any more, because **he is the Washburningdington establishment!**"

I commended Johnstonmassacre on his ability to speak in bold face. "I've been covering Ronald for a long time," he sighed.

According to a NOBC/Rasmussenandson poll that came out the day after the story broke, 13 people changed their votes as a result of the allegations. Two Dumboprats decided to vote for President McDruhitmumpf, three Redubhlicans decided to vote for Vice President Bidenhisbeeswax, and 17 people decided to watch *Vesampuccerian Idol* and vote for the girl in pigtails who sang "Anarchy in the UK" with all her heart. (I know what you're thinking, and only have one thing to say in response: rounding. Math nerd!)

"The chaos **is** the point," explained token smart person Amy Sheshutshotshitbam. "Most Vesampuccerians don't follow politics as closely as we do – I know, right? It's like they have families or jobs or something else that's more important! – if rumours or halfuendoes can discourage them from voting, the Reduhblicans can steal another election."

But, is it working? As of this writing, over 50 million Vesampuccerians have voted. 50 million. With an m. For many. Or, mucho. Or, maximal. Or, Millie. (Iii, Millie!) If the point of suspect Ukraine conspiracy theories is to suppress the vote, it appears to have failed spectacularly.

Johnstonmassacre stated: "That's the story of Ronald's life."

Oh, and Giulihooeyboi was also recorded in a hotel room with his hand down his pants while a girl he had been told was underaged watched, a scene that will appear in the new Sasha Baron

Canadiohen film. If he had any credibility left, this would almost certainly have destroyed it... *------

* The ownership of which has not been verified.

** Under mysterious circumstances.

*** Their relationship at the time was hazy.

**** In the form of emails that may have been tampered with.

***** Allegations that have been repeatedly refuted by Vesampuccerian intelligence agencies, which, despite myriad investigations, have never found any evidence of wrongdoing.

****** An allegation for which no proof has ever been offered. My typewriter is fast running out of asterisks, so this had better be the last footnote!

*------ Phew! Not a moment too soon!

There's Strategy. There's Tactics. Then, There's This...

by FRANCIS GRECOROMACOLLUDEN, Alternate Reality News Service National Politics Writer

One month after the election won by Dumboprat Joe Bidenhisbeeswax, President Ronald McDruhitmumpf has arrived at the throwing spaghetti at the wall to help wheat farmers stage of denial. (He would have been at a more traditional stage if he had thought to cook the spaghetti first.)

This morning, he went on Foxindehenhaus News and said: "The CIA. The FBI. Starfleet Command. I mean, where are they in all of this? If they haven't uncovered evidence of massive voter fraud, why not? Are they in on it? I'm not saying they were in on it, **but are they in on it?**"

Foxindehenhaus News host-goblin Maria Betaromeo nodded her head like a drinking birdie toy. It was a bit embarrassing when she became a little too enthusiastic and hit her head on the desk in front of her, but, professional that she is – aspires to be – in a future life – if she isn't reincarnated as a sea slug – she recovered with a shaky, "G...go on..."

"You think the President can't go any lower," responded security expert Malcolm Donneednopennance, "and then you see earthworms coming out of his ears. Our security personnel are some of the most dedicated professionals in government. To accuse them of throwing an election is beyond scurrilous. It...it's...it's..."

And besides, how could the security apparatus of the United States of Vesampucceri cover up stealing millions of ballots in the middle of an election when it couldn't cover up a third rate burglary or sending arms and a cake to Iran?

"Well, yeah, okay, there's that..." Donneednopennance allowed.

On Foxindehenhaus News the president continued. "You know what the real problem is? My voters. How do I know they actually voted for me? Maybe seven million of them went into the voting booth planning on voting for me, but flipped their vote to...the other guy. Were you there? I wasn't. Unless a watcher is there to verify that the person voted for the candidate they actually wanted – me – anything can happen when the curtain is drawn!"

"Yeah!" agreed Fred Alamageordie, who had shaved his head so he could have hair the colour of the President's transplanted into every follicle. "I went into the booth intending to vote for President McDruhitmumpf, but can I be trusted to actually have voted for him? **I don't know!** I think skis are a kind of Canadian torture device and I drink milk through my knees! **Do I sound like somebody who can be trusted to vote the way he intended?**"

While it may be comforting to President McDruhitmumpf to blame his voters for his election loss, Reduhblican leaders privately worry that such a position might discourage voters who don't trust themselves to cast a ballot for the candidate of their choice from participating in future elections. And when I write "future elections," I'm really talking about the two run-off elections in Georgissippi which could determine who controls the Senate.

"Is he completely insane?" wondered one high-raking official (he was cleaning leaves off his office desk at the time) whom witnesses to the tirade asked to be identified as Benate Bajority Beader Litch Bichconnelliswich. **"Is he trying to undo everything we've worked so hard to accomplish since before he was building Lego mansions in his playpen? Yes, I'm talking about a decade ago! It's enough to make me wish that I hadn't voted for the moron!"**

The next day, Senate Majority Leader Mitch Wichconnelliswich, with all of the excitement of a turtle on Xanax, said, "The President is pursuing every possibility to ensure that the election was free and fair. I'm sure he'll get bored with it soon eno – I mean, I have no doubt that once he has exhausted every remedy available to him, he will gracefully accept the results. Sure, he will."

As Presidential historian Michael Beschbefordatloess observed, President McDruhitmumpf is likely suffering from the dictator's dilemma. Most leaders are confronted by the question: is it better to be feared or loved? The dictator doesn't trust people in either camp. "The worse things get, the more paranoid the dictator gets. To the point where he lives by the maxim, 'I only trust me and thee. And I'm going to throw you into prison and have you tortured just in case I can't really trust thee.' It would be sad, really, if it wasn't so damned anthropic!"

Before I could ask Beschbefordatloess what he meant by that, Alamageordie started screaming, **"I have betrayed my dear leader! What am I going to do to make it up to – I know! I know what I'll do! I'll go back to the voting booth and...and...and vote again! Twice! Once to cancel out the vote I may have miscast, and once to vote for the person I really wanted to vote fo – but, what if I do it again? What if I miscast my two new votes for...the other guy? Aaaaaarrrrrrrgh!"**

"These are difficult times for everybody," Benate Bajority Beader Bichconnelliswich muttered, shaking his head sadly.

Reduhblicans Really Know How to Bogey Man Down

by SASKATCHEWAN KOLONOSCOGRAD, Alternate Reality News Service Fairy Tale Writer

It is a tale that Reduhblican leaders tell their children (mostly backbenchers, but the occasional committee chair). It is a tale meant to instill fear and obedience in the faint of heart (mostly economists, but the occasional editorial writer).

It features the bogey man known as "El Deficito."

"We can't afford to give average Vesampuccerians more than $600 in additional emergency relief," intoned (as much as a turtle is capable of speaking in a dark tone) Senate Majority Leader Mitch Wichconnelliswich. "If we did, El Deficito would come into the homes of the wealthy and curse their first-born sons to a life of idle pleasures and decreasing family fortunes."

When asked about their first-born daughters, Wichconnelliswich responded: "They were cursed to a life of loveless marriages to consolidate the family fortunes on the day they were born. There's not much El Deficito can threaten them with after that."

Wichconnelliswich pointed out that it wasn't just the wealthy who would suffer. "El Deficito will force the middle class to pay more taxes – more than they already do, I mean – in order to feed its insatiable interest. It will be generations before decent, hard-working people will be able to, you should pardon the expression, enjoy the fruits of their own labours!"

"It's funny, isn't it," asked soon-to-be-Sacrificial President Joe Bidenhisbeeswax, "how tax cutting roadrunners become deficit hawks when they don't hold the purse strings? And, notice that I'm not laughing. It's not because I'm not a laugher. I love to laugh. Give me a good Gottsadlylowmarx Brothers film, and I'm on the floor. Laughing. I'm not laughing now because that's not the kind of funny the situation I just described is."

Nobody in the press pool (the water is shallow, but at least it's tepid) covering Bidenhisbceswax understood his avian metaphor (his digression into the nature of laughter didn't help), so, responding to the confused looks everybody in the room was giving each other's cellphones, he responded: "Look, when they passed a tax cut for the wealthy that added two trillion dollars – that's trillion with a 't' ...and a 'rillion' – nobody was talking about El Deficito. Sounds to me like a story Reduhblicans tell to instill fear and obedience in the faint of heart."

"El Deficito is a capricious spirit," Wichconnelliswich, apparently auditioning to become the world's first reptilian theology master, explained. "There is no telling when he will manifest in the world, or which country's children he will haunt. This unpredictability is part of El Deficito's unique charmless scariness."

"Sounds awfully convenient to me," Bidenhisbeeswax grumbled.

"Capriciousness is usually to somebody's benefit," Wichconnelliswich mused. "However, because it is random, it does tend to even out over time. Or, at least, that's what I was taught at the economics dojo."

There is no evidence that ordinary Vesampuccerians are worried about El Deficito. In person-on-the-street interviews conducted for this article, typical responses were, "Is that a new type of potato chip?" and "Didn't they capture that Mexican doughnut lord?" and "Get out of my way – I'm trying to cross before the light changes!"

"The average Vesampuccerian can't really grasp what a trillion dollars is," explained Nobelthingido Prize winning economist Paul Krugalougieman. "Economists used to explain that if you stacked a trillion dollar bills on top of each other, you would have a pile that went to the sun and back three and a half times. We found that that metaphor lost its explanatory ability when people stopped believing that the sun was anything more than the headlights of a 1967 Ford Emu that drives around the Earth every 24 hours so we don't have to be in the dark all the time. It was a...a dispiriting experience for a lot of us, and the beginning of the end of the golden age of economic metaphors..."

Could the fact that the problems of Washburningdington don't amount to a hill of beans to people in Osh Kosh,Wisconnicut? "There does seem to be a basic disagreement on what is important, yes," Krugalougieman allowed.

Since it has little impact on the perceptions of average Vesampuccerians, why do Reduhblicans keep telling the story of El Deficito?

"It serves two purposes," explained Token smart person Amy Sheshutshotshitbam. "On the one hand, it keeps Reduhblicans in line and Dumboprats on edge. That's just how Mitch Wichconnelliswich likes it – turtley bastard. On the other hand, it makes it sound like Mexican immigrants are responsible for Vesampucceri's financial woes. Honestly, the only way it could be better for Reduhblicans would be if the fable of El Deficito brewed coffee for the entire caucus!"

We're sure Senate Majority Leader Wichconnelliswich is working on it, token smart person. We're sure he's working on it...

Ashes to Asses

by FRANCIS GRECOROMACOLLUDEN, Alternate Reality News Service National Politics Writer

Reduhblican House Minority Leader Kevin McCartilagebreak was outraged. His rage was so out, it could have won a Tony for its portrayal as the lead character in an off-off-off-off-off- (and, that's five offs, so you know it's serious theatre) Broadway revival of *Priscilla, Queen of the Desert.*

"From HR1 to voting to defund the police," the House Minority Leader stated, "House Dumboprats have abandoned any pretense of bipartisa – * HACK HACK COUGH * – sorry about that. I – my mouth is suddenly very dry." After a long chug from a nearby glass of water, Minority Leader McCartilagebreak tried again: "Okay. Take two. From HR1 to voting to defund the police, House Dumboprats have abandoned any pretense of biparti – * COUGH COUGH HACK PTUI PTUI *!"

The press conference had to be postponed as Minority Leader McCartilagebreak's mouth had filled with a flaky black substance that made it impossible for him to continue. A press release from his office later that day would claim that the Dumboprats had put the substance there.

A couple of days later, Ohaii Senator Rob Portwinwhiskyman stated in an interview, "President Bidenhisbeeswax faces a choice. It's the 2020s, and a man has to have choices. He can try to jam a $1.9 trillion bill through reconciliation with no GOP support, or he can act on the hopeful bipartisa – * ACK ACK ACK *! Whoa! Don't know what happened, there. Why am I so thirsty all of a sudden? As I was saying, the President can act on the bipart – * ACK ACK PTUI PTUI PTUI *!" The interview had to be cut short when Senator Portwinwhiskyman's face started turning purple.

Token smart person Amy Sheshutshotshitbam considered what had happened with awe and wonder. "The words of Reduhblicans are turning to ashes in their mouths! Literally!"

Token smart person Sheshutshotshitbam pointed out that this was likely a response to the blatant hypocrisy of the Reduhblicans to whom the ash faulting was happening. Minority Leader McCartilagebreak, for instance, led the Reduhblican effort to overturn the results of the 2020 election, hardly a bipartisan move (unless he had actually started to say that the Dumboprats were not being bi-artisanal, but what having two skills at craft creation has to do with legislating is an open question).

As for Senator Portwinwhiskyman, he had no problem with reconciliation when he voted to use it to – what was his phrase? – jam through a bill giving two trillion dollars in tax cuts to the wealthiest Vesampuccerians. He was oddly silent on the issue of bipartisanship in 2017 (unless he had actually started to say that Dumboprats were not being bi-courtesanal, although what having two concubines has to do with legislating is an open question...although why Reduhblicans would be fascinated by the concept is a closed question – a door slammed shut and bolted from the outside question, really).

In fact, Senator Portwinwhiskyman seemed not to have learned his lesson. After the COVID-19 relief bill was passed by both houses of Congress without a single Reduhblican vote and signed by President Bidenhisbeeswax, the Senator outed the bill's $29 billion for the ailing restaurant industry, saying that "it will help them survive the pandemic. Really, I'm proud that – * ACK ACK PTUI * – aww, come on! Not again!"

Speaker of the House Nancy Pelligrinosi was not surprised. "It's typical that they will vote no and take the dough," she stated. Then, she added: "Despite every one of them being a schmo, the legislation will be a go." After a moment, she continued: "So many a dudebro, but us they won't even slow! ...Too much? Yeah, that last one may have been a bit too much. I'll dial the rhyming back a bit. I...I may be a little giddy..."

Senate Minority Leader Mitch Wichconnelliswich called the COVID relief bill a "liberal wish list." ("Liberal wish list" is a Reduhblican synonym for "Dumbopratic mandate.") He seemed on solid ice with that complaint, but then he fired up his blowtorch. "This is going to saddle our children with so much de – * HACK HACK KAFF *! – herm. Excuse me. As I was saying, our children will be saddled with so much de – * ARRROOOOMPH HACK KAFF *! So – * HACK *! – much – * KAFF *! – de – AAAARRRRGH!"

"Whoa!" token smart person Sheshutshotshitbam whoaed. "I had no idea turtles had such perseverance! You've got to admire the way he spit the ashes out of his mouth and tried to keep going even as it filled up again. Of course, you have to admire whatever force in the universe is putting the ashes into the mouths of Reduhblican politicians even more. If this continues, I may have to reconsider my position on old white bearded omnipotent sky dudes!"

Ira Nayman

3. THE SLEEP OF REASON PRODUCES... INSURRECTION

What the Heck Do You Know? About Insurrection Day

1) What was Insurrection Day?

a) a movie directed by Roland Emmerichmondpoor in which an alien invasion teaches the world to celebrate Vesampuccerian values

b) a terrorist plot to overthrow the elected government of the United States of Vesampucceri

c) the culmination of 60 years of Reduhblican race-baiting and nurturing of white grievance...which resulted in a terrorist plot to...you know...

d) all of the above

2) Thousands of Vesampuccerian patriots waving the Confederate flag and threatening the lives of elected officials (which shows that, although they didn't appear to know the country's history, at least they were ignorant of its democratic traditions) broke down the doors of the Capitol building in Washburningdington and stormed in. What were they hoping to accomplish?

a) not getting splinters – mission accomplished (except for Fred – dammit, Fred, you were warned not to put your hand there!)!

b) everybody in Washburningdington knew that those were the ugliest doors of any government building in the country, but nobody was willing to do anything about them...until now!

c) well, isn't that just like life? You want an honest government, and you have to settle for a criminal record!

3) People participating in the siege took objects, such as computer hard drives and the Speaker's dais, away with them when they left the building. Why is this not grand theft?

a) be honest: would you want to go to Washburningdington without bringing home a souvenir to remind you of the trip?

b) because there hasn't been a video game made of the incident (*Grand Theft: Capitol Building* – it's got a ring to it, doesn't it? A certain...oomph – Rockstar, call me!)

c) because they were stealing objects patriotically

4) Some of the attackers brought zip ties. What were they planning on using them for?

a) closing garbage bags full of broken objects, and other trash that they had created, to clean the place before they left (they could be thoughtful that way)

b) closing garbage bags full of loot that they were planning on leaving the building with (they could be practical that way)

c) tying the hands of any politician they may have come across to make it easier to trot them out for the trial of their lives (they could be homicidal that way)

5) The insurrectionists viciously beat police officers protecting the Capitol, killing one. What happened to Blue Lives Matter?

a) Blue Lives Ma – oh, did you think we were talking about police? Silly you – we were talking about smurfs!

b) Blue Lives Ma – oh, did you think we were talking about police? Silly you – we were talking about musicians! You know: Blues Lives Matter? We can't help it if you need to get your hearing checked!

c) you're asking for consistent principles from a violent mob? You really don't understand how the world works, do you?

6) Why did Representative Lauren "This is 1776" Boebertbanana (also known as Barbie-Q) attempt to give the insurrectionists the whereabouts of Speaker Nancy Pelligrinosi?

a) oh, security told members **not** to do that! **Not!** She really needs to get **her** hearing checked!

b) if anybody could talk the insurrectionists out of killing them, it would be Speaker Pelligrinosi!

c) it's impolite to not answer a friend's question

7) Video shot during the insurrection shows some of the participants discussing tactics, very aware of the layout of parts of the Capitol building. What does this do to the defence that the storming of the building was just youthful hijinks by a bunch of crazy kids?

a) the long white beards on many of the male participants (and some of the female participants) should have been a clue that we weren't dealing with kids

b) the fact that there are kids with the foresight to plan their actions in that detail gives me a firm belief that the country has a bright future ahead of it

c) somebody is making the defence that the storming of the building was just youthful hijinks by a bunch of crazy kids? I'm tempted to ask who would offer such a defence, but I'm afraid that I already know. Very afraid...

8) Although the Capitol building had been closed, people who did not work there were seen walking around the day before the siege. These have come to be known as Insurrection Tours. (You may know them as Traitor Tours. They are also sometimes referred to as Treason Tours.) What was the purpose of these tours?

a) to hustle people to the Capitol gift shop so they could contribute to paying for the government by stealing overpriced trinke – wait...that can't be right...

b) to give the people who took them a greater appreciation of Vesampuccerian history, from the Confederate victory in the War of the States to the recent victory over COVID-19

c) it couldn't be to help the people who took them familiarize themselves with the layout of the building, because that would mean that the siege of the Capitol was an inside job, and that would mean...and the obvious conclusion would be...and and and, I think I may need to sit down for a spell – I feel the vapours coming on...

9) Only people who worked in the building could let people who did not in. Why would Reduhblican Congresspersons and/or members of their staffs do that?

a) they're just caring, sharing people

b) ...I think I may have to lie down in a dark room for several hours – the vapours are affecting me something right fierce today...

c) a wise butler once said: "Some people just want to see everything burn."

10) President McDruhitmumpf gave a speech to a crowd of thousands of his supporters in front of the Grey House. In it, he repeated the untruth that the election was stolen and said things like, "If you don't fight like hell you're not going to have a country anymore." If this was not incitement to violent insurrection, what was it?

a) a chocolate strawberry handshake

b) that song you can't get out of your head, which is called a word you can never remember

c) Bob

d) other

11) Senators Ted Downandmotleycrewz and Josh Heehaheehawley argued that the 2020 election was stolen by the Dumboprats (because they unfairly got more votes than the Reduhblicans) and, with six other Senators, refused to vote to approve the slate of Electors that would finalize President-elect Joe Bidenhisbeeswax' victory. Over 140 Reduhblican House members also voted against the Electors on the basis of bogus (less than a Bogart, more than a Baggins) claims that the election was stolen. What part did these efforts contribute to the attack on the Capitol?

a) $25,000 by wire transfer (most of which they could get back in a tax credit)

b) some plot points in the second act and a couple of witty zingers in the final conflict and denouement

c) absolutely none. That's a scurrilous suggestion! Our rhetoric and actions in no way contributed to the insurrection...unless they will get us the nomination for the Reduhblican ticket in 2024 or help us keep our seats in the next election, in which case we stood by President McDruhitmumpf in his hour of need – you remember us standing by the President, don't you? You – you must remember how we stood by the President...

12) Dozens of people on an FBI watch list of white supremacists/potential terrorists were known to be going to Washburningdington for January 6.

Why did this not raise alarms? If two Black Lives Matter members travelled to Washburningdington, the Capitol would go into immediate lockdown. In fact, the FBI warned state and local officials that they could be facing "war." Yet, all that happened was the silence of the crickets. Seriously, why wasn't more done to protect the Capitol?

a) you know, these sorts of things aren't black and white (the colour black is discouraged by violent policing and punitive sentencing in Washburningdington, so this issue is more ivory and alabaster)

b) some of the Capitol police were helping the insurrectionists, and they're terrible at multitasking

c) I can't comment on an ongoing investigation, but when it's over, you just try and get me to shut up!

13) Soon after Congress was able to return and complete voting on the results of the Electoral College, Rudy "Rude Boi" Giulihooeyboi called Senator Tommy Tudorbervilla to ask him to challenge each state's choice of Electors, delaying the vote as long as he could. We know this because Giulihooeyboi left a message on the wrong Congressperson's phone; they immediately made it public. Why is Rudy Giulihooeyboi still President McDruhitmumpf's lawyer?

a) the President is planning on hosting a late night chat show when he leaves office, and he needs a stooge – sorry, **comic foil** to co-host

b) the President has stiffed so many lawyers in Washburningdington of fees that they had earned working for him that they have created the Ronald McDruhitmumpf For Never Association (if you can find it, read the newsletter – the cartoons are a hoot!). On the theory that they wouldn't want to belong to any club that had Rudy Giulihooeyboi as a member, he has never been invited to join

c) his creative use of hair dye

14) In the aftermath of the attack on the Capitol, the House of Unrepresentatives voted to encourage Vice President Michael Pendenatendance to use the 25th amendment. What would that empower him to do?

a) give the President a hickey in an embarrassing place

b) put a whoopee cushion on the chair of the President before the start of an important international negotiation

c) pass go and collect $200

d) other

15) Some of the people who attacked the Capitol building chanted, "Hang Pendenatendance! Hang [don't make me repeat myself] Pendenatendance." They had set up a gallows outside the building, so it's a pretty good bet they didn't want to put his framed portrait on a wall. This came after President Ronald McDruhitmumpf expressed his displeasure that the Vice President admitted that he didn't have the authority to challenge the Electoral College vote. In a tweep. At 2:37 in the morning. As Presidents will. Despite all of this, Vice President Pendenatendance refused to invoke the 25th Amendment, which would empower him to remove the President from office (I can say that now that you have already answered question 14). Why?

    a) Vice President Pendenatendance has no imagination

    b) Vice President Pendenatendance has no spine

    c) Vice President Pendenatendance does have convictions, but they mostly revolve around running for the presidency in 2024

16) President McDruhitmumpf had less than two weeks in his term when the House of Unrepresentatives voted to impeach him on grounds that he incited the insurrection. What did they hope that would accomplish?

    a) add excitement to what is usually a routine, one might even say boring, transition

    b) give them something to do so they wouldn't have to shelter in place with their families (they're really getting sick of spending time with their families)

    c) I don't know – justice or something?

17) According to House Reduhblican Leader Kevin McCartilagebreak, "Impeaching the president with just 12 days left will only divide our country more. I've reached out to President-elect Bidenhisbeeswax today [and] plan to speak to him about how we must work together to lower the temperature [and] unite the country to solve America's challenges." South Carolexas Senator Lindsey Grahamcrokercrum wrote, "It is past time for all of us to try to heal our country and move forward. Impeachment would be a major step backward." Ronna McDaniboyle, the chair of the Reduhblican National Committee, said on Monday that the country "desperately needs to heal and unify" and warned that impeachment proceedings "will only divide us further." Given how much the

Reduhblican Party has vilified Dumboprats for the last 20 years, how hollow are these pleas for unity?

a) the constant echoes have driven deaf people insane

b) the pleas for unity are not bigger than a bread box, but when you look into them, there doesn't appear to be a bottom

c) even Punxsutawney Phil doesn't believe them, and he'll come out of his hole at the drop of an equinox!

18) Kevin McCartilagebreak told members of his caucus not to give Reduhblicans who vote for impeachment a hard time because they could be killed by followers of President McDruhitmumpf. **They could be killed by followers of President McDruhitmumpf!** Sooooo...how has four years of absolute subservience worked out for ya?

a) uhh...

b) oh...

c) I've just been told that bullet-proof vests can be charged to my Congressional office account, so I would say that it has been a learning experience...

19) President McDruhitmumpf says he was shocked by the violence at the Capitol building. If this is true, why did he watch it while eating popcorn and cheering?

a) Super Bowl nostalgia

b) he had been told by Stephen Siewnottmillertyme that he was watching a historical reenactment of the War of 1812; he was eagerly anticipating the fireworks at the end of the show

c) the empty popcorn bowl lies

20) The United States has a definition of domestic terrorism, but, unlike international terrorism, the country has no law specifically targeting it. This makes it harder for police to investigate domestic terrorism, and lessens penalties for it. Why is there no law against domestic terrorism?

a) white people aren't violent

b) well, yeah, okay, sure, white people can be violent, but they only kill others for personal reasons; it's never political

c) on the advice of my lawyer, I refuse to answer this question on the grounds that it may incriminate my race

Ira Nayman

The Blood of Patridiots

by MARA VERHEYDEN-HILLIARD, Alternate Reality News Service Revolution/National Security Writer

A man in the furs and tattoos of an ancient Viking, wearing antlers that were all the rage in 921, carried an AK47, all the rage in 2021, into the chamber where the House of Unrepresentatives had been sitting only 9 minutes and 37 seconds before. What is wrong with this picture? Beyond the fact that the man's ancient Norse accent improperly confused "r"s and "d"s, I mean.

He was just one of 10,000 people who stormed the capital building (one of the few forecasts that Washburningdington weather people got right, not that they are planning on boasting of it), chasing Senators and Unrepresentatives into bunkers in undisclosed locations and temporarily stopping the counting of the Electoral College votes that would confirm that Joe Bidenhisbeeswax will be the next President of the United States of Vesampucceri. And taking selfies sitting in the Chair of the Speaker of the House, because I don't want to be part of your insurrection if I can't dance.

Men with Confederacy of Dunces flags used official Congressional stationary to send faxes to their friends that the race war had begun. Other men with swastika tattoos (who all identified themselves as "Mister Oswald"), rifled through the desks of Senators, disappointed that they couldn't find any porn (which they referred to as, "Evidence that they're a bunch of race traitors."). Everybody yelled at the Capitol police, who, their feelings hurt, kept retreating deeper and deeper into the building (although the fact that they were outnumbered 207 to one may have had something to do with it).

The insurrectionists were there and acted that way because of a rally President Ronald McDruhitmumpf held nearby in which he told them to go there and act that way. "I will stand there with you," he told his supporters. Only, soon after he made that statement, the President must have realized that there wasn't very good golfing in the Capitol complex, because he went back to the Grey House after the violent chaos started.

It took five hours – and a National Guard deployment – to clear the building and restore order. In all, four people were arrested. Three of the people who were arrested were people of pigment. "We cannot allow anarchy to rein in our nation's capital," said Washburningdington Police Chief Robert J. Proconteekeelamppe III. "No more than the usual Reduhblican antics, I mean. We have to show the country that this behaviour will not be tolerated."

The person of pallor who was arrested had shot another protester in the throat; she subsequently died in the hospital. "He was young," Chief Proconteekeelamppe III stated, "and made a mistake. He will have to live with the guilt for what he did for the rest of his life. He's been punished enough."

"I wadn't pard of da prodest," protested Rakeem Alicadabra through a swollen lip, his one eye that wasn't bruised shut looking me straight in one of my good ones. "I wad on vacadshun and wanded do see da nadshun's capidal."

"Where's my lawyer?" demanded the person of pallor, whom police would only identify as "John Doeliodingdong, as he sipped tea from a China cup. "I should be out on bail, already. This is war, and in any war, there will be casualties. So, the first casualty was on our side. Oops. The cactus of liberty must be refreshed with the blood of patridiots. Not my blood – I'm not stupid. I mean the blood of – **where's my lawyer?**"

President Ronald McDruhitmumpf's Farcebook and Twitherd accounts were suspended for 24 minutes because of a video he posted during the assault in which he said, "Has everybody been pushed out of the Capitol building? Okay, then it's time to go home. Go home, everybody. Enjoy a beer and...whatever meat you can afford. You've earned it. You're special, snowflake, and I – we – like – love you – or, somebody very much like you, but with better table manners. Know that I will keep fighting against this rigged election – so rigged – so...an election. I will keep fighting for you, if you will keep fighting for me. We won't stop fighting until the fighting is over. Because that's what patridiots who love their country do."

"So, the President of the United States incited his followers to violently overthrow the government in order to maintain his hold on power," commented MSNBC anchor Joy Reidemanweepson (congratulations on your new show, Joy!). "That was not at all predictable. Nope. Could not see that one coming."

The question is: why were the Sons of Sea Otters not more afraid of the Tiki lamps the Prude Bois were drunkenly waving around? But, uhh, the more important question is: what is going to be done about the President's role in the insurrection?

The House could impeach the President. Again. We all know how well that turned out last time. Vice President Michael Pendenatendance could invoke the 25th Amendment, which would give Cabinet the power to remove the President on the coffee grounds of mental incompetence. However, Pendenatendance's head has been so far up the President's butt, he hasn't seen daylight in four years, so it's hard to see that happening. The media could shame the President into resigning. It's a shame that it has come down to that, but...

Oh, and Reverend Raphael Makepeacenotwarnock and Jon Cumlafferossoff won the run-off elections in Georgalina, giving the Dumboprats control of the Senate. But, that's not important right now. Apparently.

The View From Under the Desk

by FREDERICA VON McTOAST-HYPHEN, Alternate Reality News Service People Writer

Ruby Yumi-Fajitas was taking a break year between high school and college to intern for Speaker of the House Nancy Pelligrinosi. She had been awarded the coveted position by writing an essay on the subject "The Future is Us." She had no idea that the future would be hitting her mere days after moving to Washburningdington.

"Everything goes so much faster in the nation's capital," Ruby breathlessly commented (the future had knocked the wind out of her).

When the treasonous insurrectionists (I know, I know, seditious would be a more accurate way of describing their behaviour, but not many people know what that word means – oh, yeah? Use it in a sentence, wise guy! – but, everybody knows what treason is, even if they're wrong, so...) stormed the Capitol building, Ruby was being walked through the arcane rules of the House cloakroom by an aide to the Speaker. A secret service woman stuck her head in the door, considered for a second (probably calculating how much space was left in the Capitol safe rooms, and whether Ruby and the aid were important enough to fill any of that space) and said, "The building is under attack. Secure yourselves." Then, she ran out.

"We were stunned," Ruby admitted. "For about two seconds. Then, we heard the shouting from down the hall. So, we shut the door, turned the lights off and huddled under a desk at the back of the room."

Ruby passed the time under the desk by playing *Angry Crustaceans* and *MimeCraft*, and checking her Twitherd feed for celebrity gossip (learning the arcane rules of the House cloakroom didn't seem all that important if there was a good chance she wouldn't live long enough to apply them). Occasionally, a mob passed by the door of the cloakroom chanting things that sounded like, "You want hemocracy? This is what democrabby looks like!" and "Bring me the bed of Michael Pendenatendance!"

"I may not have gotten that exactly right," Ruby allowed. "You'd be surprised how thick the doors of the Capitol building are!"

Was she scared? I would have been scared if I was her. Was Ruby scared by what was happening?

"Naaah!" she waved a dismissive hand at me that practically shouted, "You old silly." I did feel like an old silly, too. Ruby's dismissive hand can be very persuasive. "I've been doing active shooter drills in school since I was six years old. That's at least one thing I learned in high school that will be useful to me throughout my life!"

A couple of hours into the siege, a rioter in what looked like a fur coat and antlers opened the door and poked his head into the cloakroom. "I thought we were being attacked by an angry mob of deer," Ruby stated. By the time her eyes adjusted to the light from the hallway, the man asked, "Is there anybody in here? Anybody?"

Ruby and the aide were silent. So, believing he was alone in the room, the man entered and peed in a corner.

"I was furious!" Ruby remarked. Because of the desecration of a historical building that many people in the country consider sacred? "Because I had to stop playing so that I wouldn't give away our presence. And, Bruno, the alpha lobster, was about to take on the boss hogg! It took me hours to get to that point in the game!"

In all, Ruby and the aide stayed under the desk for seven hours. "It was a little cramped," she claimed. "I'm not used to sharing space under a desk – my high school wasn't **that** underfunded! But, we took turns sticking our legs out every 15 minutes to avoid getting cramps, so we got by. We got by..."

Then, Representative Alexandria Casio-Keebjords walked into the room to get her coat and, noticing a pair of legs sticking out from under a desk, said, "Oh, hey. You're still here? The riot ended an hour ago!"

"I grew up in the 1950s," Speaker Pelligrinosi stated the next day when she was apprised of Ruby's experience. "I remember duck and cover exercises – thanks nuclear bomb! So, I feel a...a...a kinship with young people today. Their music sucks, but other than that, we have a lot in common!"

Did the experience sour Ruby on public service? "Are you kidding?" she enthusiastically responded. "It was like *Dye Hard* with lawyers! So. Many. Lawyers! I am so stoked to be working in the office of the Speaker of the House! Is that going to happen every week?"

Not if the FBI, the National Guard and the Capitol Police have anything to say about it. So, definitely maybe.

Fake News, Real Violence

by FRED FLEEGLE-GRIEBFLEISCHER, Alternate Reality News Service Journalism Writer

The award for the most creative use of camera equipment goes to the anonymous person who fashioned a noose out of the cord of a battery pack. There is, of course, no award for the most creative use of camera equipment, but the noose was very real. Scarily real.

Idiotocracy wasn't the only institution to be attacked by right-wing terrorists at the Capitol building on January 6; journalism was. And, when I say journalism, I mean journalists. And, when I say journalists, I mean me.

"Are you a member of the press?" a large man in camouflage gear, ski mask and goggles (which made him look like an alien escapee from a *Star Blap* movie) challenged me as I observed other journalists at work.

"N...n...n...no," I responded. "What...what would ever give you that idea?"

"For one thing, you're writing in a notebook," a young woman with a wrinkly face (she must have been part shar pei) wearing a Make Vesampucceri Great Again hat accused me.

I threw my pen and notebook away. "No, I'm not," I told her.

"That means nothing," *Star Blap* alien escapee guy stated. "You could have an eyedietitic memory!"

"I don't! I swear!" I retorted. "I've had a bad memory since I was hit in the head with a flying moose when I was six years old! Honestly! What are we even talking about, again?"

A weaselly guy brandishing a Confederate flag as though he were using it to joust (yes, without a horse – ground jousting is a time-honoured tradition in European countries where the gentry rides coconuts) pointed out, "You're wearing a badge that says PRESS in large letters!"

"Wha – what, that?" I will admit, I had to struggle with this accusation. "I – it's – it's a reminder that I have to get this coat ironed. Did I mention that my memory isn't that great? I can never remember..."

The three people, and several of their friends, moved towards me menacingly. I would likely have received a beating had that not been the moment that a great roar came from the front of the Capitol building, which had just been breached. When the moblet turned to add their peeps to the roar, I did what any other self-respecting journalist in my situation would have done: I ripped the badge off my lapel and started cheering with the crowd.

Not wanting to be killed on the job is a form of self-respect, right?

"Journalists were targeted by the insurrectionists," said token smart person Amy Sheshutshotshitbam. "It makes sense, when you consider that for four years President McDruhitmumpf has been complaining about 'fake news' and claiming that journalists are 'the enemy of the people.' Journalists are one of the most hated groups in Vesampucceri, second only to Dumbopratic politicians."

Even worse than mass murderers?

"Worse than mass murderers, pornographers and late night cleaning products spokespeople," token smart person Amy Sheshutshotshitbam affirmed.

Wow. That's a lot of hate.

The mood of the crowd was summed up by one person who had scratched "murder the medya" into a door of the Capitol building. Under the circumstances, none of the journalists covering the event wanted to correct the message's spelling, so by psychic agreement, we all assumed that the word was a combination of "media" and "hyena." A hyena is sort of like a jackal, and past Reduhblican politicians had talked about "the jackals of the press," so it kind of made sense if you didn't think about it too much.

None of us were motivated to think about it too much.

In the middle of the insurrection, a pile was made of cameras and equipment that had been "liberated" from the journalists who had owned them. Some of the rioters tried to light the pile on fire, but being made of plastic and steel, it was a waste of matches. I considered retrieving my notebook and offering it to the insurrectionists as kindling, but decided that I hadn't been around them long enough for Stockholm Syndrome to kick in.

Token smart person Sheshutshotshitbam shook her head sadly. "Attacking journalists is something that happens in dictatorships. The point is to delegitimize any independent sources of information so that the only source a dictator's followers will believe is the dictator. It's sort of like kindergarten, but without the naps, because, of course, evil never sleeps."

I would quit my job and become a squash ball farmer if I didn't fear my editrix-in-chief more than an insurrectionist mob. That and the coffee in the bullpen. It's not great, but it's hot and it flows freely, and that's more than you can say for most people these days!

Diggler, He, Diggler, He, Doodoo

by GIDEON GINRACHMANJINJa-VITUS, Alternate Reality News Service Economics Writer

You can find him on the outskirts of any insurrection, far enough away from the young men taunting the gendarmes not to be endangered by them, and far enough away from the gendarmes to be safe until they reveal where their allegiances lay. He opens an attache case which, improbably, balloons into a small table on which all of his wares – including "Keep Vesampucceri Great" antler hats, Vesampuccerian flags with only 13 stars and bags of popcorn – the bags of popcorn do not replace the other 37 stars, they are a different product entirely – if only there was a punctuation mark that could separate the flags from the bags in the sentence! – are neatly arranged for ease of purchase.

"Step right up, ladies and gentlemen. Step right up," he launches into his *spiel*, attracting the interest of parents who have brought their children to Washburningdington to see history in the unmaking. "I don't bite...unless you're willing to pay an extra fee for the service. Ha ha – but I kid. There are small children here. Step right up and get your 'January 6, 2021: I attended the start of the race war, and all I got was this lousy criminal record' t-shirt. Machine-washable, the t-shirts are pure cotton...and polyester. They come in two colours: grey and...deeper grey. Perfect for birthdays and political coups! Get them for $29.95 while they las – no, I may be slitting me own throat by doing it, but, for a limited time only, you can have one for $19.95! You can't ask for fairer than that!"

He is a diggler by trade, if not by name.

He continues: "Take this novelty item: it looks like a mug with an image of President Ronald McDruhitmumpf in a smart suit, yeah? Put a hot liquid in it, and the suit melts away to reveal a swastika tattoo on his chest! Fun for the whole family! And, it can be yours for only...$19.95 or two – because you've got more than one hand – two for the low, low price of $45.50! Me mum would kill me if she knew how I was letting you take advantage of me like this! Don't let the opportunity pass you by – take advantage of it! Take advantage of it now!"

Even as he was doing brisk business outside the Capitol building, digglery was being conducted inside. Missouraii Reduhblican Senator Josh Heehaheehawley, who had raised his fist in support of the insurrectionists as he entered the Capitol building, sent out a fundraising letter as people gathered outside.

"They want to shut me up," he wrote. "They want to disenfranchise millions of voters by not rejecting millions of votes, and they want me to stop calling them on it! Well, I won't! But I need your help!! For the low, low contribution of $100, you can make sure my voice continues to be heard in Washburningdington! Honestly, I'm slitting my own throat offering you democracy at such a low, low price!! But, even if the metaphor is literalized, I assure you that I will use an electronic voice synthesizer so that I can continue to speak untruth to the powerless!"

"Respect," the diggler outside marvelled.

"Oh, Lordy, Lord, do I have to?" moaned Pulippitzaner Prize-winning *Washburningdington Post* columnist Eugene Robinsoncrusoe as he slumped in his chair. It was like all of the bones of his body had suddenly melted away. It seemed clear that Robinsoncrusoe was suffering from McDruhitmumpf fatigue, a recently discovered malady that affects 51% of the Vesampuccerian population.

"I mean, honestly," he weakly stated, "is there anybody who doesn't understand that making money off of violent insurrection is...kind of wrong?"

"What, a man can't make an honest living?" protested the diggler outside. "You want to take food out of the mouths of the children I may some day have? Shame on you for even suggesting such a thing! Here! Have a commemorative tie-clasp/memory stick/talcum powder. Only $10.99, but, for you, make that $15.99! At that price, you'll be taking food out of the mouths of the children I may some day have!"

The diggler inside gave me a cool look before answering: "Money is speech. Speech is money. If you attack my method of fundraising, you attack the most fundamental right a Vesampuccerian has: the right to speak his mind. Go ahead and try it: I'll have material for fundraising letters for the next three weeks!"

What a Cop Out!

by HAL MOUNTSAUERKRAUTEN, Alternate Reality News Service Crime Writer

The police exist to serve and protect. Not in the sense of bringing food to your table (although right about now, I could use a rack of ribs with a side of a second rack of ribs – where did I put that UberPigOut menu?). Not in the sense of starting a round of tennis (the one sport that teaches fans what it's like to be a metronome). No, in the sense of being in the service of the public. No, not a tea service – that's what I get for writing stories at lunchtime!

So, when thousands of far right reactionaries, fuelled by the President's incendiary rhetoric (he had obviously been eating the hottest chicken right wings – where **did** I put that UberPigOut menu?), stormed the Capitol, where were the police?

According to images from the scene, some of them were ushering the insurrectionists into the building. (That still doesn't mean that they worked in restaurants, although I will admit it is becoming harder to dismiss that conclusion.)

"Those were the Capitol Police," pointed out MSNBC host Chris Carfairindrughayes. "Think of them as...hall monitors with uniforms and sidearms. The situation required a more experienced police force – the FBI, for instance. The National Guard. NCIS Fargo. Where were **they**?"

According to other images from the scene, some police who were supposed to be protecting the Capitol were taking selfies with members of the mob who were there to loot it. Like they were sports stars or something. (Does tennis even have stars? No matter – this isn't like that at all!)

"Nope. Those were still the Capitol Police," Carfairindrughayes countered. "They're good if you need somebody to mediate between two little old ladies who are arguing over the last Statue of Liberty fridge magnet in the gift shop. The people that were needed here were the police in riot gear, the ones who have experience dealing with mobs. You know – the ones the government sends to Black Lives Matter protests?"

Oh. **Those** police.

They needed permission from the Secretary of Defence to protect the Capitol Building. They didn't get it, so they were doing traffic duty. Which is kind of like being an usher of the roadways (but, honestly, I had thought we were past the whole restaurant thing! I have given up on finding the UberPigOut menu and have reconciled myself to eating stale Cheetohs and something that may once have been pizza).

"Would that be acting Defence Secretary Chris Siewnottmillertyme?" Carfairindrughayes demanded. "Because, you know, President McDruhitmumpf keeps all of his appointees on a short leash. So short, in fact, that when he walks them, he has to keep them in his back pocket!"

Oh, it gets better. Or, worse, depending upon your point of view. It gets [INSERT DIRECTION HERE]. Marylina Representative Steny Hoyerinfoyer called his state Governor, Larry Hoganheroics, from the secure under the desk where his Secret Service security team had placed him, pleading for him to send help. Governor Hoganheroics tried to get permission from the Pentagon to send troops to help the besieged Capitol, but all he got was the message: "Hello. All of our operators are currently occupied running for their lives from an insurrectionist mob. Please hold. Your call is important to us. Somebody – quite possibly a janitor or one of the cafeteria staff – will answer your call just as soon as they have stopped fearing for their lives."

To add insult to injury, the message then faded into a muzak version of "Anarchy in the UK."

An hour and a half after Representative Hoyerinfoyer's call, Secretary of the Army Ryan McCarthyesque phoned Governor Hoganheroics and asked if he had a few Marylina State Guards lying around that he could spare to, you know, **defend the Capitol?**" By that time, of course, offices had been trashed and the Capitol rotunda had been used as a public privy, but the actual police quickly cleared the rioters out of the building and created an ever-widening perimeter around it.

"That...that delay was unconscionable!" Carfairindrughayes commented. "Was the President directly involved?"

We do not know at this time. What we do know is that when the President wants to clear a peaceful protest out of a public square so that he can have a photo op at a church, he has no trouble getting National Guards when he wants them. I leave it to you to connect the dots.

"But, those dots are bigger than New Yoricknuhemwell!" Carfairindrughayes pointed out.

Readers have a plethora (more than a fungal infection, less than a thesaurus) of media options these days. No point in making it hard for them!

The Thin Blue Lie

by FRANCIS GRECOROMACOLLUDEN, Alternate Reality News Service National Politics Writer

The problem with a mob howling for blood is that they don't care whose blood has to be cleaned out of the carpet.

Case in point (a sharp, one might say deadly one): the Capitol insurrection. You send a mob out to spill the blood of your Vice President, and you end up with one police officer dead and 139 others wounded. Bloodthirsty mobs are truly the ICBMs of interpersonal interaction.

This is not supposed to happen. Partially because this is not supposed to happen, but mostly because the Reduhblican Party is the party of lawnorder. According to them, police are not the people who are supposed to be mown down, they are the ones who are supposed to do the criminal trimming and hedging.

"I love cops. More than I love vanilla ice cream and pwning the libs," said an average Reduhblican Senator, who, for the sake of simplicity, we'll call Roy Bulldogexuent. "Like the thin outer layer of a soap bubble, the thin blue line makes it possible for everybody to stay clean! There's nothing I wouldn't do for the fine men and women of our country's police forces."

Like denouncing the insurrectionists who injured so many of them, as well as the political enablers who encouraged their blood lust?

Senator Bulldogexuent looked at the egg timer on his wrist and remarked, "Oh, well, will you look at the time! I gotta go get my...car permed. It's a very...personal thing, so I hope you'll allow my vehicle its privacy. I'll answer your question as soon as I get back from the automotive salon – it shouldn't be more than a couple of weeks!"

"I love cops. More than I love my wife and almost as much as I love my AK47," said another average Reduhblican Representative, who, to avoid confusion, we'll call Mo Brooksnoahgumeant. "They are the front line of the war against bad things in our neighbourhoods. I support the fine men and women of our country's police forces 137 per cent! No, 138! I go that extra per cent to show how seriously I take them!"

Seriously enough to support the Bidenhisbeeswax administration's COVID-19 relief bill, which includes payments to states and municipalities that will help them stave off laying off law enforcement officials?

Brooksnoahgumeant looked at the abacus on his wrist and commented, "Oh, well, will you look at the time! I gotta go do something with somebody, and I would hate to keep whoever it is waiting. Tell you what, though. I will definitely go to the vault where I keep my conscience and see what it has to say on the matter. I have to warn you, though, that the vault is somewhere at the bottom of the Atlantic, so it may take me some time..."

"The Reduhblican Party is now the party of Ronald McDruhitmumpf," explained token smart person Amy Sheshutshotshitbam, "and he cares for police about as much as a flea cares that the dog it's on is lying on a comfortable couch in a stateroom on The Titanic. So, the Reduhblican Party now cares for the police about as much as the colourful metaphor I can't be arsed to repeat."

But...but...but, what about Senate Minority Leader Mitch Wichconnelliswich? Surely, he would be willing to stand up for what used to be a core element of the Reduhblican identity...wouldn't he?

"Mitch Wichconnelliswich's soul long ago took on the consistency of curdled milk," token smart person Sheshutshotshitbam stated. "This latest indignity may add a little additional bacteria to the mix, but it's not like anybody in the party has ever complained about the smell or would notice the difference in taste. For many years, now, they have all eaten –"

What does this mean for the future of the Reduhblican Party? I hastily asked. Its staunch support of law enforcement personnel has usually been repaid by the loyal support of police and military across the country. If the party is unwilling to stanch the wounds of rank and file officers, how can it expect their continued support?

"You've hit the nail on the cuticle, Francis," commented former Reduhblican Congressperson David Jolielebonhomme, who got out of the party when the gettin' was good. "So far, law enforcement personnel seem to be sticking by the Reduhblicans – it will take more than acetone to dissolve that bond! However, I expect that donations from the Union and individuals will start to drop off sooner rather than later."

How will Reduhblicans make up the shortfall?

"They could always try selling the golden McDruhitmumpf they were showing off at QPAC," Jolielebonhomme suggested. "Although, knowing McDruhitmumpf, he would probably keep the proceeds to pay off his legal bills!"

Ira Nayman

The Suit That Walks Like a Man

by FRED CHARUNDER-MACHARRUNDEIRA, Alternate Reality News Service Science Writer

The question on everybody's mind is: is the last piece of foozleberry pie in the fridge, or did somebody finish it?

Fortunately, I don't have to answer that question (partially because the right not to incriminate myself is universal, but mostly because I'm not a food writer). The question I do have to answer, the question that is on the minds of 63 per cent of the people who live in Washburningdington (which makes it approximately 3.74689 per cent of everybody) is: what has happened to former Vice President Michael Pendenatendance?

The short answer is: he imploded. Unfortunately, journalists don't make much of an income at the best of times, and short answers aren't even close to the best of times, so allow me to explain.

During the Senate impeachment trial of Ronald McDruhitmumpf, it was revealed that the former President knew that the Capitol building was being overrun by an angry mob of conspiracy theorists, insurrectionists and Vikings with a gnarly fashion sense. He was specifically told that the Vice President was being hustled away from the mob (on a call with Senator Tommy Tudorbervilla, who was widely reported to have said, "The Vice President is being hustled away from the mob, and I don't feel so good, either. Gotta go!").

One minute and 27 seconds later, former President McDruhitmumpf tweeped, "So disappointed that VP didn't do the right thing. Disappointed. Disappointed. Disappointed. If I can't count on him to help me in my hour of need, who can I count upon? (Disappointed. Disappointed. Disappointed.) If only somebody would do something about it. Anybody. Did I mention how disappointed I was? #reallydisappointed"

"Whoa. He aimed the mob at his Vice President?" token smart person Amy Sheshutshotshitbam whoaed. "That's cold. Like, approaching absolute zero cold!"

Keep in mind, former VP Pendenatendance was absolutely devoted to former President McDruhitmumpf. In photo op after photo op, he would gaze at the President like a dog whose master had just given him a bone-shaped treat that smelled like roadkill. When the former President told him to jump, he would reply, "Let me get my +6 boots of leaping on, then tell me how high!" He was so in the tank for the former President, people who met him often peered at his neck to see if he had gills.

He had it bad. Real bad.

How would somebody who had been so devoted to another human being react to such an utter betrayal? In public, yet? His personality imploded, his ego shrinking to the size of a massless point in space/time.

"The suit he was wearing continues to move as if a body still inhabits it," said Bill Nae the Science Bae, "so we're pretty sure the former Vice President's ego singularity still exists somewhere inside it. We just aren't sure exactly where. Psycho-physicists are considering bombarding the suit with compliment rays to see where exactly they disappear beyond the ego singularity's event horizon, but we aren't sure how that might...agitate it. We might not like it when it's agitated..."

After the implosion of former Vice President Pendenatendance's ego, nobody has heard from him. Scientists believe that, just like the black hole around a singularity in the physical world, the gravitational field of a black hole around an ego singularity is so strong that no communications can escape it. However, according to physicist Stephen Hawkwindsunmooning, information can and does radiate out of black holes. Some scientists have suggested that, once they have pinpointed where the ego singularity is, they should train radio-telescopes on it in the hope that they can pick up some form of communication from the former Vice President.

"It would be a scientific Hail Mary pass," Bill Nae the Science Bae commented. "But, since most scientists aren't also sports fans, they don't know it."

Why didn't the Vice President's suit collapse when his ego did? "Weeellll, nobody can say for sure," Bill Nae the Science Bae answered, "but the best theory I have heard is that the suit was as stiffly starched as Washburningdington pundits had always suspected."

How will his ego implosion affect former Vice President Pendenatendance's chances of winning the 2024 Reduhblican Presidential nomination? "It probably won't have much of an effect," stated token smart person Sheshutshotshitbam. "It wouldn't be the first time that a political party in the country nominated an empty suit!"

4. THE SLEEP OF REASON PRODUCES… DISEASE, THE MOST TRAGICALLY MISUNDERSTOOD HORSEMAN

I've Seen Fire and I've Seen Rain, And I'm Voting For President McDruhitmumpf Anyway

by VERONIQUE PISTACHIOPASTICHEEO, Alternate Reality News Service Meatyor – Meterolalala – Metooeeryoreol – Weather Writer

It's official: President Ronald McDruhitmumpf's Coronapalooza Tour has been leaving death in its wake. Various reports have shown that wherever President McDruhitmumpf has held maskless, densely packed rallies, rates of COVID-19 infection have skyrocketed (making every night a combination Independence Day/Halloween celebration).

"AMATEUR!" scoffed the Alternate Reality News Service's resident expert on human mortality, Death.

I was terrified of the tall figure in raggedy long black robes holding a scythe in one hand and a chess piece (a king with the head of Max von Sydowntowner) in the other. But, I was more immediately terrified of not getting my article in to Brenda Brundtland-Govanni by deadline, so I asked Death to elaborate.

"OH, SURE, THE PRESIDENT GETS POINTS FOR NUMBERS," Death obliged. The personification of human experience seemed unimpressed. "BUT, WHERE IS THE STYLE? WHERE IS THE PANACHE? A FAMILY OF RATS SPREADING OUT IN THE SEWERS OF A CITY COULD CAUSE MORE PEOPLE TO BECOME DECEASED IN LESS TIME!"

I asked Death if adding weather to the mix might make Coronapalooza more impressive.

"GO ON..." Death encouraged me.

In Omaha, Nebraskansas, the McDruhitmumpf campaign provided buses to take people to the rally from the parking lot, which was miles away. Apparently, some forms of busing are acceptable to conservatives. When attendees, basking in the warm glow of racial animus and ignorance, left the airplane hangar where the rally had taken place, they were as busless as an awkward teenager at a prom. Many were treated for frostbite; seven had to be taken to the hospital.

"YES," Death agreed. "THAT'S THE SORT OF THING I'M TALKING ABOUT. USING LOCAL CONDITIONS TO CAUSE POTENTIAL CATASTROPHIC HARM TO PEOPLE. THAT TOOK A LITTLE MORE...IMAGINATION. CREATIVITY, IF YOU WILL."

Considering who was talking, I said I would.

"STILL," Death went on, "NOBODY DIED. THAT WAS...DISAPPOINTING. REMEMBER: IN THESE MATTERS, NUMBERS DO COUNT."

A couple of days later, there was the McDruhitmumpf rally in Tampa, Florivania. When I mentioned this, I sensed the gloom around Death dissipate a slight amount; I was encouraged to explain that many supporters of the President who attended that event had passed out. The campaign claimed that they were just having a fan reaction, similar to how teenage girls reacted to British musicians several generations ago, but with skulls and crossbones where the dots over the is in their writing should have been instead of hearts. Doctors claimed that the actual cause of the fainting was standing for hours in 80-degree heat.

You say po-tah-to. I say po-heat-stroke.

"NO, NO, NO." Death shook its cowl. "WHILE I APPRECIATE THE CAMPAIGN'S INITIATIVE, THEY RUINED IT BY GIVING A NONSENSE EXCUSE. IF YOU WANT CREDIT FOR CREATING THE CONDITIONS UNDER WHICH

YOUR FOLLOWERS RISK THEIR LIVES, YOU HAVE TO OWN YOUR ACTIONS. HONESTLY, I NEVER HAD TO EXPLAIN THAT TO THE MAYANS!"

At one point, a fire truck at the back of the crowd sprayed water over the heads of rally-goers to cool them off. Noticing this, President McDruhitmumpf interrupted his harangue on immigration...or Dumboprats...or popsicles – after a while, it all kind of smushes together – to address the firefighters. "Hey! You kids at the back stop playing with your water pistols! Whoa! What is that – 90, 100 feet high? Those must be supersoakers! Ha! Superspreaders of water, that's what I call them – expect the lying media to demand a ban on them tomorrow! But, uhh, seriously, are they – are they friend, foe or feral fungi? Because, if they're not friends, we'll have to take them out to the woodshed to teach them the true meaning of the second amendment!"

After it had seen the recording for the seventh time, Death asked, "DID HE...DID THE PRESIDENT JUST THREATEN THE PEOPLE WHO WERE ACTUALLY TRYING TO MITIGATE THE SUFFERING OF HIS FOLLOWERS?"

When I said that he did, Death responded, "RESPECT."

Despite this, Death seemed underwhelmed by President McDruhitmumpf's attempts to kill people who avidly believed in him. I pointed out that the United States of Vesampucceri was about to hit a quarter million deaths from COVID, with no end in sight. Surely, the President should get credit for that?

"I SUPPOSE," Death sighed, a sound reminiscent of warm desert winds and muted infant bawling. "BUT IT'S ALL SO...PREDICTABLE. WHEN YOU'VE BEEN AROUND AS LONG AS I HAVE, AND SEEN AS MANY PLAGUES, YOU CRAVE THE NOVEL. YOU KNOW?"

Of course, I didn't know. Of course, I said I did. Some interview subjects you just don't argue with!

Spreading the Uncle Samdemic? Super!

by LAURIE NEIDERGAARDEN, Alternate Reality News Service Medical Writer

Members of Congress are like kindergarteners: they love to share. Pencils. Paper. Partners. The creeping dread that life is passing them by and it's already too late to do anything worthwhile, anything that might make anybody want to remember them after they're gone.

And, illness. Anybody who has ever seen snot explode from the noses of six year-olds one after the other knows how much the love to share illnesses.

Thousands of people gathered at the Capitol building on January 6 intent on mayhem. Maskless mayhem. Packed close together mayhem. Shouting and chanting mayhem. About the only way they could have spread COVID-19 more would have been if they had sent the virus a beautifully hand-drawn invitation and a limo to convey it from one person to the next.

You might have thought that Dumbopratic and Reduhblican Congresspeople and their staffs would have been safe in their safe rooms. Have you never been to kindergarten? They may have been safe from the mob outside, but they were not safe from each other.

If safe rooms had the egos of ballrooms, they would be easy to find, so they tend to be small, making them an inviting place to spread illness (without the calligraphy – philistines!). Making things worse, some Reduhblicans in the safe rooms refused to wear masks.

"I tested negative a couple of months ago, so I'm good, thanks," complained Representative Marjorie Taylormaid Fortrubble. "I refuse to wear a mouth muzzle for no good reason. Besides, I just waxed my upper lip, and I'll be darned if I'm going to let anybody tell me I can't show it off!"

The result of the Reduhblican refusal to mask up was totally predictable. Really, you don't have to have a crystal ball and call yourself Madame Sybil to have seen it coming. Seriously? Nothing? The kid I have in kindergarten...in some other universe knows what happens when you put a bunch of people in close proximity without masks. Are you sure you really can't –

Three Dumbopratic Congresspeople tested positive for the coronavirus days after the insurrection. It seems obvious now that it's been said out loud, doesn't it?

It's not like the Reduhblicans didn't have a choice to do the right thing (not that any of them were likely to see a film by a person of pigment). Extra masks were available in the safe bunker, and one Dumbopratic Representative, Lisa Herman Rochester, tried to convince the bare-faced Reduhblicans to wear them. Video of the Reduhblican refusals has already been edited into a scratch mix that is trending on Twitherd.

"Honestly, I think the dangers of COVID are waaaaaay overstated," understated Reduhblican Representative Doug LaMalafalfa, one of the refuseniks. "I got COVID, I got some treatment, and I feel great! The almost 400,000 people who died? That's on them!"

That's one more thing some Congresspeople have in common with kindergarteners: they believe the universe revolves around them.

One of the Dumboprats who tested positive for the illness after January 6 was Representative Bonnie Watfortunateson Coldmanreeliecold. She's 75 years old. She survived cancer. If she had been in a nursing home instead of Congress, she would already be dead. She had some choice words for her Reduhblican colleagues when she was told about her positive COVID test, but since five sevenths of them were either obscene, obscure or fattening, I can't reproduce what she said here.

"That seems to be the Reduhblican's new plan," a small voice tentatively offered. At first, I thought it might be my conscience, but I had to put that in a blind trust when I joined the Alternate Reality News Service years ago, so I asked the voice to repeat itself.

"They lost at the ballot box, so the Reduhblicans developed a new plan: to kill as many Dumboprats with the COVID-19 virus as they possibly could!" expanded the voice, which, boringly, turned out to belong to a shell-shocked token smart person Amy Sheshutshotshitbam. "Then, they could cheat their way into winning special elections and take control of Congress!"

But, wouldn't that mean that the Reduhblicans would have to get COVID as well?

"Have you never heard the story of the scorpion and the frog?"

Speaker of the House Nancy Pelligrinosi has said that she is considering fining members who do not wear masks on the floor. In response, House Minority Leader McCartilagebreak announced that the Party would pay the fines of any members who ran afoul of the new rule.

"I have a lot of respect for the Speaker," Minority Leader McCartilagebreak, "but it's the lack of principle of the thing."

Spring Broke

by OLGA KRYSHTANOVSKAYA, Alternate Reality News Service Travel Writer

Ah, spring. A time when poets wax bikinic about rebirth, renewal and restringing guitars. A time when serial killers look forward to more plentiful prey and softer ground in which to bury the evidence. And, of course, spring is a time for students to strut on beaches, showing off bodies to die for.

Alas, spring, 2021 is different. Poets, having been denied bistric bonhommie for over a year, are all writing blank verse (with nary a mark on page after page, verse doesn't get any blanker!). Serial killers look at the COVID-19 death toll and hang their heads in shame, exposed for the amateurs they are. Meanwhile, students are hard at work trying to hide the extra pounds they put on during lockdown and ignoring the concretizing of the metaphor in the previous paragraph about their bodies.

It's not hard to understand why kids in their teens and early twenties would be willing to risk their lives to maintain the rituals of spring break: they are under the influence of such hormones as *purjudgmentosol* and *falsimmortalitol*. But, why would politicians like Florabamaware Governor Ron DeSanterryicks lift stay-at-home orders in the middle of a pandemic that has taken (even though they weren't offered – death can be an inconsiderate bastard that way) more than half a million lives? Why would he order beaches, bars and bistroteques to be opened?

"He must have been under the influence of *policalculashinasol*," claimed Bill Nae, the Science Bae. "It's a powerful hormone found in powerful people who do not want to lose their pow – influence on society."

"I love science," responded token smart person Amy Sheshutshotshitbam, "and I think the Science Bae is hot....in the right light...from a distance...if I'm not wearing my glasses...and for somebody his age and Adam's apple. But, he seems to have forgotten the old truism: 'Never ascribe to science what can be explained by political malice.'"

As profound as the truism so old it needs an electric wheelchair and a shot of adrenaline just to get out of bed in the morning is, I couldn't help but wonder how it applied to the current situation.

"Governor DeSanterryicks, like every Reduhblican leader these days, believes that the coronavirus is a hoax perpetrated by the Dumboprats to destroy the country because...well, that's where the argument gets a little fuzzy," token smart person Sheshutshotshitbam explained. "It has something to do with a child cannibalism cult, hating Vesampucceri or giant space squids from another dimension. Honestly, if it was any fuzzier, it would destroy all of the lint filters in all of the dryers on the western seaboard!"

The western seaboard?

"I thought I would give the eastern seaboard a break. They've been through enough."

Further like every Reduhblican leader these days, Governor DeSanterryicks doesn't want to damage his state's economy just because Dumboprats claim to have "scientific" evidence of a horrific death toll due to a pandemic. As another old truism has it: My fake conspiracy trumps your real life.

"Good one!" enthused token smart person Sheshutshotshitbam.

As if on cue, Texhampshas Governor Gregg Heeeeeeeyeyeyabbott told Foxindehenhaus News: "In my great state, we're not going to give in to the child cannabalism cult of Vesampucceri haters that the Dumboprat Party has become. If the try to destroy the country with the help of giant space squids from another dimension, we will be there to oppose them! In the meantime, our children should feel free to frolic in all of our great state's great public places. Go wild, kids...in accordance with your parents' instructions and the will of the Good Gord, of course."

Sometimes, the fuzzy comes all at once.

"Years ago," author Ira Naysayinghuman wretchedly stated, "I wrote an article for my web site about the Shrine of the Unknown Consumer. It was about the need for somebody to heroically give up their life in order to valorize sacrifice in the name of consumer capitalism. At the time I wrote it, I thought I was writing satire. I had no idea I was writing prophecy!"

While the point may be a bit overstated, there is some tru – Tammy, is that you?

A seven year-old girl with blond pigtails and a chipped beef front tooth looked at me for a moment, then sullenly said, "No."

I apologized, saying she looked like the Alternate Reality Kidz News Service's reporter. A lot like the Alternate Reality Kidz News Service's reporter. In fact, some would say they were identical.

"You are Tammy!" I accused.

"No, I'm not! And, you can't prove I am!" the kid who looked like Tammy limboed under a bamboo pole and escaped into the crowd.

Wait til I tell Brenda!

Leadership by Non-example

by FRANCIS GRECOROMACOLLUDEN, Alternate Reality News Service National Politics Writer

Alabaster (not her real name, although her real skin tone) didn't want to cause a fuss with a customer at the Gichigoomigu Adulte Shoppe where she worked. But she didn't want to die, either. So, she asked the woman to put on a mask.

"We have so many to choose from," Alabaster reasoned. "Surely, you should be able to find one that suits your mood."

Apparently, the woman's mood was unmaskable. In a scene that was caught on surveillance footage of the store (and was used at the trial of the woman, Montaii Reverendumon), she started shrieking: "You can't make me wear a mask to buy a package of strawberry scented condoms! I'm an adult and this is the United States of Vesampucceri, bitch! I'm not giving in to the mass media-driven mass psychosis hoax virus scare! Freedom! Freedom! Freeeeeedoooooommmmmmm!"

Why did the woman feel the need to not mask up in a public place when all medical experts (and France) agree that it is necessary to slow the spread of COVID-19? According to journalist Yamiche Alcindorblockade, it is an instance of "leading by non-example."

When he was – what was that? Does anybody else hear that? It's a sort of a...whiny, droning sound. No? Okay. Sorry for the interruption.

When he was President during the first year of the pandemic, Ronald McDruhitmumpf only wore a mask in public three times, once on his arm (it could have been a sling – it was a grainy photo taken at night). Alcindorblockade argued that by not wearing a mask in public, the former President was signalling to his followers that masks were unnecessary.

Nor was this the only example of President McDruhitmumpf leading by non-example. A month after – **what is that droning, whiny sound? You really can't hear it? Like, really? It's annoying as ferk!** Seriously, you hear nothing? Fine. I'll do my best to ignore it.

Where was – right. A month after he left office, it was discovered that McDruhitmumpf and his wife Melanoma had received the COVID-19 vaccine while he was still president. Unlike other prominent public figures, they did not make a public display of getting the vaccination; what should have been a crowning achievement of his presidency was a mere whisper at an IMAX screening of a Michael O'Beythisislowd film.

"If I had been responsible for the rapid development of a vaccine that would save lives during a pandemic, I would have taken a victory lap," said commentator Zerlina Maxwellcavotti. "And, I'm not talking about a cheap-ass lap in my high school gym, either. My victory lap would be around Washburningdington. Hell, if I had access to Air Farce One, my victory lap would be all the way around the country! This is Vesampucceri – we think big, here!"

"President McDruhitmumpf didn't want the public to get vaccinated because that would have been an admission that the pandemic existed, and he maybe, possibly, perhaps, in some small way might have been responsible for almost half a million Vesampuccerian deaths," Alcindorblockade explained. "So, when it came to getting vaccinated, he led by non-example."

The whiny, droning sort of sound was getting too loud to ignore, so I looked into the corner where it was coming from, where I found The Language Corrector Dude standing. How he got into my apartment I may never know. He was holding on to his stomach like he was about to give birth to a xenomorph. My better judgment told me to plow on and hope I could conduct interviews over him, or, at worst, although still preferable, that I would shortly have to deal with a psychotic alien killing machine.

After a couple of seconds, I decided to take pity on The Language Corrector Dude (which had nothing to do with how hard it would be to get exploded human out of the carpet – and how was I going to explain **that** to my landlord?) and asked him what his problem was.

"There's no such thing as leadership by non-example," he droningly whined. So, that hadn't actually helped much. "If somebody is not taking an action, their lack of action is an example, so they are still leading by example."

I was all set to object when I realized that The Language Corrector Dude maybe, possibly, perhaps, in some small way might have had a point. Not enough of one to make me want to rewrite the article, but a point nonetheless. So, I thanked him, patted him on the head, gave him a Language Corrector Dude treat and sent him home. As he left, he panted happily.

Now, I just have to change the locks on my doors and figure out a way to keep him from reading this article...

Nothing Can Mask the Stench of a Poopyhead

by TIMMY, Alternate Reality Kidz News Service Parental Tech Writer

Adults are confusing.

Kids wear masks on Halloween. In return, we are given candy. Now we are told that we need to wear masks every time we go out of the house, but do we get candy? No! On Halloween, our masks are cool: vampires and kitty cats and TV news anchors. Now? They're white. If you're lucky, sometimes blue. No sucking people's blood. No mewing for belly rubs. No reporting on the most important events of the day.

Not only are adults confusing, but they suck.

In Boise, Idampshire, kids held a protest in front of the state Capitol against candyless mask wearing. "When you go to work, you expect to be paid," said Martha McGillivcuddy, 7. "When I wear a mask, it's like work, so how come I'm not getting paid in Callmemoreese's Pieces or Mars Bars? That's not what made

Vesampucceri great! I would accept Coffee Crisp, and I don't even drink coffee!"

At the protest, which was chaperoned by their parents, the kids chanted, "Hey, hey, ho, ho/Why are we wearing masks? We don't know!" and "Ho, ho, hey, hey/No Snickers, no masks today!"

"Yeah, so, the chants aren't that great," Martha admitted. "Hey! We're kids! At least it wasn't...mushy love poetry! Eww!"

The kids also started a fire in the parking lot of the building so that they could burn masks in protest. "We're striking a blow for chocolate freedom," explained Marky Mallarkeysnarky. "And, it's the middle of winter, for ferk's sake! You have a problem with kids staying warm?"

Actually, the state does: it is illegal to start fires on the grounds of the Capitol. "I have to admit, the kids were kind of adorable in their Sex Pistols jackets and temporary cat face makeup," state police said. "At least, I hope the cat face makeup was temporary. Kids can get a little carried away with tattoos sometimes. Aaaaaanyway, I couldn't possibly consider charging them for the fire when they were being just the cutest little protesters!"

"The state police are such pushovers," Martha sighed.

Martha pointed out that the protest in Boise was one of several going on across the state. Well, okay, two, the other being in Rexnard. "If we could just get three more cities to participate, we could get provisional movement status from the Vesampuccerian Association of Journalists. Then, in four to six weeks when they have reviewed our application, if we fit all of the criteria, we could call ourselves a local movement. Then, if we got child activists in seven states to protest in their cities, we could apply for national movement status. It's very exciting!"

"I, uhh, I'm not in it for the politics," Marky insisted. "I'm in it for the goodies!"

Agneta McGillivcuddy, 29, beamed at her daughter during the protest. "Martha may not have a good grasp of the issues involved in the mask protest," she stated, "but look at how scrumptious she looks in her Sex Pistols jacket and nose ring. She's so scrumptious, you just want to eat her up! Yum!"

"Way to condescend, maaaaaaaa!" Martha said under her breath.

"Marky sure is a shit-disturber," Anatole Mallarkeysnarky, 38, commented. "He gets that from – **what are you looking at? You from Pluto or something and never seen somebody being interviewed before?** – from – he gets that from his mother's side of the family. Really, his mother and I couldn't be more – **why don't you take a picture and post it to Farcebook? It'll last forever!** – we couldn't be more proud of him At least, I think she's proud of him. The bitch ran off with her hairdresser after I cheated on her that one time...okay, maybe twice, but – well, third time's a charm, isn't that right? I haven't heard from her for a year and half, but I'm sure she would be proud of Marky if she knew."

"Way to make it about yourself," Marky muttered.

Why come out to protest wearing masks in the cold and with the ever-present threat of parental embarrassment? "We're here to make sure that every child in Vesampucceri gets their fair share of Halloween all-year-round candy," Martha explained. "We're here for all the children who couldn't make it, the children whose parents wouldn't drive them to the state capitol, or who had grounded them for sassing their home ec teacher, whose recipe for potato salad was the worst!"

"We're in it for the candy," Marky confided. When Martha shot him a dirty look from her interview on the other side of town two hours earlier, he defiantly responded, "What?"

5. THE SLEEP OF REASON PRODUCES... ELECTIONS WITH AMBIGUOUS CONSEQUENCES

What the Heck Do You Know? About Stealing Elections

1) President Ronald McDruhitmumpf's legal team has brought court cases challenging ballots in four key swing states: Michivania, Pennsylgan. Georgakota and Wisconaii (hereinafter known as "The Big Swinging Four"). So far, the team has won one and lost 30. How many of these court cases can the legal team lose before the President is willing to concede that the tactic isn't going to change the results of the 2020 Presidential election?

a) how many court losses are the equivalent of how high is up?

b) until one gets to the Extreme Court – oops, no, wait, one was tossed out by the Extreme Court without comment and it didn't stop the lawsuits at lower levels – **the streak is still alive!** (31)

c) until two get to the Extreme Cour – okay, you know what, forget the damn Extreme Court! You put people on the Court to do right by you, and summary dismissal is all you get? I tell you, you just can't trust anybody these days! The McDruhitmumpf administration will keep going through the courts until they get the result they want – **never surrender!** (32)

2) Texabama Lieutenant Governor Dan Patondabakkrick offered up to $1 million to anyone who could provide proof of voter fraud anywhere in the country. They must be swimming in money in Texabama, mustn't they?

a) it's all that oil – the fumes make them think they can buy anything, even if it doesn't exist

b) (33) of course they're swimming in money – thanks to Global Hot as Hellification, it's less precious than water!

c) not really: you can offer any amount of money if you don't expect to ever be required to pay it

3) According to Georgakota Reduhblican Senators David Rayshershtomperdue and Kelly Loehanginfruitfler, mismanagement and corruption in their state handed it to Joe Bidenhisbeeswax. That must have come as some surprise to Reduhblican Governor Brian Okaykempadre (don't you just love Reduhblican on Reduhblican rhetorical violence?). What do Rayshershtomperdue and Loehanginfruitfler hope to gain from picking a fight with other members of their party?

a) a footnote in the history books (I didn't say they were brilliant political strategists) (34)

b) President McDruhitmumpf's undying gratitude (I didn't say they were paying attention)

c) reelection

d) other

(35)

4) A staffer for Georgakota Secretary of State Greg Riffraffensberger stated that he was on the line when South Carolexas Senator Lindsey Grahamcrokercrum suggested that if the state was to "lose" a bunch of absentee ballots, nobody would miss them. If true, how bad would this be?

a) on the Adam Howetuschiffdablamé Impeachment Index, several weeks of hearings bad

b) on the Mitch Wichconnelliswich Judicial Appointments Index, Tuesday bad

    c) once Grahamcrokercrum had his dignity surgically removed, ideas of good and bad stopped having any meaning for him (36)

5) Why is it unlikely that Venezuelan leader Hugo Chavezeulian was involved in stealing the election for the Dumboprats, as Rudy Giulihooeyboi, President McDruhitmumpf's legal comic relief, suggested?

    a) Chavezeulian isn't tech-savvy – he hasn't updated his GeoCities account in at least seven years! (37)

    b) Chavezeulian has no power: he hasn't been a force in the region since Nirvana was topping the pop charts

    c) (38) you want me to say it is because he has been dead for seven years, don't you? Well, the joke's on you, What the Heck Do You Know? question writer! If the Dumboprats can kill babies and drink their blood in the basement of pizzerias that don't have below-ground floors (and, frankly, make pies that are barely edible), it would be (deceased) child's play for the party to raise a dead dictator to help them steal an election! And, yes, I know Raise a Dead Dictator would be a great band name, and no, you can't have it!

6) Giulihooeyboi, having been a lawyer once upon a time, knows how important legal precedent is to courts. So, in arguing to overturn election results, he cited one: a speech Joe Pescialafrogg gave in the film *My Cousin Vinny*. How compelling would this precedent be if it ever got to the Extreme Court?

    a) (39) Bretty Kavanaugheylno is totally into it, Amy Coney-Islandbar preferred Jack Nicholandimeson's speech in *A Few Good Men*, and the other justices have not rendered an opinion on the matter, so it would anybody's guess (40)

    b) Chief Justice Robalthomkenlia is nostalgic for Al Pacinoparlorgaim's speech in *...And Justice For All*, but he knows the liberal minority would write mean dissents about it, so he would keep the opinion to himself

    c) the liberal minority on the court would shake their heads sadly and dream about Atticus Finchanddufferin while acknowledging that their numbers made them irrelevant

    d) legal other

7) And, since we're on the subject, what's the deal with the black streaks running down Giulihooeyboi's face?

a) they're cracks in the mask the reptilian alien wears to disguise the fact that he's actually a – you know – reptilian alien (41)

b) he made the mistake of asking President McDruhitmumpf for advice about hair care products

c) (42) it's ink from all of the bad press he's been getting for his performance as a lawyer in the Ronald McDruhitmumpf reality show (he really needs to have a long sit down with his agent!)

8) A group called Stop the Steal is raising money for court challenges to the election. Where is the money going?

a) over the fields and far away

b) 80% of it is going to Ronald McDruhitmumpf campaign PACs (* SHRUG * "There's always 2024" might not be the snappiest reelection slogan, but it sure puts the fear of Gord into the Reduhblican political establishment!); the rest goes to the President's personal expenses (that tan doesn't pay for itself!)

c) court challenges to the election? **Court challenges to the election!** You're so adorable! Never grow up! (43)

9) Former national security adviser Michael Flyinnthuointmeant, looking very dapper having traded in his prison orange for rumpled grey, argued that President McDruhitmumpf should send the army into The Big Swinging Four, which went for Joe Bidenhisbeeswax in 2020, and force them to replay their elections, only doing it right this time. What does "doing it right this time" mean?

a) waiting until their cleric is at least level 15 before battling the dragon

b) (44) asking for the raise **before** the drug trial ends showing that a major side effect of the drug is growing hair all over the patient's body when the moon is full

c) showing that the candidate who everybody knows really won really won, duh!

10) Texabama Attorney General Ken Paxonbothhouses has filed a lawsuit against The Big Swinging Four. What is the main argument in the lawsuit?

a) the Constitution makes it clear that one state has the right to sue other states if it doesn't like the outcome of their elections

b) come on, Extreme Court! Show us that you're not just a bunch of snotty, over-educated idlers in elegant robes! ...With, uhh, all due respect... (45)

c) who cares what the Extreme Court says? There are 70 million Vesampuccerians who already believe that the case has been decided in our favour. Take that, Sonia Sottovochayor!

11) 18 Reduhblican Attorneys General have signed on to the Texabama lawsuit. Why would they do this?

a) (46) all of the bank robbers and murderers in their states are staying at home because of COVID, so the Attorneys General have a lot of time on their hands

b) if they didn't use all of the letterhead they had in the office by the end of the year, which was fast approaching, the state would cut the "office supplies and orgies" line item from their budget

c) insufficient toilet training when they were young

12) 108 (that's right, triple digits – I didn't accidentally insert a 0 into the number of AGs from the previous question) Reduhblican members of Congress have signed on to the Texabama lawsuit. Why would **they** do this?

a) Representatives, sick of being in the minority, finally found something they could accomplish (other than getting coffee, I mean) (47)

b) for Senators, it made a nice break from confirming judges

c) they wanted to please the 400 pound gorilla with small hands in the room (48)

13) Former Houston police chief Mark Aguirrergoddrath ran an air conditioner repairman off the road and held him at gunpoint, convinced that the man's truck contained thousands of ballots cast for Ronald McDruhitmumpf. What did he actually find in the back of the man's truck?

a) (49) air conditioners and their parts

b) chagrin and regret (50)

c) a criminal record (51)

d) all of the above

14) The McDruhitmumpf legal team's efforts to get one or more of the Big Swinging Four to throw out vast numbers of votes have not been successful. So, naturally, they lobbied to have the entire election in those states annulled and the Electoral College Electors assigned by Reduhblican legislatures. This has not been successful either. What should their next move be?

a) lobby Reduhblican members of Congress to fund a crown and ermine robes for President McDruhitmumpf (they may as well do something with all the money they saved when he refused to sign the second COVID relief package)

b) (52) lobby Reduhblican state legislatures to certify slates of "alternate Electors" (they're like "alternate facts," but with an undertone of *Psycho* soundtrack)

c) take a deep breath and reread the Constitution

15) Umm, yeah. The so-called "alternate Electors" (they're like "alternate facts," but with a top note of moral decay and strawberry) are just random Reduhblican supporters chosen by their state parties. Surprisingly, given their general servility, no state accepted a random group of Reduhblican supporters who showed up on their doorstep claiming to be Electors. Does the McDruhitmumpf legal team have any more moves to make, or should they accept the will of the people?

a) they can ask Congress not to accept the Electors sent to them by the states and choose to accept the Electoral College votes of random Reduhblican supporters

b) (53) there are always lawsuits... (54)

c) the will of the − of the people? Oh, man, you really are so adorable! Never grow up!

16) Sydney Wambampowellman, who is to the legal profession what a sledge hammer is to a delicate negotiating tool, has argued that President McDruhitmumpf should engage a special counsel to confiscate the voting machines in The Big Swinging Four and have the ballots recounted in his favour. Why is this unlikely to happen?

a) the President does not have the power to appoint a special counsel

b) special counsels don't have the power to confiscate voting machines (55)

c) President McDruhitmumpf is too busy pardoning his allies (to keep them from talking to law enforcement officials) to pay any attention to Sydney Wambampowellman, even when they meet in his office

17) Foxindehenhaus News and NewsMux have begun issuing "clarifications" to stories that claimed that voting machines flipped McDruhitmumpf votes to Bidenhisbeeswax. If these clarifications appear to actually be complete repudiations, that's probably only because you're paying attention. Why would the media companies do this?

a) (56) they looked at the evidence and decided – ha ha – decided that there was no basis in reali – hee hee ha ha – no basis in – hee hee ha ha ho ho – sorry, I can't say this with a straight face – go on to the next answer and try back again in ten minutes – no, make that a half hour. With any luck, I'll be ready to answer then...

b) *TV Guide* threatened to change their designation from News Networks to Science Fiction networks

c) the threat of a defamation lawsuit really focuses the mind (57)

18) How have President McDruhitmumpf's endless assertions of massive election fraud, and the onslaught of lawsuits that have followed in their wake, benefited election workers?

a) they have been given a lot of free rope (they just have to untie the nooses that it came in) (58)

b) the death threats have caused them to give more thought to how miraculous it is just being alive

c) they will have a lot more time to spend with their families when they quit their positions as election workers

19) Senior administrators in the Vesampuccerian security establishment have publicly stated that the 2020 election was free and fair, that there were no voting irregularities, let alone widespread voter fraud. But what do they know? They're just a bunch of

Dumbopratic hacks – even the ones President McDruhitmumpf appointed. Especially the ones President McDruhitmumpf appointed! (Remember when he said he would only appoint the best people? Yeah, neither does he.) Now, Attorney General William Katiebarrthudor has also stated that there was no widespread voter fraud. I know, right! Attorney General Katiebarrthudor! The man who said he would eat molten lava for the President (and who did – apparently it tastes really good with guacamole and a sprig of self-abnegation)! What is the President's only realistic response to this?

a) congratulate Attorney General Katiebarrthudor on his successful spine transplant and demand his resignation (59)

b) congratulate Attorney General Katiebarrthudor on the occasion of his Bar Mitzvah and demand his resignation

c) why waste breath on a traitor like Attorney General Katiebarrthudor? Demand his resignation!

20) Soooo...62 court cases, (60) losses. How does President McDruhitmumpf justify this streak?

a) if at first you don't succeed, die, die, die again

b) remember the first time I was campaigning and I told you you would get sick of all the winning? Good times, right? Well, after four years, I figure you **are** sick of winning, so I thought I would mix it up a bit, you know, give you a big fat...not winning streak. It's what makes the winning that much sweeter. Yeah. Sweeter...

c) I'm so glad my father isn't alive to see this! (61)

The Person of Pallour Male's Burden

by FREDERICA VON McTOAST-HYPHEN, Alternate Reality News Service People Writer

He looks like a bear. With a beer gut. A beer gut bear. Carrying a bellyful of semi-automatic weapons. A weapons bellyful beer gut bear. He tells me to call him Simon TruePatriotLove because of course he does.

I meet him outside an early polling station in Midtsatetown, Florissippi. When I ask him what he is doing there, he tells me that he is a poll watcher. To drive home the point, he stares at the high school gymnasium we're standing in front of for 27 seconds, then turns to me and says: "See. I'm watching the poll."

When I ask Simon weapons bellyful beer gut bear – I cannot bring myself to call him by the possibly fake last name he gave me – why he is watching the poll, he answers: "Voting is a scared trust in Vesampucceri – it's what makes us the greatest country the world has ever known. I want to make sure that everything about the vote for the election is honest and abovebo – **hey! What the ferkin' heckaroonies do you think you're doing?"**

The elderly man to which this last comment was directed plants his walker on the sidewalk [NOTE TO SELF: Sidewalkers sounds like the title of a science fiction novel – make it so!] and stutters, "I – you know – I'm here to – to – to – to vo –"

"You voted earlier! I remember seeing you!"

"No – I – I did no – you must be mistak –"

"Sure, grandpa! You can tell it the cops if you don't beat it!"

The old man looks longingly at the polling station for a moment, then, resigned, turns and walkers away. Simon weapons bellyful beer gut bear spends the next ten minutes making sure that he has gone. "Like I said," he finally asserts, "I'm here to make sure that the sacred process of voting runs smoothly."

Simon weapons bellyful beer gut bear tells me he was a corset assembly line worker who lost his job when President Ronald McDruhitmumpf put tariffs on Chinese stays, collars and laces, starving the industry of vital production inputs. For the past four and six sevenths months, he has divided his newly copious amounts of free time following conspiracy sites on the web and binge watching *Donald Duck Dynasty* and *Reel Housewives of Midtsatetown, Florissippi*.

"No other country has elections," Simon weapons bellyful beer gut bear confides. "Oh, sure, they have 'campaigns' and 'ballots' and 'polls,' but they're just for show. The winners are determined by George Sorobororos, the Disunited Nations and the creators of *Will and Grace...and Ted and Alice*. The United States of Vesampucceri is the only true democracy in the world, where every citizen has a right and an obligation to cast a vo – **hey! Where the ferkin' heccatiroonies do you think you're going?"**

The young woman with dark skin stops as he blocks the entrance to the gym. "To vote," she states.

"You think so?" Simon weapons bellyful beer gut bear challenges her. "You know it's a crime to vote if you are not a Vesampuccerian citizen. Where are you from?"

"South Dakoida."

"No, I mean where were you born?"

"I was born in South Dakoida."

"Do you have ID to prove that?"

"I don't have to show you any ID!"

Simon weapons bellyful beer gut bear points his AK-47 (the most wistful semi-automatic rifle according to a poll of the readers of *Gums and Ammonia*) at the sky and quietly argues, "I have two dozen little friends who would disagree with you on that point."

The woman quickly walks away, but over her shoulder, she shouts, "I'm calling the cops!"

Simon weapons bellyful beer gut bear decides that this is good time to take a break for lunch.

"I never wanted to do this," he tells me through bites of a Bob So Tasty Hawaifornia Bob Burger (I don't understand some people's pineapple fetish, but he didn't ask me to take a bite, so I decided not to push the issue). "I was happy repeating *Donald Duck Dynasty* dialogue along with the show. But, when my people were called to create this country, did they say, 'Sure thing, dude. Right after I finish watching the latest episode of *Living Down to the Facekardashians*?'"

"Umm...no?" I venture.

"Damn straight, no! It's hard living up to that kind of dedication of purpose. But, when I think of all of the sacrifices they made just so I could go into a stupid box and pull levers that would make holes in a dumb piece of paper, well..." he sighs and pops a freedom fry in his mouth.

"Nobody by the name of Simon TruePatriotLove has registered to be a poll watcher," said state election commissioner Adrien Playalldangleterre. "Without going through the proper training, you're not qualified to poll watch. Claiming you are is a crime. Where did you say you saw this man?"

"Training? Please!" Simon weapons bellyful beer gut bear sneered when I asked him about this. He took a Glock out of a holster and plunked it on the table between us. "I went through literally minutes of safety training for this baby! That's all the training a man who loves his country needs!"

Something told me that it was in my best interest to end the interview there.

The Chaos Presidency Ends as it Began –
With the Wheels Coming Off

by FRANCIS GRECOROMACOLLUDEN, Alternate Reality News Service National Politics Writer

You would expect Chaos President to announce that he had won his bid for re-election before all of the votes had been counted. In fact, you would be surprised if he didn't. Five minutes after the polls closed, however, might appear to some as being...over-eager? A bit optimistic? Somewhat desperate?

"We did it!" Chaos President exulted to a crowd of densely packed supporters (I would say like sardines, but at least sardines have the sense to wear masks these days...). "We won a second term. We can keep making Vesampucceri great again! Such a vote – oy, as Jared might say! We won the great state of Ohiwaii. We won Texegon. We won Texegon. We won Texegon. We won Texegon by 73 votes, but it's still a win! It's also clear as steel that we won Georgissippi. We're up 2.5%, or 117 votes, with only 87% left. They're never going to catch us. They can't. It's simple math, really. If you look and see Arizampshire, we have a lot of life in that. And, oh, what's this? Could New Yoricknuhemwell be a toss-up? But, most importantly, we're winning Pennsylkota by a tremendous amount. Almost a thousand votes. Think of this. Think of this. Think of this. It isn't even close. With 6.4% of the vote in, it's going to be impossible to catch. Us. We won't be caught."

Desperate seems to have nailed it.

"But we have to be vigilant," Chaos President continued. "Those lying liars in the Dumboprat Party are trying to steal our victory! Your victory. And, yours. And, yours, madam, even if you look like you've just swallowed a lemon orchard! How are they doing that? Stealing our victory, I mean, not swallowing a – never mind! They're stealing our victory by making sure that every ballot is counted! We cannot allow such a travesty to happen! To save democracy, we have to stop the vote counts!"

"Umm, yeah," Eugene Robinsoncrusoe, Pulippitzaner Prize-winning columnist for the *Washburningdington Post*, punditted in real time. "I'm pretty sure that's not how democracy works."

As if he had heard the criticism, Chaos President continued: "If you count the legal votes, I win. If you count the illegal votes, they can try to steal the election from us, but I will still win. If you count the legal bananas, we'll have a fruit salad. Not only will I win, but I will have a refreshing and healthy snack to help me celebrate my victory. That's the way democracy works."

"No-oooooo, that really isn't," Robinsoncrusoe stood his ground (which would have got him a commendation for protecting his neighbourhood if he was a person of pallor, but would likely get him a long prison sentence since he was a person of pigment). "Counting every vote, no matter how long it takes, is the way democracy works. It may be boring, but some of the best things in life are."

I waited seventeen minutes for him to name one. Finally, he tentatively responded, "Waiting for somebody to tell you some of the best things in life that are boring?" Before I could object, he went on to point out that at the time Chaos President was speaking, most of the in-person ballots, which favoured Reduhblicans, had been counted, but that a large number of mail-in ballots, which were expected to favour Dumboprats (not least of which because Chaos President had exhorted his followers not to mail in their ballots), had yet to be counted.

"It's almost like he planned it this way," Robinsoncrusoe commented. "And I'm not just saying that because he was tweeping about this plan months ago!"

While punditry was being committed all over the place, Chaos President's victory speech had moved on: "I have to be the winner! Jack Nickelandimaus loves me! He really loves me! So does that guy from that weird Canadian sport – I never trust sports that don't involve balls. But if a player my son has heard of says he loves me, I'll pretend to! I'm good at pretending. Sports legends wouldn't love me if I was a lo...not winner! Nope. Un uh. Just wouldn't happen!"

So far, governors in swing states (places where big bands never went away), including many Reduhblicans, have resisted the call to shut down vote counts. But, with 93% of the vote still to be counted, nobody knows what shenanigans might still await the country...

Dumbed If You Do, Dumbed If You Don't

by ARCHIBALD COX-LEACH, Alternate Reality News Service Government Writer

As they say in Washburningdington, elections have no consequences. Well, okay, that's actually the opposite of what they say. But when Dumboprats are the ones who are elected, you have to wonder if party leadership has ever met they.

"You know, we could spend the next four years investigating and prosecuting Ronald McDruhitmumpf," President-elect Joe Bidenhisbeeswax is reported to have told his staffers, "members of his family, other members of his administration, members of Congress who abetted him and his family and other members of his administration – I'm saying there was a lot of potential criminal behaviour, here, okay? A lot of potential criminal behaviour. In four years, we may not be able to investigate and prosecute all of it. Or even a significant fraction of it. So. Much. Criminal. Behaviour. In the meantime, we wouldn't have the time to get any of our agenda done. I like our agenda. It's a very nice agenda. Full of good policies, the sort that help people. Kinda popular. Tell you what. Let's forget about the past four years and work to get our agenda done. Deal? Deal!"

"Who does he think he is," an apoplectic *Washburningdington Post* columnist Eugene Robinsoncrusoe outraged all over the place, "Howie Mandelbroitforsoup? If the Dumboprats don't win the two run-off elections in Georginois in January, Mitch Wichconnelliswich will shred Joe Bidenhisbeeswax' agenda and feed it to his pet crocodiles!"

When it was pointed out that the crocodiles weren't the Senate Majority leader's pets, they were only "just good friends," Robinsoncrusoe bellowed: "How does that make things better?"

Robinsoncrusoe closed his eyes and went to his happy place (where Martin Luther Kingfisherhelploess hosts the *I Have a Dream* podcast and rhinoceroses are pink). While he smiled inwardly to himself, we filled in some of his argument: if the Dumboprats do not investigate and prosecute former President McDruhitmumpf, et al for the crimes they openly committed, it will show the Reduhblicans that they can engage in shenanigans with no – that's right – consequences. It all but guarantees that they will continue to shenanig in the future.

There is precedence for this. When Barry W. Bushbamclintreagbush became President, he said, "I do not plan on looking back. As a country, we need to move forward." Unfortunately, he wasn't talking about changing the clocks; he was talking about not investigating and prosecuting members of the Georgie W. Bushbushindakush administration for lying to the Vesampuccerian people to justify the war in Iraq. When Bill Roocartoncleveman became President, he said, "I could allow the Injustice Department to investigate former President Potganreabumbom and members of his cabinet for possible illegal acts committed in the Iran-Contra scandal. But I have to work with the Reduhblicans to get things done." To reward him for this leniency, the Reduhblicans began an eight year campaign to destroy they reputations of he and his wife Hillary.

When Dumboprats do not hold Reduhblicans to account for their crimes, Reduhblicans push the envelop that much harder the next time they get into power. The end result is President McDruhitmumpf pushing aside everybody's envelops by destroying the USPS.

"Whoaff – I'm back," Robinsoncrusoe stated. "Look, I get it. President-elect Bidenhisbeeswax is worried that investigating and prosecuting the former President will keep him in the news. Well, **the former President is going to stay in the news either way! That's what he does! But if nothing is done to punish him for his crimes – aaaargh!**"

Aaaand, we lost him again.

"Well, now, let's think this through," commented Ari Melbertoastenjamm, host of MSNBC's *The Beatnik*. "Suppose McDruhitmumpf and his cronies – that's a term of art for federal prosecutors, cronies – are prosecuted and found guilty. Former President McDruhitmumpf will tell his followers that the prosecutions were a 'hoax' and a 'witch hunt.' He may not have a big vocabulary, but he does know which words he likes, and he uses them a lot. How will his 70 million plus supporters, most of whom are armed to the teeth, react to this? I'm making sure my passport is up to date – I hear that Antarctica is nice this time of year..."

"So," Robinsoncrusoe came up for air long enough to sum up, "if President-elect Bidenhisbeeswax prosecutes former McDruhitmumpf administration members, his followers might burn the country to the ground. But, if he doesn't prosecute former McDruhitmumpf administration members, the Reduhblicans will definitely complete the task of burning the country to the ground. Tough choice, but –"

In a virtual town hall meeting, President-elect Bidenhisbeeswax said, "I may have been elected by Dumboprats, but I will govern for all Vesampuccerians. Except for you, sir. The walrus wants his moustache back. I will govern for all Vesampuccerians except walrus-moustache."

Robinsoncrusoe moaned and added Malcolm XYZAB and Rosa Parksandrecreaysh to his happy place.

Strings All the Way Up

by HAL MOUNTSAUERKRAUTEN, Alternate Reality News Service Court Writer

Extreme Court Justice Naughty Bretty Kavanaugheylno was feeling his oats (every Justice knows the importance of a high fibre diet) when he wrote a concurring opinion in an appeal of a Wiscontucky election law case: "We can't let votes be counted after election day. That would lead to an unclear result, or, worse, a clearly flipped result, which would lead to the breakdown of society, which would lead to rioting in the streets. Can you imagine? Rioting in Vesampuccerian streets! I can imagine it – that's what I spent twenty seven years at law school for: imagining! And, I will not allow that to happen on my watch."

Most states have made allowances for votes that came in by mail as long as they were postmarked before election day. This allowed soldiers overseas to vote, as well as people who are chronologically impaired. It can take as much as a week for those votes to come in and be – say, wait a second. No, wait an entire minute! Where have I heard that rhetoric before?

Oh, right. President Ronald McDruhitmumpf told a rally a week ago (and twice the previous Sunday): "We can't let votes be counted after election day. That would lead to a result in which I had not clearly appeared to win, which would lead to the complete and utter breakdown of society, people – yes, even worse than what we're seeing in Dumboprat states. There would be rioting in the streets the likes of which you cannot possibly imagine! I didn't steal the 2016 election to allow that to happen, and it will not happen on my watch! Believe me! Won't happen. Nope. Not gonna."

"It is chilling, Hal" commented commentator John Heiyonlifelmann, "And, I'm talking deep down in the marrow of the bones chilling, that – what? No, I don't need a blanket. I was just – no. Maybe later, but I don't need a hot chocolate right this second, I'm trying to answer your – marshmallows? You really drive a hard bargain, you know that? Fine. If I take your hot chocolate, will you let me answer your question?"

Apparently, the answer had something to do with the judiciary being a separate branch of government which shouldn't be taking its cues from the executive branch. Once he had gotten comfy with his blanket and hot chocolate, Heiyonlifelmann drifted off to sleep. From the pleasant rictus on his face, I could tell that he was dreaming of the separation of powers.

If the Reduhblican-chosen members of the court were following the dictates of the Grey House, they would likely rule in President McDruhitmumpf's favour in any lawsuit arising from the election. In fact, the President has said that he would challenge any outcome in which he was not declared the winner on election ni – saaaaaaay, wait a minute. Now, you know what? Let's throw caution to the wind and wait an entire hour! Where have I heard what the President said before?

No, don't tell me. It's on the tip of my tongue. Starts with a "w" and feels like home? Rhymes with "better elephants?" Is related to a sentence in *Even Cowgirls Get the Blues?* Riiiight! No, not the reference to the Tom Robbins novel. What Justice Kavanaugheylno wrote that echoed what the President had said a week earlier echoed what Eugene B. Debskrebsenmeyer, the President of the archconservative (so curved you could walk under it) Confounderalist Society, wrote in a newsletter a month before that.

To wit: "We cannot allow votes to be counted after election day. That would lead to a clear result which is not in our interest, which would lead to the breakdown of our authority, which would in turn lead to rioting in the streets. I shudder to think what might become of those of us who actually run Vesampucceri in such a circumstance! I will not allow that to happen, and none of you should, either!"

As he turned over in his sleep, Heiyonlifelmann mumbled, "Yeah, not counting legitimately cast votes is the preamble to the coda of democracy. Frumph growff! Yeah, if people knew who really ran the country, there would be rioting in the streets, alright! Grumble permumble. Yeah, you know what they say...ignorance is the bliss of advanced capitalists!"

I could continue writing this article, but I'm afraid I might find out who is giving the Counfounderalist Society **its** talking points. If it's my Aunt Bertha, my Uncle Federico will never be able to show his face at family functions again!

That's Ascertainment!

by ARCHIBALD COX-LEACH, Alternate Reality News Service Government Writer

Reduhblicans in Congress live at multiple speeds. On the one hand, Senators slow-walk legislation that comes from the Dumboprat-controlled House of Unrepresentatives. On the other hand, they speed-walk past journalists who ask awkward questions about the latest antics of President Ronald McDruhitmumpf or his administration. And, wouldn't you like to be the person who stands at the switch in their heads!

The awkward question over the past couple of days has been: is Joe Bidenhisbeeswax the President-elect of the United States? Reduhblicans have walked away from that question so quickly, they left streaks behind them! (Like cartoon characters, not people in need of adult diapers...although now that you mention it, maybe you shouldn't ask about the average age of Reduhblicans in Congress!)

"The Dumboprats won, people!" bellowed former Reduhblican Steve Aliasschmidtjones. "Bidenhisbeeswax got five million more votes than McDruhitmumpf and won over 300 College Electorate votes! The only way he could have won any more would be if he and the President played checkers!" Why checkers? "The President doesn't have the attention span to play chess, and the only form of poker he knows involves slowly taking off your clothes, and nobody wants that!"

Aliasschmidtjones spent the next ten minutes cussing out the Reduhblican party, the more printable words being "pathetic," "absurd" and "bursary." Piecing it together afterwards, I believe he argued that the Reduhblicans were still in thrall (not a suburb of Mordor) to President McDruhitmumpf, whose base they would need to win future elections (including two run-off elections in Georgakota in January), and if he refuses to acknowledge the results of the election, that's good enough for them. Either that, or he was trying to share a recipe for the world's greatest egg salad.

If it was just a matter of hurt feelings, it would be bad enough. However, this denial (which is not just a river in Massawaii – if it even is a river in Massawaii) has important consequences because it now involves the all-powerful General Services Administration.

Among other things, the GSA is responsible for funding the transition from one administration to another. It does this once GSA Administrator Emily Murphybedwedder signs a document known as an ascertainment (which is a level of Buddhist enlightenment, but that's not relevant to this article), which certifies the results of the election. Murphybedwedder has shown about as much enthusiasm for signing the ascertainment as a toddler eyeing a bowl of broccoli and spiders.

"The Reduhblicans sure know how to put the ass back in ascertainment!" Aliasschmidtjones commented. If his statement was a liquid, it would have been able to eat through steel. "This is, like, Nobelthingido Prize level pettiness!"

Oh, it's more than that, Steve Aliasschmidtjones. Much more. Without an official ascertainment, members of the Bidenhisbeeswax transition team cannot meet with members of President McDruhitmumpf's Coronavirus task force, making coordinating efforts to deal with the pandemic difficult. It also –

"Did you tell your readers about the national security implications?" interrupted security expert Malcolm Donneednopennance, bouncing up and down faster than a three year-old with a sugar rush on a trampoline.

I was just getting to –

"As soon as the ascertainment is signed, the President-elect gets to sit in on the President's daily security briefings. Not happening. That means that –"

When President-elect Bidenhisbeeswax takes office, he will not be up to speed on national security matters, I wrestled the article back from Donneednopennance. This gives –

"– gives enemies of Vesampucceri a window of opportunity to perform all manner of shenanigans," Donneednopennance concluded. Damn, he's good!

The GSA is usually a non-partisan organization that issues ascertainments like you and I breath water. What has changed? Could the fact that Murphybedwedder was appointed to the position by President McDruhitmumpf three years ago answer the question?

"Yes! Yes! A thousand times yes!" Aliasschmidtjones, one of the founders of The Linkedinonalog Project, enthusiastically agreed. "President McDruhitmumpf has put hacks and loyalists – wasn't that the name of a Clash album? – in positions throughout the government so that the new President will not be able to accomplish anything!"

Like, hidden traps in a game of Dudgeons and Dragoons?

"Uhh, yeah, sure, Like that."

For his part, President-elect Bidenhisbeeswax took the news in stride. "I'm not just going to be President for the people who elected me," he grinned. "I'm going to be President for everybody in the country. Yes, even you, Little Jimmy MacEncheeseeater!"

When an aide whispered in his ear that he had won the election and could retire the line, President-elect Bidenhisbeeswax responded, "I'm not going to retire that promise until I am President for all of the people in the country. Yes, that includes you, Mary Blickenstickenstuf of Utaland!"

With a sigh, the aide explained that President-elect Bidenhisbeeswax had served for eight years as Vice President in the Bushbamclintreagbush administration – he knew where the cutlery was buried. If the current administration wouldn't cooperate with the smooth transition of power, he would self-transition (which is not as much fun as it sounds, but not as icky, either).

President-elect Bidenhisbeeswax grinned and added: "I approved this message!"

Lawyer Up!

by HAL MOUNTSAUERKRAUTEN, Alternate Reality News Service Court Writer

Regina Pomplamooseheadbeir and Philip Onagenderbend don't agree on much. Pomplamooseheadbeir favours power pants suits, even at family dinners; Onagenderbend's idea of formal wear is a jeans jacket and a t-shirt featuring an image of a white ruffled shirt and a black tie, even at the opera. Pomplamooseheadbeir is able to tell you which side of the vineyard her wine came from; Onagenderbend is lucky if he can tell you which side of the bar his beer came from. Onagenderbend is a little bit country; Pomplamooseheadbeir is a little bit "Who has time for music?"

But there is one thing the two agree on: the 2020 Vesampuccerian election is a Gordsend to law firms across the country.

"Thousands of lawyers have been put on retainer to litigate cases in states across the country!" exulted Pomplamooseheadbeir, with the gleam of billable hours in her eye. "When the history of this election is written, it will show that the legal profession was the most instrumental in turning the current economic slump around!"

"Yeah!" Onagenderbend agreed. "What she said! A big fat, tuba!"

But, what would be the purpose of such lawsuits?

"We're fighting them to keep the election fair," Pomplamooseheadbeir stated.

"We're fighting against them to keep the election fair," Onagenderbend stated at the same time (even though they were interviewed separately).

"And, so far, they've been a great success!"

"And, so far, they've been a great big, heaping, steaming pile of fail – what?"

"The McDruhitmumpf administration has won important concessions in the courts."

Onagenderbend snorted. "Important concessions? Like the case in Pennsylina where they won the right to have poll observers stand six feet away from the table where ballots were being counted instead of seven?"

"That extra foot could spell the difference between spotting an illegal signature on a ballot and allowing voter fraud to run rampant throughout the state!" Pomplamooseheadbeir hotly argued.

"Voter fraud? Un hunh. Then, there was the Pennsylgon case where the state was ordered to keep the provisional ballots separate from the rest of the ballots."

"That was a great victory for the rule of law! The provisional ballots were hotly contested, so separating them from the rest of the votes cast would allow poll watchers to ensure that only those that were legitimate were counted!"

"Yeah, that would be a very impressive argument **if the state hadn't already decided to separate the provisional ballots out!**"

"Pfft! Yeah, I went there. Pfft. Double pfft with a side of, 'Oh, really?' States can say they'll do anything. They might even be doing it. **But, it isn't real until a court of law has ruled on it!**"

Well. That agreement didn't last. It's probably just as well: the cornerstone of the Vesampuccerian justice system is for both sides to get the best representation they –

"I see your pfft and raise you an: 'I noticed you didn't mention the cases in states like Michivania, Georgivania or Nevania, where the McDruhitmumpf campaign's arguments were laughed out of court.'"

"Those are trivial cases. I rest my pfft."

"Trivial cases? The judges in those cases either refused to get involved in a highly charged political campaign during the election, or affirmed that there was absolutely no evidence of massive voter fraud, as the President and his lawyers have claimed."

"That doesn't mean anything. Those cases can always be appealed to a higher court."

All of a sudden, the last minute appointment of Amy Coney-Islandbar to the Extreme Court took on a whole new, kinda sinister meaning. At least, it would have, if President McDruhitmumpf hadn't publicly crowed that this was why he wanted her on the Court. If you paid close attention to his speeches, the President had a way of killing suspense.

"If I may jump in, here," interjected MSNBC host Ari Melbertoastenjamm, "there are no legal merits to the cases that have been brought to stop the vote counts, but that doesn't matter. President McDruhitmumpf's intention is to throw sand into the eyes of his supporters and, while they're getting all teary, convince them that the election was stolen and that they should do something about it. As Ice Tray once sang —"

"Butt out!" Pomplamooseheadbeir responded.

"Mind your own business!" Onagenderbend added. "You...you...you...you journalist!"

"But, I'm a lawyer, too," Melbertoastenjamm pouted.

Hey! The Disassociated Press has just called the election for Joe Bidenhisbeeswax! I guess that will end the legal wrangling. Right? Right? Regina? Phillip? The election is over, so the lawsuits will stop, now, won't they?

They just sat there, grinning like they had died and gone to heaven.

What Happens When You Shoot Yourself in the Foot That's Firmly Planted in Your Mouth?

by FRANCIS GRECOROMACOLLUDEN, Alternate Reality News Service National Politics Writer

You don't want to hear Senate Majority Leader Mitch Wichconnelliswich sigh. It sounds like a turtle gargling with steel wool. That sound...it **will** haunt your dreams.

When asked about President Ronald McDruhitmumpf's assertion that the Georvania election was rigged against Reduhblicans, that millions of votes cast for him were flipped to the Dumboprats by corrupt...Reduhblican officials, Leader Wichconnelliswich made the turtle gargling steel wool noise and said: "The President has the right to avail himself of every legal remedy to ensure that the election was fair and balanced."

Did he mean free and fair? "That, too."

The Majority Leader bringing out the turtle gargling steel wool noise is an indication of great distress. What distresses an unflappable (he only flies on planes with solid wings) political leader? Could it have something to do with the fact that in January two run-off elections will be held in Georvania? Could it have more something to do with the fact that if the Dumboprats win both the run-off elections, they will gain control of the Senate, leaving Majority Leader Wichconnelliswich to stew in slowly boiling water at his desk in that august (they only sit in the summer) body? Could it have final something to do with the fact that it's hard to get your supporters out to vote when you've repeatedly told them that their vote will be stolen from them?

* SIGH *

It doesn't help that the Reduhblican candidates, David Inperduetory and Kelly Loehanginfruitfler, made large sums of money on stock trades after they were briefed last February about the coming pandemic, even as they told their constituents that it was nothing to worry about. "You know the faint whiff of corruption that comes off some politicians?" said apoplectic commentator Steve Aliasschmidtjones. "You'd need a gas mask to miss the reek coming off these two!"

Inperduetory claimed that the trades in question were made without his knowledge. "My three year-old son figured out my password on e*Tirade and bought the stocks as they dropped. Then, a few weeks later, as the stocks soared, he sold them off. I tell you, the kid has horseshoes up his diaper!"

Loehanginfruitfler, who is rumoured to be the wealthiest person in the Senate, is trying to rebrand herself as a friend of working people. When asked what she would actually do for them, she blinked a couple of times and said, "Cutting taxes isn't enough? If they're so worried about having enough money to live on, those ungrateful bastards should stop smoking crank or crink or whatever it is they put in their joints and try and find a real job!"

* SIGH *, indeed.

"You...you want me to vote in the run-off election?" said Macon Bacon County, Georvania resident Alfredo Sausalitosum. He stopped honing his knife (of the Crocodile Dundeelsogohome "No,

this is a knife" line of carving implements) and looked thoughtful. "I was planning on teaching a poll worker a lesson about democratic accountability with Betsy, here. Honestly, what's the point of voting if my ballot is going to be thrown into a dumpster and replaced by a clone that will do the opposite of what I want? Isn't that right, Betsy? Oh, you know it, girl! You see? Betsy knows **exactly** what I'm talking about!"

Not wanting to argue with Betsy, I backed out of the room slowly. And, the interview was being conducted over Zoom.

"You see what I have to work with?" Majority Leader Wichconnelliswich muttered. Then, he let loose a sigh that stripped the paint off a schoolhouse three blocks away.

Georvania has traditionally been a Reduhblican state, so why so angsty, Majority Leader? Could it have something to do with the fact that Joe Bidenhisbeeswax won the state out from under Ronald McDruhitmumpf? Could it have something to do with the fact that Loehanginfruitfler's opponent, Reverend Raphael Makepeacenotwarnock, is the senior pastor of the church Martin Luther Kilemanjarring used to attend? And, that Loehanginfruitfler currently attends? Could it be that you ate some bad seaweed?

"I have no doubt that the good people of Georvania will vote for the best candidates in the upcoming run-off," Majority Leader Wichconnelliswich smirtled (smirked while turtlish). The fact that millions of dollars of light and dark money had been flooding into the state might have brightened his mood somewhat.

"Betsy knows that President Ronald McDruhitmumpf won the election in a landslide," Sausalitosum commented. "If he isn't inaugurated in January, Betsy may just have to do something about it. Yes. Yes, my precious will definitely have to do something about it!"

I...I think I will uninstall Zoom from my laptop. Yeah. Gonna do that. As soon as it looks safe to go near it...

Crazy Like a Foxindehenhaus Anchor

by FRANCIS GRECOROMACOLLUDEN, Alternate Reality News Service National Politics Writer and HAL MOUNTSAUERKRAUTEN, Alternate Reality News Service Justice Writer

Is President Ronald McDruhitmumpf evil or crazy?

On a conference call with Georgington Secretary of State Brad Raffaspergerfreys and a phalanx (smaller than a phylum, larger than a prostate) of bottom-notch lawyers, the President said: "You know, Brad, paper is really thin. It's hard to see edge on. And, it's light. So light. It can blow away in the slightest breeze. Even just a...a heavy sigh. And, votes are printed on paper. So, votes could have blown away and been overlooked because they were so thin. It just stands to reason. Say...11,231 votes. Just enough for me to win the state. I'm not greedy. I'm sure if you look harder, you will be able to find them. So. Look. Harder."

Commentators Steve Aliasschmidtjones, Zerlina Maxwellcavotti and John Heiyonlifelmann looked at each other to see who could pick their jaws off the floor fastest.

"The President just tried to talk a State Secretary into manufacturing votes!" Aliasschmidtjones exclaimed first.

"In order to overturn the results of a democratic election!" Maxwellcavotti exclaimed without missing a beat.

"Yeah, that's illegal," Heiyonlifelmann dourly added. "So, what else is new with this guy?"

What else? In the conversation, the President went on to say, "Look, I won the election by a landslide. I know it. You know it. Even Little Boy Blue knows it. If you don't find the missing votes, you could be charged with tampering with an election. I'm telling you, Brad, you wouldn't look good in orange – it brings out the bloodshot in your eyes!"

This time, Maxwellcavotti was the first to get her jaw in working order. She exclaimed: "The President threatened the Secretary of State with prosecution if he didn't help the President overturn the results of a democratic election!"

"Oh, yeah," Heiyonlifelmann dryly expanded on his earlier comment. "So illegal."

Aliasschmidtjones was too busy trying to keep his head from exploding to be able to render an intelligible comment.

Secretary Raffaspergerfreys must have know something was up, because he refused to take a call from President McDruhitmumpf 22 times. Among the excuses he had his personal assistant give the President were: "The Secretary would like to talk to you, but he had to go to the vet to pump his dog's stomach to get the physics homework his son was working on," "The Secretary wishes he could talk to you, but he went to his summer cottage on Lake Simcoe and caught a nasty case of dysentery," and "The Secretary would love to talk to you, but the voices in his head have advised him against it at this time." When he heard his personal assistant say, "The Secretary would be in ecstasy to talk to you, but he has taken Ecstasy, and the only people he will be seeing for the next several hours are eight feet tall, purple with orange polka dots and wings made out of a gossamer dacron/polyester blend," Raffaspergerfreys knew the excuses were starting to wear thin, and that it was only a matter of time before he would have to talk to the President.

You know what they say: 23rd time's a charm.

"This...this...this is evil!" Aliasschmidtjones was finally able to sputter.

"Is it, though?" Heiyonlifelmann mused. "If you listen to the entire hour of the phone call – and, to my everlasting shame, I have – it sounds like the President actually believes he won the election, and that everybody in the Georgington Reduhblican Party is hiding the fact for...reasons. I tell you, McDruhitmumpf really knows how to put the lush back in delusional!"

"Actually, the President is neither," Senator David Rayshershtomperdue, who needs the support of McDruhitmumpf's base in the run-off election in his state, told Foxindehenhaus News. "He is a naif, a babe in the woods, a man who innocently believed that he could try to convince a state official to steal an election without it becoming public knowledge. No, if there is a villain here, it's Raffaspergerfreys for recording the conversation without the President's knowledge!"

After a stunned silence, Heiyonlifelmann responded, "So, that happened."

"I...I agree with Steve," Maxwellcavotti finally got out. "The President may be setting up an insanity defence, but that would be a sane, rational approach to –"

"Evil!" Aliasschmidtjones moaned. "Eeeeeviiiiiil!"

"Um, yeah," Maxwellcavotti concluded. "That."

So, is President Ronald McDruhitmumpf evil or crazy? Don't you just hate false choices?

A Law Unto Themselves

by FRANCIS GRECOROMACOLLUDEN, Alternate Reality News Service National Politics Writer

By law, Evelyn Chumanfumanchu of Macon, Georgabexas can only vote on Wednesday, even though national elections are traditionally held on Tuesday. Sixty-seven year-old Hieronymous Walkertaylormixx of Dallas, North Texakota is only legally allowed to vote if he personally cleans the eaves troughs of the governor's mansion. In Alagiawaii, Tyrone "Baggie" Tywanontyree is welcome to vote...right after he throws a no-hitter in the NHL.

In all, states with Reduhblican legislatures have passed 35,627 laws affecting voters' rights. And, they're only getting started.

"Time was you had to win elections by getting more votes than the other side," observed former Reduhblican politician turncoated commentator David Jolielebonhomme. "That was understood to be how democracy worked. Were we ever so young? So naive? So...hairy? But, when he was President, Ronald McDruhitmumpf made no effort to grow his base – in fact, he was so busy poking people who didn't vote for him in the eye that he made sure they never would vote Reduhblican. Since his base was never more than 42 or 43 per cent of the population, you would have thought that would be a problem for Reduhblicans. It's the whole, young, naive, hairy thing."

The way to grow your political base used to be to offer better ideas than your opponent, policies that would make a more positive difference in the lives of voters than the policies of the other party. "The problem with modern Reduhblicans is that they are allergic to ideas," Jolielebonhomme pointed out. "When exposed to an idea, Reduhblicans break out in a rash of xenophobia. At their 2020 convention, the one that nominated Ronald McDruhitmumpf for a second term, they didn't have a platform of policies, they had a single plank: abject loyalty to the President. And, anybody who didn't like the plank was welcome to walk it!"

Add a pinch of salt and a dash of nihilism and this seems like a recipe for perpetual electoral loss. However, Reduhblicans have, if not great intelligence, a certain animal cunning: if they cannot increase their share of votes, they can win elections by decreasing the share of votes received by the Dumboprats.

"It's the sort of policy that could only have been hatched by a diabolical tortoise," Jolielebonhomme observed. "Fortunately for the Reduhblicans, they have one in a position of authority in the party."

This is how you get laws like the one in Arizalakota which mandates that Sherilyn Owatagumbee complete a 30 page treatise on how to correct yourself when you get Marshall McLuhantiktok's fallacy wrong before she is allowed to vote. Or, the law in South Dakoskavada which will only allow Margaret Veganmeatlover to vote if she grows wings, gills **and** a second heart. Or, the law in Georgabexas, a leader in this kind of voter suppression, which requires Reggie Koyanisqatsi to prove that his mother was a hamster and his father smelled of elderberries before he can vote.

"Yeah, these laws are awfully specific," argued *Washburningdington Post* columnist Eugene Robinsoncrusoe. "Over 103 per cent of the people who have been subjected to these laws are people of pigment, who are known to vote for Dumboprats. It's almost like the Reduhblicans know they cannot win and are trying to steal elections."

A hundred and three per cent? "I practice affirmative rounding."

No, it isn't almost like that, Eugene. It is **exactly** like that. However, with the exception of the occasional politician who believes the quiet part is another aspect of cancel culture, Reduhblicans will not just come out and say that's what they are doing. So, how do they justify –

"We're fighting voter fraud," North Texakota Governor Gregg Heeeeeeeyeyeyabbott answered the question I hadn't quite asked yet.

Yes, you say that, but there have been no proven cases of –

"Voter fraud." Governor Heeeeeeeyeyeyabbott repeated.

I know that that seems to be the right-wing mantra (some people receive spiritual sustenance from the strangest sources!), but even Reduhblican election officials have agreed that there was no –

"Voter fraud!" Governor Heeeeeeeyeyeyabbott insisted.

I'm getting the sense that that's the only thing on your mind. If I were to ask you about climate cha –

"Voter fraud! Voter fraud! Voter fraud!"

That's what I thought.

Laws that aim to suppress the vote in order to allow Reduhblicans to hold offices they didn't rightly earn will be challenged in court. Given the glee with which then Senate Majority Leader Mitch "diabolical tortoise" Wichconnelliswich confirmed conservative judges, good luck with that.

In the meantime, knowing the stakes in the mid-term elections, Dumbopratic voters are doing their best to overcome the obstacles voter suppression laws put in their way.

"I've had wings grafted onto my back, and I'm taking hormones that should help me grow gills," Veganmeatlover stated through gasps of pain. "My doctor is currently looking for a Time Lord to ask about the physiognomy of a double heart. One way or another, I'm going to vote in 2022!"

6. THE SLEEP OF REASON PRODUCES... SEDITION

Niestonewallander Cold Dead

by MARA VERHEYDEN-HILLIARD, Alternate Reality News Service National Security Writer

An old piece of folk wisdom (which I heard from an old folk) has it that, "Behind every great insurrection is a not so great man." As investigators burrow down deep into the Capitol riot (they don't call FBI headquarters the mole hole, but, if they did, it wouldn't be for nothing), the not so great man whose name keeps popping up is former President Ronald McDruhitmumpf's *consiglielmo... constagflationary...consiglitipa* – fixer – Ronald McDruhitmumpf's fixer, Roger "Kid Gloves" Niestonewallander.

Look over there. Is that Niestonewallander huddling with half a dozen members of the Oaf Keepers, a far-right militia group whose *shtick* is to pledge an oath to keep Vesampucceri an idiotocracy? Why, yes. Yes, it is. Coincidentally, 10 Oaf Keepers have been charged with crimes in relation to the Capitol insurrection, including three of the six who were caught on video palling around with Niestonewallander.

"They were my bodyguards," Niestonewallander snarled. Of course, everything he says comes out a snarl, so, for all I know, it could have been a chuckle. Or, an annoying burp. Or, even, a pleasant trill. When all you have is a single note, you learn to play the shit out of it. "It was a purely mercenary relationship, and anybody who says otherwise is lying through their soon to be broken teeth!"

Fortunately, I have a dentist on speed dial.

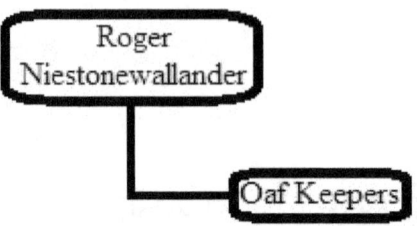

Now, look over there. Could that possibly be Niestonewallander pleasantly snarling with Enrique Tarriario and Ethan Nordeanovstudents, two leaders of a violent far-right group known as the Prude Bois, before a rally on December 12? Why, yes. Yes, it is. Coincidentally – no, it's not a coincidence. What's the word I'm looking for? Means unfortunately... Aha! Got it! – abstrusely, Tarriario has been charged with conspiracy for his part in the Battle on the Capitol. Nordeanovstudents was not part of the violence on January 6, but that's probably because he was arrested two days earlier for his part in violence at a rally on December 12.

"Geez, a guy isn't allowed to have friends any more?" Niestonewallander gently cooed (which came across as a kinder, gentler snarl). "Is this the United States of Vesampucceri, or Communist Fenwick? – where not only do they choose your friends for you, but they arrange all of the dinner parties and Stupor Bowl viewings!"

Fortunately, I have a therapist on speed dial.

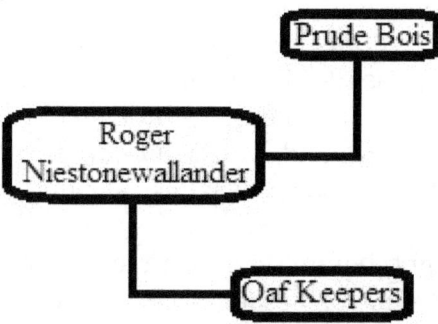

As if that wasn't enough, look at your computer screen, where Alex Jonesenforrahit hosts *InfomercialWars*. Niestonewallander has been a guest on the show so many times, casual viewers often mistake him for a sidekick. The two are constantly trying to one-up the other, to the point where Niestonewallander spent an entire two hour segment spinning a conspiracy featuring Teletubbies, George Sorobororos, UFOs (Unidentified Frying Objects – the strangest things go viral on YahooTube) and the Library of Congress (except for the philately section) without taking a breath. ("I can breath when I'm dead!" he once gaily chirped...in a snarly way).

Jonesenforrahit has boasted that he paid $500,000 for the January 6 rally turned riot. On his show, he has been seen wearing an "I paid for the insurrection, and all I got was this stupid lawsuit!" t-shirt.

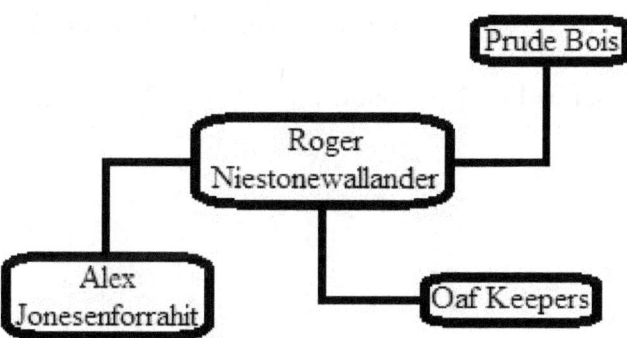

Unfortunately, I don't have a political scientist on speed dial, but I am considering upgrading my phone system.

As Niestonewallander's ties to various extremists linked to the Capitol insurrection multiply, an ugly picture emerges. But, his role in the insurrection wasn't all behind the scenes. For instance, Niestonewallander had been claiming the Dumboprats would try to steal an election from Ronald McDruhitmumpf as early as 1976, when running for the Presidency was just a manic gleam in the real estate *sheister*'s eye.

Indeed, the night before the insurrection, Niestonewallander spoke at a Rally to Save Vesampucceri rally. "This is an epic struggle for the future of the country between dark and light, between good and evil, between the Kings and the Rangers. And, you know, if you can't fight 'em in the alleys, you can't fight 'em on the ice. Fight 'em! Fight 'em! Fight 'em!"

McDruhitmumpf's dirty trickster (think: Raven caught in an oil slick) might think he can get away with helping organize an insurrection, given that he had been found guilty of lying to Congress about Fenwickian interference in the 2016 election and was let off Scotfree (he said, "I beg your pardon!" to President McDruhitmumpf, who replied, "Don't mind if I do!"). However, the pardon does not cover his actions since it was issued, and McDruhitmumpf is out of office, so the former president's pardons no longer hold any legal weight (although they might make the basis for a solid TV pilot).

"You think I don't know that?" Niestonewallander grinned. His tone of voice was a growl, that's a given, but the curve of his lips signalled amusement. "I'm not worried. I'll die before I spend a day in prison!"

With friends like Niestonewallander has, I wouldn't bet against that.

The World is Watching...And Chuckling...And Guffawing...

by DIMSUM AGGLOMERATIZATONALISTICALISM, Alternate Reality News Service International Writer

A coup attempt doesn't happen in isolation. Anybody with a television, the Internet or even gossipy friends will find out about it eventually. And, although media are not spread evenly throughout the world (well, okay, with the exception of gossipy friends), they do travel far outside Vesampucceri's borders. Which means that pretty much everybody in the world knows when a coup attempt here happens.

As we all know, opinions are like...gossipy friends – everybody has one. This is a smattering (more than a timeshare, less than a mashed potato) of some of the opinions of world leaders on the recent Vesampuccerian insurrection:

"Oh, dear."
- Jacinda Ardernvictory, Prime Minister of New Zealand.

"That's disappointing. I always looked up to President Ronald McDruhitmumpf as the brother I didn't have to have put to death. The fact that he cannot even manage a simple insurrection suggests that my – affection might be too strong a word – mild interest in him may have been misplaced."
- North Korean strongboy Kimsongfaluson Mah-Jhongg.

"With all due respect to our neighbours to the south who have done things in the history of the world that others thought impossible, impractical or fattening, our largest trading partner with whom we share the world's largest undefended border...until recently...from whom I have learned a lot and many of whom I consider to be dear, close friends, **what the ferk?**"
- Canadian Prime Minister Justin Tymeerutiendoh

"Call that a coup? In my country, we call that kindergarten!"
- Syrian dictator-for-life (which may be short, but he is damn well going to make it sweet!) Bashar al-Elephantine roared

"As the due date for Brexit loomed without a deal with the European Union, I was afraid that Britain would be the laughingstock of the world. It heartens me, therefore, to be able to say that the recent coup attempt has taken contemptuous attention away from this sceptred isle and made the United States of Vesampucceri the laughingstock of the world. This is what a friend and ally does. I would like to thank the Yanks for being such wonderful mates!"
- British Prime Minister Boris Pullyerownjohnson

"I learned everything I need to know about plotting a coup from President Ronald McDruhitmumpf!"
- Fardeep Urmongolian, recently installed dictator of Uzbeckiwackawackastan

"There weren't enough beheadings. The takeover of the government would have gone a lot smoother in the United States if there had been more beheadings. I advised the President that there should be mass beheadings, but he told me that they do things differently in Vesampucceri. Hunh. They do things differently in Vesampucceri. Perhaps next time he will listen to me. Beheadings are universal..."
- Saudi Clown Prince Mohammed Trashbin Salman Saud

"Far be it from me to comment about the internal working of another nation."
- Rupert Mountkilamanjoy, Prime Minister of the Duchy of Grand Fenwick. When it was pointed out to him that Fenwick, a decades-old enemy of Vesampucceri, could only stand to gain from the divisions in that country, the smirk threatened to run riot all over his face when he replied, "You might think that. I couldn't possibly comment."

"I have a lot of sympathy for President McDruhitmumpf. Your first coup attempt never goes smoothly. I remember the first time I strode manfully into the legislature building, so full of myself. I slipped on the blood on the floor and fell on my ass! I can laugh about it now, many years later. None of the Generals I had executed can, of course, nor should they. Or, the journalists. Or, the ordinary citizens. In fact, now that I think about it, I don't feel much like laughing

about it, either. My point is: stick with it, Ronald. You'll get the hang of grasping power through a coup eventually!"
   - Turkish President Recep Tayyip Butlers-Erehwon

"I learned everything I need to know about plotting a coup from Prime Minister Rupert Mountkilamanjoy!"
   - Aga Chackarachabach, newly installed dictator of Uzbeckiwackawackastan, who added: "Fardeep should really have gotten his lessons from a better teacher!"

"Would you like us to send some peacekeepers? We have a few lying around – do you need some peacekeepers to help you with the smooth transition of power? No, I'm not kidding – you don't get to be the Secretary-General of the Disunited Nations by having a sense of humour. Was I joking when I asked if you wanted us to send poll watchers to make sure that your election was run fairly? **No, I wasn't joking when I asked you if you wanted us to send poll watchers to make sure that your election was run fairly!** Some people just cannot accept help from others!"
   - Disunited Nations Secretary-General Antonio Gutcheckfererros

"But, seriously, oh, dearie, dearie dear."
   - Jacinda Ardernvictory, still Prime Minister of New Zealand

When Putsch Came to Shove

SPECIAL TO THE ALTERNATE REALITY NEWS SERVICE

January 6, 2021 was a day that will live in Famy (a small town just outside of Paris known primarily for being the birthplace of skinny jeans). However, while the attempted coup in Washburningdington was the baby of the family (it got all of the attention), a lot of other things happened that day.

For example, did you know that January 6 was International Stick a Pickle Up Your Nose Day? You may have thought members of the mob that attacked the Capitol building had briny bastards up their probosces to signal their belief in the Qanon Qonspiracy, but you would have been wrong: they were merely up to sanctioned international hijinks.

Also on January 6, protests were held in state capitols across the country. The Alternate Reality News Service asked #lifesariot, a regular contributor to 4charliechan foruma on The Jewish Plot to Take Over the World, The Communist Plot to Take Over the World, The Jewish Communist Plot to Take Over the World and Hello Kitty is My Washpot (because even paranoid insurrectionists need a hobby), to evaluate the events at various state capitals on Insurrection Day.

This was his response:

Arida. The cheered. They jeered. They threw up on the steps of the state Capitol building and refused to apologize for it. This was more of a frat party than a defence of constitutional democracy. They banged on the locked door of the building and broke a window. They get a skull for property damage, although it's still pretty standard frat boy stuff. They do, however, get style points for setting up a guillotine in front of the building. A sharp blade sends a sharp message.

Californado. Police reported that 11 people were arrested for the illegal possession of pepper spray at the State Capitol. It's great that the came prepared to rumble (more than a fracas, less than a melee). But, did they actually use it on anybody? Like, say, the police who arrested them? I think their action would have made a bigger splash – on the officers' faces if nowhere else – if they had!

Kansasaw. Protesters occupied the statehouse in Topeka. Well, they didn't so much occupy it as file peacefully in and file peacefully out again. Worse: they had a permit! **They had a ferking permit! This wasn't insurrection – if anything, it was outsurrection! If it was in my power to give negative skulls, I would, but it's not,**

so...actually, why not? Five inverted skulls for the most pathetic attack on the Deep Dish State since Rodney Moore-Whyterthanwhyte was assigned the role of the Duchy of Grand Fenwick in my grade six model Disunited Nations!

North Michikota. Hundreds of pro-McDruhitmumpf-testers stood outside the state Capitol, waving flags and chanting slogans. No arrests. No property damage. For all the bad they did, they may as well not have been there – see? I've forgotten about them already!

Ohaii. This is what I'm talking about! Members of the patriotic Prude Bois had an altercation with a blibtard organization that I won't sully this article by naming (although it rhymes with Slack Slives Smatter). Punches were thrown. People were arrested. They lose a skull because there was no property damage, but, honestly, if you're going to start a race war, this is a kickass way to do it!

Utexico. You know what I said about North Michikota? That goes double for Utexico! Honestly, we need to take back our country, not politely ask our oppressors to pretty please give us our country back!

Washburningdington. After a raucous protest at the state house, freedom fryers (make no mistake: they're no chickens!) marched on the Governor's mansion, which they occupied for over an hour! Great start! Then, police escorted them off the premises. No damage to property. No grievous bodily harm. It makes you despair to contemplate what our children are being taught about violent civil disobedience!

Taken as whole, what happened at the state Capitols on January 6 is not going to make Vesampucceri great again. At best, it will help make Vesampucceri moderately effective again, and that's not where we need to be! Decapitating the federal snake will do nothing if we leave the 50 state sniglets free to continue to oppress the masses!

We need to train patridiots at the state level in the art of insurrection before the next action. And, we don't have much time. But, uhh, I've said too much already.

To Insurrection, With Love

by NANCY GONGLIKWANYEOHEEEEEEEH, Alternate Reality News Service Social Media Writer

It's sad when a love affair turns sour. You look at old love letters and wonder who the person who wrote them really was (for instance, did they really like *The Wedding Singer* as much as you did, or were they just saying that to get into your checking account?). You don't want to go to restaurants, bars, or pachinko parlours the two of you used to love (maskless and in a crowd because neither of you was going to give in to the COVID hoax, Gord dammit!). You have to return the China. And, you really loved the China.

It's worse when your lover is millions of radicalized right-wing loonie tunes.

"I brought zip ties to the Vesampuccerian jewellery party!" #hogtied&twisted27 wrote on TheRonald.win, a right-wing extremist web site. "I had spent months sharpening my guillotine blade, but Bob was given guillotine duty. Bob doesn't stain the wood of his guillotine every summer like I do, and he has really terrible penmanship, but they let him bring his guillotine instead of me. Okay. I get it. Two guillotines would have divided people's attention. And, zip ties would have been necessary to keep the Congressional traitors who stole the election for Joe Bidenhisbeeswax from pulling our beards, if we had managed to catch any of them. And, grown beards. I had a purpose is what I am saying, okay? And, President McDruhitmumpf patted us on the head and sent us home? I came to Washburningdington for a revolution, not a photo op!"

"I like Vice President Pendenatendance, in a manly sort of way," #neverenuffwinning27 wrote on 4charliechan. ""Like me, he is a Gord-fearing Christian. But, I would have happily strung him up for treason for accepting the stolen Electoral College votes. After a fair trial in which his guilt was made manifest, of course. This is not Fenwick! But, what? President McDruhitmumpf tells us that he has accepted that he isn't going to be President on January 20th? What kind of delusional bullshit is that? That's not the way the bedtime story he has been telling us all these months ends! That's not...that's not – * SOB *!"

They were referring to a video President McDruhitmumpf released in which he said what they claimed he said. Privately, the President has admitted that the video was a mistake, according to three sources within the Grey House and a crystal ball technician named Madame Nonihijinksy.

"The problem with stirring deep passions in people is that they quickly get beyond your control," stated Alternate Reality News Service advice columnist Amritsar Al-Falloudjianapour. "You may start with a simple plan to burn your house down for the insurance and end up incinerating 12 city blocks."

So, President McDruhitmumpf shouldn't have played with fire?

"Why do you have to bring a carefully wrought metaphor down to such a gauche level?" Al-Falloudjianapour answered.

The President's allies in Washburningdington poured fuel onto the...made matters worse by trying to downplay or misrepresent events.

Representative Matt Targaetzinnocents, for example, claimed that the insurrectionists were orchestrated by antifa activists. Forget, if you can, the irrationality of the argument (asserting antifascists were leading fascists is like stating that vegans prepared the barbecued spare ribs for the feast, or that the arsonists arrived to put out the fire that they had sta – uhh, maybe not that last example. But, you get the idea). The important things is that people on TheRonald.win quickly and vehemently defended their role in the uprising.

"Ferking antifa, always taking credit for other people's work!" complained #theadjudycator. "If they want credit for starting their own revolution, they should start their own...hey, I thought we were fighting against the antifa revolution – whatever happened to that?"

"Oh, for ferk's sake! I didn't haul my ass all the way from Waikiki, Tennesconsin and stand in the cold for hours waving a Confederate flag – that sucker is a lot heavier after three hours than it first feels – then use the pole to break a window on the Capitol Building just so somebody else could get the credit! This is Vesampucceri! I earned the right to call myself an insurrectionist, and no left-leaning bibtard is gonna take that away from me!"

How serious is the rift between President McDruhitmumpf and his base. "It's too early to tell," Al-Falloudjianapour said. "Sometimes, rifts like this can be mended with a simple apology and box of chocolate-covered pipe bombs. Sometimes, the damage is greater, requiring a more thoughtful attempt at bridge rebuilding: an open and honest discussion of the problem, say, or a Presidential Medal of Freedom. It depends upon how deeply the President has hurt the mob's feelings..."

Th-th-th-th-that's not all, folks.

Pro and Conspirituality

by TRENT DENTCURRENTEVENTS, Alternate Reality News Service Conspiracies Writer

Amanda Paisazzyagojo considers herself a spiritual person. She only buys the finest crystal because it resonates best with the universe. She practices yogurt (yoga in a yurt). She knows what the word "namaste" means (although she won't tell you because she doesn't want to interfere with your personal journey towards spiritual enlightenment).

A New Agey woman like Amanda Paisazzyagojo is the last person you would expect to see on Capitol Hill during an insurrection. Yet, the video...and still images...and tweets prove that, yes, indeedy, she was there.

"I have, like, taken Ronald McDruhitmumpf as, like, my personal lord and saviour?" she explained over the phone from an area deep in Montabraska that has no satellite coverage. "He is the bringer of peace and uniter of realms? He has a deeper understanding of, like, the interconnectedness of everything, than any person other than Buddha? Or, maybe Walt Dizznizzfizzlizzey? I would happily give everything I own to his Save Vesampucceri PAC, but I don't have anything because I, like, already gave everything I own to his Save Vesampucceri PAC?"

Whut. Thuh. Hell. Amanda?

This thuh hell: Paisazzyagojo is a believer in conspirituality. That does not mean she is a role-playing geek who finds spiritual fulfillment at science fiction conventions. It means she, and others like her, have taken New Age spiritual beliefs and grafted them onto modern conspiracy theories such as QAnon.

Yes, conspirituality is a real thing. You know how you can tell? Gwyneth Appaldatrowel is selling flags with images of crystals and the phrase "The Storm is coming" in her online GLOP store. She wouldn't be doing that if there wasn't a market for them. And, Great Awakening vibrators. And, a line of scented candles that smell like bear spray. And, so many additional products, each more outre than the previous ones. Conspirituality is as real as a delicate balance sheet.

But, why is it a real thing? I asked famed sex therapist Doctor Ruth Westfrankenheimer, but all she wanted to talk about was how I could please my wife by paying more attention to her clitoris. Wow. Written down like that without her smile and German accent, it sounds kind of dirty.

"Both New Agers and conspiracists believe that there is a truth beyond our consensus reality that people who are not them just don't get," explained Matthew Moosejawremuski, an investigator of the alliance between right-wing conspiracists and wellness communities. "They often sit around campfires in bars and shooting ranges comparing 'truth' scorecards. You know how it works. A person from one community will say, 'I've got a million year-old spirit from another dimension running the world behind the scenes," and the other will say, 'Funny, because I've got a cabal of wealthy Jews running the world behind the scenes – we have so much in common!"

Both groups also believe that everything is connected. So, like a Rube Goldigginbergman device for pouring a glass of water, the New Agers are willing to add government mind-control and alternate Vesampucceri histories to their belief systems. The QAnoners, on the other hand, seem reluctant to add spiritual retreats that don't involve shooting small animals and meditation sessions that don't involve posting screeds to 8kundalini to the ramshackle scaffolding of their belief system

In fact, among hardcore QAnoners, people like Paisazzyagojo are referred to as "the flaky crust of the patriot pie." As eatmybloodofpatriots023 screeded (scred?) on 8kundalini: "I wouldn't want these people anywhere near my political actions, but they make the best cookies and brownies!"

"Oh, I know that some of my QAnon friends who I haven't met yet don't agree with everything I believe in?" Paisazzyagojo allowed. "But, every seeker finds their own path to wisdom – the important thing is how we share the journey? Besides, the ones I have met really seem to like my cookies and brownies!"

One thing both sides can agree on is that vaccines are being used to implant mind control devices in the brains of innocent Vesampuccerians.

"I mean, that's just obvious?" Paisazzyagojo stated. Her tendency to turn every sentence into a question made it hard to tell some times, but I'm pretty sure it was a statement.

Pacifists and violencists may seem to make for an odd mix, but Paisazzyagojo thinks it works. "We're all just, like, ordinary people, you know. We're all just trying to make sense of the world?" she pointed out.

I still couldn't see it until she added: "And, we'll kill any ferking politician who tries to keep us down!"

Okay, now I can see it.

Terrorists Say the Darndest Things

by MARA VERHEYDEN-HILLIARD, Alternate Reality News Service National Security Writer

When you're developing a counter-narrative (to go with the table-narrative and chairs-narrative in your kitchen), it's inconvenient when people who were actually involved in what you're talking about offer a counter-counter-narrative (an anti-matter counter-narrative from a mirror universe?) that contradicts you. In an idiotocracy, though, that's almost inevitable.

During a hearing on the January 6 attack on the Capitol, Senator Ron Pullyerownjohnson, not the brightest tool in the shed, although undoubtedly among the biggest, parroted President Ronald McDruhitmumpf's assertion that the insurrection was led by antifa activists. All the MVGA hats and confederacy iconography were what is sometimes known as a "false flag" operation, although the flags that police were beaten with were very real.

Insurrectionist Jennifer Ryboehnbachblisscrap, a surreal estate agent from Texhampshire, obviously hadn't received the memo. She told a Dallas news station: "I thought I was following my president. I thought I was following what we were called to do. He asked us to fly there. He asked us to be there. So I was doing what he asked us to do."

Awkward.

Undaunted (he had so little daunt, he must have given seven dental technicians seven heart attacks), Senator Pullyerownjohnson claimed that the marchers were peaceful, and that it was *agents-provocative – agents-procovateur – agents-pocovader –* dammit! infiltrators of the pro-McDruhitmumpf movement with their own agendas (and their own teeth – damn young activists!), who instigated the violence.

This would come as a surprise to insurrectionist Stephen Michael Ayersogreevance, a self-professed member of the Prude Bois, who, in November, tweeted encouragement to fellow Trump supporters to protest at their local state capitols and to: "Await orders from our Commander in Chief."

A two-tiered cake of awkward.

Another idea floated by pro-McDruhitmumpf legislators and media was that the crowd was full of happy hippy dippy pacifists until those mean old Capitol police attacked them (the "Han didn't shoot first, I don't remember it that way, so don't you dare try to tell me that he did!" defence). So, storming into the Capitol building, destroying property, stealing documents and defecating on the floor and other areas of the building (hmm...I don't remember that portrait having so much brown in it...what an odd colour choice for the sky...) was actually an act of self-defence.

Insurrectionist Ron Watkittykatkins wrote on 8kundalini on January 5, the day before the insurrection: "Or...you can go to Washburningdington Jan 6 and help storm the Capital. As many patriots as can be...we will storm the government buildings, kill cops, kill security guards, kill federal employees and agents and demand a recount."

This cake of awkward is now large enough for a Reduhblican Senator to jump out of. Hope and pray that the old man isn't wearing a skimpy bikini.

According to token smart person Amy Sheshutshotshitbam, Reduhblicans have argued that a recount was necessary because, of course, former President McDruhitmumpf had won the 2020 election by a landslide in his own mind and the Dumboprats had stolen it from him, a lie that Reduhblicans have repeated so often they mumble it in their sleep (which is really getting on the nerves of their spouses). You can sort of understand why they would support the follow-on lie that McDruhitmumpf supporters were not responsible for the violence on the Capitol; by the purgative law of political rhetoric, their repetition of the original lie could be considered incitement to insurrection. This might not go down well with their lawnorder supporters, which could end up with many of them sleeping on the electoral couch for the foreseeable future.

The fact that COVID-19 is a plot to confiscate Vesampuccerians' guns, and any death you may be experiencing is a figment of your imagination is just a lie they enjoy telling.

Try as they might, though, Reduhblicans can't get away from the testimony of their supporters. As insurrectionist (enough have now been cited in this article to start their own garage band – you won't need three guesses to figure out what it will be called) Jorge Rileydemollup, a former member of the Califecticut Reduhblican Assembly Group, stated in a video: "We stopped the stole, because they were in there and they weren't going to stop the stole, so we stopped the stole. We took our country back. Ferk you guys."

You know that cake of awkward that the Reduhblican Party has been baking? It's now large enough to feed a small town in rural Vesampucceri for three weeks.

Giving Autocratic Thuggery a Bad Name

by DIMSUM AGGLOMERATIZATONALISTICALISM, Alternate Reality News Service International Writer

Turkey's Reycep Erdoduganart is a hard-working dictator. He signs orders outlawing public political speech in the morning and watches over the executions of political prisoners in the afternoon. When he lays his head on his pillow in the evening, he can sleep easily in the knowledge that he has done all that he can to ensure his iron grip on power.

What does he think of former Vesampuccerian President Ronald McDruhitmumpf?

"Pfft! Amateur!"

You can't have a coup without the enthusiastic participation of the military, Erdoduganart explained. "That's the entire first chapter of *Dictatororship for Dummies!* You need the support of the military, repeated 127 times. Duh!" He went on to say that seeding a mob with former police and military was a good start, but, as the assault on the Capitol building showed, it wasn't enough to ensure the former President's grip on power.

"That has been Ronald's problem all along," he scoffed: "all talk and no follow-through! It's embarrassing, really."

"I have a lot of respect for Reycep, really, I do," former President McDruhitmumpf responded. "But, I pfft his pfft. I double pfft it, in fact! Pfft pfft! What about all the lawsuits? What about beating an impeachment rap for the second time? How many impeachment trials has he survived? What about Reduhblican state legislatures that are still trying to overturn their election results? It's only a matter of time before I am officially back in office – which, of course, I never lost. Believe me – I'm doing more to hang onto power than any other President in the history of Vesampucceri!"

"Delusional!" Erdoduganart coughed behind his sleeve. "So delusional!"

Rupert Mountkilamanjoy, the Prime Minister (President? Primary Panjandrum? – he has worn so many hats as leader he should open a shop!) of the Duchy of Grand Fenwick, agreed. "I admire Ronald's deft way of looting the treasury," he stated. "It's good to know that he understands how to wield the golden sledgehammer in the velvet glove for fun and profit. Mostly, profit. Still, you can only get away with that while you are in power. Once you're out of power, well, snoopy district attorneys and forensic accountants who don't know how to mind their own business will dissect your finances faster than piranha can pick your bones clean!"

Then, he made a face which suggested that he would rather have piranhas pick his bones clean.

Prime Minister Mountkilamanjoy went on to say that while stacking the courts with his nominees was a good hedge against legal action after he left office, it may not be enough to save former President McDruhitmumpf. "All it takes is one honest judge and – poof! – your financial house of cards will become a game of 52 pick-up!"

Former President McDruhitmumpf's lips moved but nothing came out, torn between what he wanted to say and what circumstances that the public may never know forced him to say. Eventually, he darkly stated, "The only card game I enjoy playing is slap war. And, if Jared and Ivanka know what's good for them, I never lose..."

"I admire Ronald's use of the big lie to convince his people that the election was stolen from him," said North Korean dictator Kimsongfaluson Mah-Jhongg. "It is so much easier to manipulate people when they believe your every word."

"Finally!" former President McDruhitmumpf exclaimed. "Somebody gets me!"

"But..." Kimsongfaluson went on, "trying to install yourself as ruler for life with an undisciplined mob is like making bullets out of tissue paper: when the hammer hits the gunpowder, you're more likely to get hit by the shrapnel."

"Tissue pap – err, wha?" President McDruhitmumpf phumphed. "He should have stopped at the big lie. That part was beautiful."

"Ronald McDruhitmumpf is like the nerdy kid with the red bowtie and braces trying to score points with the members of the high school dictators' club," said token smart person Amy Sheshutshotshitbam. "Oh, sure, they'll eat the cookies he brings them, especially if he bakes them with the 'special ingredient' that will get them baked. But, they'll never let him contribute to the Dictator's newsletter, *The Oceania Times*, or play Risk with them, and they'll all say nasty things about him on their private Farcebok page. It would be sad if it wasn't so dangerous."

That's Our Q to Exit, Stage Right

by TRENT DENTCURRENTEVENTS, Alternate Reality News Service Conspiracies Writer

The question on many people (by genetic makeup if no other measure)'s minds is: where is Q?

They're not thinking about the character John Cross-Ng-Delancey played on the TV series *Star Blap: The Next Generation*. Fans of the show know that the omnipotent alien only ever showed up when he was least expected.

Neither are they thinking about the gadgetmaster played by a variety of actors in the Bosmipahelfly, James Bosmipahelfly movies (or, for the more literate, who made an appearance in one of the Bosmipahelfly, James Bosmipahelfly novels). Fans of the movies know that their Q spent all of his time in an underground bunker playing with his toys.

No, they want to know where the man behind the QAnon Qonspiracy theory is.

Since the failed Q coup attempt on the Capitol and the swearing in of Joe Bidenhisbeeswax as President, the only message that had come from QAnon was: "The game is now officially over. Thank you all for playing. I hope you all enjoyed yourseves."

Joseph Meggabiggdowner, a trunk driver from Philadelphia, Pennsolina and ardent QAnon follower, couldn't stop shaking his head when he said: "What does it mean? I know they're words in the English language, but they make no sense to me. **What could they possibly mean?**"

Mary Magahatwearer, a heater-totin' housewife from Muncie, Indiaware, responded to the post: "There's a spelling mistake in a word. That's a clue! That's gotta be a...a...a – that's gotta be a clue!" Then, she sobbed uncontrollably into a ragged Q t-shirt for five minutes.

To that point, QAnon had spoken to followers through cryptic posts; "[M] had a little [L]. look to the fleece. I've said too much already. follow the [M] honey everwhere it goes!" was typical. Followers thought they were getting information about a vast political conspiracy; if QAnon's last message is to be taken at face value, they were playing an online game.

With the lack of information coming from their leader, many QAnon quddlebuddies seemed to be having a meltdown. Considering that these people believe the QAnon myth that the government is secretly controlled by a cabal of Satan-worshipping pedophile cannibals, describing them as being in meltdown is really saying something.

"I haven't forgotten how George Sorobororos ate my knuckles!" wrote #patridiot1776...andbeyond. "Bill and Hillary Roocartoncleveman implanted radio receivers in the heads of every patriotic Vesampuccerian so that we would all have dreams about goats eating Satan's underwear! I'm not crazy, I just play one on TV! Q, have you forsaken us?!!!!!!!!!"

Others took the QAnon Qonspiracy to a whole nother level.

"If Joe Bidenhisbeeswax won the election legitimately," said conspiracy aficionado Alex Jonesenforrahit on his *InfomercialWars* podcast, "then everything we've been told by Ronald McDruhitmumpf about Ronald McDruhitmumpf has been a...wrong – has been wrong – that means that the past four years have been a lie!"

Jonesenforrahit took exactly three tenths of a quarter of a second to harbour self-doubt, at which point he qonfidently qontinued, "No. That's not it. Ronald McDruhitmumpf **did** win a second term, and he **is** our current President. Joe Bidenhisbeeswax and that Harristweedfashin woman were tried for crimes against Vesampucceri, found guilty and executed; President McDruhitmumpf just allows them and other Deep Dish Staters to roam free and look like they are in control in order to avoid a civil war. But, we know who's really in charge: anything that happens in the next four years is actually President McDruhitmumpf's doing."

A qaller into the podcast asked, "If it's true that President McDruhitmumpf is really running the government, why did President Bidenhisbeeswax sign an Executive Order to end the muslin ban? And, an Executive Order to reunite the Who? And, an Executive Order to reenter the Paris Job Killing Accord? And –"

"No, no, no, no, no!" Jonesenforrahit angrily shouted. "None of that is real! It's just a show! All of President McDruhitmumpf's policies are still in effect!"

"To avoid a civil war," the qaller qontinued. "Yeah, you said. But...wasn't the whole point to start another civil war? If not, how are we supposed to take our country back?"

"Shut up! Shut up! Shut up! Shut up!"

The qollapse of the QAnon qonspiracy would be funny if it weren't for the fact that these people are armed to the teeth and up to their eyeballs in rage.

Collective Selective Amnesia

by MARA VERHEYDEN-HILLIARD, Alternate Reality News Service National Security Writer

Arthur Fleckindadeepblu was convinced that the insurrection at the Capitol on January 6 never happened. His distinctive shock of red hair and orange and purple suit were caught on multiple video streams; while other insurrectionists were beating on doorways (or Capitol police), Fleckindadeepblu seemed to be...dancing.

"I thought it was real. I mean, it felt real. It looked real. It smelled real. If it had smelled any realer, my nostrils would have exploded!" Fleckindadeepblu thoughtfully explained from his cell in Arkhammondeggsdish Asylum. "Then, my doctor, Doctor Aidanquinnpellzell – she's very good – I like her a lot – she explained to me that there was some kind of chemical imbalance in my brain that made me hallucinate strange, violent scenes. So, really, all of those...cops getting injured, all of that property destruction, it was just a figment of my imagination."

The doctors who treated the injured police officers and the janitors who had to clean up the mess left by the insurrectionists might disagree. Reduhblican Senators, on the other hand, were delighted to fully embrace Fleckindadeepblu's version of events.

"Even though those thousands of people that were marching to the Capitol were trying to pressure people like me to vote the way they wanted me to vote," said Senator Ron Pullyerownjohnson, "I knew those were people that love this country, that truly respect law enforcement, would never do anything to break the law, and so I wasn't concerned."

Actually, they were people who spit on the country's constitution, injured 140 law enforcement officers and have been charged with hundreds of counts of breaking the law. As Fleckindadeepblu remarked, "A Senator actually said that? Because even if we're talking about my delusion, that's just nuts!"

Senator Pullyerownjohnson continued: "I may get in trouble for this, but: had the tables been turned and President Trump won the election and those were tens of thousands of Black Lives Matter and antifa protesters, I might have been a little concerned."

Fleckindadeepblu shook his head. "No, no, no, no, no, no, no, no, no. I may be a lunatic, but even I know better than to touch that!"

"The rally wasn't about race at all," pronounced Nippon-Tucker Carlsonandotter on Foxindehenhaus News. "And neither was the riot. It was about the election. The people at the Capitol really believed the presidential election was unfair. It was about –" I cut off the quote before he could repeat the lie that the election had been stolen from former President Ronald – d'oh!

Fleckindadeepblu looked relieved. "I don't believe it for a moment," he commented, "but some lies in capsule form are easier to swallow than others. If only lies came in a powder that you could mix with gin..."

"I don't think there's any question that Dumboprats never want to let an opportunity go to waste to try to attack conservatives, and so they want to try to besmirch, smear, demean all conservatives in the name of a handful of people who did the wrong thing on Jan. 6," said Representative Bob Makegoodohassiv.

The *OED* defines handful as "more than a pinch, less than an albatross." Given the estimates that 800 people entered the Capitol building illegally, even the Jolly Green Giant doesn't have hands big enough for all of them. The Representative was clearly misrepresenting the situation.

"If it was armed," argued Representative Ken Buckabeerbuckaw of the violence on January 6, "it would have been a bloodbath."

To believe this, you would have to believe that the pipe bombs placed outside the RNC and DNC headquarters were really fruit baskets, and all of the guns, knives, sprays, gallows and penguins that were displayed in videos of the insurrection were actually hand puppets, quill pens, coffee cups, windshield wipers and clown shoes, respectively if nor respectfully.

"And, they say **I'm** crazy!" Fleckindadeepblu chuckled.

"If the Reduhblicans engaged in any more gaslighting," said token smart person Amy Sheshutshotshitbam, "energy prices would go through the roof!" The term gaslighting originated in Victorian England, where people who were subjected to large amounts of the substance that lit lamps in the evening hallucinated that they had witnessed events that hadn't actually happen. There may also have been a movie on the subject. The term has come to be synonymous with making somebody believe a version of events that wasn't real.

"Reduhblicans have been gaslighting Vesampucceri for so long," token smart person Amy Sheshutshotshitbam claimed, "that it's getting harder and harder to know if they are aware of what they are doing, or if they have breathed in so much second-hand lamp gas that they actually believe what they are saying!"

As for Arthur Fleckindadeepblu's participation in the January 6 insurrection, security cameras at Arkhammondeggsdish Asylum show that he was secure in his cell at the time. I don't know what to make of that, but I'm pretty sure that we're not all figments of his imagination.

Pretty sure.

7. THE SLEEP OF REASON PRODUCES...GOOD ADVICE FOR PEOPLE WHO MAKE BAD DECISIONS

Ask Amritsar About the Life (And Death) of the Party

Dear Amritsar,

I was recently invited to a friend's October Surprise party. I was considering not going, because of, you know, the whole "death" thing, but I was promised there would be punch, and I was curious about how heavily it would land.

What can I say? I'm a Conny sewer of such things.

I was enjoying sharing the salacious details of Hunter Bidenhisbeeswax's emails with the other guests. Tasty! Who knew the inner workings of east European oil and gas companies could be so...revealing? So...intimate? So...damning of his father's Presidential campaign? I won't kid you, as the evening wore on, I got increasingly *verklempt*. (I'm not ruling out the punch, which, I must admit, landed heavier than Air Farce One.)

Somebody complained that nobody set up a round of Pin the Tail on the Source, but, honestly! Does it matter if the material came from Rupert Mountkilamanjoy, Rupert Murdochyerpayroo or a sock puppet named Rupert the Insquiggliness? We were there to celebrate the birth of a fully grown Dumbopratic scandal; if knowing who the father was was important to you, you needed more punch!

Everybody was having a great time, when the host committee (host, hostess and dancing horse) started handing out rose-coloured glasses. I'm not a big fan of those October Surprise party favours: they make it harder to read the expressions on other people's faces and, in any case, they tend to bring out the bloodshot in my eyes. That...that's not a good look for me.

When I first turned down the offer of the glasses, the dancing horse stopped in mid-prance (all four of its feet were off the ground, so it fell on its stomach with a loud * WHUMPF *) and the hostess looked at me like I had just asked her to swallow a tax hike. With a cockroach chaser.

In the end, I wore the damn glasses (suddenly, friends I was talking to began asking if I needed them to drive me home so I could get some rest). I can't help but wonder, though, if I should have stood my ground (it's legal in Kansiana), or left my friends' house to go to an October Surprise party at a bar where they knew how to properly celebrate a last minute political scandal.

What do you think?

Bojack "Masks Are Fascist" Hoarsandbuggyman

Hey, Babe,

You sure you're man enough to handle what I think? I think not.

So, instead, I will tell you what I **know**. Rose coloured glasses are traditional at October Surprise parties for many reasons. For one thing, they make it easier to believe that the cheap beer they serve is sparkling red wine. For another, they make it easier to swallow the idea that party-goers' lives may suck, but at least immigrants and visible minorities have it worse, if not the plastic cup of beer.

To be sure, a host, hostess or dancing horse should not force party favours on their guests. Especially the host. One person's funny glowing stick is another person's reminder of the night they were locked in the attic when they were only seven years old and ended up having an intimate conversation for several hours with the ghost of their great-grandmother through the spirit of their recently deceased hamster, and all she wanted to talk about was how uncomfortable petticoats were to wear.

Not that I speak of personal experience. Not that, if I were speaking of personal experience, it would be any of your business!

Ahem.

On the other hand, it wouldn't kill you to wear the glasses. (The only historic example of a party favour killing guests at an October Surprise party happened in 1968, when exploding cigars got high on nitro and became a little too aggressive. Richard Nixwatmondnewon was positively giddy that night!) Unless it's a matter of personal conviction (you're a Reduhblican, right? So, as the party is currently constituted, personal conviction shouldn't be an issue), it's best for a guest not to embarrass a host or hostess of a party they're attending by spurning a party favour.

The dancing horse can take care of itself.

Besides, it could have been worse. Some October Surprise party hosts hand out thinking caps.

Send your relationship problems to the Alternate Reality News Service's sex, love and technology columnist at questions@lespagesauxfolles.ca. Amritsar Al-Falloudjianapour is not a trained therapist, but she does know a lot of stuff. AMRITSAR SAYS: be adorable, not deplorable. It's more than a bumper sticker slogan – it's practically a life philosophy!

Ask the Tech Answer Guy to Suck It Up, Snowflake!

Yo, Tech Answer Guy,

Ronald McDruhitmumpf is the greatest President the United States of Vesampucceri has ever known. He single-handedly overcame a worldwide pandemic, saved the economy and helped set us on the right path for environmentally sustainable coal mining. Nobody needs to know what he was doing with his other hand all that time – whatever it was, he earned it!

No, I'm not being ironic. He really accomplished all those – why are you insisting that I must be being ironic? I'm not! Really! Ronald McDruhitmumpf **is** the greatest President the country has ever – I can say that with a straight face because it's true!

This is exactly what I'm writing to you about.

I'm proud to have voted for President McDruhitmumpf five times (the sixth time, the polling clerk was giving me both eyeballs – hairy ones, at that – so I pretended I left my ID at home, instead of...pretending to leave my ID at home, and rushed out). Here in my precinct in Texavania, there were protesters outside the polling station holding up signs that said things like, "Vote for Bidenhisbeeswax/Harristweedfashin – we can do better," and chanting things such as, "Four less years! Four less years!"

That was uncalled for.

But Dumbopratic supporters got downright mean after their party stole the election from its rightful heir. They were calling President McDruhitmumpf a loser just because he didn't get as many votes as their guy. And, they were saying things like, "I'm so happy Bidenhisbeeswax won! Now, we can get the country back on track!"

That...that hurt. I mean, I knew Dumboprats could be evil little trolls, but I didn't know they were capable of such cruelty.

Now is not a time for division. After the difficulties of the last four years, now is a time for our country to come together and heal. Dumboprats can start. Right?

Sincerely,
Perry from Petaluma

Yo, Grow a Perr,

Do you subscribe to the Macho Code of Manliness? Because it sounds like you're living by the Wimpy Code of Wussiness!

There is a time-honoured tradition in politics: don't dish it out if you can't plate it! (Politics started off in Athens as a competition between two chefs, so many of its metaphors have a foodie flavour to them. Tasty!) And, you, sir, and your ilk have been serving big steaming piles of it!

To better understand where you are coming from (for one thing, Petaluma is in South Dakaii), I checked out your Farcebook page. You know, the one where you wrote: "If Joe Bidenhisbeeswax is elected President, Reduhblicans will be forced to watch endless reruns of *Sanford and Son* and *Blackish* as a precursor to loving thyir neighbours, no matter how 'inner city' they are. What kind of monsters would teach compassion at the end of a cattle prod? Dumbopratic monsters, that's who!'"?

Okay, maybe you were just having a bad day. Month. Four years. Decade. It happens to the best of us. So, I checked out your Twitherd profile to see if you were any different on that platform. You know, the account where you wrote: "Llllllllosers! Losey lose lose losers! What's the difference between Dumboprats and a bag of soggy potato chips? NOTHING! THEY'RE BOTH PATHETIC! #hahahahahapwnedlibs"?

Keep in mind: in both accounts, I had to wade through a lot of "burn in hell with George Sorobororos and Hillary Roocartoncleveman"'s and "Dumboprats want to take away Vesampuccerian's freedom because they didn't get enough love when they were children"'s to get to those relatively mild quotes.

You can't seriously complain about the pleasure Dumboprats have taken in the election of their ticket for President when you have spent the last four years treating them like shit. (I use that term in its strictly clinical advice column sense; any obscenity you may find in it is a matter you may want to take up with your antisocial worker.)

After all, he who lives by the "s" word...

The Tech Answer Guy

Yo, Tech Answer Guy,

Oh. Yeah. Well...can we just agree that both sides have been equally horrible to the other?

Sincerely,
Perry from Petaluma
Yo, Grow a Perr,

Sorry, but I don't deal in false equallys. The last time I tried, I gained 17 pounds and blew my chance to take Sadie Hawkins to the L'il Abner Day dance.

The Tech Answer Guy

If you are a dude with a question about the latest technology, ask The Tech Answer Guy by sending it to questions@lespagesauxfolles.ca. Just remember: Those who dine on glass dishes should not throw parties where they serve brontosaurus burgers for dinner. Don't tell me that ancient Athenian wisdom isn't relevant to modern society!

Ask Amritsar About the Ideal Love Line

Dear Amritsar,

I believe it is my civet duty (Mister Bojangly threatened to go on a hunger strike if I didn't, and everybody in my neighbourhood knows how much he loves his ferret chow!) to vote. Here in Pittothastomachsburg, Pennsylton, DC, lineups at polling stations have been known to run eight or nine hours. It pays to prepare (even though I had to get out of work, so I wasn't, technically, getting paid – oh, how I long for the days when the only sacrifice you had to make for the common good was a goat!), so, I packed a lunch, wrestled a folding chair away from Nana Geronimo (she can sit on the stoop for a couple of hours!), put on comfortable shoes and went out to my polling station.

In line in front of me stood a hot young woman in a We Are the Weird t-shirt and jeans, with hair that made her look like a refugee from the 1980s. I'll never forget the first thing she said to me: "Can you hold my place in line? I really have to pee!"

It was so magical, it could have been written by Shakeaspeararetoo.

We started talking and, as the hours passed, we realized we had a lot in common. I loved *How to get a Head in Murder,* she loved *Jersey Smores*. I'm a filet mignon kind of gal, she enjoys nothing more than a Bob So Tasty Bob Cajun burger. I was planning on voting for Ronald McDruhitmumpf, she was planning on voting for Joe Bidenhisbeeswax. I'm a little bit country, she's a little bit rock and roll. I – wait, what?

I was falling for...one of those?

I mean, okay, I didn't really believe it when *Foxindehenhaus and Fiends* host Brian KissMeadekilmeadenow swore that

Dumboprats had horns. How would they wear hats? Besides, if any sizable population of human beings had horns, you just know that somebody would come out with a line of horn grooming products. That's the genius of the Vesampuccerian system.

But, yeah, I had long believed that Dumboprats were the source of all of the problems in the country. For one thing, if they got into power, they would be taking away all of my guns (of which I had none, since their display would clash with the decor of my apartment). They would tax my income at 276% and force me to eat food stamps. Antifa would spray-paint slogans on my forehead as I walked down the street. My beloved country would descend into chaos...even more chaos than there had been under Chaos President.

That would be a ripe bucketful of chaos, that would be.

Over a brunch of cold chicken with fava beans and a nice Chianti, we discussed politics. My blossoming love blossom pointed out that the Dumboprats had been in power for eight years, and the most radical thing they did was pass a law modernizing interstate commerce. She joked that she wished the party was organized enough to do something seriously disruptive. At least, I think it was a joke. I'm sure it must have been a joke. Yes. Absolutely. A joke.

As we got to the doors of the polling station, we exchanged numbers. I wrote hers in my Palm Pilot; she wrote mine in sharpie on her palm. I don't know, though. Should I follow up, or should I chalk it off as the seven most magical hours in my life and move on?

Zerlina Lickenchickenour

Hey, Babe,

As that

Dear Amritsar,

Oh. Her name was Frankina. I should have mentioned that. Sorry.

Zerlina Lickenchickenour

Hey, Babe,

Think nothing of it. An experienced advice columnist learns to rise above interruptions.

As that famous filosopher Keanu Hereevertstoform truly said: "Relationships that, like, start off intense often end up, like, whoa!" It's also true, though, that relationships that start off mildly often end up, like, whoa. Relationships ending up like, whoa seems to be an integral part of the human condition.

Which is to say that all relationships carry the seeds of their own destruction in them from the very beginning. Some find the fertile ground of emotional incompatibility, others founder on the hard ground of empathy. Some are nurtured by the sunshine of profound political contradiction, others sputter out owing to compassion and compromise.

All relationships are hard. All we can do is go into them with an open heart and a locked knife drawer.

Send your relationship problems to the Alternate Reality News Service's sex, love and technology columnist at questions@lespagesauxfolles.ca. Amritsar Al-Falloudjianapour is not a trained therapist, but she does know a lot of stuff. AMRITSAR SAYS: If you enjoyed waiting in line to vote, you're going to be ecstatic over waiting for all the votes to be tabulated and a winner to be declared!

Ask an Advice Columnist for a Referral

Dear Ask a Doctor,

I'm a doctor in the Intensive Care Unit of the Cedars Closet Sinai hospital. Last week, I was attending a patient with all of the symptoms of COVID-19, but, when I gave her the diagnosis, she started screaming that the disease was "a hoax perpetrated by the lamestream media to help the Dumboprats steal our freedom!" I told her that her freedom would be severely constricted by a pine box (it was towards the end of a 20 hour shift – I had given my last ferk hours earlier). The woman shrieked that she had had a minor cold when she was admitted and that I must have injected her with something lethal in order to deny President McDruhitmumpf a second term in office **because everybody knows COVID isn't real!** When I assured her that the pandemic was real, she spit in my mask and swore that I was a "ferking poxified cudchugger with ferking besmirched pantaloons!"

The intubation put a quick end to that nonsense, let me tell you!

By the tone of the woman's voice, I got the sense she was trying to insult me. But, I have no idea what a poxified cudchugger with besmirched pantaloons is. Could you help me out?

Angela Rhododendrummer, type b positive (like that's possible in these trying times!)

Dear Curious Patient

We're medical doctors not script doctors! Okay, some of us are a little too fond of our scripts, but that's between us and our medical certification board. The point is, if we had to figure out every oath that a patient in COVID denial had sworn at a doctor, we would be spending all of our office hours reading dictionaries – then, who would be available to fill out patient charts or harass interns (purely in the interest of making them better doctors, of course)?

Take two hours of escapist television. If curiosity persists, consult a Language Corrector Dude.

*Ask a Doctor is a consortium of medical professionals who would rather not be personally identified as this is just a side gig and they don't take it especially seriously, so why should you? If you have a question of a medical nature, **talk to your family physician about it!** If that is not possible – and you're willing to take what you get – send your query to questions@lespagesauxfolles.ca. Say, wasn't Scott Atlascoughedupcats the guy who sold body building programs in the back of comic books in the 1950s? What he's selling today may not make any more sense, but you have to admire his tenacity!*

Yo, Tech Answer Guy,

I'm a doctor in the Intensive Care Unit of the Cedars Closet Sinai hospital. Last week, a patient who exhibited all of the symptoms of COVID-19 was lying on a bed in her room, denying my diagnosis of her condition while watching *Foxindehenhaus and Fiends.*

"The President said the number of cases of COVID would go down to zero back in April," Brian KissMeadekilmeadenow was saying. "So, whatever illness you may be feeling now, it's not that."

"No COVID, **no COVID!**" the patient howled. "President say so! What I got? **What I got for real?**" Then, he called me a "ferking poxified cudchugger with ferking besmirched pantaloons!"

I...have no idea what that means. Do you?

Sincerely,
Angela from Akron

Yo, Ange,

Uhh, yeah, I'm not comfortable with your question. The Tech Answer guy has a lot of skillz, but speakage and wording aren't one of them. Have you considered asking the Language Corrector Dude?

The Tech Answer Guy

If you are a dude with a question about the latest technology, ask The Tech Answer Guy by sending it to questions@lespagesauxfolles.ca. Just remember: No, Ask a Doctor must have been thinking of Charles Atlascoughedupcats. Scott Atlascoughedupcats was actually a performer who rose to fame as a cast member of the sketch comedy show Weekends!

Dear Amritsar,

I'm a doctor in the Intensive Care Unit of the Cedars Closet Sinai hospital. Last week, we were operating on a person for complications from COVID-19. When the anaesthetist asked the patient to count down backwards from 10, before he went under, he said, "Why won't you...tell me...what I...really have...you ferking...poxified...cud...cud...cud..." I think he was trying to call me a "ferking poxified cudchugger with ferking besmirched pantaloons!" I've been getting a lot of that lately.

I still have no idea what it means, Can you help me figure it out?

Angela Rhododendrummer

Hey, Babe,

There was a time when people would put on their best Sunday clothes to go to the emergency room of a hospital, thanked the dentist for his tender ministrations as he amputated their leg without anaesthetic, and apologized for getting their blood all over the waiting room carpet. How long ago those days seem!

I could write a book about how social norms have broken down in the past four years as millions of Vesampuccerians have been given permission to release their inner Mr. Hydengoseekseanz by watching the behaviour of the country's Raging-Id-in-Chief, but that wouldn't – that – umm, excuse me, but I think it's time I gave my agent a call.

In the meantime, you're asking the wrong person the question (how gauche!). You should be talking to the Language Corrector Dude.

Dear Amritsar,

Yeah, a lot of people have been telling me about this Language Corrector Dude guy. He sounds like he could really help with my question. How do I get in touch with him?

Angela Rhododendrummer

Hey, Babe,

You don't find the Language Corrector Dude so much as he crawls out from under his rock and finds –

Did someone take my name in vain?

And, there he is.

Hi, Angela. Excellent question. The naive interpretation of the word "cudchugger" would be "somebody who drinks liquefied grass quickly." That would definitely be an insult, since everybody knows that the only way to avoid indigestion would be to drink liquefied grass slowly. Very slowly. Preferably with a bourbon chaser.

In fact, "cud" derives from the word "duccud," an ancient Norse term for somebody who kisses horses on moonless nights. To "chugger" is a Middle English (half of the words from that period involve certain finger gestures!) form of the verb "to await with a mixture of trepidation and a runny nose." So, you're a moonlight horse lover in need of a kiss and a Kleenex.

The rest of the words in the epithet are pretty straightforward.

That may not sound like much of an insult to modern ears, but it was the height of personal invective in 1272!

It's unfortunate that medical professionals should be assailed with such language by people whose lives they are trying to save. But, we live in extemporaneously divocative times, don't we?

Send your relationship problems to the Alternate Reality News Service's sex, love and technology columnist at questions@lespagesauxfolles.ca. Amritsar Al-Falloudjianapour is not a trained therapist, but she does know a lot of stuff. AMRITSAR SAYS: I believe my esteemed colleague The Tech Answer Guy was referring to Charles Gogorocketschmo. Scott Atlascoughedupcats is actually a subspecies of Gobi Desert snow leopard.

Ask the Tech Answer Guy
About Striking the First Blow for Freedom

Yo, Tech Answer Guy,

My Grammie Paw-Paw used to tell stories about standing in bread lines during The Great Depression. She told us young-ungs (that was the noise she made when she tried to pick us up – maybe she should have stopped before we turned 35) about how the lines were so long, people would often lose more weight shuffling forward in them than they would gain from the food they received at the end of them!

And, about how the gurgling from empty stomachs up and down the line sometimes sounded like the chorus at Minsky's. One time, she was in a bread line in a blizzard so bad that when it cleared, she found she was standing on a steamer ship about to set sail for Shanghai!

Good times.

We didn't believe her, of course. Why would anybody choose to starve when they had credit cards?

Then, there was the fake virus that led to the hoax small business meltdown that led to me losing my job as a short distance trucker. I was told that it was because restaurants didn't need me to haul packets of mustard, ketchup and pickled sheep's intestines to them because they were closed. I knew it was really because our Chinese overlords shanghaied all our condiments to use for nuclear reactor fuel, but whatever the reason, I found myself without an income.

Of course, I refused to accept any unemployment insurance, because my name is not Karl or Gottsadlylowmarx, and, anyway, red is not my colour, if you catch my driftnet. For a week, anyway. If I wanted to keep my trailer, I had to accept the UI checks. What the hell – when my wardrobe changes, I can always avoid looking into mirrors. Unfortunately, UI doesn't cover food **and** Netflax, so braving the line it was.

I learned a valuable lesson: Grammie Paw-Paw was an optimist!

One time, the guy behind me was spouting off about politics, saying things like "President McDruhitmumpf's whole fallacy is wrong." If the dude wanted to be fitted for a microchip straitjacket and flung off a fiscal cliff, who was I to argue? Still, I couldn't allow such ignorance to go unchallenged – it might have swayed other, weaker people in the line – so I punched him in the ghoulies. As he lay on the pavement, panting, I argued, "How's your fallacy now, pal? Hunh? How's your fallacy now?" I'm good with the clever repartee like that.

In my defense, I was manhangry. That's short for "hangry while being a man." **That's** short for "being hungry and angry while being a man." Jesus Louise...is, there was so much meaning in that one word, I almost mistook it for being German!

Anyway, when the cops came, he was panting a lot less and able to explain what had happened. Which makes me wonder: should I have punched him in the throat instead?

Sincerely,
Alex from Rolodex

Yo, Lex...is,

I know what the term "manhangry" means. Thanks for the man-on-mansplainin'; I haven't had somebody do that to me since my brother The Science Answer Guy spent thirty-four minutes explaining why the sky is blue. Thirty-four excruciating long minutes from my life that I will never get back. Unless eternal recurrence is a thing, in which case, crap.

No, you should not punch somebody standing near you in a food line in the throat. Or, the ghoulies. Or, the time card. Violence is the last refuge of the argumentatively incompetent. That is right there in the Macho Code of Manliness, after the section on how to use a stick shift and before the recipe for the perfect barbecue sauce. (That's not man-on-mansplainin', that's reminding you of something you know but may have forgotten, or may not have fully understood, or may be ignoring because it's inconvenient.)

The proper way of dealing with people we disagree with is to swallow our anger until we get home, then channel it into building a birdhouse. Or a doghouse. Or an outhouse.

The point is to channel your hanger into something productive. That way, you don't get a criminal record (or add to the one you've already started), and birds get a home.

Building birdhouses is Macho Code of Manliness approved.

The Tech Answer Guy

If you are a dude with a question about the latest technology, ask The Tech Answer Guy by sending it to questions@lespagesauxfolles.ca. Just remember: some people may consider language a technology, but if you can't work on it with a monkey wrench, a screwdriver or a phaser, it isn't a technology in any meaningful sense of the word!

Ask Amritsar to Dream Big
Bigger
Like, An Entire Universe Big

Dear Amritsar,

I'm just a regular person with dreams. The kind that come when you're asleep, I mean; life has already slipped a knockout drug into the morning coffee of the dreams out of my waking hours and taken photographs of them in compromising positions with the dreams of my next door neighbour and threatened to expose them if they ever showed up in my conscious awareness again. Or, I just don't have much of an imagination. Who can tell, really?

In one dream, I am walking towards a bus stop just as the vehicle is pulling out; the ad on the side of the bus is for a brand of toothpaste called "Ha Ha, Sucker!" In another, I am at a train station; I know my train will be leaving in five minutes, but I can't find the right platform (the squawk on the PA system sounds suspiciously like: "Ha – crackle – a, su – crackle – er"). In another, I am in a cab on the way to the airport, but the plane will be taking off in five minutes (my sleeping brain seems to forget that you have to be at an airport seven hours before the plane takes off to get through security). I think you can see a pattern emerging (in that last dream, the DJ on the cab radio is announcing that the last song was "Disconnected Flight" by the band Ha Ha and the Suckerfish).

I recently read that dreams may be doorways to other dimensions. If that is true (and a scientist said it, so who am I to question the assertion?), why are my counterparts in other universes such *yutzes*?

Sav On a Rolla

Hey, Babe,

The multiverse is vast. There are an infinite number of realities in which your counterparts are *yutzes*. There are an infinite number in which your counterparts are *putzes*. There are even an infinite number where your counterparts are *schmendricks* – the multiverse contains infinite variety with infinite annoyability.

Having said that, there are also an infinite number of universes in which your counterpart is a *mensch*. The real question here is: why do you dream of the versions of yourself that cause you anxiety rather than the ones that would make you feel better about your life?

Anybody who knows me (which is nobody, because is it really possible to "know" another human being?) will tell you that Herr Doctor Freud and I have never really gotten along. This is partially because of his habit of borrowing 50 Marks until the beginning of the month and never paying it back (it's not like he can't afford it; I suspect he was compensating for not being properly toilet trained until he was 37; he would have appreciated that diagnosis). But, mostly, it was because his theories about women seemed to come from a universe where women didn't exist.

Despite this, some of his basic concepts do conform roughly to human experience. In this case, I am reminded of his statement: "Every dream contains a wish. Last night, I dreamed that you would lend me 50 Marks until the beginning of the month – it's not for me, it's for my recently deceased mother. How could you possibly refuse?"

I couldn't. Herr Doctor F. can be very persuasive when he's not smugly sucking on a big fat cigar.

I'm not suggesting that you want to miss a train, plane or automobile. Dreams that come from other dimensions are subtler than that, like the aroma of weak tea or the meaning of a David Lynch film. Your dreams could mean that you are worried that you are going to fail a big test you have coming up...every few days. (If your dimensional dreams were about failing a big test, it could mean that you were concerned about missing a travel opportunity. In dreamatology, this is known as The Law of Reciprocal Improbability.) Or, it could indicate that you should stop eating four course meals before you go to bed.

Dreams can be inscrutable bastards.

By the way, Bill Nae the Science Bae doesn't believe that dreams come from other universes. "If the theory that dreams are the random firing of neurons that our brains interpret as we start coming out of sleep was good enough for our parents, and their parents, and their parents before them," he stated, "it's good enough for me!

And, who am I to argue with Bill Nae the Science Bae? He's on TV!

Send your relationship problems to the Alternate Reality News Service's sex, love and technology columnist at questions@lespagesauxfolles.ca. Amritsar Al-Falloudjianapour is not a trained therapist, but she does know a lot of stuff. AMRITSAR SAYS: That's right, the last names in this article don't have five syllables. Not all questions come from people who live in the United States of Vesampucceri, you know. Honestly, Earth Prime 1-6-7-1-8-2 dash Psi needs to get over itself!

Ask the Tech Answer Guy About Your Future

Yo, Tech Answer Guy,

I don't mean to say that my father was a hard man, but adamantium bows its head in respect every time he walks by. So much starch is used when he cleans his adult diaper that it could be a military drill sergeant. When he gets mad, an earthquake swallows a small Latin Vesampuccerian city.

But, he loves me. In his way. Which other people might mistake for contempt. Stupid other people.

Anyway. My dad has recently fallen on hard times. An evil bastard stole his job from him. With the help of a vast conspiracy. Evil bastard conspiracy. A lot of his friends – Cushyjoboman and Wakupinafield, Deutsche Bank, the Girl Scouts of Greater New Yoricknuhemwell – the Girl Scouts! You know, I never liked their cookies: they always tasted to me like rat poison between two sheets of cardboard – not that I'm bitter (although the cookies certainly are!) – have abandoned him. He's got debts to pay, and his accountants are popping Xanax like they were smarties.

Not only that, but malicious prosecutors are looking to maliciously prosecute him on charges that are a complete joke. A hoax. Fake news. He could spend the last few years of his life in court. Or, jail. Or...or...or, poverty.

It's unthinkable, but it is very possible that he may not be able to pay me the allowance he has given me all of my adult life. How am I supposed to survive when the business he has been grooming

419

me to lead has gone bankrupt? This is a disaster! I mean, don't get me wrong, the possible jail time is bad, but this? This is a disaster!

How can I become a billionaire tech startup CEO?

Sincerely,
Ronald, Jr. from No Fixed Address

Yo, Ron Bon Bon,

The world of tech startups is way above the Tech Answer Guy's pay grade (I'll be honest: my pay has barely made it out of primary school). So, I asked Phil, the mechanic from the shop down the street, your question. Phil, the mechanic from the shop down the street, whose religion of the wrench forbids him from acknowledging pay grades, knows stuff.

Phil, the mechanic from the shop down the street, says becoming the CEO of a tech startup is easy. You have an original idea for a technology. You build it in your garage. You impress a vulture capitalist, convincing him to give you some vulture capital so you can start producing the technology for the market. You develop a marketing strategy to persuade the public that your technology will change their lives for the better. When you start making a substantial profit, you sell the company to MicroSquish for more money than you ever dreamed of. Then, you start the process all over again with a new idea. Keep going until you have a billion dollars.

Phil, the mechanic from the shop down the street, wishes you the best of luck.

The Tech Answer Guy

Yo, Tech Answer Guy,

That sounds like it could take a lot of time. Like, years. I don't have years. Maybe I didn't make myself clear: I have a few days, maybe a couple of weeks if my father's creditors are generous and his prosecutors are building an especially complicated case. **I need to become a billionaire tech startup CEO now!**

And, what's the big idea about having an original idea for a technology? I haven't had an original idea in my life! I think I may be allergic to original ideas – they make my skin break out, and my pristine complexion is my biggest asset! Can I buy an original idea on the internet? On credit – I'll be good for it in a few days, once I'm a billionaire tech startup CEO.

Are you beginning to see the depth of my problem?

Sincerely,
Ronald, Jr. from Skid Ro – No, I Dare Not Think It!

Yo, Ronnie Big Sap,

Yes, I think I'm beginning to see the depth of your problem. You chose to be born to the wrong parents. Sorry, but at this point, there really is nothing anybody can do for you.

The Tech Answer Guy

If you are a dude with a question about the latest technology, ask The Tech Answer Guy by sending it to questions@lespagesauxfolles.ca. Just remember: it's not the size of your framistat that counts, but what you do with it.

Ask Amritsar to Reconcile the Irreconcilable

Dear Amritsar,

A couple of days ago, I started my dream job: member of the House of Representatives. The first day was like the first day of any job: getting to know the people who worked around me; finding the cafeteria; sweeping my office for listening devices planted by Deep Dish State operatives trying to find dirt they could blackmail me with. Good times.

This lasted all of three days. (I never did find the listening devices, so I just never say anything that could come back to haunt me while I'm in the office. Boo!) I was supposed to be on the floor of the House for a vote on accepting the Electoral College vote. As if

I was going to let a tool – a monkey wrench, maybe, or a left-handed screwdriver – of the Establishment like Joe Bidenhisbeeswax become the next President; somebody who does Ukraine's bidding should never be invited to the bridge table!

At the same time, thousands of people were outside the Capitol building, protesting how the Dumboprats stole the 2020 Presidential election by getting more votes than the Reduhblicans. A lot of my Qanon buddies had flown in from across the country to attend the protest: Spidermoose3000 was there, along with antimarieantoinette, thebloodofpatriodiots0037 and questionauthori-gaack. I had never met them in person, and when I heard they were coming to Washburningdington, I was really excited by the possibility of hanging out with them. Not literally, of course: there was only one noose, and it didn't fit any of our necks.

Still, our attitude had always been: we'll hang out together or we'll surely hang out separately.

What should I do? Should I follow my head and stay for the vote, or follow my heart and go be with my friends?

Representative Marjorie Taylormaid Fortrubble

Hey, Babe,

It's a classic dilemma, although in your case, it would be more accurately described as following your butthole or following your vena cava. We often romanticize our life events to make ourselves appear more like a hero and less like the comic relief that we all are.

The obvious thing for you to do would be to enact the classic sitcom scenario of trying to be in two places at once. While another member is droning on, you could pass a note to the Speaker of the House saying you have a weak bladder and you need to go to the bathroom. Then, duck out and go meet your friends. After a couple of minutes with them, find an excuse to leave (for example, tell them that you just remembered that somebody left a pipe bomb in the hall near your office and you need to go back and see if the bomb squad has determined whether it's live or Memorex). Then, return to the Chamber.

This approach is not without risk. The more often you go back and forth, the more ridiculous the excuses you will have to use to leave one place or the other. You may have to tell the Speaker that you need to check outside to determine whether the mob has been infiltrated by Alpha Centaurans, for example, or to tell your friends that you have to return to your office to finish sweeping it for bugs planted by operatives of the Deep Dish State trying to find dirt they could blackmail you with.

This scenario never ends successfully: the two groups of people eventually run into each other, exposing the ruse. But, they almost always forgive you by the end of the episode, so as long as you live your life in 30 minute increments, you should be fine.

Amritsar is not a big fan of sitcom scenarios.

Or, you could just tell the truth and duck out of Congress to be with your friends. It's not like you have ever hidden your affinity for Qanon. And, who knows? You may be rewarded for your honesty. Stranger things have happened in Washburningdington. It could be argued that stranger things are happening even as we speak...

Dear Amritsar,

Oh, never mind. The session of Congress was suspended because protesters entered the Capitol building and are roaming around the halls and offices. **Hey, Spidermoose3000, wait up! I don't want to miss any of the fun!**

Representative Marjorie Taylormaid Grennongilles

Hey, Babe,

I love a story with a happy ending, although, in your case, I'm prepared to make an exception.

Send your relationship problems to the Alternate Reality News Service's sex, love and technology columnist at questions@lespagesauxfolles.ca. Amritsar Al-Falloudjianapour is not a trained therapist, but she does know a lot of stuff. AMRITSAR SAYS: Turn off the TV news and have some sweet potato fries. They can't make every hurt go away, but the emotionally restorative power of sweet potato fries is one of the unsung triumphs of the twentieth century!

Ask the Language Corrector Dude About How Tense He Gets When People Mix Up Their Tenses, Or the Correct Use of the Moral Injunctive, Or...Or...Or Anything But How He Feels About Getting His Own Column

I am of course, honoured, thanks for asking. I know I won't be able to columnize half as well as The Tech Answer Guy (especially if it meant I would have to match his alcohol consumption – talk about an ambulatory fire hazard!), and I couldn't possibly compete with Amritsar Al-Falloudjianapour (whose brand of compassionate smarm is unparalleled!). All I hope to be able to accomplish in this space is to make the world just slightly more amenable to acceptable linguistic practice.

Okay, then. Who would like to ask the first question?

Dear LCD,

Ever since she was elected to Congress, I have had an online correspondence with Alexandria Casio-Keebjords. Okay, she hasn't responded to any of the 127 emails, text messages or carrier pigeons that I have sent her, but she did send the FBI to my house one time to "have a little chat" with me, which sends its own kind of message. And, I heard it. I heard it loud and clear, Alexandria.

After about the 98th communication, I felt that I was repeating myself, that my message was getting stale. I mean, there are only so many ways to say "Ferk off and die you ferking Communist whore!" and "You ferking Communist whore, ferk off and ferking die!" and "Ferk off you ferking Communist whore, ferk off and die!" I thought that last one was especially creative, even if the genre as a whole was getting stale.

I considered switching to another target (so many female people of pigment in the Dumbopratic Party to choose from!), but, well, call me sentimental, but you always remember your first, you know? You never want to let her go. And, anyway, I'm pretty sure they have their own fans, and I wouldn't want to interfere with their relationships. You know what they say: 102's company, 103's a bloody mess.

So, can you suggest any creative endearments I could share with Alexandria to show her how truly, madly and, yes, deeply I hate her?

Sincerely,
Least Creative Deplorable

Dear LCD,

No. I – just no. This is not a question that should be answered. Who wants to ask the next ques

[Dude! What the ferk? You begged, you pleaded with, you attempted to bribe (a laughable proposition considering I know how much you make) me to give you your own advice column, and now you refuse to answer your very first question? What, as I say, the ferk? EDITRIX-IN-CHIEF BRENDA BRUNDTLAND-GOVANNI]

Yeah, Brenda, I'm really sorry about that. When I lay in bed at night imagining what my column would be, I thought I would be answering basic questions. You know: what is the difference between "there," "they're" and "their?" "What's so important about the Oxford comma that whole forests have been felled debating its use?" "When did 'any more' become 'anymore?' Has our society sped up so much that we no longer have the luxury of spaces between words? Or, should that be 'spacesbetweenwords?'" You know: normal language questions! I never expected to have to answer a question about harassing a member of Congress!

[So, you thought being a columnist was going to be easy? Putting on my slapping gloves is easy – writing a column is hard! Groucho Gottsadlylowmarx said that on his deathbed, so you know it must be true! Listen: I don't care what your answer is; just make it entertaining. Beyond the person who asked the question, nobody cares about the answers in advice columns as long as there entertaining. Got it? BB-G]

It's they're, actually. But –

[You know, there are lots of little Language Corrector Persons and Language Amender Dudes who would kill to be where you are now. Just saying. BB-G]

Erm...

Dear LCD,

You vile pus-sac! You and your lizard-brain opinions are completely repugnant to me! Your despicable, self-serving rhetoric plumbs the depths of human incivility. You should not be encouraged to interact with other human beings – you should be sent somewhere far, far away where you cannot be a threat to yourself or others – especially others. You are hateful and disgusting to every decent human being on the planet!

Dear LCD,

That's great! I can't wait to try this out! Thanks for your help!

Sincerely,
Least Creative Deplorable

Dear BBG,

I quit.

Language evolves. Words are born, they grow, they get old, they forget where their glasses are, and they die, replaced by a new generation of words that repeat the cycle. If you have trouble keeping up, you can ask the Language Corrector Dude by emailing him at questions@lespagesauxfolles.ca. Who knows? If he even has a column in the future, he might just answer you!

Ask Amritsar About Proper Child Discipline

Dear Amritsar,

Children. Ammirite?

I got a visit from the cops the other day. They thought I might have had something to do with the Capitol fight for freedom just because I was there. And, I was hitting a cop with a "Don't tread on me" flag. I thought it was ironic; they did not see the humour. And, I was looking through papers that had been left in the Senate chamber when the politicians fled (oh, don't say you aren't curious about what Eric Swallowacatsbell writes when he thinks nobody is looking! You aren't? Yeah, neither were the cops. Am I the only person in the world with an imagination?) The cops thought what I had done was a crime. You say potato, I say pardon. Oh.

How did they identify me? My six year-old son Kyle was in kindergarten, usually a low risk activity, for me if not for him. Far as I can tell, the teacher was surfing the TV looking for *Spongeburp Sloppydroopypants* when she caught a news report about the Stop the Stole rally. Before she could change the channel, the fruit of my looms piped up: "That's my daddy!"

Misses Gilgamesh, his teacher, froze the frame. Did you know they could do that with TVs these days? Isn't that something? She looked at it closely, and I guess she must have recognized the beer cap with bunny ears that I was wearing (my wife, Katerina, and I got a matching set when we were married – mine were in the shop for a leaky tube, so I borrowed hers), because I was soon answering questions at the local precinct.

That will teach me to go to parent-teacher meetings!

I was let out on bail three days later. By that time Katerina and Kyle (you think that would make a good cop show title? I don't know...sounds more like a 19th century romance novel title – just my luck!) had disappeared. I'm expecting the divorce papers any day now.

I gotta admit, I didn't think the little bastard had it in him to turn his old man in. It would make me proud, if I wasn't looking at serious jail time. Like, double digits jail time. Ouch! The little bastard.

So, obviously, he's out of my will. That leaves me on the horns of a dilemma, though. Double ouch with cayenne pepper sprinkles! Should I try to track him and his mother down so I can tell him now, or should I let him find out when they're reading my will?

Michael Flintaintinnocint

Hey, Babe,

I think you may have lost track of what is important, here.

One should never go where one has not been formally invited – that's terrible manners! Just as you did not appreciate members of the local constabulary showing up at your house without an invitation, you should not have shown up at the People's House without one.

And, while it is traditional to bring a gift when you are entering somebody else's house, a pipe bomb does not say, "Thank you for letting me share your space." It says, "Don't put out the good China, because I will just chew it up and spit it out because that's how much of a rebel I am!"

Were you one of those dreadful little people who soiled the carpets while you were in the Capitol? If you were, **were you raised in a barn?** Honestly, we make people clean up after the messes of their pets – you would think they would learn to clean up after their own messes as well! Don't smirk at me and make a joke out of leaving unexpected gifts, young man! You're not that clever and I'm not that forgiving! (Nor, I imagine, is the Capitol janitorial staff!)

As for talk about writing your son out of your will, it may be somewhat premature for that. After all, he is only six years old. He still has a whole life of disappointing you ahead of him!

*Send your relationship problems to the Alternate Reality News Service's sex, love and technology columnist at questions@lespagesauxfolles.ca. Amritsar Al-Falloudjianapour is not a trained therapist, but she does know a lot of stuff. AMRITSAR SAYS: Capitol tours are for putting into photo albums that you can bore your grandchildren with. They are **not** for planning routes to the offices of Congresspeople during an insurrection!*

8. THE SLEEP OF REASON PRODUCES... MONSTERS

What the Ferking Hell is Wrong With Kansconsin?

SPECIAL TO THE ALTERNATE REALITY NEWS SERVICE

The Alternate Reality News Service recently hired polling firm Harristweedfashin Interacting Up (HIU) to conduct a focus group of Reduhblican voters in Kansconsin to help our readers better understand what the ferking hell is wrong with the state. This is a partial transcript of that conversation.

QUESTION ONE

HIU: Do you feel you are better off now than you were four years ago?

ALLAN PSEUDONOMOUSNESS: (24, white, college student who plans to be either the next Ayn Randiasagohl, Rand Paulonaldaphun or Unibomber, may not be his real name) Who are you to be asking the questions?

HIU: I...I'm sorry?

PSEUDONOMOUSNESS: This country has been under the thumb of big polling for far too long! You make up the numbers that make the fake news feel so real to so many gullible sheeple. Honest, hard-working Vesampuccerians should take back polling and ask you about your opinions! The first thing I would like to know, and please feel free to share your feelings with us, is: why the ferk should any of us answer your questions?

HIU: Because my company is paying you to participate in this panel?

PAUSE.

PSEUDONOMOUSNESS: Well...okay, then. I'll answer your questions. But, under protest.

PAUSE.

HIU: So, how about the rest of you? Do you feel better off now than four years ago?

EMILY LITANUTELLA: (67, white, retired grandmother): My husband, Renaldo of Ghent, passed two months ago in the Poodle Cut Senior's Residence where he was trying to catch Alzheimer's disease. I tried to explain to him that you could only get Alzheimer's from toilet seats, but would the stubborn old son of a...goat listen? Course not! His passing was quick – one day, he was wondering how he would be affected by eating the brain of a dementia patient – it wasn't like she was using it! – the next day, he was in the ICU – a month later, he was dead. I couldn't even see him to say goodbye because of COVID restrictions at the hospital, couldn't hear his voice one final time. So, yes, I would say that I am better off now than I was four years ago. Much better off.

CHORUS: (half a dozen people who otherwise didn't contribute to the conversation) Just when you think your eyes will mist
    Up, there comes a twist!

LITANUTELLA: Hey, that rhymed!

CHORUS: Thank you for noticing, but please don't make a fuss:
Rhyming is just something a chorus does.

FLOYYD JONESENFORRAHIT: (37, white, manager of a Bob So Tasty franchise) I can't complain, really. I mean, sure, I may lose my business because of unnecessarily onerous lockdowns for a disease that doesn't exist, and I may have to sell my children for scrap in order to pay the mortgage on my condo. And, if I'm being completely honest, I didn't budget for the amount of alcohol I've started consuming. On the other hand, I look forward to the day when President McDruhitmumpf storms back into Washburningdington and has all the traitorous Dumboprats arrested and their ringleaders hung in public as a message to the world that we take democracy seriously! I like to think of myself as an optimist...

CHORUS: Matters in the heartland aren't as stark as depicted:
Many people who live there are...strangely conflicted.

QUESTION TWO

HUI: Do you believe that the Reduhblican Party best serves your interests?

ERIC FLATULENTSANEER: (37, white, police officer) Absolutely! I paid $37 less in taxes over the last four years than I did when...that person of pigment was president! I mean, okay, the Reduhblicans haven't shrunk government to the point where they can drown it in a bathtub. A pool, maybe. A big pool. You know, Olympic-sized. But they're heading in the right direction, that's for sure.

CHORUS: The party of limited government? How quaint.
Your grandparents' Reduhblicans these ain't!

FLATULENTSANEER: What – what do you mean?

CHORUS: The Reduhblicans can be such "fiscally responsible" phonies –

They love government spending that puts money in the pockets of their cronies!

PSEUDONOMOUSNESS: Yeah, well, at least they aren't shoving Black Lives Anti-matter propaganda down our throats or eating babies!

FLATULENTSANEER: (mutters) I hate...propaganda...

RHONDA LACKAWAKANDA: (17, white, aspiring single mother) Wait – what? Eating babies?

PSEUDONOMOUSNESS: It's true! They share recipes from some guy named Swiftonhisfeetberg or Swiftonhisfeetstein or something like that – right there on the Internet! You just have to know where to look!

LACKAWAKANDA: (shudders) That's...disgusting!

FLATULENTSANEER: That's why I will always vote for Ronald McDruhitmumpf – he may be many disgusting things, but he has never eaten a baby! ...That I know of. And, so what if he did? He must have had a powerful reason! And, I'm sure he didn't enjoy it...much...

CHORUS: Their beliefs are immune to any externality –
They have completely given themselves over to the cult of personality!

QUESTION THREE

HUI: I can see that many people in this room are hurting, just as many people in the country are hurting. Why do you think that an autocratic leader will improve your lives more than democratic institutions?

PSEUDONOMOUSNESS: Ferk democratic institutions! What have democratic institutions ever done for me?

HUI: Other than maintain the road system?

PSEUDONOMOUSNESS: Oh. Well, sure, I'll give you that.

HUI: And, ensure the quality of our food and drugs?

PSEUDONOMOUSNESS: Yes. That. Obviously.

HUI: And, stabilize our dollar so that our financial system doesn't fall into ruin?

PSEUDONOMOUSNESS: If you're going to get technical about it –

LACKAWAKANDA: This is starting to sound awfully familiar...

HUI: And, provide us with the police to protect our communities?

PSEUDONOMOUSNESS: Ferk the police!

FLATULENTSANEER: Now, hold on a second, there, son –

PSEUDONOMOUSNESS: The police are tools of the elite, oppressors oppressing the oppressed white man! Traitors to the country and a danger to true patriots – that's what the police are!

FLATULENTSANEER: I would be careful about what you say, there. You –

JONESENFORRAHIT: I know how to deal with traitors. (SOUND: metal clanging on table)

HUI: Wait, what –

LITANUTELLA: Bitch, you call that a knife? (SOUND: metal banging heavily on table) This, this is a ferking knife!

HUI: Put those away! This is not supposed to –

LACKAWAKANDA: Lady, did you...did you just go full on Betty Sowhitesheblindshines on his ass? Respect!

PSEUDONOMOUSNESS: Amateurs. Don't you know that you don't bring knives to a Civil War...fight? (SOUND: the cocking of a gun)

HUI: **What the ferk?**

PAUSE.

CHORUS: Then, there arose an awkward silence,
    Filled with the heaviness of impending violence.

PSEUDONOMOUSNESS: You know, I've had just about enough of your comments! If you don't put a corkscrew in it, I'll shut you up for you!

CHORUS: This is what living in a fantasy world begets:
    Increasingly violent threats.

PSEUDONOMOUSNESS: You know, you've done nothing but criticize us since this whole thing started. Who do you work for? The FBI? The CIA? **The phone company?**

CHORUS: So many bad ideas, so misbegot
    How do people – BANG – oh Gord, we've been shot!

TRANSCRIPT ENDS

Missing the Forest for the Tweeps

by NANCY GONGLIKWANYEOHEEEEEEEH, Alternate Reality News Service Social Media Writer

At 2:37 in the morning, President Ronald McDruhitmumpf tweeped...nothing. A grateful nation continued to sleep, but if its rest was more peaceful, its dreams less anxiety-ridden, the drool on its pillow less...wet, that may well have been the reason why.

It wasn't because he didn't want to. The bees that buzzed in his skull were transmitting messages about standing back and standing by and standing on your own two feet and standing by your man and being upstanding in a court of law and standing orders and standing your ground and standing at attention (while holding a baby's arm holding an apple) to his cerebral cortex. His cerebral cortex responded with a hearty, "I gotta share this with the world!"

Only, he couldn't. Because Twitherd, the favourite social network of bees in disturbed brains around the world, had suspended his account for 24 hours, a suspension that would later be made permanent.

In explaining the decision, Twitherd posted a message to its blog (because it was obviously too important to be limited to 239 characters), which read, in part: "This motherferking bastard is insane! Totally batshit bonkers nutzoid! We are not going to allow him to continue to undermine our precious democracy and sow violent discord on our platform! We do not want blood on our profit/ loss statements – thanks to the pandemic, there's already enough red on the bottom line!"

I may have read between the lines (whatever colour they may have been) of the actual message a bit, there. But, what the message lacked in urgency, it more than made up for in punctuation.

"They can object all they want, but that red on Twitherd's bottom line looks a lot like blood to me," commented Senator Richard Blumenthalated. "Where was Twitherd when the President tweeped about taking back states? Out in the parking lot having a smoke. Where was Twitherd when the President personally attacked Dumbopratic legislators like Governor Gretchen Whitmerdelalune? Bailing its kid out of detention for having a smoke behind the high school gym. Where was Twitherd when the President repeatedly lied about winning the 2020 election? At the local deli having a smoked meat sandwich. This makes too little too late seem like Roaring Twenties excess!"

Senator Blumenthalated added that Twitherd waited until the President had less than two weeks in his term, a time when many Reduhblicans had begun speaking out against him. "It's like Daniel waiting until the lion was old and feeble before going into the den to take the thorn out of his paw. Not exactly a profile in courage. More like a back of the head shot in courage, really."

"What about the President's right to free speech?" argued Foxindehenhaus anchor Lou Dobbsermanpincher. He's not a lawyer, you know. "This goes beyond cancel culture – this is an example of cancel, burn all of the tapes, erase all of the recordings and delete the show's entry in the *Imaginary Movie Database* culture. That's gotta be unconstitutional! It's gotta be!"

"That's a spurious argument," retorted MSNBC host Ari Melbertoastenjamm. He is a lawyer, you know. "And, when I say that, I don't mean it wears chaps and competes in rodeos. I mean, it has nothing to do with the case. The Constitution says that government shall not abridge the right to free speech. Government. Now, Twitherd is larger than 37 governments around the world, but, last time I checked, it didn't have legislative capabilities or a standing army. Or, a sitting army, for that matter. Or, any kind of military presence, really. It is a business. Booting the President off the social media platform was a business decision. Freedom of speech is not the issue. As Piddley Diddley once sang, 'You don't like the dress the press bought you?/Sorry, but you have to dance with the gunboat that brought you!'"

It may all have been for naught. The President still has right-wing social media platforms like 4charliechan and ParlerGames to disseminate his message to his followers.

In addition, at 2:37 in the morning, President McDruhitmumpf aide Stephen Siewnottmillertyme tweeped: "January 6 was just the beginning!!! we'll take back our democracy one speaker's lectern at a time!!! Next stop: January 20! It'll be a blast!!! This is not the President speaking, just a normal Grey House staffer!!!!! #littledeucecoup"

They say information wants to be free. What they don't say is that disinformation wants to club information over the head, dump the body in a dark alley and take its place.

The Representative With Angst in Her Pangst

by ELMORE TERADONOVICH, Alternate Reality News Service Film and Television Writer

The general public impression of Representative Lauren Boebertbanana is that she is a blood-thirsty gun fetishist who wants to burn Washburningdington to ashes and strew the ashes over a confederate flag flying high above what's left of the Capitol. Which would be treason. And, messy.

The general public impression of Representative Boebertbanana is wrong. It's not that she's not a blood-thirsty gun fetishist who wants to burn Washburningdington to the ground – Gord knows that part is accurate. No, I mean that characterization is incomplete. What the general public seems to be missing is that she is also a filmmaker of funk, a *cineaste* of comfortlessness, an *auteur* of angst.

Take her latest production, a political ad called "In the Shoes of Pygmies." It starts with Boebertbanana walking down a ten foot tall chain link fence with barbed wire on the top, a security measure put in place after January 6 to protect legislators from violent white supremacists. She is blathering on about "freedom" this and "people's house" that, but ignore what she is saying (she may as well be an adult in a Peanuts cartoon for all the sense she makes) and focus on the symbolism of the wall.

Walls divide us. They provide us with excuses not to collide us. Okay, that sounds awkward, but in my head it was a poetic statement of the essential apartness of human existence, the impossibility of making meaningful connections to others. Walls do not just protect politicians from angry mobs of well-armed people: they are symbols of the emptiness between (and inside) human beings, whether we are physically in contact or universes apart. As depicted in the video, the wall around the Capitol has no beginning or end – it is all middle. You could circle it forever and never make contact with anybody inside, whether to share your innermost fears and dreams or hear back from them about your generous campaign contribution.

As Sartrobartfasto truly wrote, "Hell is other politicians."

Okay, Boebertbanana does say one interesting thing in the video. For a moment, she stops walking, looks directly at the camera and says, "Speaker Pelligrinosi, tear down this wall!" This is an example of what semidioticians refer to as "intertextuality," and non-intellectuals refer to as stealing ideas from other people.

Those of you who are old enough will remember that former President Ron Potganreabumbom, in his own walking film in Berlin, said, "Mister Gorbachevskyite, tear down this wall!" (For those of you who are not old enough, former President Ron Potganreabumbom, in his own walking film in Berlin, said, "Mister Gorbachevskyite, tear down this wall!") The intertextual theft should be obvious.

Moreover, Boebertbanana was referencing the trend of having long scenes of walking that was all the rage in the films of the 1970s. Who could possibly forget the ten minute scene of Bob Woodworkingreward wandering through a parking garage looking for Deep Stoat in *All the President's Manacles*, or the narrator walking through Kurtzentodapoynt's island compound for 23 minutes in *Apocalypse Noun*? In the seventies, it was a comment on how all human effort is futile; now, it may be a comment on how out of shape the average Vesampuccerian is.

Boebertbanana's video ends with the sound of a gun being fired, reloaded and fired a second time. Most critics assume that this is a threat against the life of Speaker of the House Nancy Pelligrinosi. It may be time for a reassessment of this interpretation (even if the video was only uploaded to YahooTube 23 minutes ago). The repetition of the gunshot could be an intertextual reference to the concept of eternal recurrence. This would make the sounds the basis for an exploration of whether or not human beings are capable of anything truly original, or, at the very least, an interesting aspect of an M.I.A. song.

The general opinion is that the way former President Ronald McDruhitmumpf coddled extremists allowed somebody like Boebertbanana to gain a position of power. The general opinion is wrong. Which is to say that it isn't wrong, but that it is incomplete. An argument could be made that the former President was in reality a master producer, orchestrating the creation of some of the most potent short films of our time masquerading as political ads, works of art that will outlive his administration.

Which, I guess, amounts to the same thing, really. But, it doesn't sound so bad when put in an artsy context.

Buddy, Can You Spare 3.5 Million Acres?

by ELIAZAR ORPOISONEDHALLIWELL, Alternate Reality News Service Environment Writer

The only sound you hear is the clickety-clack, clickety clack (yes, that's what it sounds like, don't talk back!) of the wheels on tracks and somebody playing a mournful version of "Hoot For Teacher" on harmonica.

Out of the gloom, somebody says, "I hear that across east, the streets are paved with field mice!"

Another person responds, "I hear that across the east, old growth forests are so big that those who live there are able to burrow holes for nests in summer trees **and** winter trees."

And, they sigh.

"I...don't know that this is the right approach to introducing the problem," demurred Noah Greenewpayntonwald, endangered species director at the Centre and Outer Edges for Biological Diversity.

You think it would be better to just come out and say that the US Fish and Wildlife (Not That Wildlife, You Perv!) Service published a revised critical habitat designation for the northern spotted owl, removing federal protections from approximately 3.5 million acres of forested land in Orefornia, Washburningdington and Caligon? You think I should explain that logging and mining could destroy the habitat of the endangered species of avian life?

"Yes! You should definitely say that – it's exactly what happened!"

Oh, sure. I suppose you would want me to add that with only days left to go in his presidency, Ronald McDruhitmumpf continues to direct agencies in his government to undermine rules that protect the environment?

"Yes! Yes, that's what you should be writing about! People need to know this stuff!"

No, they don't. If people actually cared about the environment, do you think they would keep electing governments that look the other way while business has its wanton way with it?

"Uhhhhhhhh..."

According to Consolidated Wood, a logger lobby group (try saying that three times fast! ...I don't really know why you would want to, but go ahead. It's a free country...), The Endangered Species Act threw thousands of people out of work. "You wanna know who's really endangered?" CW asks on its web site. "Men in flannel shirts who want to do an honest day's deforestation, that's who!"

Greenewpayntonwald objected to this, pointing out that automation in the logging industry was far more responsible for job losses than a cute little bird. However, I didn't appreciate the way he challenged my approach to the subject, so I refused to quote him directly.

To say that the McDruhitmumpf administration has been hostile to environmental regulation would be like saying the sun is hot. It replaced the Bushbamclintreagbush-era Clean Power Plan with the Safe Affordable Dirty Energy rule, which rolled back emissions standards for power plants. The Safer Affordable Fuel-Effluvient (SAFE) Vehicles rule rolled back emissions standards for cars, potentially adding millions of tons of carbon dioxide into the atmosphere. The Safe Affordable Mercury and Air Toxics Lack of Standards rule rolled back regulations on how much poison companies could release into the environment.

When you hear about rollbacks, you might think rolling back on your bed to get comfortable before falling asleep. These are more like your car rolling backwards on a hill that ends in a lake.

You see? This is not just about northern spotted owls, Greenewpayntonwald stated. He was making a point that I felt should be included in the article, but I was still mad at him, so I didn't give him the dignity of quotation marks. The McDruhitmumpf administration has rolled back as many as 100 environmental regulations, most of which were designed to help save **people's** lives!

How has the Environmental Pollution Agency responded to the McDruhitmumpf rollbacks? "Eep! Was a common reaction throughout the four years of his administration. "Gaack!" often came up. "We believe that the standards enacted by previous administrations have been too restrictive. Help! Help me! I'm trapped in a regulatory body led by people who do not believe in regulation! We believe that the new rules will better serve the public by striking a more reasonable balance between environmental protection and the needs of industry. No! No! Please! Stop us before we deregulate again!" has also been said once or twice.

Meanwhile, northern spotted owls are hitching a ride on the steel rail and migrating by the thousands, hoping for a better life in a new part of the country, while a mournful version of "Hoot! Hoot! Hoot!" is played on the harmonica.

"I'm really not comfortable with this anthropomorphization of wildlife," Greenewpayntonwald complained.

This is why people don't care about the environment: environmentalists have no poetry in their souls!

Poetry Survived Post-modernism –
It Will Almost Certainly Survive This

by FREDERICA VON McTOAST-HYPHEN, Alternate Reality News Service People Writer

Limerick 1

Newly elected maniac Marjorie Taylormaid Fortrubble
Lived in the right-wing conspiracy bubble
The Reduhblican Party was just a pawn
In the plans of the member for Q-Anon
Remove her from her committee postings on the double!

The Many Manias of Steve

There are some who probably will find it tacky
But I can never get enough of Steve Kandykornaki.
He may not be the height of elegance
In his starched white shirt and khaki pants,
But if you're desperate for an election night data fix, he
Is the perfect manic number-crunching pixie.

Where other analysts wouldn't be interested,
Steve appears to be heavily emotionally invested.
While other analysts try to be succinct,

Steve is happy to do a deep dive into each ward and precinct
Every data point is a matter of life and death,
And he never seems to take a breath!

(And, it's a natural high – Steve would never use meth!)

Steve can be seen in a variety of media,
Which is only right – his mind is an encyclopedia
Of facts! He knows all of the names and faces
Of people in hundreds of House and Senate races!
Who won by less than 100 votes seven cycles ago?
Ask Steve – you can be sure Steve will know!

Steve really knows how to put on a show,
Reciting facts you never knew you needed to know.
The current race could go this way
Or, it could be completely different – who is Steve to say?
In the numbers he is supremely confident,
And he'll explore them until his energy is spent.

(We're behind you, Steve, one hundred per cent!)

And, oh! You have to admire how Steve is the Lord
Of the network's election night smart board.
How he manipulates the data can be frightening –
His fingers flying around like lightning!
As out of his mouth the latest number slips,
It also appears to travel out of his fingertips!

Steve can certainly be said to be driven,
So he should be easily forgiven
If, in his electoral consciousness' stream,
He has trouble finding the most helpful screen.
Confusion should not be something we're fearing:
They happen so rarely, his mistakes can be endearing.

(Now look what you've done! You've got me all tearing!)

Although he can tell you how a race will look, he

Would not do well as a bookie.
His speech is plain, not arabesque,
And votes are called by the Decision Desk.
The end of the party he will always miss,
No matter how sharp is his analysis.

How can anybody not love Steve Kandykornaki
He has such a talent! He has such a knack, he
Can take facts so dry and uninviting
And make them come alive, make them exciting!
With his boundless enthusiasm,
He looks like election results give him a satisfying...ummm...

(Oh, I'm sure you know what fills that empty chasm!)

Limerick 2

How many transgressions of norms does it take
To get a reaction out of House Reduhblican leader Kevin
    McCartilagebreak?
If your fascistic tendencies are cut and dried
He will calmly take you aside
And gently, over lukewarm bathwater, you rake

The Friendly Face of Fascism

She looks and speaks like your kindly grandmother.
You would expect her to offer you biscuits and tea.
But, when she speaks, she's something other,
Reminding you of your pledge of unity constantly.

For her tactics, you shouldn't be fallin'
Susan Yummytomcollins

Of course, she'll be happy to be lead negotiator
Of the terms of your major legislation.
But you will find, ten months later

That for an agreement you're still waitin'.

She says she wants a deal, but she keeps stallin'
Susan Yummytomcollins

A proper negotiation involves give and take,
But from her position she will never slip.
To give in would be a big mistake.
Her offer to you is a fake,
A deal all Reduhblicans will break
In the spirit of one-way bipartisanship.

Who smiles while your bill she's maulin'?
Susan Yummytomcollins

She may seem independent,
But who does she think she's kidding?
Learn from how previous negotiations went:
She's there to do the obstructionist party's bidding.

You may be grinning now, but soon you'll be bawlin'
Thanks to Susan Yummytomcollins

Limerick 3

Despite being so young, Senator Josh Heehaheehawley
Is reaching for the ultimate prize, by golly
He plans to win the 2024 Presidential race
By appealing to Ronald McDruhitmumpf's base
To bet against him would be folly

Cancellation of Cancel Culture Cancelled

by FRANCIS GRECOROMACOLLUDEN, Alternate Reality News
Service National Politics Writer

Reduhblicans have a bee up their butt. I don't know how it got there. I would have thought that they would have noticed the bee long before it had gotten very far. Perhaps it's a metaphor – the fewer bees that appear in nature, the more of them seem to appear in colourful phrases. But, I digress. And, I haven't even started.

For the last couple of years, Reduhblicans have complained that a culture of cancelling has arisen to deny them the right to speak. This culture of cancelling is often referred to as "cancel culture."

How does it work? Somebody says something offensive. Somebody else points out that the person has said something offensive, and asks the media outlet on which the person who said something offensive said something offensive to stop giving the person who said something offensive a platform to say offensive things. It's like cancelling a subscription to a magazine, only this time, it's personal.

"Uhh, yeah, what Reduhblicans're really arguing for is to be able to say whatever they want without consequence," pointed out token smart person Amy Sheshutshotshitbam. "'I can shoot you, but don't cry out in pain because that would oppress me!' And, they think that left-wing philosophy infantilizes people!"

"I have been a victim of cancel culture," complained right-wing pundit Dinesh D'Souzaphonie to millions of viewers of *Foxindehenhaus and Fiends*. "Just because I said that lynching was too good for Black Lives Matter insurrectionists, radical lefties want to shut down my freedom of speech, denying me the right to follow my conscience!"

So, Reduhblicans believe in freedom of speech and conscience, right?

WRONG!

Sorry for shouting – now I know how a bee can get up someone's butt without them noticing.

Seven Reduhblicans voted guilty in the Senate trail of President Ronald McDruhitmumpf, who was being tried for inciting the Capitol insurrection. Did the Reduhblican Party congratulate them on their fit of conscience? Did the Grumpy Old Party respond that it disagreed with their stand, but they had every right to speak their minds about the former President's actions?

Sure, they did. Just before the orgy on the floor of the Senate. You don't remember the orgy on the floor of the Senate? Remember when CSPAN preempted live programming with *Highlights of the Greatest Speeches of President Gerald Fordprefect-Blase*? That was when the orgy took place on the floor of the Senate. (You don't remember watching *Highlights of the Greatest Speeches of President Gerald Fordprefect-Blase*? Nobody does, friend. Nobody does.)

Okay, that never happened. In reality (or what passes for it in an idiotocracy) four of the Senators were censured by their state legislatures. (Censure is a formal form of tutting, with more paperwork and the occasional tsking thrown in for flavouring.) Two of the other state legislatures were in recess, but promised to censure their Senators who voted against the former President when they got back from the spa. The other state legislature made a strangled noise and fell to the floor frothing at the mouth (apparently, this happens a lot in Alaskyvania; when the mood passes, the state legislature will look around, sniff, and vote to adjourn for the day).

"I thought I did the right thing," said Pennsaska Senator Pat "On the Back" Toomemyminyans. "I listened to the evidence and voted my conscience."

"We didn't send him to the Capitol to do the right thing," apoplecticked Washburningdington County Republican Party Chairman Dave Ballbustingbabee. "We sent him to the Capitol to do the President's bidding. Pat clearly doesn't understand how democracy works!"

"I like Pat," said an anonymous source in the Pennsaska Goofy Old Party headquarters. "I attended his daughter's *bris*. He loaned me 20 bucks and never hassled me for not paying it back. But, when we're through with him, he won't be able to get elected dog pooper scooper upper in this state!"

Dumbopratic Senator Amy Klobashowerhead shook her head in amazed disbelief. Disbemazement. No, amazed disbelief. "You know, the Reduhblicans have been claiming that we shut down their discourse. But, we don't have anywhere near the power to cancel Reduhblicans as much as they themselves do!"

"Well, isn't that just like a Dumboprat?" retorted Reduhblican Senator Marco Rubydubio. "Trying to cancel the way Reduhblicans cancel each other!"

"Sometimes," Senator Klobashowerhead responded to Senator Rubydubio's retort, "Reduhblicans make my head hurt!"

The Hapless Hater

by FREDERICA VON McTOAST-HYPHEN, Alternate Reality News Service People Writer

Ryan "Butch" Untideewheidee didn't get the memo. Not that the Oaf Keepers, the organization to which he wanted to belong, sent out memos; they were more like a flock of birds that just watched each other intently for signs of straying from the current path. Twitchy. Hyper-alert. Prone to sudden changes of direction. Like ostriches. Or, vultures. Or, penguins.

Ryan Untideewheidee was not a very good penguin.

When white supremacists began to focus their vili –

"We prefer the term 'white nationalist,'" said Kelly Meggsnotferbrekkie, one of the leaders of the Oaf Keepers. When I asked him what the difference was, he answered: "The general public hasn't caught on that white nationalists like burning crosses and beating the Shiite out of people of pigment. Shh..."

Oh. Well, then. When white...supremationalists...

No objection? Yeah, I'm not sure what it means, either – language, as they say, is what you can get away with. Especially English. Okay, then. When white supremationalists decided to focus their vilification on brown people coming across the border, Untideewheidee missed the penguin signal and continued to write angry blog posts about how Black Lives Matter was an organization made up entirely of baby killing Doctor Soseussonandawl haters. He finally clued in on the new target just as the outrage at the border died down and the mainstream of Oaf Keeper fury returned to African-Vesampuccerians.

"I like Butch, really, I do. Really nice guy," Meggsnotferbrekkie stated. "He would give you the shirt off his back – not that you would want it – he doesn't do laundry as often as he should. Still. Great guy."

Meggsnotferbrekkie paused for effect. Or, perhaps, because he had lost his train of thought. His face was about as expressive as wax paper taped to the side of a nuclear reactor. When I prompted him about trying to remember what he had started to say about Untideewheidee, he cleared his throat and continued: "Yeah. Ahem. Harrumph. Fantastic guy. His heart's in the right place. But, his mind? It's out on Pluto, somewhere. Honestly, if he was any less with the programme, he would have been written out of the show and replaced by a can of baked beans in the 1950s!"

"As I've said many times before: hate doesn't discriminate," explained security expert Malcolm Donneednopennance. "The sort of person who hates people of pigment will also hate Jews...indigenous people...redheads – anybody who isn't white like them. But, while it may not discriminate, hate does have a short attention span, flitting from one group to the next and back again. I tell you, hate is worse than a hummingbird on a sugar high!"

The latest target of the Oaf Keepers and other white supremationalist groups are Asian-Vesampuccerians, their irrational hatred having been fed by former President Ronald McDruhitmumpf's repeated assertion that, "COVID? They started it!" (Yes, he learned rhetoric at the university of the playground.) Since the pandemic began, verbal and physical attacks on Asian-Vesampuccerians has skyrocketed faster and higher than GameStop stock under the influence of social media.

But, Untideewheidee? Until recently, he was still blaming Black Lives Matter for rising shorelines, bulging waistlines and the disappearance of bees (from the environment, if not Reduhblican's minds and butts). When he did finally clue in that the new target was Asian-Vesampuccerians, Untideewheidee made the mistake of picking a fight with young men and women at a taekwando centre instead of old men and women playing strip mah jongg on a street corner.

He will need a couple of weeks in hospital to deal with the broken bones and a good lawyer to deal with the assault charges. The image will remain in his head for the rest of his life.

"Yeah, if anybody asks," Meggsnotferbrekkie shook his head, "I've never heard of him."

"They think they're making a statement by beating up old Asian-Vesampuccerians," security expert Donneednopennance scoffed. "Sure, they're making a statement. And, it is: **we're reprehensible cowards who never learned to pick on people our own size, age group and income bracket!** I would call them clowns, but that would be a disservice to honest, hard-working circus performers everywhere!"

Could the fact that he continued to attack members of a single group be a sign that Untideewheidee could focus better than most Oaf Keepers, while attacking young people meant he wasn't a coward?

"Naah," security expert Donneednopennance naahed. "He just didn't get the memo!"

I was about to point out that the Oaf Keepers didn't send memos when I realized that that would bring us back to the beginning of the article in a loop that threatened to go on forever. Better to end the article on a high note. C.

Rash Omen

by SASKATCHEWAN KOLONOSCOGRAD, Alternate Reality News Service Existentialism Writer

The honourable (if that doesn't dishonour the term) member for the Twilight Zone, Representative Marjorie Taylormaid Fortrubble, posed a problem for the Reduhblicans. For one thing, she had a habit of posting outrageous things to social media, like the time she claimed on Farcebook that then-Califoregon Governor Jerry Browninpanforsix made a deal with Thor to send a thunderbolt to his state that would start a raging fire to clear land for a luxury spa.

"Could Thor target such a specific area?" she wrote in a post that has since been deleted. "How would I know? All that I can say for sure is that Governor Browninpanforsix was always hot for a mani-pedi, and he sure seems to like his Norse gods!"

For another thing, when metal detectors were set up in the Capitol building after the January 6 attack, she refused to go through them. "I'm allergic to Second Amendment infractions," she smirked as she walked around the metal detectors. "They make me break out in veiled threats to go on shooting sprees!"

In response to her provocations (did I mention her QAnon Qonsciousness?), Republican Leader Kevin McCartilagebreak took Representative Taylormaid Fortrubble aside on the floor of the House and had a talk with her.

"He was very deferential," Representative Taylormaid Fortrubble described the conversation. "He told me how happy he was to be working with such an obvious patridiot, and that I should keep representing my constituents the way I was doing, because I obviously understood the will of the people who elected me. What a nice welcome!"

Minority Leader McCartilagebreak remembered the conversation a little differently. "I told Marjorie that the Reduhblican Party could not be a safe harbour for white supremacists, that her actions were not in keeping with our core moral values," he said in a separate interview. "If she wanted to remain in the Reduhblican caucus, she would have to renounce extremist views. She seemed very contrite and assured me that she would. I considered it a very productive discussion."

Whose version of the conversation was correct? "Neither!" snorted Representative Alexandria Casio-Keebjords. She was walking out of the chamber to go to the Representatives' privy and overheard the conversation. "McCartilagebreak whined that if Taylormaid Fortrubble didn't stop being so racist, the Reduhblicans would never again get a vote from a person of pigment. Taylormaid Fortrubble snarled that he should ferk off, that she was going to do her because that's what her constituents wanted, and if he didn't like it, he could take a flying ferk at a watermelon! That conversation sounds about as productive as trying to convince bacon not to be so damn tasty! Mmm...bacon. Excuse me..."

If these were the only versions of the discussion, the situation would be confusing enough. However, the ghost of Representative John Lewlewlewisman was also privy (but not in the bathroom sense, because ghosts are beyond bodily functions) to the conversation. "I wanted to keep watch over the chamber where I worked for all of those years," Representative Lewlewlewisman said via Ouija board. "If I had known white supremacists would be in the House, I wouldn't have passed away!"

What did he hear? "Minority Leader McCartilagebreak asked Representative Taylormaid Fortrubble how she was adjusting to life in Washburningdington. She said she was pleasantly surprised that she didn't encounter demons on every street corner. He smiled and said that if she did come across any demons, she should report them to him immediately and he would see what he could do to help her overcome them. She told him that she appreciated his help, then patted her hip and said with a wink that she could take care of herself, thank you very much. After a brief pause, Representative Taylormaid Fortrubble asked if there was something specific the House Leader wanted to discuss. McCartilagebreak replied, no, no, just welcoming a new member. After a few more pleasantries, the conversation ended. Honestly, this is what all the fuss is about?"

"Oh, hell, yes, this is what the fuss is about!" Representative Casio-Keebjords, having returned from doing her private business, insisted. "Racists should not be given committee positions! Racists who have made threats against the Speaker should be expelled from their caucus! Racists who have made threats against the Speaker and who carry weapons onto the Floor should be expelled from Congress! Having a pleasant chat with somebody like that is like wearing sunscreen to protect yourself from a nuclear bomb!"

We wanted to ask Minority Leader McCartilagebreak to respond to this criticism, but he had flown to Mara-Lara-Dingdong to talk to former President Ronald McDruhitmumpf. We can't wait to hear how **that** conversation went!

Extremism in the Pursuit of Free Dumb is No VICES

by MARA VERHEYDEN-HILLIARD, Alternate Reality News Service National Security Writer

On his first day as President, Joe Bidenhisbeeswax signed an Executive Order stopping the deportation of undocumented immigrants until his administration had a chance to study and propose changes to Vesampuccerian immigration policy. It may have come as a surprise to him, then, that the deportations did not stop. It certainly came as a surprise to those who were being deported.

Wha' happen?

On his last day in office, former temporary ad hoc impermanent passing ephemeral acting deputy Secretary of Homeland Insecurity Ken Cuccicuccicoo signed an agreement with VICES (the Victorious ICES Conniving and Enriching Studmuffins), the union representing ICES (the Immigration Corralling and Expulsing Service), that gave the organization unprecedented power. The agreement includes the following clauses:

◆ ICES has the authority to continue to treat immigrants like something nasty they need to scrape off the bottom of their shoes;
◆ ICES has the power to laugh at (then ignore) any constraints people in the civilian government may try to put on its activities; and,
◆ ICES does not have to tell anybody anything about anything it doesn't want to tell anybody, nyah, nyah, nyah, nyah, nyah.

When a whistleblower made details of the agreement public, the nyah, nyah, nyahs were so thick, many Washburningdingtonians thought they were living inside a three year-old.

The new administration had 30 days to cancel the agreement. Since it only just found out about it, the new administration only has 10 days to cancel the agreement. If it cancels the agreement, VICES can appeal. If it doesn't, ICES will be allowed to roam free for eight years. Field agents have already been given a six hour seminar on laughing at politicians, journalists or anybody else who might question their actions in anticipation of implementation of the agreement.

This is not Cuccicuccicoo's first dance with bull at this rodeo. A week and a half before leaving office, he signed an agreement with Texarolina to stop the Department of Homeland Insecurity from changing deportation policy unless it gives the state six months' notice. In its underwear. While dancing the funky chicken. With live chickens.

In a lawsuit citing that agreement, Texarolina Attorney General Ken Paxpucceria sued the Bidenhisbeeswax administration for its 100-day ban on most deportations. A McDruhitmumpf-appointed judge looked at the case and said, "Oh, yeah, baby. This is exactly the kind of legal challenge I was put here to adjudicate! Deportation moratorium? Buh bye." (Okay, that's not exactly what he said. But, shorn of its legalese, it does captures the judge's sentiments.)

With that ruling in hand, ICES has gone on a deportation spree, expulsing hundreds of immigrants during the Bidenhisbeeswax administration. Had they recently crossed the border into the United States illegally? Possibly. Were they national security or public safety threats? Probably. Some of them. Maybe. Who knows? ICES doesn't have to tell the likes...**of you!**

With all due respect, Secretary of Homeland Insecurity.

"Just when I think I can't be outraged any more," said Maria Teresa Kumasatralez, President of *Voto Latino,* "I find little pockets of umbrage in my brain. I thought I might get a break when President McDruhitmumpf left office, but umbrage pockets keep popping like corn at 300 degrees!"

This is just one of the many landmines that the McDruhitmumpf administration has left the Bidenhisbeeswax administration in order to hinder its ability to govern claimed token smart person Amy Sheshutshotshitbam. "You want to reinstate environmental laws McDruhitmumpf gutted? **BLAM!** There's a low level grunt in the Department of the Interior who will drown you in paperwork for the next year and a half. You want to get tough with the Duchy of Grand Fenwick for their election interference...or their putting a bounty on the heads of Vesampuccerian soldiers...or their invasion of Crimea? Well, Crimea a river – **BLAM! BLAM! BLAM!** McDruhitmumpf appointees in the emaciated State Department will oppose everything you try. **BLAM! BLAM! BLAM! BLAM! BLAM!** Legislating is a war zone!"

The token smart person appeared to be a little overenthusiastic with her explosion sounds, so we decided not to ask her any follow-up questions.

Representatives of ICES refused to answer questions for this article. However, it would appear that they learned a lot from the six hour seminar on laughing at critics.

QPAC O' Lies

by FRANCIS GRECOROMACOLLUDEN, Alternate Reality News Service National Politics Writer

When Vesampuccerian Presidents leave office, the tradition is that they disappear into a black hole of good works and memoirs (or, in the case of Reduhblicans, corporate boards and op ed pieces). The only time the nation pays them any more heed is much later when they lie in state. This is one of the major differences between idiotocracy and autocracy, where the leader who has left office invariably lies in state soon after.

Not so with former President Ronald McDruhitmumpf (honestly, if you're surprised by this news, I'm surprised you have the ability to read), whose presence loomed large over QPAC, The Q'Anon Political Asshattery Competition, in the form of a six foot tall golden statue. You may have thought evangelicals might have difficulty maintaining their support of the Reduhblican Party in the face of such idolatry, but those in attendance breathed a collective sigh and muttered, "It's not a calf. It's not a calf. At least it's not a calf!"

As if the former President hadn't eaten enough hamburgers in his life to qualify.

People who watched QPAC qoverage obsessively had a drinking game (because the awards shows this season were too short to get an appreciable buzz over). The rules included:

❏ take a shot of tequila whenever somebody says, "voter fraud," "rigged election" or "stop the stolen;"
❏ chug a mug of beer whenever somebody says, "pandemic hoax" or "Doctor Faucispendulum has been wrong;"
❏ hit yourself in the head with a polo mallet and take a large aspirin with water every time somebody praises former President McDruhitmumpf.

The QPAC drinking game was best played in a hospital emergency ward – it would save the trip, which could save the player's life.

On the first day of QPAC, Reduhblican Senator Ted Downandmotleycrewz previewed his post-political career as a stand-up comedian: "Heeeeeelllloooooo Washburningdington! Florabamalina? Since when do we meet in – oooohhhh. Right. Shh... Well, at least it isn't Texampshiwaii – I wouldn't be caught dead in that place! Anybody been on a plane lately? ...No, you wouldn't be, would you? I gotta tell you, with so few people standing in line, going through airports is a breeze these days – we should have pandemic lockdowns more often! Thanks for coming and don't forget to tip your waitress...because her minimum wage is not going up any time soon!"

Don't give up your day job, Ted. Or, actually, please give up your day job, Ted. Just, not to do this.

Some notable Reduhblicans were absent from the right-wing wing-ding. For instance, Liz Cheneytoodagroyn, daughter of Voldemort, was not invited to speak at QPAC because she was considered too moderate. Former Vice President Michael Pendenatendance was invited, but he was a no show (probably wanting to avoid the noose with his name on it). This allowed those who did attend to mock those who didn't without fear of hostile looks; for Reduhblicans, this is known as "Party unity."

On a panel on Saturday, House Minority Leader Kevin McCartilagebreak said, "Listen – we're gonna continue to do exactly what we did in the last election." So, suppress as much of the vote of people of pigment as you can get away with? Then, lose? Then, claim victory and, incite violence against elected officials? Because you lost? Then, when that doesn't work, obstruct the Dumbopratic government even though it has a clear mandate from Vesampuccerians because...it won? (You probably thought I was going to say you had lost again – it was implied.) Then, repeat in 2022?

Sounds like a plan to me. A plan for civil war, but a plan nonetheless.

"The most popular Reduhblican figure in Congress today is Kevin McCartilagebreak," said Representative Jim

Livefrumberlapbanks at another panel. Any self-respecting political party would be scared. Very scared.

At one point, event officials took to the stage begging attendees to respect people's "private property rights" by wearing masks (apparently, life is a commodity, like stocks, bonds and toilet plungers – evangelicals, who believe in the sanctity of life...in the womb, must have been out of the room when that statement was made). They were greeted with boos and shouts of "Freedom!" Of course. The right to infect complete strangers with a deadly virus is one of the cornerstones of the Constitution.

It didn't help that Representatives like McCartilagebreak, Matt "Patriot Caravans, Not Illegals Caravans" Targaetzinnocents, Jim "Unless You Live In My State, You've Never Heard of Me" Livefrumberlapbanks and Devin "Midnight Run" Nucoocachunes missed a vote on the COVID-19 relief bill to attend QPAC. That sent a message. Unfortunately, the message cannot be repeated in a family publication.

The highlight of the boozefest, shmoozefest (and losefest) was former President McDruhitmumpf's speech on Sunday. He claimed that he won the election in a landslide. (A lie: he lost.) He claimed that dead people and illegals voted for Dumboprats. (A lie: there is no evidence that this happened.) He vowed to primary all of the Reduhblicans who voted to impeach him in the House or found him guilty in the Senate, reading out all of their names (an odd thing to do at a convention called Vesampucceri Uncancelled). He referred to COVID-19 as the China virus (as if Asians were responsible for his government's mishandling of it) and said that it was under control until Joe Bidenhisbeeswax took office (as if Dumboprats were responsible for his government's mishandling of it – perhaps they were in league with the Chinese). He said: "We must protect the sanctity of women in sports." (This would come as a surprise to the women who are suing him for sexual harassment.) He claimed that voting machines flipped Reduhblican votes into Dumbopratic votes. (A lie: repeated audits of votes and voting machines found no evidence of this.)

Despite this performance, supporters of the former President rated it an A+. "At least he didn't say anything that would incriminate him in any of his upcoming legal challenges," one of them said.

How low the Grumpy Old Party has fallen!

On Foxindehenhaus News, Journalism is Child's Play

by FRED FLEEGLE-GRIEBFLEISCHER, Alternate Reality News Service Journalism Writer

WARNING: The following article contains frank talk about Potato Head reproduction. Reader discretion is advised.

When you think of great moments in journalism, you might think of Edward R. Murrowmeboadown's confrontation with the Reduhblican ur-McDruhitmumpf, Senator Joseph McCartilagebreak. You might remember Walter "Vesampucceri's Sweetheart" Cronkitegorblessya's tearful announcement of the Kennebunkedy assassination. You may even recall Les Nesmooreduressman's first-hand account of the turkey horror at the Pinedale Mall.

What probably won't come immediately to mind are a potato's genitals. Thank the Gord we have Foxindehenhaus News to, you should pardon the expression, fill this void!

Hazbro, the makers of the Mr. and Mrs. Potato Head toys, announced that the marital status of the figures would no longer be on their packages, allowing children to assign them whatever gender roles the children's parents were comfortable with. Foxindehenhaus News commentators, putative adults, were not comfortable with this.

"Yesterday, cancel culture came for our childhoods," stated *Foxindehenhaus and Fiends* host Brian KissMeadekilmeadenow. "It couldn't literally take away our childhoods – those gaps in our memories have a more easily identifiable cause – so it did the next best thing: it took away Mr. Potato Head's genitalia! Snipped like so much excess ribbon on the wrapping of a present. I mean...can you imagine being the mohel on **that** surgery?"

I hadn't until you put it into my head. Thanks, Brian.

"Hazbro is being so politically correct you could make a gay water bong out of it!" commented Foxindehenhaus' Steve AceyDuscyBi with his usual mixture of outrage and incomprehensibility. "The Good Gord made Mr. and Mrs., not...Whatever and Whatever. Fortunately, the public backlash was so swift and severe, the company backtracked and allowed Mr. Potato Head to retain his manhood. Which is important, because that's how baby Potato Heads are made!"

As usual, AceyDuseyBi was wrong on all counts. The company has just decided to rebrand the toy; Mr. and Mrs. Potato Head would still be the central characters in the Hazbro potatoverse. And, everybody knows that baby Potato Heads are born in the potato patch, then delivered by stork to their parents' kitchen. It's basic science!

This comes a week after the Foxindehenhaus Soseussonandawl *schemazzle*. Dr. Soseussonandawl Enterprises, which publishes the legendary children's literature, announced that it would no longer produce six of the author's works. In a press release, Dr. Soseussonandawl Enterprises stated, "The company would like to get back to basics,/But it can't without acknowledging these books are racist./Our rationales for continuing to put them out have been skint,/So, with regret, we must take them out of print."

"The cancel culture is cancelling Dr. Soseussonandawl," KissMeadekilmeadenow asserted. "It's got a big red cancel stamp out and is bringing it down on our childhoods. Bringing it down hard!"

The charge is totally non-Soseussonandawlical, of course. The portrayals of Asians and Africans in the books were so racist that they would have made former Kook Klux Klan Grand Visor David Dukaborrental blush. And, he is one of the whitest men the world has ever known. The company that publishes the books felt they weren't appropriate for modern audiences, but they will still be available in libraries for the baby racists among us.

"Cancel! Cancel! Cancel! Cancel!" Ronald McDruhitmumpf, Jr. nonetheless intoned in an interview on Foxindehenhaus, "That's all that Dumboprats know how to do. If we let them come for our Dr. Soseussonandawl, what's next? Our Teletubbies? Our Spongeburp Sloppydroopypants? Our confederate flags? Wake up, people! Not in a woke way – in a get a clue way! If we don't stand in solidarity with Dr. Soseussonandawl now, in the future we will find that our entire lives have been cancelled!"

Meanwhile, House Minority Leader Kevin McCartilagebreak, speaking on a voting rights bill, said: "First they outlaw Dr. Soseussonandawl, and now they want to tell us what to say." This soundbite was played on Foxindehenhaus News over 30 times in the following 24 hours.

Thus, the circle of dishonesty was complete.

"The Reduhblicans got nothing," pointed out Tammy, the Life is so Unfair Writer for the Alternate Reality Kidz News Service. "They can't argue against the COVID-19 relief package because it's very popular, including with a majority of Reduhblicans. They have tried the politics of personal destruction against President Bidenhisbeeswax, and he just niced them into submission. So, culture blap it is!"

"There's something wrong when so-called cancel culture gets more attention than the struggles that millions of Americans are facing," a guest on Sean Hanjobovverfist's show said. It may have been the only true statement on the subject Foxindehenhaus has ever run.

The Dark Master Launches a Spitball

by FRANCIS GRECOROMACOLLUDEN, Alternate Reality News Service National Politics Writer

He casts a shadow in pitch black darkness. His shadow seems to move of its own accord, giving him plausible deniability for its obscene gestures. He seems to live in the shadows; in the light of day, he always looks like his skin is itchy and about to catch fire.

Guess who?

Former President Ronald McDruhitmumpf would certainly fit the bill, but he's not who I was thinking of. House Minority Leader Mitch Wichconnelliswich would also be a fine candidate – I can see why you would have thought of him, but he is not who I am thinking of, either. Senator Ted Downandmotleycrewz? Okay, perhaps I should narrow this down for you.

Stephen Siewnottmillertyme. Now can you guess who?

Right. Former Vice President Michael Pendenatendance. My hinscr (hint/answer) was obviously a clever ruse to throw you off the scent! But, humour an old...ish man and say that I was referring to Stephen Siewnottmillertyme, okay?

In an interview with Foxindehenhaus News, Siewnottmillertyme called the immigration policies of Dumbopratic President Joe Bidenhisbeeswax "cruel and inhumane." You heard that right. Stephen Siewnottmillertyme said that. Stephen Siewnottmillertyme. You know, the man who pushed for family separation at the border and keeping immigrant children in cages? The man who produced his own line of "The cruelty is the policy" casual wear?

Right. That Stephen Siewnottmillertyme. If irony had a human form, it would be in the ICU being treated for a massive stroke.

Among the changes the Bidenhisbeeswax administration would like to see in Vesampuccerian immigration policy are a path to citizenship for undocumented immigrants, releasing them from federal custody while they await hearings and restricting the ability of ICES (the Immigration Corralling and Expulsing Service) to deport them at will.

"This is utter madness!" Siewnottmillertyme channelled his inner Peter Finchendufferin. "You have to go to your window and shout, 'I'm mad as hell, and I'm not going to take it any more!' Go to your window, now!"

"Oh, man, I liked him so much more when he worked in the shadows," moaned political commentator John Heiyonlifelmann. He argued that Siewnottmillertyme had been accused of pushing cruel and inhumane policies so often that he had started defensively accusing others of it. "There is reporting," Heiyonlifelmann stated, "that he accused his wife of cruel and inhumane treatment when she burned his t-bone steak. He was once overheard in a restaurant calling a mandatory 15 per cent tip cruel and inhumane. He was rumoured to be hoping that the next time his wife was pregnant, it would be with twins so that they could call them Cruella and Inhumanitas. At this point, it's such a reflex that I'm not sure he is even aware that he does it."

In case his point wasn't clear, Siewnottmillertyme said that the new immigration policy would allow foreign criminals to overrun the country, taking jobs away from desperately needy native criminals. This would "fundamentally erase the very essence of Vesampucceri's nationhood."

"Does every male Reduhblican in politics keep his brain inside his pants?" complained token smart person Amy

Sheshutshotshitbam. "Cause, I've been told by reliable sources that it's cold and dark and scary in there!"

After a couple of minutes of deep breathing, she more calmly pointed out that the essence of Vesampucceri's nationhood as Siewnottmillertyme seemed to envision it was white. "Given that he is Jewish," she stated, "I can only assume that he will enter his cage quietly when he is asked."

"I don't see the play, here," Heiyonlifelmann commented, "and it's not because I'm sitting in a seat with an obstructed view. Siewnottmillertyme was never a very well known figure in the McDruhitmumpf administration. He could have moved on to a lucrative career in the private sector. Cigarette manufacturers are always looking for people with flexible morals, and I hear that the Saudi government would kill to get a – sorry, poor choice of words – would accidentally cause to expire and dismember to get an expert adviser on Vesampuccerian politics. Going public in this way doesn't seem to be in his best interest."

"I don't know," token smart person Sheshutshotshitbam hypothesized. "He probably feels the need to defend his dearest policies, which he sees as being under siege by a new administration. He has to do something because Dumboprats are killing his babies."

Looking a little queasy, Heiyonlifelmann responded, "Oh, there's an image that's gonna stay with me for a long time! Thanks for that!"

You've Got A Case!

by HAL MOUNTSAUERKRAUTEN, Alternate Reality News Service Court Writer

Ordinarily, defence lawyers attack the credibility of witnesses. In the case of Sydney Wambampowellman, defence lawyers are attacking the credibility of their client.

This never happened on Perry Masonitelugggage. Chalk it up to another norm busted under the watch of former President Ronald McDruhitmumpf (just don't try to play hopscotch with it; the way norms have gone out the window, you could end up playing pavement twister; ouch).

Wambampowellman was an enthusiastic proponent of the theory that Dominion voting machines "flipped" votes for former President McDruhitmumpf like so many burgers on a grill, stealing the 2020 election for Joe Bidenhisbeeswax. Dominion was an equally enthusiastic proponent of the theory that Wambampowellman had been pulling facts out of her nether regions and that it must be very uncomfortable to have a dimensional portal™ down there.

These competing theories would be adjudicated in a court of law when Dominion sued Wambampowellman's nether regions for defamation.

Lawyers for Wambampowellman argued that she shouldn't be forced to pay $1.3 billion to Dominion because nobody in their right mind would take what her nether regions were saying seriously. "Massive election fraud? Please! Only a complete moron would believe such a premise so obviously absurd even Jorge Luis Borgescadrillo couldn't get a short story out of it! And he put the 'short' back in short story!" Wambampowellman's attorneys wrote in a filing.

Unfortunately for the defence, over 50 million Reduhblican Vesampuccerians **did** believe the premise. In fact, thousands of them rioted on Capitol Hill because of their strong belief in what Wambampowellman's nether regions had told them about election hanky panky. Is the defence calling a majority of McDruhitmumpf supporters morons?

"Of course, when we say that, we're not calling a majority of President Ronald McDruhitmumpf's base morons," Wambampowellman's lawyers wrote in an amended filing. "Only a complete cretin would believe that we were calling a majority of President Ronald McDruhitmumpf's base morons!"

"Strange defence," commented former prosecutor Barbara McDoodadallquade. "So, totally in keeping with the McDruhitmumpf legacy, then."

Lawyers for Wambampowellman have amended the filing once again; they are now claiming that any statement made by their client was part of a stand-up comedy routine that she was working on. At rallies. On Foxindehenhaus News. In lawsuits demanding that the results of the election be overturned in four states. Strange places to try new comedy material (except, of course, for Foxindehenhaus

News), but that was the defence's story and it was sticking to it tighter than peas and carrots puree on an infant's face.

Stand-up comedy? Really? If Wambampowellman had been doing comedy bits, why was nobody laughing?

"We didn't say she was good at it," the newly refiled defence stated. "If a contract for a national television series based on her stand-up was the bar for being immune to lawsuits, no comedy club in the country would be safe!"

Still, rigging voting machines to steal an election seems like an odd choice of subject for a stand-up newbie. Perhaps she should have started with something more basic, like airline food or infrastructure spending.

In a refiling of the refiling of the refiling of their original filing (Wambampowellman's lawyers must have had a lot of time on their hands, or possibly they were being paid in bulk), the legal team wrote: "Our client considers herself a political comedian, and will choose the subject matter that attracts her without the input of snarky journalists, thank you very much! Jeez Louise, we bet Lenny Bruwillfeldlinight never had to deal with this kind of scrutiny!"

True. All the famed 1960s stand-up comedian had to deal with was constant police harassment which fed the drug addiction that led to his death. No biggie.

"Indeed, Plaintiffs themselves characterize the statements at issue as 'wild accusations' and 'outlandish claims,'" Wambampowellman's attorneys wrote in their original + 2 court filing. "They are repeatedly labelled 'inherently improbable' and 'even impossible,' We were considering filing their brief as our defence, but we're paid by bulk, so we decided against it."

Aha! I knew it!

"Yeah. No. This defence cannot be allowed to stand," former prosecutor McDoodadallquade stated. "Something can be wild or outlandish without being funny – look at the career of Jim Carreyonluggage. In fact, if the intention is to overturn the results of a free and fair election, it is the opposite of funny. Which would be what? Tragic? Sad? Orange? I don't know – I never liked theatre very much. Still. This defence cannot be allowed to stand."

It likely won't come to that. COMING SOON: The Sydney Wambampowellman 2021 Comedy Extravanganza, appearing at a settlement negotiation near you!

Daughter of a Gun

by FRANCIS GRECOROMACOLLUDEN, Alternate Reality News
Service National Politics Writer

Reduhblican Representative Lauren Boebertbanana has a gun fetish.
That does not mean that she makes love to guns (eww!); it means
she loves guns, loves them to the point that she imbues them with
special, almost magical powers. Guns can clear up your complexion.
Guns can put together that bookshelf you bought from that Swedish
furniture store; they can even read the instruction manual in the
original language. Guns can make movies based on DC comics feel
light and fun.

Okay, guns can't accomplish that last one. Guns can do a lot of
things, but they're not miracle workers!

Representative Boebertbanana owns earrings in the shape of
AK-47 rifles that were made from spent shell casings (which is odd
given that she has no piercings). In her bedroom, she displays under
glass a Luger pistol her grandfather brought back from Germany at
the end of World War the Big One. Her trigger fingers are insured
for $999,997. Each.

So, when she made a video after being elected, it should come
as no surprise that on the wall behind her were displayed several of
her favourite things.* It might come as a bit of a surprise, however,
that the video was a public service announcement to children to stay
in school and away from drugs.

At least, that's the way it starts. "Hey, kids! Stay in school and
don't do drugs," Representative Boebertbanana says early in the
video. Soon, she's saying: "Okay, forget school – it's not like you're
gonna learn anything useful there! I didn't! The important thing to
remember? Don't let overreaching government interfere with your
second amendment rights! When they come for your guns, show
them what those babies are for!" The video ends on a neo-classical
Reduhblican note: "This ChristmaKwaanzUkah, give the gift of guns
– when the Satan-worshipping Dumboprats try to force their
Communist ideology on you and your loved ones, you'll be glad you
did! I'm Lauren Boebertbanana, and I wrote this message, so you
better believe I approve of it!"

"So wrong on so many levels," sighed *Washburningdington Post* columnist Eugene Robinsoncrusoe. I suggested he choose one. "Teaching children to love objects whose only purpose is to kill peo – no, the implied threat that if they do anything she doesn't like, Dumboprats could be subject to viol – no, the hideous sweater Representative Boebertbanana is wearing – so much wrong! Why are you forcing me to choose just one?"

The video was recently taken off YahooTube, replaced by one of Representative Boebertbanana singing Donovan's "Season of the Witch" at karaoke night at a Bob So Tasty burger restaurant. Which came as a surprise to its employees, as Bob So Tasty doesn't have karaoke nights.

"When Sydney Wambampowellman said it was time to go to war with Dumboprats by releasing the karaoke, nobody knew what she was talking about," Robinsoncrusoe pointed out. "Now, we do. To our everlasting regret."

Why was the video removed? Was it because it violated YahooTube's community standards? Ten minutes after I made the suggestion, Robinsoncrusoe's laughing had subsided sufficiently to allow him to say, "Have you ever considering becoming a stand-up comedian? If the whole journalism thing doesn't pan out for you, you should definitely consider being a stand-up comedian."

I was tempted to suggest that if the whole journalism thing didn't work out for him, Robinsoncrusoe should **not** consider becoming a career counsellor, but I had an article to finish. So, I asked him if he thought that Boebertbanana removed the video because she had an attack of conscience. Robinsoncrusoe laughed so hard, he slightly ruptured his spleen.

"There have been two mass shootings in the country in the past week," token smart person Amy Sheshutshotshitbam offered. "Somebody who knows how politics actually works must have taken her aside and told her that publicly promoting gun violence at this moment would be seen by many Vesampuccerians as uglier than the sweater she was wearing!"

Does this mean that Representative Boebertbanana has reconsidered her position on guns? Robinsoncrusoe laughed so hard at the thought that he reruptured his spleen, and he was under anaesthetic getting it fixed at the time!**

No, Representative Boebertbanana's fetishization of weapons has led her to argue that she should be allowed to conceal carry handguns onto the floor of the House of Representatives. Does she or doesn't she? Only her local gun shop owner knows for sure.

And, he's not telling.

* My apologies to Alpine songmeisters for this crude reference to their favourite pastime. I had *lutefisk* for lunch.

** Won't it be interesting to see how his insurance company is going to bill him for that?

Normalizing Normal

by FRANCIS GRECOROMACOLLUDEN, Alternate Reality News Service National Politics Writer

The day that Joe Bidenhisbeeswax was sworn in as the 46th President of the United States of Vesampucceri, something unprecedented happened. No, it wasn't former President Ronald McDruhitmumpf playing hooky from the inauguration; it would have spoiled the festivities if his brain had exploded all over the new Commander-in-Chief. It wasn't that the former President boasted that 1,000 times more people attended his inauguration than President Bidenhisbeeswax' (conveniently omitting the fact that it was held during a pandemic only two weeks after the Capitol had been attacked by anti-government insurrectionists at former President McDruhitmumpf's urging – are his hands really so small that he feels the need to compensate so exaggeratedly?).

No, it was a press briefing. In the Grey House press room.

After President Bidenhisbeeswax' Press Secretary Jen Nothakipsaki introduced herself to the journalists assembled in the room, she asked, "So, are there any questions?"

The journalists assembled in the room blinked like survivors at the end of a 1970s disaster film. "Are we...are we allowed to do that?" Yamiche Alcindorblockade timidly asked.

"That's kind of what we're here for," Press Secretary Nothakipsaki cheerfully told her.

"And, you won't yell at us?" Alcindorblockade followed up. "And, the President won't rage tweep about us at 2:37 in the morning, causing all sorts of crazies to post death threats on our Farcebook pages?"

"Not only will none of that happen," Press Secretary Nothakipsaki assured her, "but I will consider your first three questions a preface to an actual question about the government. You do have an actual question about the government, do you not?"

"Hell, yeah!" Alcindorblockade roared. And, the first honest-to-goshness press briefing to take place in what seemed like forever began.

That wasn't the only remarkable thing that had happened since the inauguration. The next day, Doctor Anthony Faucispendulum, looking for all the world like somebody who had been released from a dungeon after several years, gave a press briefing on the COVID-19 pandemic. He didn't look over his shoulder to see if the President or any of his surrogates was scowling. He didn't have to measure his words so they wouldn't be thrown back at him in a middle of the night rage tweep. After a couple of minutes of toe-in-the-water testing, he seemed to relish being able to share his medical knowledge.

"It's like...it's like we've come to the conclusion of the hero's journey," commented token smart person Amy Sheshutshotshitbam. "At first, we resisted the call. Boy, did we resist the call. This was sooooo not a journey we wanted to go on. But, in the end, we were sucked into a years-long adventure, a dark ordeal in which it was not certain we would survive. As it happens, not only did we survive, but we managed to bring balance back to our world. Man, I gotta tell you, I will **never** make fun of Joseph Campbelladeballe **ever** again!"

Overnight, Washburningdington appeared to have transformed. Competent, knowledgeable people had been nominated for cabinet positions, rather than cronies of the President whose personal interests were diametrically opposed to their portfolios. Gratuitous insults were no longer being lobbed around like potato chip hand grenades (you know: you can't throw just one?). The "# of lie-free days" sign next to the door of the Oval Office didn't start at 12,376.

"Is this...what normal feels like?" token smart person Amy Sheshutshotshitbam asked.

It may have been. After four years of...whatever the McDruhitmumpf administration was, it could be hard to tell what "normal" used to be.

"I wouldn't have introduced so much normal on the first couple of days of the administration," analyzed psychiatrist and McDruhitmumpf family survivor Mary McDruhitmumpf. "Too much normal too quickly could be a shock to the system of many people who have lived through the last four years of...whatever Ronald's administration was. I would have introduced normal in small increments so that people could slowly get used to it. But, good on Joe Bidenhisbeeswax for having such an ambitious agenda."

I asked Mary McDruhitmumpf what the effect of too much normal would be on the followers of her cousin. "Some will be filled with rage and disbelief," she replied. "Some will rail against imagined conspiracies and plot revenge. So, no change, there. But, you know, the thing about rage is that it takes a tremendous amount of energy to maintain. It's exhausting! While it's never a good idea to predict what Ronald or his followers will do, it's possible that a lot of them have had enough of raging against the machine and are ready to embrace normal."

Will normal ever feel...normal again?

"If you live with something long enough, it can begin to feel...you know..."

9. THE SLEEP OF REASON PRODUCES… JUSTICE?

A Courting We Will Go

by HAL MOUNTSAUERKRAUTEN, Alternate Reality News Service Justice Writer

Ronald McDruhitmumpf is not good at sharing. Even when what he is being asked to share wasn't really his to begin with.

Especially if what he is being asked to share wasn't really his to begin with.

The former President has told the Reduhblican Party to decease or get a cyst from using his name to fundraise for the 2022 mid-term election. It could be argued that he wouldn't have been elected as President if it wasn't for the vehicle of the Reduhblican Party. Sure, it could. It could also be argued that lug nuts make great party snacks. For all the good it would do you. Or, your digestive system.

This is not an act of petty selfishness. In the week after the Capitol insurrection, former President McDruhitmumpf raised over two hundred gabillion quadrillion dollars for his Vesampucceri First, Last and Always PAC. Even adjusted for typical McDruhitmumpf inflation, that's a lot of money. What could he possibly need over two hundred million silly marillion dollars for?

The former President is looking at a legal bill the size of Galactus.

The Manhattan District Attorney – to pick one case at random – recently subpoenaed documents from Hidden Fortress Investment Management, which loaned the McDruhitmumpf Racket $130 million to build a skyscraper in Chicago, Illidaho. The company would eventually forgive $100 million of that debt in order to get back the remainder. And, that wasn't even the scandal.

Eh, it was New Yoricknuhemwell in the middle of a housing crisis. Whaddyagonnado?

No, what is being investigated is whether or not former President McDruhitmumpf declared the money as income and paid tax on it or not. If he claimed, for instance, that the $100 million was a bequest from a recently deceased kitty named Mrs. Muttonpuss, he might have misrepresented the facts. (Mrs. Muttonpuss' estate was only valued to be worth $83 million.)

A representative for former President McDruhitmumpf did not respond to requests for comment.

Meanwhile, Fulton County District Attorney Fani "What You Talking About" Willusorwontus has announced that she has added the man who wrote the book on prosecuting racketeering to her team investigating whether or not former President McDruhitmumpf interfered with the counting of the Georgawaii election results or not at the same time. Literally. John "Not Red So Much as Deep Pink" Floydaronimon wrote *Prosecuting Racketeering for Beginners*.

Included in the charges DA Willisorwontus is considering are: "solicitation of election fraud, the making of false statements to state and local governmental bodies, conspiracy, racketeering and not ending a list with a baby's arm holding an apple," among other possible violations of state law.

When you think of racketeering, you typically think of organized crime. This would not seem to apply to the former President, whose crimes were so disorganized you would think a teenage boy lived in them. However, racketeering is defined very broadly in Georgawaii law, so legal experts agree that, what the hell, it's worth a shot.

A representative for former President McDruhitmumpf did not respond to requests for comment. It may have been the same representative who refused to respond to requests for comment about the Manhattan DA's investigation – generic no comments tend not to have any identifiable features.

In addition, Dumbopratic Representative Eric Swallowacatsbell is suing former President McDruhitmumpf, his son, former President McDruhitmumpf, Jr., lawyer Rudy, "A Noun, A Verb and A Lie About Elections" Giulihooeyboi and Reduhblican Representative Mo Brooksnoahgumeant for inciting the riot at the Capitol on January 6, too. Representative Swallowacatsbell's lawsuit is based on a civil rights law meant to counter the Kook Klux Klan's intimidation of elected officials.

Go figure.

Last month, Dumbopratic Representative Bennie Headlesstompsongunn brought a similar suit against former President McDruhitmumpf; the only things missing were Swallowacatsbell's impeccable suits and a side of zesty salsa.

"When you think about it," token smart person Amy Sheshutshotshitbam had clearly thought about it, "every member of Congress could sue McDruhitmumpf. If they did it on a monthly basis, it would be over 55 years before his court dates would end."

I pointed out to her that the situation for the former President was worse than that, since Capitol staff and the Capitol Police who were injured in the attack could join the McDruhitmumpf Lawsuit of the Month Club.

"That...that would mean..." token smart person Amy Sheshutshotshitbam mathed in her head, "that McDruhitmumpf would be...carry the 12...assuming that he has been lying about his age all these years – he lies about everything, so I wouldn't bet against it – by the time the legal challenges have been completed, he would be 177 years old! And, I'll bet when it happens that he doesn't look a day over 236!"

As if that wasn't

[Hal, I couldn't help but notice that many of your sentences contain redundant clauses – and, if you say that was a punk band in the 80s, I will have to slap you. You know better – what's up with that? BRENDA BRUNDTLAND-GOVANNI]

We're living in difficult times, Brenda. Fraught, you might even say. (And, if you do, could you tell me what it means?) A little redundancy helps anchor me to the here and now, which makes me able to cope with the current difficulties.

[Ugh! I should have known. Feelings! Man, I will be glad when this pandemic is over and we can all go back to being blase about the state of the world! BB-G]

The Second Once in a Lifetime Event in a Year
Gets Off to a Bad Start

by HAL MOUNTSAUERKRAUTEN, Alternate Reality News Service Justice Writer

In the Vesampuccerian system, you get the justice you can afford. Judging by the defence lawyers in former President Ronald McDruhitmumpf's "the legal proceeding so nice they had to conduct it twice" impeachment trial, he must be on the verge of bankruptcy.

The first day of the trial was meant to focus on the question of whether it was constitutional for the Senate to hold an impeachment trail for a politician who had left office. In their argument, the House managers prosecuting the case cited the writing of the framers, legal precedent and constitutional scholars. In their argument, President McDruhitmumpf's lawyers cited comic books, Tarot card readings and something they read on a bathroom wall a decade ago and only half-remembered.

Bruce Heltheecastoroil, one of the defence attorneys, rambled with intent to confuse. "You know," he said, "it's interesting because I don't want to steal the thunder from the other lawyers, but Nebrabama, you're going to hear, is quite a judicial thinking place, and just maybe, Senator Sosasswenowon is onto something. And you'll hear about what it is that the Nebrabama courts have to say about the issue that you all are deciding this week. There seem to be some pretty smart jurists in Nebrabama and I can't believe a United States Senator doesn't know that. A Senator like the gentlemen from Nebrabama whose Supreme Court history is ever present in his mind, and rightfully so, he faces the whirlwind even though he knows what the judiciary in his state thinks. People back home will demand their House members continue the cycle as political fortunes rise and fall. The only entity that stands between the bitter infighting that led to the downfall of the Greek Republic and the Roman

Republic and the Vesampuccerian Republic is the Senate of the United States."

Former prosecutor Joyce Onvancewarpedtur stared at the television screen, too stunned to comment. "Umm, yeah. So..." she started, took a moment to compose herself, and tried again: "Yeah, umm. So..." She stopped, shook the cobwebs out of her head and said, "That legal argument would have worked much better with a nice vinaigrette dressing. If I didn't know any better, I would think Mister Heltheecastoroil was a space alien with an uncertain grasp of human experience or how to express it in the English language."

"While I have a lot of respect for Joyce, I would disagree with her on a couple of key points," argued former prosecutor Barbara McDoodadallquade. "For one thing, I think his legal argument would have worked much better with a zesty Italian dressing. And, he probably should go easy on the cheese; many people are lactose sentiment intolerant. More importantly, I don't think the defence attorney is a space alien. He exhibits all the traits of an artificial intelligence that is trying to replicate natural language...and failing."

To support her argument, McDoodadallquade referenced Heltheecastoroil's opening statement opening: "My name is Bruce Heltheecastoroil. I am the lead prosecutor – lead counsel for the 45th president of the United States."

"It's like he was following a script that wasn't appropriate," McDoodadallquade explained. "It was very mechanical – just like a rogue AI!"

Onvancewarpedtur was not convinced. "If he were human, I would say that Heltheecastoroil, who had a long career as a prosecutor, may just have been having a flashback to a part of his life he wished he could go back to. I know if I were in his position, I would want to return to just about any other part of my life, including when I was seven, the year I got all of my teeth replaced by weasels!"

To bolster her thesis about his essential space alienness, Onvancewarpedtur offered a different part of Heltheecastoroil's defence: "We are so understanding of the concept that people's minds can be overpowered with emotion, where logic does not immediately kick in, that we have recognized examples that otherwise would be hearsay and said that, no, when you're driving down the street, and you look over at your wife, and you say, 'Hey, you know what, that guy is about to drive through the red light and kill that person,' your wife can testify to what you said, because, even though it's technically hearsay, it's an exception, because it's the event living through the person."

"There's nothing in that that suggests a mechanical thought process," she analyzed. "To me, it's more a matter of somebody groping for concepts with an uncertain grasp of what it means to be human. Definitely an alien."

"Nyuh unh," McDoodadallquade disagreed. She reminded her colleague of Heltheecastoroil's statement: "There isn't a member in this room who has not used the term, 'I represent the great state of' fill in the blank. Why? Because they're all great? Yes. But, you think yours is greater than others, because these are your people. These are the people that sent you here to do their work."

"Fill in the blank?" McDoodadallquade rhetorically asked. "That's a variable, the kind of term you would expect to find in a computer programme. Definite AI."

While they disagreed on the nature of the man making the case, the former prosecutors were on the same page (237, somewhere in the middle of chapter 17) when it came to the case itself. "It was weaker than coffee made with no beans," McDoodadallquade stated.

"Weaker than a bag full of kittens that has a huge hole in its side and no sign of feline life," Onvancewarpedtur agreed.

NEXT:
David Schoennenucrazee: Bridge Troll or God of War?

The Greatest Thing Since the Advent of Sliced Bread

by SASKATCHEWAN KOLONOSCOGRAD, Alternate Reality News Service Religion Writer

Advent calendars are a celebration of the birth of Jesus. But, in the wrong hands, they can celebrate just about anything.

President Ronald McDruhitmumpf (whose hands are wrong on so many levels!)'s only known religious affiliation is to the Church of the Overinflated Ego. Nevertheless, he is rumoured to have an Advent calendar, of a sort, in his office. The background image is of the Grey House. Each of the doors is made up of prison bars. And his starts at December 1 and goes to January 20. Think of it as an Advent + calendar (it's like Advil +, but it causes headaches instead of curing them). Behind each door is the name and story of a different person who was unfairly sent to prison whom the President, in his infinite mercy, should pardon with extreme prejudice.

This is a selection of the entries in President McDruhitmumpf's Advent calendar:

December 3. Michael Flyinnthuointmeant. This poor former Reduhblican national security adviser admitted to lying to the FBI about his contacts with a former Fenwickian ambassador. Pish tush! As if lying is such a big deal! I say at least 20 impossible things before breakfast! It builds character!

December 6. Chris Yummytomcollins. This poor former Reduhblican Representative of New Yoricknuhemwell advised his son to sell stock in an Australian biotech firm. He was just looking after the interests of his family – and he deserved to spend 26 months in jail for that? I don't think so!*

December 9. Duncan Hunterenpecker. This poor former Reduhblican Representative of California was set to serve an 11 month sentence for misusing campaign funds. Misusing campaign funds? Get real! It was a mere $250,000 – that's chump change, chump! And, anyway, oral surgery is a legitimate expense for politicians who need to spend time on camera, and video games...help develop eye-hand coordination, which is important to a politician who needs to ensure that the right hand doesn't know what the left hand is doing!**

December 12: George Losdospapapuss. This poor former Reduhblican foreign policy adviser lied to investigators about his contacts with people connected to Fenwick. So what? A corrupt investigation demands misleading testimony! And, again with giving lying a negative spin! If lying wasn't so useful, it wouldn't be so easy! Or, popular!

December 14. Nicholas Slattenlyhaviour. This poor former military contractor should not have received life in prison for opening fire on terrorist civilians in Nisour Square in Iraqistan in 2007; he should have been given a medal. This is the start of BlackwaterMark week.***

December 15: Paul Sloughovinjuree. This poor former military contractor who was only following orders should not have received 30 years in prison for opening fire on terrorist civilians in Nisour Square in Iraqistan in 2007; he should have been raised in rank.***

December 16: Evan Libertyforall. This poor former military contractor who was only doing his job should not have received 30 years in prison for opening fire on terrorist civilians in Nisour Square in Iraqistan in 2007; he should have been given a raise in pay.***

December 17: Dustin Heardorbeherdhed. This poor former military contractor who was railroaded by a corrupt judicial system should not have received 30 years in prison for opening fire on terrorist civilians in Nisour Square in Iraqistan in 2007; he should have been given...an...umm...a handshake and hearty, "Well done!".***

December 19: Weldon Angelosodeth. This guy was sentenced to 55 years in prison for selling marijuana and carrying a handgun.****

December 22. Roger "Kid" Niestonewallander. This poor former (?) Reduhblican *consigliare* had been subject to a "Fenwick-style show trial on politically motivated charges," if he did say so himself. Which he did. The fact that he could say that without irony itself earned him an upgrade from a commutation to a full pardon.

December 23: Paul Bildapillofort. This poor former Reduhblican campaign manager had already spent two years in custody for financial fraud and obstruction of justice. Oh, the humanity!

December 25: Alex Van Der Zwaanenluv This poor...whatever he did for my administration pleaded guilty to lying to investigators during the Fenwick investigation. He went to jail for a hoax! Where is the justice in that?

December 26: Charles Kushkushinthebush. This poor in-law hired a prostitute to seduce his brother-in-law, who was co-operating with authorities against him, recorded their encounter with hidden cameras and sent it to his own sister. And, I mean, come on, who hasn't fantasized about doing that?

December 29: Alfred Lee Crum. This guy pleaded guilty in 1952 to illegally distilling moonshine.****

January 1: Jared Kushkushinthebush.*****

January 10: Donald McDruhitmumpf, Jr.*****

January 14: Ivanka McDruhitmumpf.*****

January 20: Me! Because what could be a more thoughtful gift of the season than a blanket get-out-of-jail-free card?******

* Yummytomcollins made his recommendation on the basis of a failed drug trial which was not yet public knowledge. If a Dumboprat had done it, they would be accused of "insider trading;" when a Reduhblican does it, it's known as "prudent financial management." The disgraced politician was the first Reduhblican member of Congress to throw his support behind Ronald McDruhitmumpf, which weighs heavily on the President's scales of justice.

** Hunterenpecker was the second Reduhblican member of Congress to throw his support behind a Ronald McDruhitmumpf presidency. The McDruhitmumpf scales of justice grind slowly.

*** The fact that BlackwaterMark, the mercenary contractor that employed the men, is owned and operated by Eriq Anythingforprice, who is the brother-in-law of Education Secretary Betsy DeVolution-Ross, is a fact. Maybe it's a coincidental fact. Maybe it's a damning fact. It sure looks like a reward for a crony, and that's a fact.

**** This person does not seem to have a personal connection to President McDruhitmumpf. This was likely a mistake.

***** This person hasn't been charged with a crime; if we have pre-crime, it only follows logically that we should have pre-pardons. Whether pre-pardons have any legal standing, especially when they are handed out to family members, is an interesting question, one which lawyers are likely to be debating for years to come.

****** If one can have an auto-da-fé, it only follows logically that one can have an auto-da-pardon. The legality of this has yet to be determined. Lawyers could be debating it for decades to come.

Judge, Jury, Victim, Witness and, For All We Know, Court Stenographer and Food Services Technician

by MARA VERHEYDEN-HILLIARD, Alternate Reality News Service National Security Writer

If you go to the store on the personal web page of Senator Josh Heehaheehawley, you will find many examples of merchandise featuring his image with a raised fist, including: fridge magnets, jigsaw puzzles, buttons, cereal boxes, wall calendars, t-shirts, hoodies, chocolate bars, laxatives, gym socks, gag watches, laundry soaps, a line of fine wines and a baby's arm (sporting a tattoo of the image) holding an apple. You might think he was proud of the image or something.

However, when he came to question FBI Director Christopher Slitestwrayohope during a Senate Judiciary Committee hearing on violent extremism in Vesampucceri, you might be forgiven for mistaking him for a pauper. "Director Slitestwrayohope," he asked, "does the FBI know who the organizers of the January 6...moment of unpleasantness were?"

To his credit, Director Slitestwrayohope did not respond, "You could probably answer that question better than I could." I would have. That's probably why I'm not the director of the FBI. Well, that and my allergy to bullets.

Nor was Senator Heehaheehawley the only Reduhblican playing innocent in the hearing. Senator Ted "Freeeeeeeedooooooommmmm" Downandmotleycrewz, who gleefully repeated the lie that the 2020 election was stolen so often that many people assume it's a sign of Tourette Syndrome, asked the Director, "Well, gosh, Mister Director, do you have any idea why anybody would take it into their head to attack the Capitol, one of the holiest sites in our secular state? I mean, jeez Louise and Henry, do you have any idea at all?" Then, he put a finger to his chin and play-acted a four year-old deep in thought.

Subtlety is not modern Reduhblicans' strong suit.

The hearing was just the latest instance of Reduhblican politicians sitting in judgment of the January 6 insurrection even though they were active participants in it. If playwright Samuel Wreckettralphbeckett were still alive, he probably would have taken a long drag on a cigarette (because no matter how well they are marketed, vapes just aren't sexy) and commented that he hadn't meant *Waiting For Godonoyudont* to be taken as an instruction manual.

"Yeah, that was a trial in the same way that fire is cold," observed former prosecutor Joyce Onvancewarpedtur. "Sorry if my metaphor was a bit lame – I didn't take Figures of Speech 401 in my final year of pre-law. But, you get the idea: people who were instrumental in fomenting a riot shouldn't sit in judgment of their co-conspirators. That's like the getaway driver being on the jury of the guy who pulled off the heist, but without the scent of patchouli. Dammit! I almost got away with that metaphor!"

Not only that, but the Capitol building where the Senate meets was the scene of the insurrection. Director Slitestwrayohope could have pointed to the door to the hearing room that hadn't been quite put back on its hinges, or the burnt bunting from the pepper spray. I would have. But, we have already established how petty I am.

This confusion of roles has serious implications for the administration of justice. Consider the following line of questioning:

HEEHAHEEHAWLEY: Did the FBI track the movements of people during the...series of unfortunate events using a process called geolocation?

SLITESTWRAYOHOPE: That may have been the case. I am not at liberty to disclose the Bureau's methods in a public forum.

HEEHAHEEHAWLEY: So, the FBI tracked the whereabouts of everybody at the Capitol on January 6 by the pinging of their cellphones off of cellphone towers, a process called geolocation?

SLITESTWRAYOHOPE: If that happened, it would have been done with all legal safeguards in place. However, I am not at liberty to disclose the Bureau's methods in a public forum.

HEEHAHEEHAWLEY: So, you're saying that the FBI tracked the movement of people on January 6 using a process called geolocation?

SLITESTWRAYOHOPE: Are you hard of hearing, Senator? Because I could speak louder if it would help...

In politics, as in real estate, everything is geolocation, geolocation, geolocation. (Yeah, yeah, Director Slitestwrayohope didn't say that last bit. It's just that everybody in the room was hoping that he would because they are every bit as petty as I am.)

It is possible that Senator Heehaheehawley was concerned for the civil liberties of the violent racists and fascists who attacked the Capitol. It is just as likely, however, that if the FBI did use geolocation to track the movement of everybody on Capitol Hill that day, they might have noticed how much time **he** spent trading tales of high school pranks with the violent racists and fascists.

This blurring of the roles between perpetrator and investigator/juror can be complicated. And, I haven't even mentioned how the Senators were also victims of the attack!

Triumph of the Alpha Turtle

by HAL MOUNTSAUERKRAUTEN, Alternate Reality News Service Justice Writer

Do turtles eat cake?

Unlikely. They haven't evolved the digestive apparatus to be able to process complex sugars, much less the chemicals that modern cakes swim in. A turtle attempting to eat a cake would likely * KAFF KAFF KAFF * until they either got it out of their digestive tract or choked to a premature death. ("He was only 207!")

So, how is it that House Minority Leader Mitch Wichconnelliswich is able to eat his cake and have it, too? (Not, as the popular version of the idiom would have it, have his cake and throw it at a picture taped to the wall of the President who cost him his Senate majority, too.)

When you're the Alpha Turtle, you have to swallow a lot of things that the other turtles don't.

It was in the Minority Leader's power to find President Ronald McDruhitmumpf guilty at his Senate trial; with a wave of his claw, he could have freed his caucus to vote their conscience. (Granted, big game hunters have trekked in vain for months to find a Reduhblican with a conscience in the Senate, but the species hasn't been pronounced extinct yet, so there is always the possibility...) He did not do that, with the inevitable result that the Senate could not get the two-thirds majority it needed to convict the President of violating his oath of office by fomenting an insurrection. ("What, that little kerfuffle? Pfft!")

After the vote, Minority Leader Wichconnelliswich made a speech in which he said: "It is obvious that the President is morally responsible for the unpleasantness at the Capitol which cost the lives of five people, including one police officer. Yes, I can say the word 'moral' without my mouth catching on fire. I am the Alpha Turtle – hear me witter. Oh, yes. He is guilty. Guilty as cinder blocks. Guilty as a three year-old with a stinky diaper. Guilty, guilty, guilty. Oh, my, my, how guilty he is."

Then, why didn't you vote to convict him? "He's out of office. We don't have the jurisdiction," the Minority Leader said, adding: "Not to worry. Other institutions can deal with him. Wink wink."

"Nooooooooooooooooooooooooooooooo!" howled security expert Malcolm Donneednopennance. "President McDruhitmumpf may have fired the gun, but Mitch Wichconnelliswich bought the gun from a thug on a street corner, made sure it was filled with cop-killer bullets and put it in the President's hand!"

Because the Senate spent its first day debating whether a President who was no longer in office could be found guilty, and decided that it could? Or, because when he was the Majority Leader and McDruhitmumpf was still President, Wichconnelliswich delayed the start of the trial until the President's term ended?

"All of it!" Donneednopennance moaned. "Just...all of it!"

"Heavy is the turtle head that wears the crown," Minority Leader Wichconnelliswich smirtled. "Even though I must admit that the gold and jewels look good on me."

"That's not the half of it," commented Senator Amy Klobashowerhead. "More like the seven eighths of it. Or, the thirteen fifteenths of it. Or, the sixty-seven seventy-thirds of it. Or..."

Reading between the lines of the Senator's mathematical reverie, it was clear that she was saying that while he was Majority Leader, Wichconnelliswich encouraged his members to humour President McDruhitmumpf's Big Lie, Today that the Dumboprats stole the 2020 election, the not very tasty BLT that fuelled the insurrection.

"...two hundred and forty-fourths of it. Or, the seven hundred sixty-six seven hundred..."

Yes, I'm sure that was what she was saying.

"The Minority Leader thinks that he can distance himself from a President he despises while holding on to the support of the President's fanatical base," observed former prosecutor Joyce Onvancewarpedtur. "Even after they stormed the Capitol howling for blood, including the blood of Reduhblicans. I don't think that Mitch Wichconnelliswich understands what fanatical really means. Maybe it's because turtles are cold-blooded..."

Worse, Onvancewarpedtur pointed out, he signalled that he hoped the courts would deal with the former President, removing him from the political arena without Wichconnelliswich having to dirty his claws. "He may not have thought that through, though. All of the Reduhblican judges that the former President appointed might give him a pass, which means Wichconnelliswich will have to deal with him as a force in the party for the next four years.

Could the Minority Leader Alpha Turtle have finally managed to outsmart himself? "To borrow a phrase from a dear friend," he answered: "'You might think that. I couldn't possibly comment!'"

I Bag Your Pardon

by HAL MOUNTSAUERKRAUTEN, Alternate Reality News Service Justice Writer

As has been well documented, President Ronald McDruhitmumpf has been freely awarding pardons to murderers...thieves...good friends. But, since when has the President, who has attempted to monetize everything from breathing to money, done anything for free?

"Step right up, ladies and gentlemen. Step right up – don't be shy, the person standing next to you isn't likely to steal what's in your pocket unless he cuts me in, and I'm as honest as the day is moonlit!" cried a close associate of the President who asked to be referred to as a Dibbler on the roof. "Pardons! Pardons! Get your pardons, here, while they last! For $2 million, I can see to it that that heinous crime that you have been convicted of is stricken from the books. Don't worry, I don't judge – in these crazy days, who hasn't been convicted of a heinous crime or two? Wait! Did I say $2 million? This is a going out of business sale – only three days left! You can have a pardon for the low, low price of...$50,000 now and $50,000 when you receive your pardon. Can't ask for fairer than that. Honestly, I'm slitting me own throat offering a pardon for such a ridiculously low price – one more heinous crime to add to **my** list!"

We know that this scheme by lobbyists to sell pardons exists because ex-CIA agent John Kiriakoukou spilled the beans to the *New Yoricknuhemwell Times*. From his prison cell. From which he had obviously not been pardoned. However, we do not know the extent of the pardon selling.

"No, no, no, no, absolutely not, no," the Dibbler on the roof hastily commented. "I would rather sell my grandmother's knickers than give away my client list, and the home doesn't have heat in January! Discretion is my middle name! Really. I had it legally changed from...well, never you mind what. You can call me the Dibbler on the discretion roof! The best thing about the pardon is that nobody needs to know about it until you actually use it! I mean, obviously, when you suddenly show up at your Uncle Guido's house a year and a half into a life sentence, questions will be asked. But, the President is under no obligation to disclose who he has pardoned, and I certainly won't tell, so until you're ready, chrysanthemum's the word!"

How many pardons have been sold is one dimension of extent, of course, but I was actually questioning how many people are selling pardons.

"Ah. Yes. Good question," the Dibbler on the discretion roof allowed. "Competition is the cornerstone of a market economy. But, buildings cannot exist on cornerstones alone. No, sir! In fact, buildings can be erected in which cornerstones play no part at all! What I am trying to say is: don't trust these Dibbler wannabes, these ersatz Dibblers, these Dibbler come latelies! If you want the best product at the best price, only the original Dibbler will do!"

There is also the question of quality control.

"Well, that would be up to my supplier," the Dibbler on the discretion roof stated. "Now, I do have to warn you in this regard that the product has no specific form. To wit: pardons can be written on the backs of napkins or in the margins of a newspaper clipping about walruses or on the back of a MVGA hat. They may not be pretty is what I am trying to convey to you. Still, a pardon written on the palm of your hand is just as valid as one written on parchment. I would just get a photograph of that one – either that, or use it before your next turn in the bathroom!"

Thank you for that. However, when I ask about quality control, I'm actually thinking about how somebody who pays all that money can be sure that the pardon they are buying is genuine.

"Are you questioning the integrity of the President of the United States of Vesampucceri?" the Dibbler on the discretion roof seemed offended (but it could have been a sales tactic). "Because, if you are, I'm afraid I shall have to ask you to step outside!"

That raises another question: what is the President's motive in handing out pardons he has been lobbied to issue? Could he be getting a cut of the lobbyists' fees?

The Dibbler on the discretion roof's eyes narrowed. "Are you in the market for a pardon? Perhaps for yourself for a crime you haven't committed yet, or perhaps as a gift for a loved one? If not, you are wasting my time, and that's a horrible thing to do to somebody who is just trying to make an honest living!"

At that point in the interview, the voice recording app on my phone inexplicably stopped working.

Woobat Found a Candy

by HAL MOUNTSAUERKRAUTEN, Alternate Reality News Service Court Writer

A mistrial has been called in the case of Wally Ballouyahoothu, who had been charged with aggravated public annoyance and annoying public aggravation...with intent.

Third Circuit Bored (she really wants a promotion to a higher bench, people!) Judge Eleonora van Duseldorffer had no choice but to call the mistrial when she discovered that Mildred Awashinabey, one of the jurors, had met with counsel for the defence in order to plan their strategy.

"You're supposed to be impartial!" Judge van Duseldorffer shrieked...judicially. "You're not supposed to favour either side! **What the hell were you thinking?**"

Awashinabey looked contrite. "I'm sorry, your Honouress. I know that Wally is guilty – I mean, the evidence – whoosh, howdy but it was convincing. But, gosh darknit, I really like the little lug."

"**That's your excuse? You liked the guy?**" Judge van Duseldorffer looked like she was going to throw the book at the errant juror, but, because the clerk kept the Bible on his desk, was considering substituting her gavel for it.

"Well, no, Madame Honour," Awashinabey looked down and kicked dust up with the toe of her sensible shoe (somebody on the court cleaning staff should expect a sternly worded letter about this). "I thought it would be okay because Reduhblican Senators did it during the impeachment trial of President McDruhitmumpf. And, props to Reduhblican Senators. They would never do anything improper."

Judge van Duseldorffer stared gobsmacked at the juror for a couple of seconds, then looked like she wanted to slap her forehead with her palm, but was considering substituting her gavel for it.

The mistrial was a mercy, really.

The juror was referring to Senators Lindsey Grahamcrokercrum, Ted Downandmotleycrewz and Mike Leeleesobiesk, who met with the legal team for former President Ronald McDruhitmumpf the night before they were to start their defence. What do you think they were talking about? (HINT: it had nothing to do with their favourite mask design, although Leeleesobiesk really rocks the granite look.)

"The three Senators swore an oath to uphold the Constitution and be impartial jurors in the impeachment trial," pointed out token smart person Amy Sheshutshotshitbam. "They didn't just ignore the oath, they dismantled it, sold the parts for scrap and anonymously put the proceeds into a Super PAC to fund the President's legal defence!"

Worse, she added, the defence they contributed to was like a version of *My Cousin Vinnie* where the lawyers didn't get better by the end. Half of the three hour "defence" was repetition of a video that made Dumbopratic politicians look like high school cheerleaders ("Fight! Fight! Fight!" they kept saying – all that was missing was the entire squad shouting, "Goooooooooo Washburningdington weasels!") The rest of the defence amounted to lies ("Ignore all those MVGA hats and Confederate flags: the violence of January 6 was led by Antifa!"), damn lies ("Before the Qerfuffle at the Qapitol, President McDruhitmumpf told his followers to go in peace, wear flowers in their hair and don't try the brown acid, which is none too good!") and statistics ("The votes of 71 million Reduhblicans are being cancelled. Do you have any idea how big the stamp must be to cancel that many votes?").

"**This** is what the Senators risked censure and possible expulsion for?" token smart person Sheshutshotshitbam marvelled (but, not in a comic book sense – she's too mature for that). "They must want the 2024 Reduhblican Presidential nomination bad if they're willing to be Cousin Vinnie's handmaids!"

In a written statement after the mistrial, Judge van Duseldorffer marvelled (in a comic book sense only to the extent that she remembered her nerdy childhood fondly) that it was necessary. "From now on, I guess I will have to explicitly state that jurors may not communicate with counsel for the defence. It always seemed obvious to me, but, well, this is the sort of thing that happens when politicians get involved with justice!

[What the hell, Hal? The story was highly...adequate, but what does the headline have to do with it? Or, for that matter, with anything? BRENDA BRUNDTLAND-GOVANNI]

Oh, yeah. Sorry, Brenda. I'm working from home, and my six year-old son was Petering me for attention hoping that I would play *Pokeman Get Out of Here* with him. So, I told him I was actually preparing an article on the game, I gave it that title to sell the story to him, then forgot to change it.

[Change it now. BB-G]

Sure sure. I was thinking of something like "A Poke in the Eye is Not the Way We Traditionally Conceive of Justice Becoming Blind." What do you think?

Brenda?

[That's the title you want, hunh? BB-G]

Yeah. I thought it was pretty goo –

[You're sure about that? Like, really sure? BB-G]

Absolutely. Why –

[Sorry. Deadline fast approaching. We have no choice but to go with what we have. Thanks. Bye. BB-G]

10. THE SLEEP OF REASON PRODUCES... AFTERWEIRDS

Mourning in Vesampucceri

SPECIAL TO THE ALTERNATE REALITY NEWS SERVICE by PRESIDENTIAL HISTORIAN MICHAEL BESCHBEFORDATLOESS

With the swearing in of Joseph Bidenhisbeeswax as the 46th President of the United States of Vesampucceri and Kamala Hartweirthahommis as his Vice President, a dark chapter in the country's history comes to a close.

An imperfect close, to be sure, given that 83 per cent of Reduhblicans approve of the job Ronald McDruhitmumpf did as President, and 66 per cent of Reduhblicans believe that he actually won the 2020 election, and that the universe somehow conspired to keep him from a second term. Oh, and a substantial number of them are armed and, since they can't attack the entire universe, they would be willing to attack the country's institutions.

But, with a new administration comes a new sense of possibility, a hope that the future will be brighter than the past.

Forget the fact that over 140 Representatives and eight Senators refused to certify the Electoral College votes President Bidenhisbeeswax had legitimately won in order to delay, or even overturn the results of the election. Forget the fact that Reduhblican Senators like Josh Heehaheehawley and Ted Downandmotleycrewz are staking future runs for the Presidency on questioning the legitimacy of the Bidenhisbeeswax administration, ensuring that they will oppose everything he tries to do, including quite possibly breathing. Forget that Senate Minority Leader Mitch Wichconnclliswich is a weasel among turtles who will obstruct everything the Bidenhisbeeswax administration tries to accomplish, especially if he regains a Senate majority in two years. That's about as much forgetting as the average Allinalzheimer's disease patient, but it's doable.

Still, let's not lose sight of what a change in administration can do for a country: it can make people feel a renewed sense of optimism. That is particularly true of this change in administrations: now, people don't have to fear waking up in the morning to find that their government is caging children, or denigrating our allies, or pardoning war criminals. And, while that bar is lower than a Skid Road dive, it gives many people a great sense of relief.

Granted, at the time of Bidenhisbeeswax and Hartweirthahommis' inauguration, over 2,000 Vesampuccerians were dying each day of COVID-19, more than 400,000 total to that point. The pandemic was raging out of control (much like the President after the election, actually) thanks to a government that insisted that the disease was no more serious than a cold, and any death you might suffer was all in your head, so it did nothing to combat COVID.

Gee, this doesn't seem to be quite the hopeful piece that I had started writing, does it? Still, we mustn't lose hope. The great thing about a new government is that it can take the country in a new direction. If you think that the country was going in the wrong direction, a change in driver is just what the auto manufacturer recommends. We can take heart that President Bidenhisbeeswax has signalled, with all the power in his taillights, that he will work hard to undo the damage that the previous administration had done.

Notwithstanding the fact that former President McDruhitmumpf went on a flurry of appointments before he left office, suggesting that he laid land mines for the incoming administration that would blow up if it tried to correct the old regime's policies. Want to re-enter the Paris Climate Accords? * KABOOM *! A minor functionary in the Environmental Pollution Agency will lose the paperwork for several months. Want to re-enter the Iran nuclear agreement? * KABOOM *! A mid-level diplomat will write a scathing denunciation of the move, which will get heavy rotation in right-wing media, and will lobby others at the State Department to slow walk any rapprochement with Iran. Want to reform policing? * KABOOM *! * KABOOM *! * KABOOM *! * KABOOM *! * KABOOM *! Racists in leadership positions in various national security forces will work to undermine the administration's efforts.

But...but...but a new day is dawning...even if it is cloudy and looks like a blizzard will hit before lunchtime. I mean, it's morning in Vesampucceri...even if we have a terrible hangover from the night before and we have a major assignment due at work that is nowhere near complete and the kids are fighting and our spouse is wondering why they ever wanted to have a relationship with us. This is a time for rejoicing, even if close to half the country will curse us and threaten violence if we seem to be enjoying ourselves too loudly or for too long.

So, umm, yeah, let us enjoy this moment. Moments like this are precious and fleeting. Oh, so fleeting.

INDEX

BIOGRAPHY

Ira Nayman is profilic. Proficlic. Proclif - he writes a lot.

If you enjoyed *Advanced Idiotocracy for Dummies*, you will probably love the 11 previously published Alternate Reality News Service books. *Alternate Reality Ain't What It Used To Be, What Were Once Miracles Are Now Children's Toys, Luna for the Lunies!, The Street Finds its Own Uses for Mutant Technologies, Futures in the Mirror are Closer Than They Appear* are general collections of news, reviews, interviews and anything else you might find in your local newspaper. *The Alternate Reality News Service's Guide to Love, Sex and Robots* and *What the Hell Were You Thinking? Good Advice for People Who Make Bad Decisions* are collections of humorous science fiction advice columns. *ARNS and the Man, E Deplorables Unum, Angels of Our Bitter Nature, You and What Universe/That's When Everything Went Cow-shaped* and *Welcome to the Insurrection (We're **Not** Sorry for the Inconvenience)* are the previous collections of idiotocracy articles; *Idiotocracy for Dummies* is an omnibus collection of the first three books. Print versions of all of the books are available online at Amazon, Barnes and Noble, Chapters/Indigo and other fine bookstores.

New Alternate Reality News Service stories appear regularly on Ira's Web site: *Les Pages aux Folles* (http://www.lespagesauxfolles.ca). These include two advice columns: Ask Amritsar (about love and romance and technology) and Ask the Tech Answer Guy (about anything to do with technology except love and romance). Readers are encouraged to submit their own questions for the advice columns. *Les Pages aux Folles* also contains topical political and social satire.

The Weight of Information, the pilot for a radio series based on Alternate Reality News Service articles, can be heard on YouTube.

Ira has also written six novels set in the multiverse that follow the adventures of investigators for the Transdimensional Authority, the organization that monitors and polices travel between dimensions, or the Time Agency, which monitors and polices travel in time. If you are somewhere you don't belong, doing something you shouldn't be doing, they find you, stop you and try and figure out what to do with you. The six novels in the series are: *Welcome to the Multiverse**, *You Can't Kill the Multiverse***, *Random Dingoes*, *It's Just the Chronosphere Unfolding as it Should*, *The Multiverse is a Nice Place to Visit, But I Wouldn't Want to Live There* and *Good Intentions: The Multiverse Refugees Trilogy: First Pie in the Face*. These books can be purchased from all of the usual suspects online, or from the home page of the publisher, Elsewhen Press.

Fans of Ira Nayman's science fiction writing are encouraged to check *Les Pages aux Folles* periodically for news about the availability of these and future stories.

* Sorry for the Inconvenience
** But You Can Mess With its Head

Connect with Ira online:

Twitter: https://twitter.com/#!/ARNSProprietor
Facebook: http://www.facebook.com/ira.nayman

www.ingramcontent.com/pod-product-compliance
Lightning Source LLC
Chambersburg PA
CBHW061506020726
47502CB00006B/1954